AUTHOR REED, R.   CLASS   F   20. AUG 01

TITLE   Beneath the gated sky.

BENEATH
THE
GATED
SKY

Books by Robert Reed

The Remarkables
Down the Bright Way
Black Milk
The Hormone Jungle
The Leeshore
*An Exaltation of Larks
*Beyond the Veil of Stars
*Beneath the Gated Sky

* A Tor Book

BENEATH THE GATED SKY

ROBERT REED

TOR®

A TOM DOHERTY ASSOCIATES BOOK
NEW YORK

077263147

BENEATH THE GATED SKY

Edited by James Frenkel

A Tor Book
Published by Tom Doherty Associates, Inc.
175 Fifth Avenue
New York, NY 10010

Tor Books on the World Wide Web:
http://www.tor.com

Tor® is a registered trademark of Tom Doherty Associates, Inc.

Library of Congress Cataloging-in-Publication Data

Reed, Robert.
    Beneath the gated sky / Robert Reed.
       p.   cm.
    Sequel to: Beyond the veil of stars.
    "A Tom Doherty Associates book."
    ISBN 0-312-86477-9
    I. Title.
    PS3568.E3696B43   1997
    813'.54—dc21   97-15363

First hardcover edition: September 1997
First trade paperback edition: September 1998

Printed in the United States of America.

0 9 8 7 6 5 4 3 2 1

In memory of my cousin
Kym Reed

THE FAMILY

AFTER SO MANY YEARS, THE HOUSE HAD GROWN EXCEEDINGLY FRAIL. Eroded white paint clung to its four faces. The wide front porch sagged with a treacherous dignity. Certain windows had survived since the nineteenth century, gradually and very gently deformed by the earth's pull. Roof tiles of amorphous silicon, forged in a twenty-first-century furnace and degraded by the relentless seasons, delivered just a trickle of their original current. And whenever the wind blew—a perpetual occurrence in that open country—the house would shudder and twist, and a creaking voice would rise up through its bones.

When she couldn't sleep, which was often, Porsche Neal would listen to the house, trying to understand its voice.

Eight generations of the same family had occupied the house. Every surface had its mementos, every corner and dusty cubbyhole its telling scars. Oak stairs slumped where boots and bare feet had struck them countless times. A rickety banister had been polished smooth by boys' butts and the gnarled hands of grandparents. Fearless handymen of uneven skill had left behind plaster patches, tangled wiring, and several plumbing nightmares. But most of the ghosts lived on the pantry wall: Hundreds of faded flat lines, each line dated and initialed, showed where dozens of children had stood at attention, another year's growth recorded with precision and a familial pride.

It was exactly the sort of house that Porsche could appreciate, what with its tangible history, and in its dark places, secrets.

On the first day, Porsche turned a Few-made sensor on the entire structure. In her bedroom closet, behind the back wall, she discovered a locked steel box. Cornell and his father were somewhere else, and the fourth member of their little family hadn't arrived yet. Sitting cross-legged on the floor, alone, she teased open the box, discovering that it was half-filled with, of all things, pornography. Relics of the twentieth century, the magazines were printed on cheap, acid-rich paper that had gone stiff and sickly yellow. She turned the pages carefully, lingering over certain photographs. Whose magazines were these, she kept wondering, and why would that long-dead soul have stockpiled all these delicious young men?

A lonely farm wife, maybe?

Or the farm wife's extremely frustrated, secretly gay husband.

Either way, the delicious men held their silence; and out of respect, Porsche set the magazines back into their box, and the box back into its hiding place.

She never mentioned her discovery, even to Cornell.

Houses are like people, she believed: Each one is entitled to her important secrets.

Porsche and Cornell shared the largest bedroom. Its furnishings had come with the house—a lumpy queen-sized bed; two shabby, mismatched chests of drawers, and a Net terminal nearly twenty years old. Her first priority was to rip down the bedroom's grimy wallpaper, then flood every likely surface with paint. Then she covered the scuffed wooden floor with a secondhand carpet. Of course Cornell teased her about building a nest. "We won't be here for more than a couple months," he argued, wrong by a long ways. She ignored him easily enough. Throw pillows and a bright gold bedspread gave the room a palpable newness. She fastened a star chart to their ceiling, Orion and the Dippers wheeling above them in the night. A framed picture of Cornell was given a prominent home on her chest of drawers. And beside it was the newest portrait of her parents and two brothers, their smiling wives and six adorable children.

Once she felt at home, Porsche sat on her bed and made calls.

She called her brothers first, then her parents, using the old terminal and public lines. Panning the terminal's eye, she showed off her new abode, then repeated their cover story three times.

They were going to be investors, she claimed. Wealth was the goal. One of their team, Timothy Kleck, was a genius in electronic surveillance. He would search the Net for opportunities such as corporate buyouts and amazing new products, and the others would invest their savings, then sit back and wait for their winnings.

It was a lie, of course, and to anyone with resources and a skeptical nature, it wouldn't seem like much of a lie.

But with luck, it might buy them a week or two of indifference.

Maybe.

Chatting with her family, Porsche never mentioned her former employer—the Cosmic Event Agency. And she certainly never alluded to her work, the strange worlds in easy reach, or anything else in the least bit incriminating.

Those topics were forbidden.

Other means were waiting when she needed a secure com line: Few-designed tricks proven on countless worlds, no amount of human cleverness or human luck able to puncture them.

Today's calls were meant to reassure both her family and any eavesdroppers.

She was chatting with her father when an associate happened past. A tall man, even taller than Porsche, knocked on the door and peered into the bedroom, his brown face watching her with an unnerving intensity, his big eyes perpetually amazed. "Hello?" he interrupted. "Am I interrupting?"

"Not at all," Porsche assured.

"Have you seen Cornell?"

"He went to town. For groceries." Porsche was sitting back on her elbows, dressed in shorts and a favorite baggy shirt, letting the late-day sun pour over her. "But while you're here . . . Timothy Kleck, this is my father, Leonard Neal."

Timothy squinted at the image.

Father was a large man, his plain face rounded with fat, his scalp as bald as granite, an easy smile showing an instant before he said, "It's good to meet you, Timothy." He had a distinct Texan twang. "My girl here says good things about you."

Timothy opened his mouth, then closed it. Then he opened it again, and a little too quietly, he said, "Oh?" He managed to swallow, then blubbered, "Hello, Mr. Neal. It's good to meet you, too."

Her father had raised poise to an art form. "Do me a huge favor, son. Call me Leonard, if you would, please."

"Leonard," the tall man repeated slowly, carefully.

Cornell had found Timothy through an advertisement on the Net. Timothy billed himself as a magician who could tease secrets out of anywhere. Cornell had hired him for two projects. The second project was a thorough background check on an intriguing woman whom he'd met while working for the CEA. Porsche, as it happened. And eventually, through persistence as much as skill, Timothy stumbled over a few oddities. Nothing was incriminating, exactly. But there were discontinuities, in her background and in her family's, too.

At the time, Timothy assumed that the Neal clan belonged to someone's elaborate witness relocation program.

No other explanation seemed reasonable.

Later, after Porsche and Cornell had quit the CEA, they approached the magician with an outrageous story. They didn't tell him everything, naturally. There was no reason for total disclosure. Yet they were honest about their lack of total candor. And Timothy was clever-smart, taking what he knew and filling in the blanks for himself.

Timothy came to the farm two days ago, and ever since he

had watched Porsche with curiosity and a kind of suspicious awe.

Now he had a second Neal in his sights. Staring at the image on the flat, sun-washed screen, he said, "So," with an air of importance. "A West Virginia native, I understand you are . . . What was the name of your hometown?"

"Mason Bottoms," Father replied, in an instant.

"I once knew someone from there. At least I think he was." Timothy smiled brightly, proud of his cleverness. "The town's gone now, isn't it?"

Father had poise, which meant he had patience, too.

And a liquid gracefulness.

Sitting in Texas, comfortable in his favorite waterchair, he smiled for a long gentle moment, then without a trace of haste, said, "Gosh, I'd love to shoot the shit, son. But I really need to be going now." Then with the purest Texan lilt, "Ya' understand?"

Daughter and father exchanged a few more words, rigorously pleasant and thoroughly bland. Then the terminal went black, and Timothy pulled an elaborate device out of a baggy pocket, using it to examine the terminal and its optical cable.

"If anyone was listening to you," he assured, "it wasn't from this end."

Porsche knew as much, but she didn't explain how she knew it. She sat up straight, angered by his rudeness and worried by his attitude. Was Timothy the sort of person you wanted at your side when you went toe-to-toe with the malignant, rapacious CEA?

The tall man was gathering himself, staring at a point just above Porsche's head.

He was avoiding her eyes.

"I have a question," he finally confessed. "Or two."

"Ask away," was her advice.

"I know about your . . . well, the fictions in your life story." He paused to breathe, one soft hand grasping the bedpost. "And Cornell's told me about the universe's real shape, what with all the alien worlds right next door—"

"What's your question?"

Like anyone with a razor-sharp, razor-narrow skill, Timothy was uneasy whenever he left his element.

Two deep breaths gave him the strength to say, "Can you tell me? About yourself, I mean."

"No," she replied, her tone flat and plain.

The man leaned against the post, disappointed and a little angry.

"But I'll make you a promise," she continued. "If things go right for us, I'll tell you everything."

He gave a hopeful nod.

"That's how it has to be," she warned.

Again, he nodded. But with a strong, almost incandescent pride, he said, "I know how to keep secrets."

She said, "Look at me, Timothy."

His eyes found hers.

"When I was a girl," she whispered, "one of my uncles liked to say, 'Secrets are living things. They have their own clear purpose, their own cloudy blood. And like any living thing, a secret deserves respect. Always, always.' "

Timothy laughed self-consciously. "Your uncle in Mason Bottoms?"

She stared at him for a long moment, then laughed in turn.

Timothy was strolling toward the door, saying, "I hope everything works out for us, if that's what it takes to know. . . ."

"I hope it works out, too," she replied.

He paused, then brightened. "Hey," he said, "maybe you'll introduce me to your uncle, too."

She didn't say one word.

But she was thinking: If you need to meet Uncle Jack, then everything has turned to shit.

Behind the old farmhouse, past a windbreak of junipers and rugged oaks and assorted mechanical junk, was a field of cultivated sunflowers.

Out in the sunflowers was a disk of hard black glass.

The disk measured thirty-three feet, one-half inch across. Years

ago, when it had first appeared, its surface was slick and fresh—
a slab of obsidian shining brightly on any clear day. But more
than twenty winters had passed, the glass slumping in places, lay-
ers of dust dulling its surface, and along its edge, countless tiny
fissures reached deeper with every freeze, then widened as each
spring's crops sent roots into the brittle glass.

The sunflowers belonged to their landlord—a good-natured
if somewhat laconic farmer who had grown up inside the old
house. While Porsche was remodeling the bedroom, the landlord was harvesting, stripping off the seeds while leaving the
ragged stalks and shredded brown leaves strewn everywhere.
After that, walking in the field was tough, sloppy work. It took
many trips out to carry the various equipment that Porsche
needed: Tools and an old toolbox, plus a collapsible pole and
the rest of the equipment that she'd purchased at the local Wal-
Mart. Cornell and his father were off helping Timothy unload a
truckful of electronic gear. Starting tomorrow, everyone would
be busy with assembling and testing the equipment. That gave
her work an urgency, which she enjoyed, and she couldn't have
asked for a sweeter afternoon than the one she found waiting
for her.

With bare hands, Porsche cleared the ground on the north
edge of the disk, then used an old posthole digger to sink a hole.
The topsoil was black and damp, thinned by farming and bol-
stered by every chemical trick. She poured in road gravel to
make a base, then paused, kneeling over the pole as she wondered what was the least difficult way to proceed.

Behind her, the dried stubble began to rustle and crack as
someone approached.

Quietly, in an unrecognizable language, Porsche asked,
"Who?"

A private voice tied to her inner ear whispered, "Nathan."

She rose, turned. A slender, white-haired man was fighting his
way through the sunflowers' stubble.

"Hello?" he called out.

She said, "Hello yourself."

"I thought you might need help." He smiled shyly, glancing at his own hands. "May I?"

"Perfect timing," she replied, smiling.

Nathan stepped out onto the glass, then paused and shook his head. "Actually, I sort of got on Timothy's nerves." The confession betrayed a genuine pain. "He's a very particular man. Have you noticed?"

"*Particular* is a good word."

"Inflexible, too. I think."

Poor Nathan. He wanted this project to go well, and he was desperate to help. Yet in his own way, he was as rigid as Timothy, but without Timothy's potent skills.

"In a minute," she offered, "you can help me with this pole."

"I'd love that."

She mixed the concrete and resin in an old bucket, and while she worked, Nathan opened the toolbox, removing a certain hammer that he held in his right hand, then his left, regarding it with an almost religious awe. Then she said, "Now, please." He put down the hammer and hurried to help. The pole gave off a solid tone when it was perfectly vertical, repeating the tone every few seconds, and Nathan held it in place while Porsche poured in the wet gray goo. Then he kept holding tight while she mixed a second batch, trying to do his job flawlessly, trying to prove Timothy wrong.

She poured the second batch, then checked the pole's orientation. Then she mixed a final batch and poured it, almost filling the hole; and only then did Nathan say, "I know you know what's best."

"Don't be so sure," she replied.

He could be a doggedly serious man. Standing on the disk, looking down at his own dusty reflection, he sighed in a large way, then said, "This just seems . . . I don't know . . . wrong somehow . . ."

"What are you standing on?" she inquired.

"I know. It's just glass."

"And not particularly good glass," she added.

He walked to the center of the disk. It was marked by a tiny hole. Years ago, Nathan had made Cornell chip off a piece of glass from that spot. Nathan was a self-taught researcher of odd phenomena. In those years, flying saucers were his passion. The mysterious black glass disks were cousins to the saucers, he had believed. They would appear at random locations world-wide, without warning or witnesses. For a little while, they generated curiosity and public debate. Then something much larger and fabulously strange happened, and the disks were nearly forgotten.

With genuine reverence, Nathan fingered the hole in the glass.

Porsche took the posthole digger and bucket back to the house. When she returned, Nathan hadn't moved, but now he was watching the wide blue sky. Their concrete and resin had stiffened enough to be trusted, a wet warm heat rising out of it. She pulled the plastic off the new backboard, then wrestled it into position. Nathan was caught in a spell; he didn't offer to help until her hand slipped, and she muttered, "Shit."

"What can I do?"

Porsche dropped the backboard, sucking on a bloody finger and understanding how Timothy must have felt.

Nathan apologized profusely. "I guess I was thinking too much . . . sorry . . . !"

She held the backboard while Nathan bolted it to the pole, and together they fastened the new hoop to the board, then the shiny net to the hoop. Porsche had owned the net for years. Each link was a chime, and every motion caused a rambling melody to play. When the net was in place, they finally extended the pole until it bleated out another happy sound, claiming that the hoop was level and ten feet tall, exactly.

Porsche had her own proven means of checking the height.

Starting at the far side of the disk, she began to run, an easy strong gait carrying her to the perfect point where she leaped high, her right arm lifted overhead, her long hand curling deftly around the hoop for a golden instant, then releasing.

She dropped onto the black earth, giggling.

"Good enough," was her verdict.

With a laser tape, glass cleaner, and cheap white paint, they began to lay out the free-throw and three-point lines.

It was almost evening when they had finished.

Clouds were blowing in from the northwest, covering the sun and bringing colder air. Through gaps in the clouds, Porsche caught a glimpse of the Asian coast, then the brown mass of Australia. In the east, night was a wave of darkness spreading across Indiana and Kentucky. Was there time enough for a quick game?

Nathan was standing close to Porsche, watching her.

With a thinly veiled horror, he said, "Imagine. Building a basketball court on the doorway to another world."

She smiled, a warning finger to her lips.

"I know," he whispered. "Don't talk about it. I know. . . . "

Nathan was a sweet, well-intentioned man who had invested his adult life in chasing extraterrestrial intelligence. His profession had made him more than a little paranoid, or his natural paranoia had brought him into that plot-crazed culture. Either way, decades of disappointment had been erased just a week ago. His son had told him an amazing story about alien worlds and a secret government project, and for dessert, Porsche had sat him down on this glass and told him an even greater secret— something that was incredible to him, and in the same breath, utterly ordinary to her.

"How's your finger?" he asked, plainly regretful.

She let him take her hand, examining the narrow brown-red scab. "It just stings a little. That's all."

Nathan pressed the back of her hand to his lips, kissing her as softly as possible.

And as softly as possible, Porsche said, "Thank you for your help," while deftly reclaiming her hand.

Sometimes in the night, Porsche would suddenly feel like a child again.

Enlivened by the hour, utterly immune to sleep, she would lie on the lumpy old bed, gazing up at the star chart, watching the false constellations turn slowly around the false Polaris; and she would speak in whispers, describing how it was to have been born alien, how she'd spent her wondrous childhood, and sometimes, in the deep heart of night, she would entrust Cornell with other secrets, too.

Porsche was born on Jarrtee—that word as close as human mouths could manage. "It's a beautiful world," she liked to say, "and not just because every world is." Larger than the earth, more massive and considerably warmer, Jarrtee was blanketed in a thick atmosphere laced with carbon dioxide and water vapor, fat clouds stacked on fatter clouds, and beneath them, a single continent crisscrossed with rugged mountains and salty land-locked seas.

A single night on Jarrtee lasted for several earthly weeks.

The blistering, storm-wracked days were equally patient.

To cope, the native jarrtees were unabashedly nocturnal. They didn't simply sleep during the day, they estivated, their metabolisms throttling down almost to nothing, their souls hovering on the cusp of death. Then with the first trace of darkness, they awakened, thin and anxious, and famished. Jarrtees lived with their extended families, and together, they held a dawn feast, eating fatty meats and nuts, and blood meals, everyone leaving the table with their stomach painfully, deliciously swollen.

"You were a vampire," Cornell teased.

"Oh, gosh, I was," she replied. "Oh, golly. I never noticed that stupid coincidence before."

Jarrtees were humanoids. Seen at a distance, in the night, they looked something like thick and pale and utterly hairless *H. sapiens*. The bodies were balanced on a pair of stout legs. Twin arms ended with thumbed hands. And there were human-style faces: An omnivorous, tooth-rich mouth beneath slitlike nostrils, and above, in enormous sockets, a pair of wide black organs that any man or octopus would recognize as eyes.

"I was a beautiful baby," Porsche assured, "and not just because every baby is."

Chalk-white at birth and no bigger than a cashew, her first nights and days were spent inside her father's belly pouch. The girl grew rapidly, even for a jarrtee. When she emerged from the pouch, as large as a human newborn, she was given a honored name. "Po-lee-een," she sang; it was as close as her human mouth could manage. Po-lee-een was an ancient hero. "But there's no special honor," she confessed. "On Jarrtee, everyone is named for at least one dead hero."

Before she was half a year old, Po-lee-een had turned into a big brave daymare of a toddler, fearless and physical, climbing everything and running everywhere while most of her peers were still hiding inside false pouches made of silk and plastic, sucking happily on toes and thumbs.

"I took a lot of falls," Porsche admitted. "But luckily, jarrtee skin is thick and tough, and the bones inside are even tougher."

"And you were hairless," Cornell mentioned, in amazement.

The woman lying with him had a thick long forest of honey-brown hair, plus a darker tangle of fur nestled between her long human legs.

"And you were chalk-white," he repeated.

"Except that as I aged," she replied, "I developed a platinum cast. And like any decent jarrtee, I covered my body with ink paintings. Ink was worn in lieu of clothes."

Cornell closed his eyes, imagining the child.

He was a handsome and lean man blessed with eternal boyishness. His delicious face was illuminated by earthglow, and it wore a complex, ever-shifting expression.

Porsche had no idea what Cornell was thinking.

The truth told, he had always been something of an enigma. They had become lovers only recently. They shared a genuine disdain for their ex-employer, the CEA; but more importantly, they shared a very rare talent. No, they weren't strangers anymore. But there was a distance. Lying on their backs, under the false stars and cracking plaster, neither could say with certainty what was passing through the other's mind.

Just as Porsche was wondering if Cornell was a little sickened, if the image of the bald little vampire girl was too much, he smiled with his closed eyes and open mouth, saying with unalloyed pleasure, "I bet you were beautiful."

She was the ultimate in exotic lovers, and sometimes that status, with its endless demands and sugary pitfalls, made her ill at ease.

Like now.

"Which makes me wonder," said Cornell. He finally opened his eyes—portals adapted to bright days on the open savanna—regarding her with a mixture of amusement and curiosity, and adoration, and perhaps a dose of suspicion. "Why?" he asked. "If it was so wonderful, why did you and your family leave Jarrtee?"

A perfectly reasonable question, and dangerous.

She said nothing for a moment—for too long, probably—then she told him, "It's a great challenge to come to a new world, to embrace a new species—"

"I'm just curious. Why emigrate when you did?"

She remained silent.

"If I'm not entitled to know, don't tell me." Then after his next breath, he said, "You have rules. Codes of conduct. Haven't I tried to respect that?" He paused again, breathed again. "But when you said that shit about great challenges and embracing a new species . . . well, you were trying to lie to me. Weren't you?"

Not entirely, no.

But she felt like a liar, and she found herself doing a liar's trick, letting her gaze leave the room.

Their bedroom window faced west. The topmost pane had rippled with time, and through the ripples she could make out the constellations that were San Francisco and Los Angeles and the urban wilderness between them. Eight billion souls stood on this world, very few of them like Porsche. Out of all those billions who had been born human, how many could she trust? With the long fingers of one hand, she took an inventory, fingers left to spare. It was a sobering exercise. She shook her head, smiled sadly, then slowly sat up in bed, letting the sheet and golden bedspread fall around her waist.

Porsche was a strong, well-built woman, and she had a matching face—the kind of face that men always remembered as being prettier than it really was. And her voice matched both, sounding a little like deep, swiftly moving water, almost rumbling as she asked, "Are you tired?"

"Exhausted," he confessed. "But between Timothy's coffee and the topic, I'm too keyed up to sleep."

She felt the same way.

Cornell waited for a moment, then with a genuine delicacy asked, "Can it be such an awful secret?"

Quietly, with a sudden amusement, Porsche said, "All right, I'll tell you. This is my secret." She turned and stared at a point behind Cornell's eyes, admitting, "Your girlfriend, given the chance, will do any stupid thing for love."

CHILDREN LIVE IN A WORLD OF RULES, AND ANY CHILD KNOWS THAT
rules come in distinct flavors: Hard laws that must be obeyed
without question, in every circumstance; and the lesser statutes
meant for youngsters who can't taste the difference between
things that are law and things that pretend to be.

Porsche always knew the difference.

When she was still quite young, her best friend and favorite accomplice in crime was a certain male cousin. "He doesn't want
me to use his jarrtee name," she admitted. "I'll call him Trinidad,
since that's what he answers to now."

The City lived at night. Sometimes the clouds would clear, and
the two cousins would sneak up onto one of the roofs in the
family compound, bare toes and clinging fingers navigating
across the steeply pitched landscape of Teflon-frosted tiles. They
loved to sit in the highest storm gutters, spying on their forty million neighbors. On the best nights, they could see the heart of
the City—a chaotic mishmash of stolid buildings and narrow
streets leading down to the rippling blackness of a deep-water
bay. Voices would rise from below, the prattle of strangers laced
with laughter, insults, and sloppy songs. Float cars hummed past
in an endless parade. Transport planes flew on silk wings. And
on occasion, a security dirigible would burrow its way through

the hot night air, passing close enough that Porsche couldn't help but reach high, hoping to touch the armored aerogel skin.

To savanna eyes, the City would seem cloaked in pure darkness. Yet to a jarrtee, the scene was a bright, even gaudy spectacle. The cumulative glow of so many candles and cold lamps made the long climb worth every hazard. But it was the driest nights, when the City's perpetual haze was blown away with the rare west wind, when they were treated to the finest show. Porsche and Trinidad would gaze up at the sky, and together, they would study the ghostly image of their own world: Dayside storm clouds bathed in orange-white sunlight; between storms, glimpses of bright water and blue-black land; and where it was night and it was clear, the gentle glow of distant city-states, all nameless, and none the equal of theirs.

The earth and Jarrtee shared at least that one seminal feature: In the recent past, without warning, both worlds forever lost sight of the stars.

Humans called it the Change.

Cornell had told his story to Porsche several times, in various moods. Twenty-five years ago, he happened to be outdoors on a clear August night, and he glanced up at the perfect moment. Without fuss, the stars and planets and moon vanished, replaced instantly with a diluted reflection of the earth itself. It was as if the world had been turned inside out, and whatever force was responsible—aliens or God, or shared madness—it was done so smoothly, so lovingly, that not even the most sensitive human-built machine felt the barest tremor.

The Change was momentous, and it was an illusion.

Seen from orbit, the earth was the same blue and snow and emerald and dirt-colored ball. Its albedo had been reduced, but not by much. On the ground, climate and the magnetic field remained unaffected, and the horizon stayed where it belonged, bending downward. And strange as it seemed, starlight continued to fall on the astonished billions. It was just that the radiations were transformed, scrubbed clean of information, their feeble energies incorporated into the magical earthglow.

The jarrtees had an elaborate, lovely name for the Change. Porsche could hear it in memory if not quite say it with her human mouth. *God-Stole-Our-Sky* was a viable translation. But as she liked to remind Cornell—too often, perhaps—translations were another kind of illusion, always unreal at their heart.

Like any good magician's trick, the Change had given its audience new ways of seeing.

The universe had more than one true shape, and eventually, both jarrtees and humans learned that powerful lesson.

Each true shape was intricate, and comprehensible, and beautiful. Porsche liked to stress the aesthetics, even though she had no particular talent with the tangled, surreal mathematics.

"God-Stole-Your-Sky," Cornell whispered, staring at the ceiling; then after a long contemplative silence, he made a very reasonable request. "Tell me more about your species. About the jarrtees."

By human standards, they were an elderly species.

No five-thousand-year fever had given birth to their civilization. The jarrtees hadn't endured a rapid explosion of science and industry. They were patient and pragmatic, taking the long view on every important issue. Order was a blessing; tradition was their blood. And the greatest heroes, like Porsche's namesake, the great Po-lee-een, had sacrificed everything defending their homes from the great enemies: Turmoil and Greed.

"Take my home city, for instance." She paused for a moment, then said, "Our written history reached back more than fifty thousand years."

Softly, Cornell said, "Shit."

"Our suburbs were older than Egypt."

Again, "Shit."

It was a stability born of evolution.

Humans arose from roving bands of interbreeding apes. But the jarrtees ascended from tightly-bound clans who built comfortable bunkers where they could estivate in safety, who moved only in times of crushing disaster, and who mated with outsiders with the greatest of care, and then only to refreshen their lineage.

"Humanoids," said Porsche, "but with the sensibilities of ants."

Technology gave the lucky clans an advantage. The luckiest dominated their region, winning new lands through long patient wars, and eventually—if it was deserved—they were able to swallow and digest every trace of their enemies.

Porsche's home city had grown that way. Over ten thousand years, a single clan had conquered the bay and flanking coastline, its population genetically intertwined but swollen a hundred times. In the past, the overgrown clans would shatter—a biological fission of sorts. But the City saved itself by playing games with jarrtee nature, inventing a tangle of subclans interlinked by careful marriages, every citizen recognizing something in everyone else around her, the society hammered together with a powerful sense of shared destiny.

"It sounds almost utopian," Cornell observed. Then a moment later, he added, "And more than a little xenophobic, too."

Fair assessments, both.

"So what's the city's name?" he inquired.

A reasonable, tenaciously human question.

She mangled the jarrtee pronounciation, then admitted, "*Home* is a reasonable translation. *Paradise* is better. But really, *the City* is as close to perfect as we'll get."

"It's that simple?"

"If you were born in the City, that's all the name you'd need." She paused, then said, "Boston. Singapore. Copernicus Prime. Three cities that we can visit, so of course we need names for them."

Cornell squinted at the poster overhead, then said, "But the jarrtees don't travel anywhere. That's what you said."

"The typical citizen couldn't imagine leaving her home territory."

"The City," he repeated, as if practicing. "The City. The City."

She placed her fingertips on his lips, with pressure, and with a firm voice, she whispered, "Listen."

He stared at the false stars, and waited.

"When I was young," she confessed, "no other world was as lovely as Jarrtee. No other City was as powerful or as feared as mine, which was a good thing. I knew my place, and it was a very precise, very safe place, and no child in the universe was half as happy as me."

Cornell turned his head, gazing into her eyes.

"I was jarrtee," she reminded him. "An alien in every sense. But frankly, if you think about it, human children aren't all that different. Are they?"

To a human child, Porsche's life would have seemed comprehensible.

She played games with a glancing resemblance to chess and basketball, and she fought with her brothers—"Winning most of the fights," she added, with an authentic pride—and at regular intervals, twenty times during each long night, Porsche would tuck her computer under a muscular arm and make the long hike to school.

A bright, curious student, Porsche was both a joy and a challenge for her assorted teachers. Motivated, she could be left alone to learn at a galloping pace. Bored, she would smoothly disrupt any class. Most of her teachers made peace by letting her read as she liked, and socialize too much, and if some topic hooked her interest, they gave her the chance to design her own elaborate projects.

Her school was older than most earthly nations. Constructed from granite and tough jarrtee mortar, it had once served as a fortification on the City's outskirts. But the City grew west toward the coastal mountains; the old fort was abandoned, left empty for years. Its vast courtyard was filled with quick weeds and slower trees, and before the first black-eyed student strolled through the front gate, a mature forest had established itself.

In the night, a jarrtee forest was gorgeous.

Lying on the old mattress, Porsche shut her human eyes and watched as the luminescent night flowers burst open, begging for insects and other night fliers to take their pollen. She saw swollen balloon birds courting each other, dancing like smoke in the air. Mud fish bellowed from their homemade ponds. And there was the endless chittering of sonar, a multitude of species lending the air an intoxicating, almost electric energy.

Yet for each celebrant of the night, one or two more species lived entirely by the day. It was as if Jarrtee were two worlds dancing together but facing in opposite directions. Porsche read volumes about the day world. At the City's many zoos, there were dozens of exhibits showing the diurnal fauna and flora on display, all existing in contrived environments, their carefully reversed lives spent behind heavily smoked glass. And she could look into the sky, imagining the brilliance beneath the clouds, and the great rains, and the fantastic fecundity that would rebuild her world while she lay underground, estivating in peace. But still, the day remained a remote, dreamlike realm, and how could she make it real?

The school's children ruled the courtyard's forest by night, but by day, a baboon-like species named *terrors* took control.

Po-lee-een, the eventual Porsche, decided to study the terrors. "With my cousin's help, please!"

But her science teacher was uneasy. Terrors estivated inside tangles of razor brush poisoned with their own spit and urine. The girl had most of the necessary skills, but she was too brave, too easily tempted by risk. And Trinidad was much the same, or worse. The teacher—a conservatively inked woman rumored to be as old as the school—agreed to the project, but only if Po-lee-een worked with an older student. Someone bright but naturally cautious. "In fact," she declared, "I know a perfect candidate. You will despise him!"

The promised boy was a year her senior, prefertile but not for long, his chin and forehead showing the first long ridges that came with manhood. "His name was Jey-im," said Porsche, her human voice half-singing, half-squealing. Then with a softer voice, she added, "He was my first lover."

Cornell was lying with her beneath the covers, a solid arm tucked beneath her head.

After a long moment, he asked, "What? Are you waiting for me to get jealous?"

"I don't know. Are you jealous?"

Another pause, then he admitted, "No. It's more bestial curiosity."

On Jarrtee, she explained, sex preceded fertility. Generations of children had used that square patch of forest as their private laboratory. Porsche and Jey-im took a tiny clearing behind a wall of blooming red trees, and after their first clumsy experiments with intercourse, they lay back and gazed at the clearing sky, admiring their world and themselves, discussing the shapes of the universe and their own vital, personal place within it.

The Jarrtee sky had changed long ago, when their grandparents were young adults.

Despite the dense, humid atmosphere, the original nights were capped with thousands of brilliant stars.

"Because your eyes were that sensitive," Cornell guessed.

"And because Jarrtee was deep inside a spiral galaxy," Porsche added. "More stars packed close together, at least in the old way of looking at the universe."

Millenia ago, the more prosperous clans had erected telescopes on their tallest mountains, intending to spy on their neighbors but naturally pointing them skyward now and again. But the atmosphere had limited science until several centuries ago. In the City, and elsewhere, clever engineers devised more powerful observatories. Vast dirigibles were built out of the lightest silks, then lashed together in the thin chill upper atmosphere and anchored in place with a lacework of diamond wires. Those airborne islands were covered with mirrors and radio dishes; finally, her nocturnal species was able to peer into the heart of the ultimate night.

"We had a few hundred years of observation and speculation," said Porsche, "then God-Stole-Our-Sky."

"How did Jim's people cope?" asked Cornell.

"Jey-im's people did awfully well, considering." She shook her head, admitting, "There was some panic, of course. Old gods and unknown aliens were given credit, or blame. Some jarrtees retreated into their deepest basements, convinced that the world was finished. And as a precaution, every clan put its security forces on alert.

"My grandparents told stories," she continued. "They saw their neighbors' moods leap from giddiness to paranoia, then to pure fatalism. Every street held some impromptu gathering. People danced and sang and spouted every possible idea about what the Change meant for them and their clans . . . which are one and the same thing, according to the average jarrtee."

"That sounds like my old neighborhood," Cornell offered.

When Cornell saw the sky change, he let out a great scream, bringing the neighbors outdoors, their faces bright with astonishment and simple terror. Then his father had stepped into the chaos, and with the composure of a prophet, or a madman, Nathan assured everyone that only an advanced and benevolent species could accomplish such a wonder. The sky was a wake-up call, and the extraterrestrials, bearing even more wondrous gifts, would surely come soon. Perhaps tomorrow, he had promised: A statement of faith and hope, and utterly wrong.

No starships swung into view over Washington, or McCool Junction.

Nor did they appear in the jarrtee sky, either.

Like humans would do over the next few decades, the jarrtees had struggled to understand what had happened, sifting and re-sifting through the same tangled and very peculiar clues.

The richest city-states, hers included, had had their own space programs. From out in the vacuum, satellites and interplanetary probes saw a home world that was essentially unchanged. The Jarrtee sun—still setting and rising on schedule—remained its orange-white self; the neighboring planets held faithful to their orbits; every star was locked in its proper place; and the physical laws of the universe acted oblivious to the impossibilities.

The Change was a local phenomenon, it seemed.

An astonishing, but limited, mystery.

The mystery ended at the edge of space. Astronauts riding inside nuclear-powered shuttles would see Jarrtee overhead one moment, then it would vanish, the old stars reappearing without the smallest complaint.

The event was stupendous enough that neighboring city-states made treaties of convenience. For the first and only time in jarrtee history, Master scientists from unrelated clans were allowed to join ranks, genius talking to genius in order to decipher the new sky. Ancient enemies suddenly pooled resources. For several glorious years, borders turned porous. And the sacrifices brought success: In a limited way, the truth was found.

The sky's new rules were complicated, and they were complicated in exactly the way that a city's building codes are baffling, laced with bylaws and exceptions, ancient riders, and nebulous statutes.

Simply put, the universe of stars and galaxies was a fiction.

Once, perhaps billions of years ago, there was such a universe. But life arose, and intelligence, and there quickly weren't enough habitable worlds for the burgeoning populations. Dead planets and big rocks could be terraformed, but for only so long. Stars could be sacrificed, their plasmatic meat used to fashion new worlds. But that took phenomenal resources, and patience, and besides, the builders—whoever they were—eventually found easier, more potent means to build homes.

Matter and space were harvested, then doctored and enlivened, obscure dimensions and bizarre mathematics reshaping the cosmos.

An artificial universe was created.

Like a wild forest chopped down for lumber, the builders took axes to the galaxies, and they left a grand subdivision in their wake—worlds nestled flush against worlds, a delicate minimum of suns illuminating each one.

Perhaps Jarrtee was forged in those times.

Or perhaps it was older, built from dust and gas, and the builders had simply incorporated it into their work.

Either way, the old sky had been left behind on purpose. That much was obvious. Like a painting of the vanished woods—a painting hung above the new home's feast table, perhaps—the stars were a simple, compelling means to show people: "This is how things once looked."

But the stars were left purposefully imperfect.

Stare hard enough at a starry sky, with enough telescopes demanding information, and the illusion melts away with that bewildering suddenness.

God-Stole-Our-Sky.

It was much the same on the earth. Except here the Change had happened twice. After the sky was lost to the earth, new telescopes were built on the moon. The Cosmic Event Agency had its own expansive fields of dishes and mirrors. And before anyone realized the danger, the moon's sky had everted in exactly the same way.

"So that's what the two of you talked about? The Change?" Cornell asked the question, then with a feathered sharpness added, "You and your Jim."

"Jey-im," she cautioned.

"I said that."

Porsche waited, then said, "Kids everywhere talk about the sky and their place under it."

With his head propped up on a forearm, Cornell did his own waiting.

"Most of a century had passed," she explained, "but educated jarrtees were still debating what had happened, and what would happen in the future." She paused, then added, "More than humans, jarrtees adore wrestling with details."

"So," Cornell began. "Did they know about the intrusions?"

Porsche said nothing.

"No?"

She shook her head, briefly.

Quantum intrusions were gateways into neighboring worlds. The CEA had found and exploited them. Porsche met Cornell while working for the agency, their souls sent to a desert world, their ignoble mission to hunt for any and all advanced technologies.

"From what you're telling me," said Cornell, "the jarrtees are more advanced than humans. Nuclear shuttles. Diamond ropes. And whatever in hell a float car is . . . !"

"And?"

"I'm just asking . . . if my species can crack open an intrusion, why couldn't the jarrtees?"

Quietly, carefully, she reminded him, "Intrusions are nearly impossible to find, and opening one of them—"

"Is an even tougher trick. I remember."

A steady, knifelike pressure was slicing Porsche in the belly.

But she said nothing inappropriate, honoring every secret. "When I was a girl," she admitted, "the jarrtees were suspicious. Their model universes showed worlds packed against worlds, and there was at least the possibility of gateways—"

"Okay," Cornell responded, watching her with an unnerving intensity.

Because she couldn't help it, Porsche gazed out the bedroom window again, focusing on the distant glow of cities.

"Did they have any idea that aliens were living among them?"

She heard the question, and she didn't.

"But if they knew gateways were possible," Cornell persisted, "then wouldn't they expect to have visitors?"

"It was . . . it was something that occurred to some of my people. Yes."

Cornell was smiling, suddenly enjoying this peculiar game.

Quietly but harshly, he said, "Lucky Jim."

The man was tired, she reminded herself. And humans were jealous apes, by nature. Porsche tried to ignore his little barbs.

"So," he continued, "did Lucky Jim ever realize just how lucky he was?"

Porsche rolled over in bed, lying on her stomach. Then with a quiet smooth force, she told her present lover: "You know, I sometimes miss that sweet boy."

JEY-IM WAS A SWEET, BRIGHT, AND STRENUOUSLY UNREMARKABLE BOY;
and Po-lee-een was strong-willed and confident, but treacher-
ously naive about love and other madnesses.

Years later, buried happily inside another species, the woman
would remember the first damning moment: The two earnest
students were slipping a homemade sensor into a terror's thorny
nest, trying to fasten it to the creature's neck. It was the last normal session at school; they needed to work carefully but quickly.
There was no time for witless nonsense, Po-lee-een warned herself. Yet her hand began to shake suddenly, and the sensor wag-
gled in the air, and because explanations lent strength, she told
herself that she must have a simple blood-fat imbalance. She
even mentioned the possibility to Jey-im, her voice sliding from
nervous curiosity into pure embarrassment. Then, bless him,
Jey-im tried to help, taking hold of her hand just to steady it. She
remembered the slick feel of his flesh and the concerned if
somewhat impatient expression on his face, particularly in the
night-colored eyes. Suddenly Po-lee-een was smelling the forest,
the pungent stink of the poisoned nest, and in particular, a delicious male flavor that lay thick against the roof of her mouth;
and despite every code of decent jarrtee conduct, it was the girl

who took the boy, grabbing him roughly and pulling him close, unable to get enough of his sweetness.

They made love twice, then lay back to admire the sky and themselves. Their dreamy conversation might never have stopped, except suddenly the school's siren voice called out the end of the session.

Springing to their feet, the lovers offered each other inadequate words, then rushed indoors and escaped school through the main gate. Jey-im's mother immediately took her boy into custody. The night had one more session, always reserved for exams, and as she did every night, the stern mother intended to stand over Jey-im as he studied—a common jarrtee tactic, particularly in ambitious families.

Po-lee-een's parents showed less good sense.

She found herself alone in her private cubicle, hopelessly distracted. Gazing into a sheet of mirrored silk, she appeared unchanged: A sleek, handsome face and the familiar big body, both decorated with strong swirls of red ink. Yet beneath the normalcy, her soul was sick, a perfectly fine lust ruined by a strange, intoxicating paranoia.

What if Jey-im confessed to his mother what he had done, she asked herself, and what if his mother considered her son too good for Po-lee-een's modest subclan?

Or worse, what if Jey-im now despised Po-lee-een because she had broken the ancient rules, forcing herself on poor him?

The exam session began on time, as all things jarrtee did. The children were lined up by age, then herded into the subbasement, each given a bleak stone room originally meant to hold prisoners taken in the old wars. The tests were a different flavor of torture; Po-lee-een sprinted through hers, then raced upstairs for the oral evaluation. Where was Jey-im? "Still chewing on his exams," their science teacher reported. "Come and sit, Po-lee-een. Show me your field notes and lab work, and your sensor's data, too."

But the sensor had never been attached to the estivating terror, and her notes were in disarray. Unaccustomed to making excuses, the girl did it badly. Then, finally, Jey-im arrived, numbed and frazzled and half-lost. Suddenly neither child was able to speak, sitting side by side, unable to see anything but the other.

Their teacher had seen this illness many times.

Out of sympathy, she allowed the lovers to slip off into the courtyard on the pretense of finally implanting their sensor.

Naturally, nothing of the kind was accomplished.

The siren announced the session's demise. As the eastern sky grew red, Po-lee-een received her sealed grades, plus a special note meant for her parents. Walking with her boy, she passed through the stainless-steel gate and crossed almost half of the wide stone plaza, the two of them comfortably close until Jey-im's mother suddenly pounced.

Jey-im allowed himself to be yanked into the float car, vanishing without a sound.

It seemed cruel and unfair, robbing them of their chance for a mournful, melodramatic good-bye.

Grumbling to herself, Po-lee-een started for home, navigating through the maze of ceramic streets, robot checkpoints, and little-used alleyways. A note from a teacher is perishable on any world, but the girl resisted temptation. Clenching the note in one hand, she entered the family compound, and Mama-ma ambushed her before she could entertain any second thoughts.

Smiling in the jarrtee fashion—big eyes shaking gently inside their sockets—Mama-ma asked sweetly, "What do you have for me, darling?"

There are no tears on Jarrtee, but in anguish, eyes grow opaque. Open-But-Blind, it is called.

With eyes white as opals, Po-lee-een confessed. Her grades were awful, her judgment was horrid, and worst of all, she had fallen in love, and in punishment she was being wracked with gnawing, unbearable fears.

It must have been an astonishing moment. Po-lee-een had given Mama-ma ample reasons to worry in the past, but it was always the girl's fearlessness. Yet, the woman must have reminded herself, Po-lee-een was still a child, and earlier than most jar-rtees, her daughter was entering the wicked hormonal years.

Grasping her from behind, Mama-ma gave a long smothering hug, and she carefully whispered the advice and bland encour-agement that could have come from mothers on a trillion worlds.

"Of course love frightens," she proclaimed. "It's all new," she said, "and it brings such risk."

Then Mama-ma confessed, "When I realized for the first time that I loved your father, I was at least as scared as you!"

Words helped, but not as intended.

Po-lee-een didn't appreciate knowing that her circumstances were less than unique. Anger helped clear her vision, and with a portion of her old poise, she handed over her grades and the teacher's note, bracing for any disaster.

But the grades were only slightly disappointing, and the note did nothing but sing praises for the studious girl.

"If only I had twenty children like your Po-lee-een," said the recorded voice. "And if only our great clan had a million bright, trustworthy citizens of her ilk . . . think how much greater our great City would be . . . !"

The fear evaporated; suddenly everything was right and good.

As the sun crawled across the Dawn Sea, Po-lee-ccn's father and uncles were working in the kitchen, busily preparing the dawn feast, and everyone else took their customary seats in the feast room. Years later, Porsche would describe the room to Cor-nell, in exacting detail. She would tell him about the limestone walls and floor adorned with venerable mural rugs, and the beams of green olivine overhead, portrait holos dangling from them on invisible diamond threads. There weren't any windows. A handful of tiny ceremonial candles filled the room with a de-licious ruddy glow. Sitting around the feast table were three grandparents, assorted aunts and Mama-ma, plus a dozen girl cousins. Po-lee-een's brothers and boy cousins waited outside the kitchen door, their bodies dipped in silver ink and silver helmets on every head. They represented the sun flames, and when Uncle Ka-ceen gave the command, the flames filed inside, returning with the first treats: Bowls of chilled blood stew and statues of Fertility herself, bloated and lovely, carved expertly from an assortment of sweetened and spiced fats.

The feast table was her family's central heirloom—a massive slab of greased marble resting on two dozen stout legs. If asked, Po-lee-een would lie, claiming that the table had been in her father's family for twenty generations. The dangerous, unmentionable truth was that her paternal grandfather had purchased it secondhand, not long after arriving on Jarrtee, and he had carefully doctored the engraved subclan emblems, making it his own.

Like the table, his family name and elaborate life story were pure fiction.

And it was the same for other grandparents, too.

Everyone at the dawn feast had been born alien, or they had descended from aliens, or they had willfully and happily married into the subterfuge. And all but the youngest children understood what the average jarrtee couldn't have imagined: With sufficient technology, and luck, a sentient soul could cross between worlds.

The rebuilt universe made it possible, within limits.

With the proper machinery and the correct intrusion, a jarrtee soul could take a long step and find herself standing on the earth.

But she wouldn't be jarrtee anymore. During the crossing, her hearts would coalesce into a single human heart. Her pink lung would grow and split in two. Her thick blood would become less salty and greedier with oxygen. Even her delicate genetics would be transformed, suddenly indistinguishable from an ape's DNA. And her new apish brain would hold the instincts, appetites, reflexes, and basic language skills necessary to blend into her surroundings.

It was an enormous transformation, and it was deceptively effortless.

In reality, few jarrtees or humans could comfortably make the transformation. The average soul can endure only so much strangeness. The kind of talent sitting at the feast table was rare, written in a person's genetics and in her upbringing, and in a thousand hidden corners of her unique soul.

Only a fraction of any species could live for long on an alien world.

And there was another enormous restriction: Only a naked soul could make the crossing.

Physical objects melted away inside the intrusion. Clothes vanished. Knives vanished. Books and steam engines and every flavor of nuclear warhead vanished, their elements incorporated into an unseen realm.

"Good fences make good neighbors," a poet says on every world; the universe, it seemed, was filled with the best possible fences.

Countless worlds were stacked close together, but not even the most violent, rapacious species could mount an invasion. Raising an army of "talents" would be difficult. And even then, the army could attack only through the miniscule intrusion, its soldiers crossing a few at a time, without weapons, and without even the formal dignity of a uniform—naked as newborns, and almost as helpless.

Even as a young girl, Porsche understood the basic rules, just as she had a sense of her family's grand origins.

Eons ago, on some forgotten world, talented people learned about the intrusions. They explored the neighboring worlds, and some found mates there, leaving after them children who inherited their talent and something of their wanderlust. And those children eventually explored the next worlds, and the next, helping the talent spread through the universe.

An enormous, extremely diffuse family evolved.

Scarce on almost every world, they coined an appropriate and humble name for themselves: the Few.

They lived on millions of worlds.

Billions more had been visited, once or often. In Jarrtee's past, perhaps in the early days of the City, a stranger must have appeared. He would have looked and smelled like any local citizen—olfactory cues are important among the jarrtee—and he would have had a ready explanation for being a stranger. Undoubtedly, he would have charmed everyone, then taken a wife, making babies until the day he vanished again, leaving nothing behind but perishable memories and a resilient thread of his self.

The Few didn't usually linger on brutal or primitive worlds.

They preferred civilizations that were comfortable and charming, particularly those advanced enough to cause their sky to Change.

Where they were scarce, they lived in secrecy.

Out of fifty billion jarrtees, there were barely ten thousand of the Few. Less than fifty of them lived in the City, more than half inside her family's compound.

Her grandparents had immigrated to Jarrtee just before God-Stole-Our-Sky, then carefully grafted themselves into the rigid clan structure. It had been difficult, treacherous work, but once accepted, their reward was to live in a beautiful place, part of a rich and mature culture, their loyalties perfectly divided between their clan and the Few.

Po-lee-een fully expected to grow up and grow old on Jarrtee. She would leave occasionally, exploring famous worlds and embracing their famous species. And she was too curious and courageous not to wander, mapping new worlds if she was lucky enough. But on that particular morning, in the midst of the feast, she was pure jarrtee; and like any jarrtee, she saw the future as a tower set on the far horizon, built from basalt and the toughest mortar, built entirely for her, entirely finished and waiting patiently for her.

Forever, the tower would wait. If necessary.

In the Few, important questions weren't asked haphazardly, and every answer was dressed in camouflage.

Keeping secrets was an ancient habit.

Po-lee-een always sat beside Trinidad's mother. Early in the festivities, she turned to her aunt, wondering aloud, "How did Uncle Ka-ceen know you would make a good wife?"

Her aunt was a gorgeous woman who inked her flesh with wondrously intricate patterns, accenting her elegant long face and a body that by jarrtee standards was a little too narrow. Almost delicate, in fact. Aunt Me-meel hadn't been born into the Few; the girl was really asking, "How could my uncle know that he could trust you?" But if her aunt was offended, she didn't show it, smiling peacefully and taking a last long bite of cold fat, then setting down her knives while saying with pride: "Dear, he simply knew that I would be."

"But how could he know?"

Me-meel hesitated, then leaned close, her mouth kissing Po-lee-een's tiny ear hole. "It is a skill," she whispered confidently. If someone were eavesdropping—a near-impossibility—he would assume that she meant it was any man's skill.

"Little one," she purred, "your Uncle Ka-ceen simply recognized himself in me."

Po-lee-een had already outgrown her aunt; "little one" was an old joke wrapped in the usual condescending tone. Not born into the Few, Me-meel had always acted a little defensive, even insecure. Which was only reasonable for a non-Few, Po-lee-een would tell herself, unaware that in her own way, she was being just as condescending.

A second wave of silvery young boys emerged from the kitchen, carrying every imaginable meat. Po-lee-een's little brother struggled beneath an enormous deep-sea fish, the fish's wide mouth filled with seaweed and shellfish left tender by hours of baking. And on his heels was her favorite cousin, a bowl of gravy set on top of his silver helmet, tilting one way, then the other, as his arms stretched out like wings.

Trinidad was the family clown, always.

Everyone laughed, except for Po-lee-een and her confidante.

Quietly, with careful delight, Me-meel asked, "Why the questions, little one? Have you met the boy who's right?"

The girl didn't speak, but her eyes answered for her.

"Good for you," Me-meel chirped.

Then her brother stumbled, and Trinidad tripped over a careless foot. Suddenly the bowl was airborne. People cried out and jumped to their feet. Except for Po-lee-een, that is. With the bowl flying at her, she remained seated, secretly making one enormous decision while reaching with both hands, catching the bowl and slowing its descent until it and its scalding cargo were resting on the glistening tabletop, barely two drops spilled and the room bursting into laughter and a foot-drumming applause.

As the eastern sky turned to fire, Po-lee-een tried to call her lover. The house AI answered, telling her that no, Jey-im was quite unavailable, but would she like to leave a message for him to find when he woke?

Too many possibilities came to mind; she settled on saying, "Tell him that his research partner called, and I hope he had good dreams."

"He will," the AI assured, severing the connection.

Bloated relatives were migrating into the deepest subbasement. The family compound had been secured for the day. Close-fitted ceramic blinds covered every window, triple doors were locked from within, and security robots patrolled the hallways and unlit rooms. Fierce winds were coming, and torrential rains, but worse than any natural force were the twisted, embittered people from the most different subclans who bumped themselves up with biorhythmic drugs, remaining awake in the daylight in order to pray on the estivators, destroying what they couldn't steal, and in the horrible cases, kidnapping entire families, then holding them for ransom, or for pleasure.

Their family compound made an inviting target. The occasional thief had slipped past the patrolling robots, escaping with money and antiques. And once, when Po-lee-een was a very young girl, a determined squad of kidnappers managed to circumvent every security device, making it to the subbasement before their leader hesitated, muttered something senseless under his breath, then died in an instant, a fat and healthy artery in his brain detonating like a bomb.

The Few had their own potent security systems, invisible and tamper-proof.

Property could be sacrificed, but if someone raised a blade against the estivators, a nearly magical fate would strike him down.

Po-lee-een felt perfectly safe in the subbasement, lying on a nest of freshly cut felt grass and night flowers. The ceiling was adorned with ancient deities, the paints luminescing in the infrared, warm faces helping to watch over her. And like good jarrtees everywhere, the family offered the appropriate prayers, then together, as one, closed their enormous eyes.

It wasn't sleep in a human sense, but there were dreams.

The gorged bodies cooled gradually. Metabolisms plunged. Happy early dreams decayed into a maelstrom of stark images, random sensations, and finally, the image of Death Herself.

Then, nothing.

Without any sense of time, weeks passed.

The grass dried and the flowers grew dark, the nest shattering gently into a fragrant golden-brown dust. And the bodies narrowed gradually, their platinum skin wrinkling lengthwise, a strange desiccated beauty growing within each of them.

Eventually, the dreams returned.

Death showed Herself again, retreating from the dreamers, her brilliance dissolving into the nourishing darkness of Life.

Waking, Po-lee-een's first duty was to her body. Shivering and sore, she gorged on sweet foods, drinking mug after mug of salted water, retrieving a portion of her old strength. Later, she learned that it had been a stormy, dangerous day. Heavy rains had left the streets waist-deep in runoff. The government admitted that hundreds had died, crushed when a tired hillside collapsed. Who knew how many thousands had really perished; the City's leaders liked to ration the horror. By the time Po-lee-een finally left for school, only a light drizzle was falling, and the streets were mostly dry. What if Jey-im had died? The question struck her suddenly, without warning. It was possible, surely. And it was logical: Why else hadn't he attempted to contact her when he woke? For a wicked moment or two, the girl actually hoped that Jey-im had drowned, giving him an excuse. Then her stomach began to twist in revulsion, and she decided that without question, she had to be the most horrible person in the world. . . .

The school's bright steel gate was raised high. Po-lee-een raced inside, ignoring her teachers' greetings. Then she was outside again, in the rain-drenched courtyard, the felt grass standing tall and rank, and the red tree in bloom again, her lover kneeling nearby, calmly examining the terrors' newest nest.

If Po-lee-een had followed her instincts, there wouldn't be any story.

She wanted to knock Jey-im on his famished ass and scream at him, demanding an explanation for why he never tried to reach her.

Yet she would never be this young again, or as foolish. And the boy, bless him, seemed genuinely happy to see her.

They made love, gracelessly and swiftly, then lay on their backs, holding hands and watching as the strong sea winds blew away the last storm clouds. Through the haze, they looked west at the sun-drenched face of Jarrtee, like a great bowl tilted on end, filled with a thousand raging storms that meant absolutely nothing to them.

Jey-im made his usual noise about their world's beauty and their blessings. But Po-lee-een remained silent, which must have surprised him. He turned his head, and for the first time, he looked at her instead of the world.

"I had good dreams," he reported. "About you, some were."

Everyone else was in class, students and teachers trying to re-master their routines. The courtyard was for the lovers.

Quietly, quietly, the girl asked, "Can I trust you?"

Eyes flickered, growing larger. Then with an even quieter voice, he replied, "I trust *you.*"

"You cannot tell."

"Tell what?"

"Promise me," she whispered. "Never, ever tell."

With both hands, Jey-im gave a solemn pledge, pressing them against both of their chests, feeling the rhythmic beating of every heart.

"You can trust me," he said. Twice.

Summoning every bit of courage, Po-lee-een told the truth.

She didn't give the whole truth, but in those moments, she showed the boy a bright narrow sliver of what was real. She gave him enough to make his eyes grow even larger, his breath held for a long moment, and finally, with a soft trembling voice, he repeated what he had just heard, as if he were sitting in class, committing an ordinary lesson to memory.

He was already aware that the universe had been rebuilt.

But the girl claimed that the worlds were tied together, and an alien from one world could step to another, his soul cloaked in the appropriate species.

Jey-im made doubting sounds.

His lover smiled with her eyes and the tilt of her bald white head.

"How do you know this, Po-lee-een?"

Silence.

"You read it somewhere," he declared hopefully. "Or it's something you dreamt, I think."

With a calm, sturdy voice, she said, "Guess again."

Jey-im was like any bright but otherwise ordinary adolescent. With his imagination outstripped, he was left with a reflexive skepticism. "That's not possible. Changing worlds, and species . . . that's *silly.*"

The girl whistled softly, showing her disappointment.

Wounded but undaunted, Jey-im asked, "How can you know all of this?"

She smiled slyly, then replied with a question.

"How would I know?"

The answer struck him suddenly, by surprise.

His eyes filled his face, gazing at Po-lee-een as if no one else existed in all of Creation.

And that was perhaps what the young girl truly wanted: To win from another soul that look of awe and helpless, utter devotion.

BETWEEN SESSIONS AT SCHOOL, JEY-IM WOULD SLIP AWAY FROM HIS mother's gaze, then he and his exotic companion would roam the City, visiting its most famous places while trying by any means to make passersby jealous.

They wandered the length of the Five Avenues and rode to the top of the Hero's Spire—the tallest building on Jarrtee, to their knowledge—then visited the docks where fishing farmers unloaded their slippery crops and mining trawlers dropped ore sucked off the bottom of the sea. They once happened to see a warship return from a skirmish with a neighboring city-state, its armored hull pitted by explosive bullets and laser blasts, but riding on its bow, in plain view, dangled the silk banner taken from the enemy's ship—a symbol of that clan, and as such, worth an eventual ransom for its safe return.

The City's spaceport lay to the west. When a launch was scheduled, they would ride out on the monoline, then claim two seats in the public galley, watching a new shuttle rise skyward on a column of plasma and blistering light.

Once, they rode past the spaceport, reaching a fortified suburb high in the coastal mountains. The City's boundaries lay much farther west, beyond several more mountain ranges, but for Jey-im they might as well have come to the end of the world.

He couldn't imagine stepping outside the walls of modern ceramics and diamond slashwire. But to Po-lee-een, it was the perfect place to ask the most unimaginable questions.

What if the the assorted clans began trading with one another? she inquired. What if a citizen could move freely between city-states? And most important, what if the world's great scientists and engineers—the revered Masters—could pool their resources?

Jey-im couldn't think in such terms. He offered a weak, baffled moan, then the simple declaration:

"The *outsiders* are too different from us!"

She was ready for that attitude. "After God-Stole-Our-Sky," she reminded him, "there was cooperation, and huge advances were made in a very few years."

He couldn't deny the logic, so he attacked the logic's source. "Is this the way aliens think, Po-lee-een?"

"It's the way I think," she said diplomatically. Then she quoted a Few saying, telling him, "Fluid thoughts make a flexible soul."

Jey-im was slow to appreciate novel philosophies. What he wanted instead were simple descriptions of other worlds and their bizarre people. Since she'd never left Jarrtee, Po-lee-een borrowed heavily from her family's exotic tales and tidbits. Humanoids were abundant in the universe, she promised his timid hearts. But in the next breath, she swore that intelligence could dress itself in every kind of physiology, every possible body. She described worlds cloaked in water, in liquid ammonia, in frigid oceans of liquid hydrocarbons, then with words painted the finned and tentacled inhabitants. There were desert worlds and nearly airless worlds, places where life existed only in the tiniest oases. There were gas giants where twenty sentient species shared the same endless skies. And there were even sunless planets where cold blind geniuses lived huddling next to the core's feeble heat.

The girl never named her sources.

As a precaution, she implied that she was an orphan, her par-

ents unrelated by flesh; and playing along with her game, Jey-im
listened intently to her descriptions, a studious excitement crossing his handsome face.

Midway through the night, they sneaked into the Master's
School—a complex of elderly buildings and modern laboratories set in the City's oldest district. The visit was Jey-im's idea. His
mother and her subclan had strong ties to the institution; perhaps eventually, he hinted, he would serve that hallowed place.

In the middle of their visit, Jey-im vanished.

Then just as suddenly, he reappeared, telling Po-lee-een that
nothing was wrong—even though she hadn't made any worried
sounds.

Later, she was invited to Jey-im's house for a midnight meal. It
was obviously his mother's idea, and the large, overly animated
woman filled every silence by talking relentlessly about nothing.
Occasionally a sister or a few cousins would pass through the
feast room, giggling like stupid balloon birds. Jey-im's father
missed the main course, delayed by some nebulous mishap in his
nebulous government office. When he finally made his grand
entrance, he screamed about damned idiots and feeble subclans
and the tainted fat that had found its way onto his platter. The
guest was barely noticed, which, Po-lee-een discovered, was exactly what she wanted. The truth told, this family was boring and
bleak, and she couldn't understand how Jey-im, or anyone, could
remain happy under these roofs.

In their quiet, polite fashion, Po-lee-een's family asked about
the boy. She answered with a diplomat's care. Mama-ma suggested sharing a meal, but her daughter had ready excuses. Jey-
im was falling behind in school and needed to study; he was ill
with a fungus infection, then bloody diarrhea; and finally, he
was grounded for a wide array of crimes that, she assured, had
nothing to do with her.

The image of Jey-im sitting at their feast table, knowing what
he knew and guessing who knew what, made the girl take pause.

Only one family member saw past the subterfuge, and that

was her favorite cousin. But that was Trinidad's talent. Without effort, he could reach inside any person and pull out every one of her terrible secrets.

She was walking to school with her cousin, and he gave her a sudden and very peculiar look. Then with a too-loud voice, he said, "You know what they're calling you? 'The golden couple.' "

"Is that so?"

"Everyone's asking, 'How does that common-born girl coax a high-born boy into her manacles?' "

Po-lee-een wasn't common-born, and Jey-im's family wasn't that important. But the words had their intended effect. "Is that what *they* are asking? Or is it you, cousin?"

"They ask," he assured. "Me? I already know exactly what you've told him."

She stopped in midstride, hugging her computer for a terrible, endless moment. "You don't know anything," she managed.

"Don't I?"

Bright black eyes sliced through the girl. She was simple, and transparent, and now her cousin was going to warn their family that she was a fool.

"Hardly," he replied, reading her thoughts. "I won't say a word."

"No?"

Laughter bled into a thin reassurance. "Po-lee-een," he purred, "you're a lot of things, but you're not an idiot."

"Thank you."

"But your Jey-im's the idiot," he warned, with hearty conviction. "And I don't think he really appreciates you, cousin."

She bristled, but said nothing.

"I won't tell," Trinidad promised, again. "Why would I want to spoil such a marvelous game?"

His advice about Jey-im was unwelcome, and it was accurate.

Po-lee-een began to notice the older girls flirting with her soulmate. But since jealousy was for the weak, she showed none. And since she refused to believe that anyone could get between them, she couldn't stop trusting the boy.

Before the night's final session, she arrived early at school, eager to check the sensors that they'd glued to three terrors. Pushing through the withered blossoms of the red trees, she heard a soft voice, then a foot being dragged through grass. Jey-im was sitting in the open, motionless. A girl was sitting beside him. They were doing nothing. They weren't even touching each other. But their heads were tilted back, eyes gazing at a private sky . . . and in that instant, Po-lee-een discovered a scalding jealousy with a temper to match.

She was shouting suddenly, startling everyone. Even herself.

"How about if I throw your fucking face into a terror's nest?" she told the girl. "How would you like that? How, how?"

The girl leaped to her feet, then fled.

But Jey-im held his ground, defending himself and the innocent girl, then blaming, of all people, Po-lee-een.

"I'm sick of your crazy stories!" he cried out. "Pretending to be so different, so special! This shit about worlds touching worlds . . . it's not true! And I'm not even going to pretend to believe you anymore!"

The girl was wounded, but she wouldn't retreat.

With a tight little voice, she said, "I'm telling the truth." Then after a deep breath, she added, "And I can prove it. Now."

Jey-im whistled, in doubt.

But there was curiosity left in him, and probably a nugget of guilt. Reluctantly, he agreed to give her another chance.

They slipped out of school while most of the students were filing inside, and she left the boy waiting at a nearby crossroads. Alone, Po-lee-een sprinted home. In a subbasement near the family's nest, inside an unlocked compartment watched over by Few-made devices, was a large, scrupulously ordinary tool belt. She had watched her Uncle Ka-ceen deactivate the safeguards, and she did the same things, then removed an old titanium club, a slightly bent staple, and an anonymous scrap of wood. Placing all three in a carrying pouch, she walked past the kitchen door, through a cloud of luscious smells, hesitating only when she heard her father's quiet voice, then pressing on, ignoring every instinct.

Jey-im was impatient and worried about his exams. In agony, he muttered, "That's a club! What do we want with a club?"

"I'm going to beat stubborn things with it," she warned. "Come with me!"

They rode the monoline south. Sprawling family compounds gave way to smaller compounds shouldered in beside one another. They disembarked at a nondescript crossroads, then walked into a narrow, nameless alley, the girl leading while the boy held back, whimpering, "What are we doing, Po-lee-een?"

The alley opened into a small, weedy courtyard. One corner of the courtyard was paved with eroded black glass. Decades ago, just before God-Stole-Our-Sky, this disk and others like it had appeared during the day. Every city-state had a few of them. The disks were minor mysteries until the stars vanished, then they were forgotten mysteries. Offering an abbreviated history, Po-lee-een knelt, arranging the wood and staple and club around the disk's center, speaking in a low quick voice, an electric surge passing through her arms, warning her that she had finished.

Jey-im watched her, not the sky.

Rising, she explained, "This disk marks an intrusion. The intrusion is tinier than an electron, and it leads to another world. A world that's safe for us."

Skeptical to the end, he asked, "How does it feel, being insane?"

She stared at Jey-im, for an instant or an age, waiting to see that imprecise quality that her uncle had seen in Aunt Me-meel. In his genes and in his soul were supposed to be the harbingers of talent; yet despite a tenacious hopefulness, all she could find was a rigid, almost granitic indifference.

A chill clarity struck her suddenly.

She turned, ready to kick the three devices out of alignment. But Jey-im had grown tired of watching the madwoman; lifting his eyes, he discovered to his utter astonishment that the sky was strewn with tiny but brilliant starlike lights.

They were beacons.

Each beacon marked an intrusion used by the Few. They were visible only to the two children, and only while they stood on the disk. But for them, the cumulative light of thousands of intrusions nearly washed away the storm-wracked face of Jarrtee.

Too late, Po-lee-een realized just how horrible things were.

In a low, horrified voice, the boy chanted:

"She is. Alien. She is."

No. She was born here, born jarrtee, and she felt ready to defend her loyalty to their species and the world. Yet there wasn't time to speak. With a frantic, almost comical gait, Jey-im began to run, quick legs carrying him through the pale, late-night weeds, arms raised overhead and his eyes cast downward, his shrill little-boy voice calling for his parents, pleading for their blessed strength.

On the earth, night had reached the western sky, leaving the bedroom in deep shadow.

Porsche could just make out her lover's narrow face, the sharp cheeks and chin softened by night and fatigue. Yet Cornell's eyes were wide awake, astonishment mixed with a fierce curiosity, and without saying any words, he begged to know what had happened next.

Porsche could pity that lust-sick girl. She couldn't forgive her for her actions or inactions, yet she easily comprehended the motives. More than two decades stood between them, yet suddenly, as she told the rest of it, she felt the hard, nervous beating of lost hearts.

"I went straight home," she explained. "My father and every uncle were busy with the dawn feast. I walked up to Father and set the club and staple and wood on the bloody chopping block—between two fish heads, I remember—and I told him. I told everyone. Everything. Fast, and honest."

Cornell waited for a long moment, then said, "And?"

"You know my father. If anything, he was too calm. Too much in control." She shook her head, saying, "He didn't blame me or even act particularly worried, which were awful signs. Perhaps the boy wouldn't tell anyone, he offered. And chances were that he wouldn't be believed. And besides, there were some tricks that the Few kept for emergencies—"

"Such as?"

"Memories," she said. "They're electrochemical signals. By definition, they're temporary possessions. Extremely perishable."

"You could erase what had happened?"

"Possibly." She shifted under the covers, suddenly uncomfortable. "Uncle Ka-ceen was the angry one. He started chopping the heads off every fish in the kitchen, screaming at me. He was a high-ranking citizen in the Few. An important man in Jarrtee's security network. 'Wait in your cubicle,' he told me. 'Wait and think about every stupid thing that you've done.' Which I did. And after a geologic age, he and Father came to tell me what they had learned. Father did the talking. Uncle Ka-ceen just seethed. And that's when I finally realized that everything had changed, suddenly and for always."

For a long moment, silence.

Then she continued, saying, "Remember when we visited the Master's School and Jey-im vanished? Well, I learned that he'd slipped away to find a certain scientist—a physicist, basically— and he asked the poor man some pointed questions about quantum intrusions. The scientist told him that such things were impossible, then asked where he had heard that nonsense. But Jey-im just ran, thankfully. And the scientist had done his duty and filled out a report with the security office. And Uncle Ka-ceen found the report inside an important someone's active file.

" 'That set off the first alarm,' my uncle interjected.

" 'Not the first alarm,' said Father, defending me but only to a point. 'Several things have happened lately. Others have been careless, too. Taken alone, none of these incidents matter. Together, we aren't sure.'

" 'Your boyfriend is talking,' Uncle Ka-ceen snarled. 'My eavesdroppers found him chattering like a mud fish. To his mother, his father. And now, high officials.'

" 'But for the moment,' said Father, 'no one seems to have decided what to do.' "

Cornell was watching Porsche, picturing the alien scene with its frothy, nearly human tensions.

"On the other hand," she admitted, "we'd already made our decision."

"To escape," he whispered.

"We held a family meeting disguised as a dawn feast. Everyone sat at the marble table, for the last time. No food. We didn't dare estivate. And with an electronic smoke screen in place, my father rose and spoke." She hesitated, for an instant. "He sounded calm, but his eyes weren't. He tried not to blame anyone, but he was the one talking because one of his children had done something unthinkable. I sat very still, wishing that I could repair the damage. I kept imagining myself doing brave, outrageous deeds that would make everything right. But the damage just kept getting bigger, and worse."

"What do you mean?"

"Since they'd come to my cubicle, the jarrtees had made certain decisions. Separate security bureaus were investigating our family history. The military had a squad watching the disk that I'd shown Jey-im. And an assortment of robots and tiny microphones were studying our home, confidently telling their masters that we were happily eating fat and blood stews, nothing out of the ordinary."

"I wouldn't believe the boy," Cornell admitted. "A crazy story like that—"

"Think like a jarrtee," was Porsche's advice. "You estivate through the long day, and you're utterly helpless. You have a long bloody history, but your enemies have always been jarrtee. They've always fought by your rules. Then you suddenly learn that in your ranks, perhaps next door, are creatures that look and smell and sound exactly like you. But they aren't you, and they live secret lives, and who knows what kinds of powers they wield?"

Cornell said nothing.

"After reporting the latest news," said Porsche, "my father took his seat. And my oldest living grandparent rose and turned, looking at each of us in turn. She looked at me last. Then she told us, 'At first light, we will embark. Arrangements are being made now.' The smallest children didn't understand, and everyone was a little scared, or a lot scared. My little brother gazed up at me, and with a serious expression, asked if he should pack his toys.

"Grandmama said, 'No.' She said, 'Where we are going, we can only take ourselves. Which is enough. Your toys and your clothes will have to care for themselves.' "

Cornell found Porsche's hand beneath the covers, squeezing hard.

"The Few have an expression," she mentioned, realizing finally that for a little while now she had been crying. "Grandmama used the expression then."

"What is it?"

She pushed her tears with her free hand, saying, " 'Misfortune always finds you, and it brings nothing but promise.' "

BLESS HIS APE HEART, CORNELL TRIED TO SAY THE RIGHT WORDS.

Speaking from a rich vein of experience, he reminded her that children make mistakes. These things happened long ago, and she'd acted out of love, and besides, he added, what was the result? Cornell had spent time with her parents and two brothers; they were the healthiest, happiest family he'd ever met. Porsche had obviously thrived in her new environment. And to bring up the obvious: Cornell never would have met her, much less earned his way into her bed, if that earlier suitor hadn't made the biggest blunder in his otherwise trivial life.

Porsche let the compliments and encouragements wash over her. Then the words stopped, and he kissed her forehead, her strong chin, and the humid terrain farther south. Indulging herself, she lay on her back, breathing a little fast and very hard, concentrating on her pleasure until she was close, then pulling him up over her and into her and burying her face into a pillow, suffocating the sobs.

Moments later, Cornell climaxed, and after a flurry of grateful grunts, he collapsed.

"Better?" he muttered.

"Diverted," she allowed.

"Good."

She lay motionless for a moment, feeling perfectly alert. Then she chimed out, "Back soon," and slipped out of bed, dressing quickly, the floor creaking and her slick sweats chirping as she moved into the pitch-black hallway, latching the bedroom door behind her.

Memory took her to the bathroom. While the ancient toilet did its lazy flush, she turned on the light and stood before the solitary mirror. Brushing out her long butterscotch hair while watching her human face, she recalled the precise moment when she first saw those nut-brown human eyes, and where she was, and the extraordinary circumstances.

Cornell would be asleep by now, she assumed.

She slipped back into the room, then into bed, trying not to rouse him. He was on his stomach, his face hidden. And lying on her back, watching the feeble glow of the poster's stars, Porsche remembered the first moment that she ever set eyes on him.

Porsche had been employed by the Cosmic Event Agency. Her case officer—a bulldog of a woman named Smith—showed off the file on a prospective employee. Even by the agency's standards, Cornell Novak had a peculiar background. There was no mother in the picture; the father was an exotic creature whom he hadn't seen in years; and Cornell himself had no lasting relationships, or long-term jobs, or ties of any kind.

The agency's elaborate, inadequate tests showed that Cornell was a natural talent. Not as gifted as Porsche, Ms. Smith conceded. But nearly so.

Eager to give their new recruit every benefit, her employers urged Porsche to introduce herself. "Encourage the boy," said the bulldog woman. "Help him see the noble good we're trying to do here."

Encouragement meant dinner.

The agency maintained a motel-like facility for its brave explorers, complete with a restaurant. Porsche arranged to meet Cornell in the lobby, and the truth told, she didn't have grand expectations. But with her first glance, she found herself remembering Aunt Me-meel and her wild claim that people with talent would somehow recognize talent in others.

She had always doubted her aunt's story. That kind of "knowing" smelled too easy.

But Cornell, bless him, proved her wrong.

Of course she didn't mention her past at dinner, or her aunts, and she managed to hide her feelings from Cornell, and to a lesser degree, from herself.

Later, when they were stationed together on High Desert, she tried to protect Cornell, giving him plum assignments and overseeing his rapid education. He was a quick learner, and he was clever. Following a hunch, he had hired Timothy Kleck during a vacation. Porsche's background was examined and found wanting. Then when the agency's mismanaged mission collapsed, and when it looked as if neither would survive, he confessed what he knew and what he suspected.

For only the second time in her life, Porsche confessed, adding that she had infiltrated the CEA in order to keep tabs on the agency's progress, and its less than noble goals.

Later they escaped High Desert. Barely.

Ms. Smith and the agency congratulated them on their success, and in the same breath warned them to never tell what had happened.

But Cornell had different plans. The agency was a sloppy, self-serving machine. He had learned that people had been hurt when they tried to go public. Some of them may have been killed. He was too much of the idealist—too much like his father—to walk away. And for a slew of good reasons, Porsche had vowed to help, their strange little family existing for no other purpose than to yank the CEA out of hiding, letting the world see it and its crimes.

Finally, she was becoming drowsy.

It was three in the morning. The not-so Big Dipper on the ceiling was pointing in an unfamiliar angle, pulling the rest of the constellations with it. Porsche closed her eyes and fell immediately into a half-dream, lying on Jarrtee again, in a stand of graceful and soft felt grass, her lover close to her. She assumed she was dreaming about Jey-im, but then Cornell rose up on his elbow, his human face utterly out of place. Touching her slitlike nostrils, he said, "So." He said, "Tell me the rest. How did you escape from that planet?"

Porsche's eyes flew open.

"Did I wake you, Po-lee-een?"

Cornell was lying beside her in bed, smiling.

"No." It was a lover's lie. "No, I was awake."

Po-lee-een had never been awake in full daylight.

She was wearing an airy black robe to protect her pale flesh, the hood raised and tied tight, and fitted over her eyes were thick obsidian goggles. She was first to climb through the back window, dropping into a narrow alleyway behind the compound. Despite goggles and the early morning shadows, the brightness of stones and mortar and the hazy sky were physically painful. The girl took a breath, then another, quelling that one pain long enough to stand beneath the window, offering both hands when a second fugitive emerged.

Trinidad slipped down the polished wall.

"Thank you," he offered, even though he had evaded her grasp.

Together, they helped their siblings and cousins, then the adults; and in turn, the adults helped ease their own frail parents to the ground, using elastic slings prepared for just this occasion.

Only Uncle Ka-ceen was missing.

The window was sealed behind them, the compound secured for the day. The house AI and security robots, and the police eavesdroppers, were being fed false data. This was an ordinary dawn, said the lie. The tenants were estivating, and as always, they were utterly harmless people.

Po-lee-een hadn't eaten.

A packet of hormones had been implanted under her silky skin, making her blood taste of dusk, not dawn.

Yet her body knew better. She was exhausted, fighting the weight of eyelids and legs, forcing herself to shuffle down the alley with the others. The only blessing was that fatigue left little room for sadness or fear, and even her gnawing sense of guilt was blunted.

The alley curled between neighboring compounds, then ended.

A long bus blocked their way, its engine humming, the windows silvery-black, and its armored body hovering just above the pavement, wearing the ornate blood-colored emblem of the military.

Po-lee-een hesitated, ready to run.

Then Father grabbed her shoulder, saying, "No. Wait."

Miracle of miracles, her missing uncle emerged from the bus, dressed in a day-duty uniform. Looking official in pantaloons and a loose shirt, he warned everyone, "Stay quiet." Then he stared at Po-lee-een—she could feel the eyes behind the military goggles—and he added, "Whatever happens, not another damned word."

She willed herself to become invisible.

Climbing on board, Po-lee-een took the first empty seat, then watched her brothers claim their own seat, as did her parents. The space beside her remained empty. Then Trinidad appeared, and he would have none of that nonsense. Not only did he sit, he patted her on the thigh, saying the delicious words:

"A new world for us. Finally."

She said nothing, but the hidden eyes smiled.

The overhead doors were sealed, and the bus accelerated. Only odd or desperate jarrtees would risk making a daylight journey, the girl knew, and they were sure to draw an official gaze. But if their vehicle was military, and if an officer accompanied them—and if he could show documentation and the proper boldness—then they wouldn't have any trouble. That's what her cousin assured her, in whispers, sketching out the general plan.

In the brilliance of day, the City became a different place. Textures and colors were transformed. Distances were stretched. Every stark building and empty crossroads seemed rich with menace. Po-lee-een held her cousin's hands, gazing out the window. People were extinct. Nothing moved, save for the rare robot. Studying the passing bus, each robot asked the central AI for guidance. And somewhere deep in the AIs, Few-made machines were doctoring the usual protocols, canceling the appropriate paranoia.

Living jarrtees would be much less predictable, unfortunately.

Using obscure avenues and modest speeds, Uncle Ka-ceen took them inland, slipping past the spaceport and finally reaching the first swatches of open country. Bad luck placed a pair of low-ranking officers at a crossroads. They wore silvered helmets and body armor, and with rip-guns in easy reach, they ordered the bus to stop, then demanded explanations.

Her uncle played his role perfectly, brittle politeness mixed with impatience. He opened his door, letting in a scorching light, then showed off his medallion of rank and their official pass, reading the pass aloud, in case the idiots were illiterates, too.

"These are Fire pilgrims," he claimed.

A strange, strict faith, the Order of Fire believed that great truths lay deep in the sun's evil, and by using the latest hormonal tricks, its priests remained awake for fat portions of the day. But what made the Order even more bizarre was that it had converts in many different clans, up and down the coastline and halfway across the world.

"They've been called by their god," Uncle Ka-ceen assured. "She's called them to her temple up on Grand Mountain, and I'm their escort."

The ranking officer seemed unimpressed.

"I obey my orders," he growled, "and then the gods. Maybe."

No one spoke.

The officer thrust his head down into the bus, more than thirty goggled faces reflected in his helmet. "Shit, you've got children in here!"

"I know that," her uncle replied.

"Children!" The man seemed volatile, short-tempered. Even with hormones and ample training, daylight was playing hell with his nerves. "This is fucking dangerous enough, even for adults!"

Uncle Ka-ceen agreed, adding, "You can appreciate why we're in such a hurry, can't you?"

The officer ignored him. Shouting at the adult pilgrims, he said, "Your god should have called you a little earlier in the night . . . the bitch . . . !"

No one agreed, or disagreed.

"You have to make sure these babies feast before you finally estivate. And if they don't feel hungry, stuff them full anyway."

"Of course," sang Mama-ma, and others.

Thinking he had won, Uncle Ka-ceen asked for his pass and permission to move.

But the officer hesitated. "If you're going toward the Grand Mountain," he muttered, "this isn't your quickest route."

"Because you're trying to block our way," her uncle replied, the scorn reflexive, and wrong.

There was a pause, then the officer growled, "Step out for a moment, please."

Uncle Ka-ceen said a soft, nonsensical word.

"What was that?"

A Few-built device emitted a hard, focused pulse, and both officers collapsed onto the hot pavement. And an instant later, the bus was accelerating, the force field beneath it shoving the limp bodies out of the way.

Exhausted or not, Po-lee-een was suddenly scared.

But her cousin chose a different attitude. Eyes smiled behind the impenetrable goggles, and he squeezed her hand, saying her full jarrtee name for the last time, then assuring her, "This is fun. A thousand times better than climbing some old roof!"

Every object adrift in space possessed its own intrusions.

Jarrtee was sprinkled with them, but the crushing majority lead to dead places—comets, moons, and nameless pebbles. There were plenty of living worlds, but relatively few had evolved the proper intelligence. Souls couldn't cross an intrusion unless some comparable intelligence lived on the other side. Plus the refugees needed an intrusion near the City, and the new world had to have been settled by the Few, and there had to be ample room for a large family to blend into the general population, and everything had to be accomplished in a bare-bones minimum of time.

Po-lee-een couldn't calculate the odds against such a paradise.

Yet they had a destination. She'd overheard enough to know they were making for an intrusion somewhere past the coastal mountains. Then as they were skating along a serpentine road, nothing around them but the sun-starved blue-black forest, her cousin bent close and said a single odd word:

"EE-arth."

"What's that?" she muttered.

"Guess." Then he squeezed her hands, saying, "My father told me about it."

She tried to say the world's name, twice.

"EE-arth is very much like Jarrtee," he joked. "Except for the differences."

"What differences?"

"A cold, thin atmosphere. More water than land. And a big yellow sun that could feast on our little orange friend."

Suddenly the bus crossed an exposed ridge. Through goggles and the tinted glass, people looked back over the ground just covered, the mountain slopes softened by the shaggy trees, the City reduced to a simple gray plain, and over the distant ocean, piled high by wind and the sun's heat, were the day's first storm clouds. An incandescent wafer lay behind the heaviest clouds, and the irony was rich enough for a child to find: Po-lee-een had never before seen Jarrtee's sun, and now she would never see it again.

"EE-arth has half our gravity," her cousin continued. "It dances with a giant moon, and wheels crazy-fast on its axis."

"How fast?"

"Nights and days come in a blur."

"It doesn't sound anything like Jarrtee." The girl was confident that she could adapt to anything, but what about Aunt Me-meel and the others not Few-born? "Tell me something familiar, please."

"Its people resemble us." In crisp detail, he described the human species. "In most technologies, they're more primitive. Their sky hasn't everted, but it will soon. And they're social animals, like us. With cities. With clanlike states. With a history of wars, but lately, like jarrtees, they're mostly at peace."

"Do they estivate?"

"They're diurnal," he warned. "But they can stay awake all night, if they want."

She tried to say *Earth* a third time.

Then she was quiet, gazing out the window, trying to commit details to memory. Again, as if for the first time, she realized what was happening, what she was about to lose. Events were too large to embrace in just moments, or in a morning. And suddenly even this strange country seemed precious, and she wanted desperately to take it with her, in her mind.

The road plunged back into forest, welcome shadows pulling over them. Then the shadows fattened as clouds poured over them, a light drizzle seeping through branches and epiphytes. At an unmarked crossroads, their bus pulled to a stop. Uncle Kaceen rose, speaking with urgency. "A patrol is waiting up ahead." He paused, listening to the voice of his eavesdroppers. "They want us," he reported. "We can't drive around them, and we won't fight."

Adults muttered among themselves, trying to agree.

"So," her uncle announced, "we're walking. It's not far, if we help each other."

Still wearing the black robes, they abandoned their vehicle, then watched it continue down a secondary road, steered by its AI. Snacks were handed out, and the children were cautioned to eat slowly. A game trail was found and followed, people climbing up into the wild mountains, keeping a disciplined line until the trail bled away. Then the parents found their children, and in smaller groups, with the help of more Few-made machines, they picked their way toward a golden destination.

Po-lee-een held her little brother's arm. Her older brother and Father helped with his mother, the woman strong but tiring, her confident voice telling everyone, "If it comes to it, leave me."

"You're not being left anywhere," Father replied, his voice scrubbed of doubt and hesitation.

"We're getting close," Mama-ma began to say. The device in her hand was indistinguishable from a jarrtee pen. "Down this slope now. Here, come this way."

A wind rose in the tall trees.

No, not a wind. It was the wash of compressed air, Po-lee-een realized. Glancing up, she caught sight of an enormous something passing overhead, and she dropped her face by reflex and made her little brother do the same.

"They're hunting us," she said softly, urgently.

It was a military dirigible, armored aerogels laid over super-strong silks that were buoyed up by vacuum bubbles. Its crew was watching the forest with delicate sensors. But woven into the black robes were electronic camouflage, hiding their body heat, obliterating their tracks, twisting light and sound until the fugitives were indistinguishable from ghosts.

The dirigible's engines pulsed, sending the enemy elsewhere.

But the danger could return any moment, sending down foot patrols, or worse, a random rain of explosives and nerve toxins.

Suddenly, with a soft, nervous voice, Father said, "Run."

Po-lee-een obeyed, pulling her brother behind her. She couldn't remember ever running out of fear; everything felt like a game, pushing downhill through the tangled brush, thinking of nothing but the finish line.

"We're close!" called out Mama-ma, from behind.

A great old twanya tree stood in her way, and Po-lee-een sidestepped it just as a figure emerged. She saw a man wearing a uniform, his pantaloons stained with plant saps and greasy dirt . . . and she didn't hesitate, leaping at the figure, driving the heel of her hand into an astonished, suddenly familiar face.

Her uncle fell backward. Stunned, limp.

Po-lee-een stood over him for a moment, consciously doing nothing. Then she offered a hand that he refused to take, picking himself off the ground, no one speaking.

In the next few moments, little knots of the family converged on the twanya tree. Trinidad waved at her, mouthing his congratulations. The ground between them was relentlessly ordinary, nothing to distinguish it from any other ground; yet everyone pointed their pens and medallions and little coins at the same precise spot.

They didn't have any means to open an intrusion.

It would have been a tremendous risk to bring a key with them. No tool was more valuable to the Few, or more jealously guarded, meaning that at regular, prearranged intervals, someone on the new world would have to open the way for them.

There was a brief, nervous wait. A gust of wind sounded exactly like a dirigible trying to maneuver, but it was just the wind of a coming storm. People prepared to wait a long while. Then, without warning, an electric sensation passed through them, in a wave, feeling both strange and familiar in equal measure.

"Children first," said Uncle Ka-ceen.

Po-lee-een was standing closest. The ground beneath her seemed to shift and flow, and she stepped forward, then took a longer step that covered less distance. Then the ground split wide, revealing a whirlpool, black as tar and spinning with a relentless majesty, nothing left of twanya trees or mountain slopes, or horizons, or Jarrtee.

Her parents and grandparents had told her what to expect, but emotions outstripped every remembered word.

She tried to squeal with excitement, with terror, with an unrestrained, inadequate joy. The long robe dissolved in an instant, followed by her body, nothing left but a sturdy *self* that walked out of simple habit.

The whirlpool swelled a million times, then abruptly shriveled down to a knotted little vein, and when she pushed into the vein, she shrank to nothing, climbing out into a wide rubbery bowl with her at the bottom, struggling uphill on newborn legs.

In reflex, she glanced at her hands, their bones too fine and long and the flesh sickly, hanging loose and adorned with a thin golden fuzz that had a name.

Hair, she thought.

She looked at her body, astonished. The legs seemed too long and thin to carry their trunk, and she was ugly, composed of senseless parts whose names lay inside her newly fashioned brain. Her chest was swollen, and she thought: *Breasts.* She groped her sexual organ, names from the proper to the vulgar occurring to her. Then a probing finger found another orifice, and aloud, with a new mouth, she shouted, "Rectum!"

A new sky emerged.

Stars sparkled in the clearest, blackest sky that could ever exist. A wild galaxy stretched overhead, pretending to be real, and the girl was thrilled, and impatient, forcing her ridiculous legs to run, carrying her out of the intrusion.

The cold struck without warning, without mercy.

Bare feet stepped onto a slippery white world, and she began to slide, losing her balance and recovering it again, her feet twisting sideways and biting at the snow, saving her from the ignominy of a face-first fall.

She gulped at the thin air, conscious of her mouth's new shape and the eerie normalcy of balloonlike lungs working fast.

Behind her, a single object—the essential key—lay on the foot-packed snow, anchored in place by the opened intrusion, looking for all the world like a simple mitten.

More children appeared, features hidden by the darkness.

Trinidad giggled, then slipped and spilled.

Po-lee-een grabbed him by the arm and lifted, and thought *penis.*

She herded the children together, making them share their warmth.

This was a different world, a different mountain slope, with a brutal winter locked over the land. Her body warned that she wasn't adapted to this climate, limbs shaking and her new teeth banging against each other. No one else was in view. What if something had gone wrong? What if there was no one to help them? But she saw strangers emerging from behind what looked like trees, and they were holding out gifts of polybutte under-wear and wool trousers and ostrich-leather boots and heavy winter coats, everything freshly purchased in scattered sporting goods stores and packed deep into the wilderness for exactly this moment.

Po-lee-een barely noticed the gifts.

What caught her gaze were the faces, starlit and showing teeth—larger and fewer in number than jarrtee teeth—and she showed her teeth in the same fashion, muttering her first clumsy words to people on her new home.

"Thank you," she said.

"Your sky," she said.

"I like . . . your sky . . . !"

THE REFUGEES WERE CLOTHED, AND WITH THE HELP OF FLASHLIGHTS, ushered down a forested ridge that opened onto a snowy meadow. Bonfires roared. Half a dozen enormous Dutch ovens were filled with stew and greasy chili, cellulose bowls and big spoons begging to be used. A hungry soul receives a hungry body when it is translated through an intrusion. No one needed encouragement to eat, and everyone stood too close to the fires, relishing the heat as they wolfed down their belated dawn feast, everyone chewing jarrtee-fashion, mouths wide open.

Father had become a tall human, the plain pink face surrounding tiny and sunken, nearly exhausted brown eyes. Mamama was smaller but not small, pretty and dark, her face streaked with quiet, reflective tears. Po-lee-een's brothers were obviously related. The intrusion had given them Father's face and Mamama's build, and if examined, their DNA would not only prove parentage, it would show the effects of a life spent on the earth: Tiny mutations, the occasional large mutation, and wrapped among their own selves, an assortment of estivating, mostly harmless viruses.

As on Jarrtee, Po-lee-een had more of her father's build and her grandparents' handsome features. And Trinidad was rooted in the same genetics, meaning that when they stood side by side, they looked like sister and brother—the long unkempt hair, the young faces eerily similar, and those tall, fast-maturing bodies fashioned around an easy, almost unconscious grace.

Between bites of white potato, the girl said, "Earth," loudly, with relish, the word natural and effortless.

Intrusions weren't passive filters; they were aggressive, relentless machines, taking cues from the immediate world before clothing any soul.

The intrusion on that high ridge had taken its cues from their hosts.

The apparent leader—a large-built woman who conspicuously didn't offer any name—explained that they were built from European and African DNA. Heritage had its significance. "This is empty country," she told them, her voice booming. "Few people come here. There was the chance that you'd pop out being Mescalero Apache."

"That's a problem?" asked Mama-ma.

The woman snorted, then said, "They're a people and language that's just about extinct. As it is, you belong to the victors."

The refugees contemplated those words.

"We've got a long march out of here," the woman warned. "The sun's up in two hours, which is soon. We'll leave then. We've got a storm bearing down on us, which is trouble. So try to rest now, if you can."

But Po-lee-een had never felt more alert.

The nameless woman and two men began to march up the mountainside, each carrying a heavy pack.

"They're going to mark the intrusion," her cousin told her. "Let's watch them. Just to make sure they do it right."

They had strong legs, handling the slope and altitude without much trouble. Starlight and the snow made it easy to navigate, even with their tiny eyes. The snow proved to be a fascinating distraction. They would stop now and again, examining the tracks that people and strange animals had left. They played with the beautiful white stuff. Delayed, they missed watching their hosts set up the equipment. But they saw a flash of dull red light, then heard a sizzling roar, the foot-mashed snow around the intrusion vaporized and the ground beneath melted, its substance transformed in myriad ways, visible and not.

The intrusion wasn't just marked, it had been capped—in effect, changed from an open route between worlds to a secured doorway. Should humans ever learn how to pass between worlds, a capped intrusion would add another barrier, requiring not a single, relatively simple key, but six distinct keys, encrypted and acting together.

It was an ancient precaution. The Few had learned and learned again: Keep strict control over your own gateways.

Some night, in a year or ten thousand years, an identical disk—a second locked doorway—would be constructed on Jarr-tee. But for the moment, capping the intrusion's far end would draw too many curious, unfriendly eyes.

Three adults were kneeling in the dark, speaking quietly as they warmed their hands over the cooling glass.

The children ignored them. The nearby snow had partly melted, and they realized quickly that the stuff could be packed into icy balls.

The big woman was doing most of the whispering. Then she hesitated, rose to her feet, and turned, snapping at the children, "What are your names?"

Po-lee-een tried to say her name, but her mouth stumbled badly.

Her cousin didn't try to answer. Instead, he called out, "First, tell me your name!"

The woman bristled, then said, "I'm not apologizing. I won't."

Apologize for what?

"I'm doing everything I can for you," she snarled. "Don't accuse me of anything but my best."

The woman had been talking about them.

"But if it was up to me," she continued, "I'd have left that stupid girl behind."

"Which girl?" asked Po-lee-een, softly.

"The idiot who created this mess!"

Po-lee-een opened her mouth, fully intending to tell the truth. But she never had the chance. With a solid grunt, Trinidad threw an icy lump of snow into the woman's chest, punching the air out of it and nearly knocking her off her feet, nearly putting her into that steaming lake of molten stone.

The woman was enraged. She charged down to the meadow and told everyone to break camp immediately. "We're getting out of here!"

It was a lucky rage. Grandparents and the smallest children slowed their hike out of the mountains. They hadn't gone far when the sun exploded over the nearby horizon, its chill golden light washing over the strange parade. Looking at the people's colorful coats and the knitted caps, Po-lee-een realized that her new eyes were picking up hues that she'd never imagined. Even when clouds spread across the sky, dulling the land, she found herself marveling at the emerald green of the pines and the indigo in a wild bird's plumage, and even the gentle pink in her own hands, exposed to the raw wind as she retied her little brother's boots, her breath visible as she asked him, and herself, "Isn't this place lovely?"

"I miss our home," was the boy's only response.

Before noon, snow was falling, the flakes delicate and intricate and taking her by surprise.

By mid-afternoon, that miracle of frozen water had reduced visibility and the beauty down to nothing. It was as if the jarrtee storms had chased them through the intrusion, cold now but still intent on punishing them. At one point, they nearly filed past a row of automobiles standing on simple wheels. Realizing their mistake, the nameless woman doubled back, unlocked one of the metal doors, then sounded the horn—a piercing scream that resembled a balloon bird's warning cry.

Po-lee-een was too tired to laugh at the coincidence, too tired to even feel her fatigue. Climbing into a cramped back seat, she was dimly aware of being out of the wind, sandwiched between her brothers and feeling negligibly warmer. Every sensation was muted. The novelty of a new body and new world were fading. Gazing out at the roaring white storm, she felt nothing but a weary despair, the earth too simple and far too small for the likes of her, a secret piece of herself vowing to leave, just as soon as she was old enough to wander.

As it happened, the big woman drove their automobile. If there was a road, it wasn't visible beneath the seamless white blanket. Father and Mama-ma were wedged into the front seat beside her. With her eternally angry voice, the woman warned them, "In this nation, people drive. You'll have to learn how."

"We will," Mama-ma said gamely.

"Can I drive too?" asked the youngest brother.

"Soon," Father promised. Then he added, "We have much to learn. We know." He was trying to sound conciliatory. "And if I haven't yet, please accept my thanks for all your welcome help."

"Tell that to *her* cousin," the woman growled, thinking of the snowball.

"I know it's an imposition," Father continued, unaware of the incident. "Little warning, and no time for the usual preparations. But I'm sure that we'll blend in soon enough."

The woman gave the slightest nod.

An uncomfortable silence descended. Finally, Father coughed, then said, "If I may ask, what are your plans for us?"

"I'm dealing with a lot of immigrants, lately," she replied. "Single adults, mostly. Young couples, sometimes. These are the first children to come past me."

"It's not the ideal age to emigrate," Mama-ma offered.

"This sky everts in a few months. Everyone should be in position, their lives nicely established, before the natives can guess what's happening."

"Very reasonable," said Father.

The woman squeezed the steering wheel until it squeaked,

then straightened her back and said, "It was decided—and not by me—that we can't risk keeping your entire family together. That would be too difficult to engineer, and too easy for someone else to doubt."

Po-lee-een's parents glanced at each other, emotions playing across their faces.

"You five will remain together, naturally. With your own family names, your own life stories—"

"No," Po-lee-een muttered, a sudden knife slicing into her belly.

"Each little family gets a different name, and a separate home. As it is," she warned, "we can't guarantee perfection with any of you. There's always that outside chance that someone will notice the incongruities."

"I understand," said Father, the words not matched by his doubting voice.

Mama-ina placed a hand on his shoulder, looking straight ahead.

Quietly, sadly, her little brother asked, "What happens to my cousins?"

"Officially, you won't have any." The woman spoke with a grim matter-of-factness. "You'll be able to talk to them through secure means, on occasion. But it'll be several years before you can see them again. And when you do, you'll have to take precautions."

Po-lee-een peered out the back window. The other vehicles were following, one after another, looking tiny and half-real in the blizzard. They seemed to be hovering on the brink of being lost, dissolving into all that ice.

"Humans are tribal, and aggressive." Their driver spoke with a quiet menace. "These apes are something like your former species, from what I hear. But they're younger. In fact, everything you'll see is young. The cities, the technology. Belief systems, too."

Her audience nodded, trying to pay close attention.

"It's an inventive species, which makes them fun, and popular.

And despite some world-killing weapons, there's a genuine peace in effect." With a dramatic flourish, she sighed. "The trouble is, this society is fundamentally, profoundly unstable. According to our computer models, any of a thousand events could wash away this peacefulness."

No one spoke for a long moment.

The driver had reached one of her destinations. "We don't dare let them know that we're here," she warned. "Judging by their history, they'd respond with fear, and probably violence. Against us and against the innocent, too."

"We understand," Mama-ma promised.

"In a few centuries, if things evolve properly, we'll begin to show ourselves. But today and tomorrow, no."

"Of course."

There was a prolonged pause, nothing audible but the rumbling engine and the endless wind.

No one so much as glanced at the girl sitting in the back seat.

Then with a bleak, clipped voice, the nameless woman told everyone, "This is my neighborhood. Whatever you do, don't fuck things up for me."

Sleep took Po-lee-een by surprise.

The sensation differed from estivating, brief and soft and finished before it had begun. When she woke again, she discovered that they were driving fast on a wide, wide highway, the mountains left behind and the sun lost and the dark land, flatter than any ground she had ever seen, empty of snow and almost devoid of vegetation.

There was a sound, a relentless clicking, that must have roused her. Sitting forward, she saw a blinking green arrow near the steering wheel. Was it telling the driver to look to her right? No, she realized. They were moving right, leaving the highway and losing momentum. A wonderland of peculiar buildings and machines and brilliant-colored lights was approaching, and some half-born skill of hers could interpret the scene—those lights were inviting passersby to stop and rest their weary ape bones.

"We can eat here," said their driver. "Afterwards, you'll be taken to the acculturation centers."

"Different centers?" Father asked, with apprehension.

"According to the slots available, yes."

Everything would always be Po-lee-een's fault. Yet she didn't feel the old shame. Had human sleep cured that pain? If so, no wonder the earth was a popular world.

They turned onto an asphalt plain, then parked behind the largest structure. A second vehicle pulled up beside them, Po-lee-een's grandparents greeting them with a jarrtee finger waggle. Nobody disembarked. The other vehicles arrived in short order, and everyone remained seated, their guides taking this last opportunity to brief them.

"This is called a truck stop," said the woman. "Stay with me, follow my lead, and don't stare at strangers. Humans find stares threatening."

Naturally, their guide would pay for their meals. But in case of disaster, she handed out leather packets filled with money— rectangular slips of colored paper covered with dense, artistic scribblings.

The brothers tasted the young leather, leaving behind tooth marks.

Almost as an afterthought, the woman told them, "You'll need names, too. Bland, blending names. And sooner is better than later, of course." Then because it was expected, she asked, "Are there any questions?"

Po-lee-een was holding one of her money papers up to the truck stop's glorious lights, a half-formed comprehension doing more to confuse than enlighten. "Ma'am," she replied, "can you tell me your name?"

The three adults turned together, in surprise.

"Why do you want to know?" the woman asked, words dripping in suspicion.

"I don't want to choose it," Po-lee-een confessed. "Even by mistake."

An icy silence took hold. Then the angry, nameless woman

climbed outside, and Father, then Mama-ma, slipped the girl mercurial looks of approval.

The cold was worse than Po-lee-een had expected, the wind cutting into her flesh. Air brakes and tired diesel engines sounded like animals, making the newcomers nervous, and the nervousness didn't end when they stepped into the warm fluorescent indoors. A tired woman, miffed by the sudden onslaught, showed each group to a different squeaky orange booth. The nameless woman gave them a brief tour of the menu, sounding out the printed words while pointing at the corresponding photographs. Then a tired waitress appeared, taking orders while attempting small talk, asking about the weather and the traffic, and how would they like their eggs, and that's funny, but the people in the other booths had also ordered double portions of sausage.

Po-lee-een's cousin sat with his back to her, plastic ivy between their heads. They weren't supposed to know each other, so she whispered, asking if he had slept. Not only had he slept, he'd had a dream. "Snow fell on the City," he told her with a wonder-struck voice. "It was very deep, and very beautiful."

"Not here," Uncle Ka-ceen growled. "Quiet, you two."

Her cousin rose, and while combing back his long hair, announced, "I've got to piss."

His guide whispered some advice, then sent him off.

The nameless woman was lecturing her parents about the dangers of high-fat diets. "In that way, humans are weak," she warned. "They're adapted to lean meat and vegetables." Then, noticing the girl rising to her feet, she asked, "What are you doing?"

"My bladder's weak."

The others chortled. But the woman, made of sterner stuff, simply said, "You want the ladies' room. Don't talk to anyone, and don't leave this building. Please."

"I won't."

Inside her human brain, carefully embossed into the tangled neurons, were the basic instructions for surviving here. But she needed coaching and practice, and more practice. At the end of one hallway were two doors wearing mysterious words and simple portraits of humans, one portrait triangular and the other tall and straight. Because she was more straight than triangular, and since the air around the first door smelled like shit—an odor she would recognize with any nose—she made the wrong guess.

Her cousin and a stranger were standing before white urinals, one trying to mimic the other's stance, their feet set apart and both gripping themselves in front, with one hand.

Glancing over his shoulder, her cousin looked at Po-lee-een, closing one eye with a slow, exaggerated motion.

She slipped back into the hallway.

The ladies' room was empty. She went straight to the toilet, giving it an experimental flush, then she used it successfully, astonished by the water lost with her urine. There was some gruesome trash in a white can. She flushed and stepped out of the stall, startled to see someone walking with her. Turning fast, she found herself staring at a very tall, very mature twelve-year-old girl trapped inside the mirror, and with an embarrassing slowness, Po-lee-een realized that she was looking at her own face, her unruly and uncombed hair, and an expression that she realized was a little surprised and very amused.

She resembled her cousin, and someone else, too.

Someone who didn't belong to her family.

Po-lee-een stood where she could see the booth, watching the nameless woman. Larger than most human women, and strong, her features and thick hair were much like those that Po-lee-een had seen in the mirror. A sudden chill took hold of the girl. Obviously, the intrusion had used that woman as a model, as the inspiration, when it was fashioning her new body out of nothingness.

Po-lee-een turned away.

Her cousin was off exploring another portion of the wonderful building. There was a market, brilliantly lit, racks and shelves filled with countless products, vivid colors, and tall words fighting for their attention. The air itself vibrated with the smells of food, causing her mouth to water. How did human beings survive this endless loss of moisture?

Customers selected items, then bartered with a woman near the door.

Po-lee-een watched the transactions, trying to learn. Then her cousin sneaked up behind her, tugging on an arm, saying, "Come here. Let me show you something."

Magazines filled a long wooden rack. The new humans stood before them, almost gawking, unable to count the titles or name half the colors. It was as if the entire planet lay in easy reach; Jar-rtee had nothing to compare with this marriage of commerce and knowledge. Was it all right to touch? Others did, so Po-lee-een mimicked them, selecting the closest magazines, flipping through the cheap pages, her tiny new eyes absorbing images of plants and animals and foreign scenes populated with humans of every shade, the sheer banal pageantry of it all making her heart beat faster, her breath almost galloping now.

Leaning against the far end of the rack, her cousin paged his way through a fat travel magazine.

She pulled a slick magazine from the highest shelf, opened it and found a naked man smiling up at her, his organ lying outside his body, something about it extremely inviting. Smiling, she held up the photograph and called out, "Hey! Look familiar?"

Her cousin glanced up, giggled.

She replaced the magazine and took the one next to it. Naked women posed for the unseen camera, proud of their organs and youth and apparent beauty. Po-lee-een was examining their enormous breasts when a man's voice came over her shoulder, a nebulous question posed.

"What do you think?"

The man was nearly as old as Father, his face half-furred, eyes reddened. She tried to avoid his eyes, as instructed, flipping through the pages and admitting, "To me, they look fat."

"I agree," he replied, his voice smiling.

She triggered a speaking advertisement. Simple circuits, a battery and speaker were woven into the paper, and a woman's voice said, "Porsche," every few moments. The photograph showed a sleek vehicle and an even sleeker woman—a tall and obviously strong human woman—and under her breath, to herself, the girl repeated the word.

"Porsche."

"She looks like you," said the older man.

Did she?

"Are you with anyone? That boy, maybe?"

"No," she lied.

"Are you traveling through?"

She nodded. Yes.

Again, the sultry voice called to her. "Porsche."

"What's a *Porsche?*" she inquired.

"You're kidding? It's the car."

She was disappointed. She'd hoped it was the woman.

"You know," said the man, "I've got a better car than that. I can give you a ride, if there's somewhere you need to be."

She closed the magazine, then set it back where she had found it—a good principle on any world.

"How about a ride?" he kept asking.

Turning, she finally stared at those red eyes. Sure enough, humans didn't like a hard stare.

He blinked, muttering, "Hey, I want to help."

"I don't think so."

"Fuck you," he said, then retreated.

Her cousin approached, closing and opening one of his eyes.

"What are you doing?" she asked.

"Winking," he said. "It's friendly. My guide showed me how."

Po-lee-een glanced at his magazine, at the big glossy photographs. It looked as if vast portions of the earth were white beaches and blue water, the sky as smooth and thin as the best jarrtee silk.

"I'm buying it," her cousin warned her.

"Our money's for emergencies."

"Our money is our money," was his response. Then he walked up to the cashier—another tired woman, the only kind of person hired by the truck stop—and with a jarrtee's two-handed formality, he gave her one of the paper rectangles.

She counted his change, then halfheartedly wished him a pleasant night.

But he didn't want to leave. Opening his magazine, he touched one of the advertisements. "What's a *Trinidad?*" he asked the cashier.

The woman squinted at the photograph, then said, "An island. I think."

"Trinidad." He smiled and told his cousin, "I like that name."

"Is it ordinary?" she had to ask.

"I hope not."

Whispering, she reminded him, "It's best to pick normal, simple names."

"It's our business. We can pick what we want," Trinidad replied, half-laughing.

"Hey, kids," said the cashier. "Back away from my counter, would you?"

They moved, but not far.

"Choose your name," urged Trinidad. "Now. Then we'll be the first to know each other's new name."

She said, "Porsche."

"I like its sound," he assured her.

Louder, she said, "My name is Porsche."

"Hey, Porsche," said the cashier, "tell your brother to get out of the way."

Porsche winked at the cashier, saying, "He's not my brother. I don't even know him."

The lined, careworn face examined both of them, the barest suggestion of a smile showing.

"Yeah," the cashier replied, "I've got that kind of brother, too."

The story wasn't finished. But dawn had reached the western sky, and Porsche was sick of talking, and she was starving, remembering that truck stop breakfast from years ago and her mouth suddenly wet. Sitting up in bed, she scratched her right breast, then her belly, saying, "And that's how we got here, and that's how I got my name."

Cornell was awake if not quite alert. Lying on his back, an arm thrown over his forehead, he stared up at the fading stars on the ceiling, and after a long thoughtful pause, said, "Now I know another one of your secrets."

"You do," she agreed amiably.

"Is that your last secret?"

She glanced at him, saying nothing.

"I thought not." Then he rolled onto his side, preparing to sleep, finally. "So what about your cousin? Trinidad, is it?"

"What about him?"

"What's he up to? Do I ever get to meet him?"

"He's around, and I hope you do."

Cornell closed his eyes, and smiled. "We've got a lot of nights left for stories, don't we?"

"We have," she promised.

"Time enough to hear all of your secrets," he muttered.

Under her breath, more to herself than Cornell, she said, "As long as they're mine to give."

ON THE FIRST OF NOVEMBER, THE FARMER CAME TO COLLECT THE
rent, and within the limits of politeness, to snoop.

"How's the house?" he inquired. "Holding up for you?"

"It's holding just fine," Cornell told him. "Thanks for asking."

"The roof staying tight?"

"So far."

"Good." He was almost exactly Cornell's age—an anonymous,
weathered face and durable clothes with the requisite seed cap
that farmers had worn for decades, the holo image of a golden
corncob riding above the long brim. "Good," he said a second
time, letting his eyes track sideways. "Can't help noticing. You do
some more work on the old shed?"

"We installed some new equipment," Cornell conceded, always smiling. "And some insulation and space heaters, too."

"You said you might," the farmer replied, entirely amiable.

The utility building was south of the farmhouse. It looked like
a giant steel worm cut in half lengthwise, then tucked into the
overgrown shelterbelt. Its garage door was closed, and so was
the smaller human door beside it. Tiny windows lined the
worm's sides, each covered with a simple black curtain. Timothy
Kleck had brought those curtains; interwoven with sophisticated

electronics, they were meant to disrupt any attempt at surveillance.

Hidden, Few-made devices were doing the same job, but Porsche hadn't mentioned them to Timothy. It was better that he and the world believed it was his cleverness that was protecting them.

After a long thoughtful stare at the black curtains, the farmer looked back at Cornell, folding the envelope roughly and shoving it into his back pocket, never so much as glancing at its contents.

"Glad to see this place taken care of," he declared.

It was Cornell's turn to say, "Good."

Porsche stood nearby, watching the laconic performance. The two men had met as boys—on this ground, on the Change Day. Their shared history helped smooth things between them. Cornell had never mentioned their project to the farmer, not even to offer the cover story about making money through electronic wizardry. And to his credit, the farmer had never asked for any explanations. Yet he was too shrewd and curious to ignore the clues. He looked between the farmhouse and the metal shed, gazing out at his field, the mysterious glass disk waiting in easy reach.

"Remember my dog? The one with pups?"

"Sure," said Cornell.

A German shepherd-wolf mix, Porsche recalled. Plus a sprinkling of artificial genes, intelligence married to a sweet obedience.

"My offer stands," said the farmer. "You can have a couple of her pups."

Cornell glanced at Porsche.

"They'll make fine guard dogs."

Porsche said, "I'm sure they would," and took several steps, approaching the two men. "It's just that we don't have a lot of time to care for puppies."

"Besides," Cornell added, "by the time they're full grown, we'll be gone."

The plain, weathered face nodded, eyes asking, "Where will you be going?"

But the farmer didn't ask the question out loud. Instead, he opened his pickup's door and started to climb into the cab, hesitating at the last moment and climbing down again, saying quietly, "I almost forgot. The other day, I had some visitors. . . ."

He had "almost forgot" nothing. He had saved the most important topic for last.

"Visitors?" Cornell asked.

"Three hunters. From the city. They wanted to hunt my land." Again, he looked at the utility building, questions framed by the eyes, and left unasked. Instead, he said simply, "Two of them did the talking. A lot of talking. The third man was older, and he didn't make a sound. He was in charge, I'm guessing."

"Did they mention us?" Cornell asked.

"Not in so many words."

Porsche stepped closer. "What did they talk about?"

"Where to find birds. The cold wet weather. And could they hunt close to your place . . . if nobody was going to be around, of course."

No one spoke for a moment.

"I told them to stay clear of here."

"Thank you," Porsche replied.

The farmer adjusted the long brim, pulling it closer to his eyes. "All of a sudden, one of the men started talking about my neighbors. Naming names. Telling me how they were using black market pesticides, and risking jail time because of it. And then he asked about me. He said to me, 'It's hard to plant crops from inside a federal penitentiary.' "

Cornell said, "Shit."

Porsche remained silent.

The farmer seem nonplussed, giving a half-shrug and climbing back into the cab. "I told them to forget hunting my birds, and get the hell off my land."

Silence.

"If you don't want guard dogs," he continued, "that's your

business. But my advice: Get whatever help you can. And if you can get your work done and get out of here soon, do it." He slammed his door, then dropped the window. "Not that I want you people gone," he added, pushing back his cap. "Even if we don't talk enough, I like the idea of having neighbors."

It was the most trusted face in the world, and Timothy Kleck had stolen it.

And he had stolen the body and name, the mannerisms and the deep bass voice, too. Then he dressed the man in a conservative gray suit and sat him behind the famous kidney-shaped desk, the trademark chords of CNN fading, and the stolen man smiled at his tiny audience, sober optimism mixed with grandfatherly wisdom. "Good evening to you," said the famous voice. "I am Hawthorne Klay, and this is a special CNN report."

He paused for a half-moment, giving the smile time to fade.

"It has been a quarter of a century since the Change, and it's been nearly as long since the United States government formed and funded the Cosmic Event Agency. The CEA was entrusted then with a simple mission: To study the Change for the benefit of the entire human species." The wide screen split in two, video clips of mammoth telescopes and scientists in white coats shown on the commentator's left. "For twenty-five years, the CEA has funded observatories on the moon, laboratories dedicated to exotic mathematics and physics, as well as projects decidedly less scientific in their scope. Every possible lead has been pursued at one time or another, and as a result, much has been learned."

The commentator vanished, replaced with a sloppy gray moonscape. But instead of blackness above, and stars, the moon itself looked down on the moon, a soft gray illusion hovering over ancient stone and dust.

"Perhaps the agency's greatest feat," said the deep voice, "was its role in causing the lunar sky to Change. And having done that, its researchers—some of the best on either world—were able to decipher why skies Change. It is a simple matter of too many telescopes peering into the unknown."

The video dissolved, returning the viewer to Hawthorne.

He had stopped smiling, a bleak sense of concern seeping from the trusted face, and his voice sounded pained, as if announcing the death of a president.

"There is, however, a dark and secret side to the CEA. In the next hour, we will show you the results of several years of investigation, including video from a secret base and interviews with former employees." The image paused for a moment, then said, "Please, remain open-minded. Much of what you see and hear will seem incredible. But remember that the Change seemed like madness at first, then simply unthinkable, yet today, everyone almost takes our new sky for granted.

"The ordinary always begins as something incredible.

"I am Hawthorne Klay, and this program is entitled: 'Death Under Alien Skies.' "

The image froze, its digital substance more rigid than any flesh.

It was still the first day in November. Four people were sitting together in the utility building, near the space heaters, coffee cups in hand.

Wearing a big smile, Porsche told Timothy, "Very, very impressive."

The tall man normally feasted on praise. But he saw too many hurdles in front of them, and he couldn't help but leak pessimistic sounds. "What comes after is what counts, and it takes time to create something people will believe—"

"I find it very believable," Nathan interjected.

"This is the easy part," Timothy growled. "I've got one more segment in the can. At this rate, it's going to take a few more months to get a finished product. And meanwhile, CNN is upgrading its security systems. Which makes it a kind of race." He paused, then added, "Frankly, I wish we were running a little bit faster."

Their original plan, discarded weeks ago, was to collect everything they could on the CEA, including Cornell's and Porsche's own testimony, then simply give it away on the Net. Millions would eventually see it, and some of those millions would believe the charges, and with luck, the truth would snowball from there.

But the Net was strewn with digital fictions. Some were elaborate and sophisticated, and most important, some of the fictions were as bizarre as anything they intended to show. Borderline religions liked to portray miracles and various paradises. Radical politicians invented conspiracies and rewrote history. It was Cornell who had pointed out that the public would have doubts about invisible intrusions leading to alien worlds, and portraying a noble collection of deep thinkers as being villains . . . well, that would shred the last of their credibility, and what good would come of it?

It was Timothy who proposed using the venerable news service and Hawthorne.

"What matters," he had argued, "is that the world believes our story. Believes it the first time it sees it. Then the government is on the defensive—not a role it relishes—and suddenly every news agency is going to chase the story. Particularly CNN, since they're the ones who exposed the scandal."

Cornell was heartened, but skeptical. "Suppose we make a genuine product. Okay. But how do we go about hijacking an entire news network?"

With the delight only known to the very clever, Timothy leaned forward in his chair, saying, "It's almost easy, really."

Since the Change, the earth had been throwing a portion of its own light back on itself. Light meant reflected sunlight, city lights, plus the rest of the EM spectrum, too. And over the last twenty years, as people grew more comfortable with the new sky, that curiosity of physics had been put to increasing good use.

A powerful burst of radio noise, directed straight overhead, would mostly escape from the earth, fanning across the old-fashioned universe. Yet at the same time, a diluted signal—a sliver of that radio shout—would rain down on wherever the antennae were pointed. The new sky allowed an alternative to communication satellites. To date, no corporation or government had sold its communication satellites as scrap, and probably none of them would ever take that chance. But the news agencies, fearing some great disaster that would cripple their satellites, decided to build emergency systems with earth-based antennae. For instance, CNN had a big automated station sleeping in northern Quebec. Given the proper commands, the station would awaken, and given more commands, it would begin transmitting, its signal pointed at each of the receiving stations visible in the everted sky.

"The system is intended for wars, comet impacts, and other bad days," Timothy reported. "It's a very durable system, and very adaptable, and if we can take control of it, I think we can make it obey only us for long enough." He had grinned at the three of them, utterly proud of his ingenuity. "And if someone manages to pull the plug early, then what happens? It looks as if some dark force is responsible. Which only helps our credibility, at least with some part of our audience."

There was a long, contemplative pause.

Behind three long fingers, Porsche was smiling. She already knew about the emergency system, but she was pleased—no, she was ecstatic—that Timothy had come up with this reasonable scheme on his own, free of her veiled suggestions.

"What we're talking about is a significant federal offense," Cornell had offered.

"On top of several other federal offenses," Timothy added.

"In pursuit of the truth, there's no genuine crime," Nathan had reminded them, nodding at his own ironclad logic.

"Is that what we're telling?" asked Timothy. "The truth?"

"Absolutely," Nathan had chortled.

Then his son, possessing a more sagacious attitude, added, "With a mask of fiction, I hope. Because when this is done, I don't want to be led off to prison. Please."

With a touch of a button, the stew of truth and fiction began where it had paused.

Hawthorne Klay dissolved, replaced with a dead man who spoke to his audience.

In life, Jordick Tiller had had long raven-colored hair, typically dirty and uncombed, and his personality could have been charitably labeled "difficult"; but in death, facing a doubting public, his resurrectors had cleaned him up and given him new clothes, his posture and his sour, whining attitude improved enormously. With a quick, charmingly nervous voice, Jordick described his abbreviated life. He named his parents and birthplace, then with a hint of shame, mentioned that he wasn't close to his family, and he had never married. If something happened to him, no one would notice. "Which," he conceded, "is probably why they hired me in the first place."

Hawthorne Klay's voice, born inside a top-flight audio simulator, asked, "Who hired you?"

"Tangent, Inc."

"The high-technology company?"

"No," Jordick replied, a glint of fear in his eyes. "That's a front, a fabrication. It was set up by the CEA. The corporate headquarters in California is where the agency does its special research. The agency hired me. It needed my help—"

"What kind of help?"

"You wouldn't believe me."

The artifical voice made a soft, understanding sound, then asked the dead man, "Are you talking about traveling to another world?"

Jordick nodded, muttering, "Maybe."

"What sort of world?"

"High Desert, we called it." The witness paused, his eyes losing their focus. "Very dry, very desolate. And lonely . . . beyond belief . . . "

"What were you doing on High Desert?"

"Searching. For intelligent life." Jordick paused. "The CEA wants to find new technologies. Fancy sources of energy, strange materials. Anything that helps our country get a jump on our competition."

"Did you find intelligent life?"

"Not at first . . . "

"But eventually?"

He nodded, sighed. "There was a place. The Breaks, we called it. Arroyos led into wet canyons, and as we moved deeper, we could *feel* something. A presence, I guess you'd call it. The flavor of an enormous intelligence."

"It sounds like exciting work."

"It wasn't. Mostly, it was boring. And hard."

"Was it dangerous?"

"Could be." He licked his lips. "Friends of mine died. In dust storms, under rock slides. And some were murdered—"

"Murdered?"

"Going to another world . . . it changes people. In big ways, it changes them. Even the strongest person can get depressed, or worse." He paused for a long moment, as if gathering himself. "Insanity is possible," he whispered. "Murderous rages . . . well, I saw them happen more than once."

"Did the agency know that?"

Jordick gave a nervous little laugh. "Oh, yeah."

"But they must have taken precautions."

"At first. They limited our shifts, gave us counseling. But when they thought we were closing in on a genuine alien, they began to push us. Longer shifts, less rest. We were deep in the canyons when a huge storm came up, and the floods trapped everyone who wasn't killed outright." He was breathing as if winded. "Remember that plane crash last summer? Out in the Pacific? Tangent, Inc. lost hundreds of employees, supposedly coming back from a vacation on Tahiti."

The screen split in two, authentic video showing rescue planes circling above a seamless blue sea. Above the scene was a complete list of the missing, compiled by Timothy, including hometowns and next-of-kin.

"They weren't on Tahiti," Jordick continued, "or even on the earth. They were lost on High Desert. They died horribly, and the CEA covered it up."

"You knew these people, didn't you?"

"They were my best friends. Some of them."

"Is that why you've decided to come forward, Mr. Tiller?"

"In part."

"What else is there, sir?"

The faraway gaze returned, then Jordick spoke with a quiet, utterly sane voice. "In our base camp, we built a cage. Like a zoo cage. It was meant to hold an alien, in case we ever caught one." He paused, then repeated, "Like a zoo cage." Shaking his head, he said, "We weren't there to make friends. We were hunting for knowledge. Methods didn't matter. Only results. Even if it meant throwing helpless creatures behind bars!" He shook his head, telling his audience, "It's not supposed to be that way. Maybe other nations can kidnap, can do anything they want, but not my country. Not my government."

There was a long pause, the screen filled with an anguished face. Then Hawthorne's voice said, "You are taking a risk, aren't you? Coming forward like this?"

"When the CEA hired me," Jordick confessed, "I signed away my free speech rights. I'm pledged to protect our nation's security, whatever that means."

"You're risking prosecution . . ."

"Worse." A watery smile collapsed into a sneer. Shaking his head, he said, "I heard rumors. From high-up people. If they even suspect that I'm talking to you, I'll suffer some terrible accident."

A disbelieving voice said, "You're talking about murder."

The witness stared out at the world, a subtle change in the light making his flesh appear ghostly. "In our world," he warned his audience, "knowledge means wealth, and it brings power. And think of all the harm people have done, chasing those two horrible dreams."

Jordick was hired and trained at the same time as Cornell. The men had crossed over to High Desert together, and Cornell had found the ill-fated man's corpse. Using Jordick as their first witness seemed appropriate. Timothy had pulled his image and voice print from the files of a more benign employer. The driving hope was that after the world had seen Jordick's interview, others would investigate him. They would learn that Jordick Tiller had been a genuine man and an employee of Tangent, Inc., and he had reportedly died in a remote area, in a vague accident, his body cremated and the anonymous ashes lost.

By contrast, the next witness was a living person.

A public spokeswoman for Tangent, Inc., Ms. Farrah Smith was an older, no-nonsense woman with a helmet of gray hair and a bulldog's charmless face. They had replicated her exactly, hoping to cause her all sorts of hell.

"We found the intrusions by accident," Ms. Smith reported. "At a weapons lab, as it happens. High-energy particles—I'm not privy to what kinds—were being disrupted at a single point. The disruption marked a flaw between the earth and a neighboring world. A quantum intrusion, we call it. Not a perfectly accurate name, but that's one reason to select that name. We don't want the competition learning anything easily."

"In simple terms," asked Hawthorne's voice, "can you describe an intrusion?"

"Tiny, tiny, tiny," she chanted. "Just about impossible to find, and that's if you know what you're doing." The witness had a guarded quality, her face like weathered stone. "If that beam of ours had been moved half a nanometer in any direction—up or down, left or right—nobody would have noticed the intrusion. But having found one helped us find the others. There is a complex, very advanced branch of mathematics that predicts where to look. And the same mathematics showed us how to open the intrusions and cross to another world."

"Which means what?"

"The CEA possesses an enormous new technology. And chances are, no one else is going to stumble across it soon. If ever."

"That's what we once thought about the atomic bomb, if I'm not mistaken. An assumed monopoly—"

"No," Ms. Smith interrupted. "During World War Two, every physics student knew about nuclear energy. But this . . . this is something much larger, and much more surprising. And in the long run, infinitely more powerful."

There was a pause; the audience asked to dwell on the idea of power.

"Your agency hires volunteers," the interviewer mentioned. "You find talented people who can pass through these intrusions . . . somehow . . . "

"I won't tell you how," she warned.

"But is it true that some of these volunteers died while working for you?"

The stony face cracked, a wetness leaking into the unblinking eyes. "We have a saying at the agency: 'Columbus didn't come home with full crews.' " She gave that logic a moment to fester, then added, "Our people are told what to expect; they're well-trained, and for their trouble, they're paid handsomely."

The interviewer waited for an instant, then observed, "You seem to accept the risks and the prize. Which makes me wonder: Why did you agree to speak to us?"

The face softened, finally. An expression of pure grief had been designed to take the audience by surprise. "Something else has happened. It's not being done by my division, but the agency is responsible—"

"What is it?"

"Murder," she reported. "Several murders, actually."

"Who has been murdered?"

Silence.

"Can you name the victims, ma'am?"

"I will . . . yes . . . " The moment was as genuine as possible, down to the eyelid twitching above pooling tears. "This," she reported, "is what happens to people who stand in the agency's way."

The image dissolved to black.

"And that's as much as I've finished," Timothy confessed. "So far."

He wasn't someone who apologized easily, but Porsche could

see the frustration in his face, in the way he slapped his bony knees, and in the way his voice, like the digital image, dissolved to black.

Borrowing faces was an easy trick; what was difficult, they were learning, was to find genuine evidence of criminal acts.

On High Desert, Cornell's team leader had told him about the arranged murders. But the man's sanity was questionable at the time, and he had died shortly afterwards. What if the agency was innocent? It was a cynical fear, and nagging. Timothy dredged it up for the umpteenth time, retracing their investigations with a hypercritical tone that made everyone brittle.

"We've got two people with connections to Tangent, and they blew off their own heads," he grumbled, passing hard copies of death certificates from one hand to the other and back again. "Plus, three known CEA employees picked the same fate, including two Ph.D.s. All were labeled suicides. Different caliber weapons, all traceable to the dead. No witnesses, but each left a suicide note." He set down the certificates, nervous fingers moving to other stacks of data. "I've helped study a few apparent suicides that turned out to be murders. I know what I'm talking about. Honestly, I think we're looking at self-inflicted wounds."

Porsche knew better than to interrupt the monologue.

It was Nathan who broke in, assuming that Timothy was seeking advice or encouragement. "Suicide notes can be faked. Easier than faces and voices can be, I should think."

The words brought no response.

Nathan turned to Porsche. "Was it last week? Someone suggested looking at the nearby motels, seeing if the killer had stayed there while committing the crime. And searching the phone records, in case the same numbers were called—"

"I mentioned those possibilities," Timothy snapped, "and they didn't lead anywhere. Which isn't a big surprise, since we're talking about elite assassins. Stupid mistakes aren't very likely."

"But everyone leaves traces of themselves," Nathan promised. "And I know you'll find them. Given time."

Kind words infuriated Timothy. He shook his head, saying, "I've spent a hundred hours a week trying to find something . . . that may not be there . . . and I don't know . . . "

"What don't you know?" asked Cornell.

"If it's worth the bother. Not to mention the danger." Timothy shook his head, adding, "I'm getting really sick of this goddamn farm."

Cornell's temper flared. He hated the idea of being abandoned, and he said it by saying nothing, chewing on his cheek, his face growing more and more flushed.

Nathan was gentler and equally unpersuasive. "I know it's difficult," he allowed. "To be a person like you, living in this place—"

"Because I'm black, you mean."

"No," Nathan replied, oblivious to the man's race. "I'm talking about your education, your worldliness."

Timothy was momentarily surprised, and vulnerable.

But Nathan couldn't see his advantage. Instead of more compliments, he changed tactics. "Besides," he declared, "you've already committed terrible crimes. If you leave us, you'll just place yourself more securely in *their* crosshairs."

It was a paranoid, flaky moment.

Pure Nathan.

Porsche had to leap into the breach. She rose, announcing, "I have an idea." She intended to recommend that everyone take a break. The rest of the day, or maybe the entire week. But as she began to frame her next sentence, a genuine idea came dribbling out, half-formed by some part of her unconscious mind.

"Three men," she sputtered.

"What?" asked Timothy, and Nathan. No one had told them about their landlord's ominous tale.

Cornell just stared at her, waiting.

She moved closer to Timothy, looking at the stacks of printouts. "We also talked, last week . . . about using security and traffic cameras . . . looking for anyone who was near two or more of the murder scenes."

"I did that," Timothy replied. "It was a long shot. The chance of two clear images is about as tiny as an intrusion—"

"How about one image?" Porsche asked.

Cornell understood. "We're looking for three men riding together. Do you have anything like that on file?"

"Two young men," Porsche added, "accompanied by someone older."

Timothy almost asked, "Why?"

But he thought better of it, framing the question for the durable, semiportable computers that lined the back wall of the old utility building.

It was a dark, relentlessly damp building. Porsche glanced up at the cot that Timothy used on most nights, sleeping in little bites. A self-imposed prison, that's what this place was. Clearly, she had to get him out more often, making the poor man enjoy himself, somehow. . . .

The search for a threesome brought a quick answer.

Or, rather, ten possible answers. Timothy dispensed hard copies after a quick enhancement. Porsche looked them over, then made a guess. But she didn't tell anyone her guess, putting all of the candidates into an envelope, then telling everyone, "Let's go enjoy a little drive. Okay?"

"A drive where?" Timothy inquired.

"Not far," Cornell promised, winking knowingly at the others.

Walking into the chill November air, Porsche whispered, checking with her Few-made eavesdroppers.

No one was within half a mile of the farmhouse.

As a precaution, she set the defensive systems to full alert. If there were trespassers, they would be eased into unconsciousness. She climbed aboard a long-bed Humvee-style truck that she'd bought third-hand, and with Cornell at her side and the other two men in the back seat, the group drove over graveled roads and up a short driveway, arriving at their landlord's house for an impromptu visit.

Set down in any modern suburb, the new house would have vanished into obscurity. An architectural vision of glass and cultured wood and carbon-fiber trim, it seemed to extrude a kind of middle-class snobbishness. However, the mud-encrusted combine parked in the front yard disarmed the snobbishness quite nicely. And the owner himself seemed entirely out of place, walking stiffer than most men of his age, coming down stairs made of Colorado River rocks and bone-white epoxies.

"By any chance," asked Porsche, "do any of these gentlemen look familiar?"

The farmer flipped through the ten photographs. When he reached the last photograph, he gave it a half-glance, then looked up and said, "Where'd this one come from?"

From California, though no one mentioned it. A security camera at an apartment building close to an apparent suicide had caught the image of three men riding together in a nondescript sedan. They were dressed like businessmen, but they sat like soldiers; that's what Porsche had thought at first glance.

"You're sure?" Timothy sputtered. "Absolutely?"

Only two faces were visible, and both of them were shown from the side. Yet the farmer tapped both with a certain unflappable authority, saying, "I don't see a lot of people in a day. So I tend to remember those that I do see pretty well."

No one spoke for a long moment.

Then the farmer handed back the photographs, saying, "This one here . . . the one riding shotgun? He's the one who didn't talk. As far as I'm concerned, he's the one you've got to keep your eye on. . . . "

THE DAY WAS MILD AND BRIGHT, THE BEST WEATHER YET IN DECEM-
ber, and after a full morning spent delving into the CEA's secret
budgets and bureaus, the team decided to treat themselves to a
long lunch. They made sandwiches, dressed in sweaters and
sweats, and sat on lawn chairs out on the glass disk, enjoying the
sun and a bottle or two of sun-colored Mexican beer.

Porsche didn't suggest playing basketball.

That was Cornell's duty, and he meant just the two of them.
But Timothy was in a rare mood, inviting himself into Cornell's
camp. Two against one sounded more reasonable, he argued.
Nathan volunteered to serve as the men's coach and the game's
referee. A plastic barrel stood behind the pole, and Porsche
opened it and pushed aside the old toolbox, the best of three
basketballs waiting at the bottom, begging to be used.

The dark glass was warm and dusty and a little slippery. Cornell faced Porsche at arm's length, his father between them, giving the ball a stiff little heave and sending it over her head. She
swatted it toward the three-point line, then sprinted past Timothy to grab it, dribbling fast between the two defenders, making
her first layup in a crisp, business-as-usual fashion.

The net sang a few notes.

"Two-zero," Nathan called out from the sunflower stubble.

It was the usual mismatch. Cornell was strong, but he had no quickness or sense of grace. And while Timothy was taller than Porsche, with long spidery arms, he spent far too much time thinking. Deliberating. Doubting. Good basketball was instinct built on practice, and when it was sweetest, it was an art form. But Timothy's main strategy was to stand like a tree, guarding the hoop with arms outstretched, and if Cornell fed him the ball, he had a fifty-fifty chance of making an uncontested two points.

Timothy's first shot danced on the hoop, then fell into Porsche's outstretched hands.

Back she went, back behind the line, then pulled up and threw a long arcing shot that barely made music, it was so perfect.

"Five-nothing!"

"We know, Dad."

Nathan shouted at his team, saying, "Play harder. That's my advice."

Obeying the coaching, Cornell drove hard toward the basket, and Porsche blocked with the relentless hands-on style that she had played years ago, in the pro women's league.

"Foul!" cried Nathan.

Cornell pulled up and shot, banking it in.

"No shot, son. You fouled her."

Knowing that words wouldn't help, Cornell stood like a statue, the ball under his arm, looking very much like a little boy with his hair swirled by the wind, his face red from exertion and from being pissed.

"It's five-two," Porsche announced. Turning to Nathan, she added, "You couldn't see it, but I hit him first."

Only because she said so, the old man allowed the basket.

"Don't patronize us," Cornell growled.

"Okay." She dropped back and fired from the far edge of the disk, dropping in another three points.

"Eight-two!" three men shouted, in a chorus.

The game wobbled along for another forty minutes. As always, Nathan lost track of the score, which was the only reason the men kept playing. Without a quantified measure of the slaughter, and managing the occasional run, little doses of hope gave them the will to keep chasing the lost cause.

Porsche discovered basketball on the plains of west Texas.

She was living at the acculturation school, acquiring and polishing the essential skills to be human, and one day, not long after she arrived, she found an old ball, half-deflated and worn slick. Not knowing any better, she pounded it into the pavement to make it bounce, and when that game grew boring, she took a long, long shot that somehow connected with the hoop, the old-fashioned rope net *whooshing* and a tiny golden joy serving as a nucleus for the next twenty years of her human life.

Her first coach was television.

Television was a popular tool at the acculturation school, serving as an enormous if badly distorting window into the human world. Porsche spent hours watching the college tournaments, astonished by the level of play and the palpable differences between the sexes. On Jarrtee, men were a little larger than women, and stronger, but noticeably slower, too. Among apes, with the size differences and hip disparities, the inequities were greater. Porsche was an exception. No one seemed to know how the intrusions worked, but one thing was self-evident: Porsche's soul demanded a big body blessed with speed and an unconscious grace. That was true on her first home, and it was even more pronounced on the earth—no reason to expect any differences on any other world.

Athletically, Porsche was just a long step short of impossible.

Without exception, her instructors warned that if she played the game in public, she would be wise to hide some portion of her talent. "Don't jump so high," was the sum total of their coaching. "And miss some of your easy shots, too."

Of course, that was the instructors' advice in every circumstance.

"Whatever the moment requires," they preached, "make sure first, last, and forever that you blend in."

Porsche lived at the acculturation school until summer.

The school was hidden on a remote ranch. A dozen thoroughly humanized faculty lived with fifty immigrants—young single adults, for the most part. Officially, the ranch belonged to a minor and extremely private religious cult. The same cult owned property in twenty states and Canada, each facility turning out people who were utterly indistinguishable from those who had always been human.

By summer, Porsche had a last name and a rich, well-documented life, including a family history that reached back for two centuries. A birth certificate filed in West Virginia carried her name, inky footprint, blood type, and other simple data. Family albums showed her growing tall in genuine locations. According to records, she had been home-schooled. In the recent years, the Neals had moved several times, usually living in backwater places, without close neighbors or notable friends. Outside investigators would be hard-pressed to say that they hadn't lived there. Sculpted out of shadow and human expectations, their cobbled-together lives had as much vitality as anyone else's.

Cash was funneled from the Few, and a fictional credit history was built. The Neals purchased an anonymous brick home in a suburb of Dallas. A swimming pool nearly filled the tiny backyard. Jarrtees were too dense to float; none of them knew how to swim. But Father insisted on lessons, and blessed with long limbs and a fearless buoyancy, Porsche was soon churning out the laps under the brilliant Texas sky.

But basketball remained her finest love. A new backboard was fitted above the garage, the chiming net singing in the wind. But their short driveway had a ridiculous tilt, emptying into the alley that ran behind their house. Bored with her home court, Porsche would dribble up and down the alley, streaking into other driveways to make a layup or fadeaway shot, then dribble away before anyone could take offense.

On her best days, she covered miles.

On one incandescent afternoon—twenty degrees cooler than a jarrtee night, but brutal for humans—a voice cried out, "What the fuck are you doing?"

With a snap of gravel, Porsche wheeled, discovering an older boy glaring at her.

"This is my fucking yard!" he snarled.

"Fuck you," she said, happy for the chance to use that vivid word. "It's your parents' yard, not yours."

The boy was fifteen, nearly sixteen, tall and passably handsome. He was also sharp enough to see her logic, changing tactics instantly.

"Well," he said, "it's my hoop you're using."

"So stop me," she replied. Then she drove past him, holding back nothing, leaping as high as possible and making the layup, then snagging the ball out of his hands.

Porsche had won her first human boyfriend. They played until the heat beat them, then met again that next morning, in the local park, playing for hours in the relative chill. He was a fearless, somewhat talented opponent, and a fair kisser who claimed to be a masterful lover. But she wasn't old enough for intercourse. Instructors and her parents had warned her about the local norms. *Restraint* was her new watchword, and when she felt like doing more than kissing and fondling, Porsche would simply think of Jey-im and the pain that she'd brought to her family, and her little lusts would bleed away, lost.

Only once did she let her restraint slip, and the boy never even knew.

In August, Father announced that the earth was ready to evert. Uncle Ka-ceen—now named Uncle Jack—had contacted him with the news. A giant array of telescopes had been completed in Utah; on its heels was a Chilean facility. The eversion would come with cloudless skies above enough telescopes. Father explained the situation, then smiled. He had a wonderful human smile, his teeth a little uneven and very white, brown eyes dancing, a deep joy running beneath the surface happiness. "Tomorrow night," he told them. "Sometime after ten o'clock, according to Jack. And the forecast for Dallas is clear skies."

Everyone was excited. But Mama-ma was quick to warn her

children, "We don't know anything, and we say less than that. We're going to watch from the back yard, unseen."

Porsche disobeyed, but not scandalously.

While Father grilled steaks for a late dinner, she slipped away. Her boyfriend was waiting in the park, their court lit up by dusk, then by blue lights on tall poles. "We're going to have a lot of fun," she told him, and that's all she told him.

They teamed up against a threesome of older boys, and because it was a special evening, Porsche let herself play full-bore. Long shots rattled home. Circus tosses ended up dropping. Their enemies were intimidated, then angry, and her boyfriend was proud at first, then bored. It ended up in a rout, the enemy off to lick wounds and the victorious pair lying on the harsh Texas grass, away from the lights, in the privacy of night, necking relentlessly as Porsche kept careful track of the time.

At exactly ten o'clock, she said, "Wait." She said, "Let's just look at the stars."

"The stars?" he gasped.

"For just a little bit," she promised. "Then we'll have some real fun."

He was a teenage boy; he assumed sex. Suddenly the picture of obedience, he stared at the sky for a solid five minutes before asking, "Am I watching for something?"

"A shooting star," she replied. "When both of us see one, you get your gift."

The sky was busy. They weren't far from DFW, and every kind of plane passed overhead, the wings still wrong-looking to Porsche, too long and frail, primitive engines whining as they drank the thin, impoverished air. Streetlights—little doses of daylight intended for a diurnal ape—washed away all but the brightest stars. What if the eversion wasn't tonight? She'd probably have to give the boy something, which would be easy enough. But what if Father came hunting for her, furious because she wasn't where she belonged? She knew exactly how that drama would play, and suddenly she was every thirteen-year-old girl, bracing herself against the coming embarrassment.

But the eversion arrived on schedule, just as Uncle Jack had promised.

The boyfriend complained twice about the paucity of meteors, but he remained hopeful, and aroused. Porsche fought the urge to blink, her breath quickening. Then abruptly, without fanfare, there were no more stars; the earth instantly filled its own heavens.

The boy made a choking sound, then shot to his feet.

"What the fuck?" he sputtered, a baffled anger bleeding into fear. Then he lifted his hands overhead, grabbing at the thin and cold earthly air as the girl below him whispered softly:

"You're very much welcome."

"Thanks for the drubbing," said her current boyfriend, the sarcasm blunted by exhaustion.

"You're very much welcome," Porsche allowed, laughing.

They were walking back across the field. Timothy and Nathan were leading the way, Timothy's fourth beer glinting in the slanting light. Suddenly he paused and looked toward the southeast, toward the graveled road, and while taking a last pull from the bottle, he pointed at an oncoming cloud of soft gray dust. "Friend?" he asked aloud. "Or fiend?"

"Neighbors," Porsche called out.

Sure enough, a familiar Humvee rumbled past the house, two people visible for an instant before they vanished behind the shelterbelt. They were an older couple who farmed sections north of theirs. They were harmless. Porsche's eavesdroppers had already warned her that they were coming, and with a voice generated directly on her audio nerve, they assured her, "They are gone."

Timothy made a partial turn, then stood motionless. He looked a little drunk and acted as if he were trying to guard the basket. His face looked sloppy. The eyes were too bright, too simple. He waited for Porsche and Cornell to step close, then with an incautious voice, he said, "I feel safe here."

"Good," said Cornell.

Timothy fell in behind them, saying, "I sweep this ground twice every week, just to be safe."

"I know," said Cornell. "And thank you."

Timothy put a hand on Porsche's shoulder, squeezing and saying with a drunken singsong, "Three times. I've found standard, government-issue bugs three times. All brought in on the backs of microrobots. Which is what our government does when it wants to be subtle."

Porsche couldn't remember Timothy ever touching her. She turned to look at him, shrugging her shoulder and pulling free in one smooth motion. "We know," she reminded him. "You showed them to us . . . remember?"

"They're hard bugs to detect," he boasted. "I can do it because I'm better than my opponents."

No one spoke.

"Yet," he sang. "I have never, ever found any trace of your eyes, Porsche."

"What eyes?" Cornell asked, by reflex.

The willowy black man grew animated, dancing around the two of them, saying, "No games. You know what I'm talking about."

Porsche touched Cornell first, then Timothy.

Quietly, carefully, she said, "I doubt if you could ever find . . . my eyes . . . "

Anger and a giddy excitement swirled together.

"Does that bother you?" she asked. "Because it shouldn't—"

"No, that's not it!" he declared, half-shouting and glancing skyward. "You've got more advanced equipment. Fine. I can come up with explanations, and I won't tell anyone . . . but I've got to know: Why do you need me? What in the hell can Timothy Kleck do for you that you can't do for yourselves?"

He was staring hard at Porsche, waiting.

"Yourselves," she echoed. "Why do you think there's anyone but me?"

His gaze flickered, dropped.

"This is my project," she assured him. "No one else is involved."

"No one?" he muttered, more surprised than dubious.

"All I have," Porsche warned, "are some simple tricks, and my three friends. And I can't do this work without you, Timothy." She said the words exactly as she had practiced them, then before he could smell what was untrue, she gestured at the reflection of the earth. "There's no one better qualified for this work than you."

It was a lie that he could believe.

Watching him smile, watching the logic win him over, Porsche wondered why almost every sentient species, given a choice, gladly selected praise before the truth.

Then Timothy repeated, "I really do feel safe here."

"You should," she replied, and her eyes slipped sideways and up, her gaze escaping into the sky.

After three quiet years on the new world, the Neal family decided to embark on an American adventure. In a rented motor home, they drove west, then north, following the continent's raw spine to the cosmopolitan campgrounds of Yellowstone. Their reserved campsite lay in the shadows of lodgepole pines. A larger motor home bearing Washington plates was already parked next door. The family's name was Vortune. Mr. Vortune was an intense man, a glowering expression beneath a dark brown mat of synthetic hair. His wife was a quiet, lovely woman, very blond and very tan. Both of them had worked three years at Boeing, and they had five children, the eldest being a feral boy named Trinidad.

There was a distinct physical resemblance between the families, but they pretended not to notice.

With the ease of people on vacation, everyone became fast friends. For a long week, they had each other over for meals, went on daylong hikes together, played croquet with a newcomer's passion, and fished the nearby river for its few remaining cutthroat trout.

Porsche played her role perfectly.

She wouldn't betray her family twice, even by accident.

Trinidad was less self-conscious. In public, he called her, "Po-lee-een," as if joking; by contrast, he hated to hear his own jarr-tee name. So much so that no one dared tease him with it.

He loved making fun of their family's precautions and the infectious paranoia.

It seemed to be an old, much-practiced game between father and son.

There was a daily argument about security issues and things less definite. Trinidad claimed that no one else in their little club lived so carefully. Not on the earth, at least. He was sick of never being given real freedom or trust. And Uncle Jack responded by quoting the Few's protocols, in scrupulous detail, then when the protocols didn't help, he would make the usual allusions to other's past mistakes, never quite looking at his niece.

Around the nightly campfire, adults blamed typical teenage rebellion. But Porsche found easy reasons to blame her uncle, too. He had always been a stiff, suspicious man, but he was worse than ever. If anything, the relative freedom of the earth gave him even more excuses to be paranoid. He was always whispering to the hidden eavesdroppers, making them examine every stranger who happened past their campsite. But that wasn't enough. If Jack Vortune was sitting outside, he glared at the passersby with his own eyes, causing more than a few strangers to turn and hurry off in the opposite direction.

"You never know when someone's watching," he reminded both families. "And even if you see the spying eyes," he would add, "you'll never know what's behind them."

No one blamed Porsche for the past. And Aunt Me-meel—now called Kay Vortune—endeared herself to the young woman, going out of her way to make small talk, and occasionally promising that everyone in her family was happier here than they ever were on Jarrtee.

"Including you?" Porsche asked.

"Particularly me," her aunt replied. "Oh, I know I was born jarrtee. But that's an accident of biology. My spirit *loves* this sweet little world."

Even at his worst, Uncle Jack never seemed angry toward Porsche or said anything unkind. But there was a palpable distance between them, glacial and persistent, and it helped Porsche tolerate—and sometimes applaud—her cousin's tiny rebellions.

On their last day together, Porsche and Trinidad slipped away to a private mountainside, sunning themselves on a slab of dark volcanic rock. Passing hikers would have guessed they were fraternal twins, blessed with the same good looks and a closeness begun in the womb. Three years apart, yet they were utterly at ease with each other, trusting and happy. Porsche certainly felt happy. She was so relaxed that when Trinidad asked a taboo question—a question absolutely forbidden outside a secured enclosure—she simply closed her eyes, then opened them, answering as if everything were perfectly normal.

"What do you know about the other worlds?" he asked. "The Few's worlds, I mean. And be honest."

Very little, in truth. She could name dozens of nearby worlds, give schoolgirl descriptions of most, and if suddenly transported to any of them, she would know the basics of finding her way home again. But even a hundred worlds were nothing compared to millions. "I'm not old enough to travel far," she explained. Then she proved that she could ask dangerous questions. "You know something, cousin. What is it?"

He waited for a moment, grinning.

"Deep inside the Few universe," he said, "are the most ancient worlds. Worlds where we've lived for ages. At least since the earth was a sloppy wet newborn, very nearly."

She knew that already. Who didn't?

"We've been there for so long, we aren't the Few anymore." He shook his head, his voice growing louder. "We've become every-one, and we live openly, in total freedom."

Porsche glanced warily at the rocky slope below them, then above.

"Every intrusion leading to a living world is left open perma-nently. You and I could walk and fly and swim and crawl our way from world to world. Pick an efficient route, and we could be-come two hundred species in an earth's day."

She said nothing.

Both of them looked up at the sun-washed whiteness of Green-land. After a long moment, Trinidad asked, "Wouldn't that be wonderful?"

One kind of wonderful, yes.

"I'd do anything to go there." He spoke as if making a con-fession, as if there was something wrong in the soul that would want such things.

Teasing him, Porsche said, "Anything?"

But she didn't mention the obvious: One life was too small to make that enormous journey.

Then Trinidad said something even more astonishing, and strange. "Did you ever realize . . . you and I are part of an invad-ing army."

"No!" she responded, in reflex. "That's ridiculous . . . stupid!"

He gave her a wink. "The Few are slow, patient conquerors." The winking eye was bright against his tanned face and the gray-black rock. "We come here and prosper, and we make nice big families, and over a few million years, we'll gradually, relentlessly make this planet our own. As human beings, maybe. As por-poises, but probably not. Most likely, as whatever follows these modified apes."

Trinidad was baiting her. He wanted to argue, she assumed. But that would increase the odds that someone would overhear them. "You're entitled to your stupid opinions," she announced, "but not to my stupid opinions." She rose and began to goat-step her way down the slope, then ran casually back to the camp-ground.

Uncle Jack was waiting.

He sat on a folding chair with a beer in one hand, eyes slicing through Porsche but not a word said. He finished the beer and started a second can before his son wandered into view. Uncle Jack set the beer down in the grass, then stood. As soon as Trinidad was in earshot, his father started talking, apparently to himself. In a low, bitter voice, he said, "I heard you. I can't believe it. Talking that way, and the whole fucking world watching you—"

For an instant, Trinidad's cockiness faltered.

Then with a teenager's easy outrage, he straightened his back and let his eyes catch fire, crying out, "You were spying on *me!*"

"Always," his father rumbled. "I'm always watching you."

"Bastard! You had no right!"

But he had every right, and people knew it. Not even Porsche came leaping to the boy's defense. Standing at a safe distance, she watched them trade insults. The worst insult was when Uncle Jack used Trinidad's jarrtee name. Trinidad took a swing at the large, powerfully built man, doubling him over with the first solid blow. Then Trinidad lost his fire, dropping his hands, standing motionless as his father found his breath, then his balance, shoving the boy down on his back and squatting on his chest, weeping great long tears, weeping as he slapped Trinidad's face, and still weeping after Porsche and her father took him by the arms, dragging him away.

The boy scrambled to his feet, his face reddened by the blows and the unbearable shame. Then his mother appeared at his side—a petite blonde with the perfect button nose of a doll— and she took Trinidad's head and pulled it down to where she could press her mouth to his ear, whispering, then pausing for a moment, then whispering something else that seemed to calm him enough that finally, finally he was crying, too.

The Vortunes made all the appropriate apologies, and the Neals pretended to be forgiving. Then the families promised to meet again next year, vacationing at the Grand Canyon, perhaps, or somewhere in Canada. Perhaps. With a year to plan, who knew where they would go?

But the promise was never kept.

Porsche's father grew ill. Cancer was found during a routine examination. In total innocence, the purely human doctor remarked, "Except for the tumor, Mr. Neal, you're in remarkable condition for a man of your age."

One testicle was removed, and tailored leukocytes were injected, hunting down any surviving traitors. The prognosis was excellent but not perfect. Father proved to be a durable, uncomplaining patient, except for the bad days, and he tried to remain philosophical, informing his family with a dry, overpracticed calmness that his fate was sealed one way or another, and if the worst happened, it would just help prove that they were humans, that they belonged here, genetic weaknesses and all, his bones in the ground and in the ground to stay.

Father recovered during the summer, thankfully. And since the Vortunes were distant friends, it was decided to delay their next adventure for a year.

But that never happened, either.

"Why not?" asked Cornell.

They were lying in bed, in the dark. It was a few hours after the basketball game. A front had come out of the northwest, bringing light snow and strong cold winds. Wind moaned against the window, rattling the old glass, making them speak louder than Porsche liked to speak, and slower, and with as much precision as the late hour allowed.

"Why not?" Cornell repeated. Then he said, "No," and placed a hand over her full mouth, saying, "I have better questions."

The wind lifted to a roar, then fell away.

Then with a puzzled tone, he asked, "Why tell me this touching little story? And why tell it to me now?"

She didn't answer him.

Instead, she pushed back the covers and rose, stepping toward the window. With the pressure of her palm, she kept the lower pane from shaking in its frame, and with a series of commands delivered in a whisper, in a mutated form of the City's jarrtee, she engaged tiny machines that were scattered about the house and its snowy white yard.

"What are you doing?"

Porsche turned, her free hand moving to her mouth, one finger laid across it.

Cornell didn't move, didn't speak.

A surge of electricity traveled along Porsche's body, telling her that the channel was open. Then she quietly and firmly said, "I need to meet with you."

Her lover nearly spoke, then hesitated.

"Face to face," she said. "Now."

There was a long pause, then her auditory nerves channeled a message straight into her mind.

"I can't meet this minute," said the familiar, welcomed voice. "Is tomorrow soon enough, cousin?"

9

EARLY THAT NEXT MORNING, PORSCHE ANNOUNCED THAT SHE WAS
going shopping.

"We need a table and chairs out here," she said, pacing in the narrow, very empty room beside the kitchen. "Nothing fancy," she promised. "Just a place to eat. Like Christmas dinner, for instance."

"Do you need help?" asked Nathan, stepping eagerly into the future dining room. "Because I'd be willing. If Mr. Kleck will let me out of today's work—"

"Take him!" Timothy shouted from the kitchen, over the hum of the microwave.

"Thanks, no," she replied. "Cornell's already agreed to go."

Cornell was standing against the faded wallpaper, smiling thinly, not quite looking at anyone's face.

"A second helper, maybe?" his father persisted.

"Sorry."

Timothy joined them, stirring a bowl of reheated chili. "I need somebody's help," he grumbled. "Two billion dollars in discretionary funds are missing from the agency's ledgers. To me, that's more fun than any furniture."

"You've got me," Nathan pledged.

Timothy's eyes grew large and round, but he kept his mouth shut.

"Back soon," Porsche promised everyone.

"Find something nice," was Nathan's parting advice.

For an instant, she imagined a long and ornate marble table filling the narrow room, its heavy fluted legs carved with the symbols of a vanished family. She halfway laughed at herself, then felt a hand pressing against the small of her back.

"Let's go," said Cornell. "Before the best deals are gone."

Porsche drove. The country lay brown and dead beneath a thin coat of dry snow, and above, a serene blue sky freshly arrived from the Arctic. Rutted roads gave way to a two-lane highway. Cornell happened to ask if anyone was following them. The on-board eavesdroppers couldn't find anyone, but of course there were many ways to follow. He nodded and dipped his head, looking toward the western sky. Then with a hand over his mouth, he asked, "Who exactly am I going to meet?"

"You'll see."

"So mysterious," he observed. "For security?"

"No," she replied. "For the sake of drama."

Eighty miles later, they reached the interstate, and continued south for twenty miles of tired pavement. A truck stop's towering windmill promised biofuels and twenty-four-hour service. Porsche pulled off and past the truck stop. A terrifically bland metal building, long as an aircraft carrier, wore a proud banner declaring:

ANTIQUES CRAFTS TREASURES

Porsche parked between out-of-state cars.

"This really is a shopping trip," Cornell muttered. "Isn't it?"

The outdoor cold was replaced with overheated, desert-dry air and the stink of assorted potpourris. The store's front was packed with Christmas wreaths and Santas made from corn-stalks, porcelain candleholders, and smiling robotic bears that disobeyed hundreds of commands. Stocky Midwestern women marched up and down the narrow aisles, hunting mythical bargains. Old high-backed chairs were tucked into the corners, bored husbands filling most of them, their sleepy eyes popping open when they saw Porsche striding past.

The bulk of the furniture was in the back, tables and breakfronts, rolltop desks, and mismatched chairs all wearing chip-coded tags, the prices falling strategically short of exorbitant. What could have been another bored husband sat behind an enormous table, elbows on the glossy wood, folded hands obscuring his mouth, his clothes utterly in keeping with the scene. But he was younger than most of the men, and his eyes were already wide open when Porsche appeared. He glanced at her, for an instant, then his eyes settled on Cornell, no trace of surprise or anger showing. But his eavesdroppers would have already warned him: Without permission, she'd brought her lover on this sudden jaunt.

The hands dropped, revealing a face younger than its years. Combed and cleaned but still unruly masses of honey-brown hair framed the boyish face. His features were Porsche's features, but sharpened by testosterone. The resemblances were obvious enough that Cornell stopped short, then said, "Trinidad," under his breath.

Porsche dropped into the hard chair beside him, trying to smile, jarrtee-fashion. Then she tugged on Cornell's arm until he sat, saying, "My famous cousin."

"And this is your Cornell," said Trinidad. He offered a long hand, then clasped his other hand around Cornell's, pumping it several times as he said, "I was wondering when we'd meet, Mr. Novak. How are you?"

"Surprised," Cornell confessed.

"I know the feeling." A big laugh was negated with a hard glance at his cousin. "What's the word I want, Porsche? *Caution? Protocol?* What?"

She didn't care if he was angry. And besides, he could have slipped away the moment he saw Cornell coming.

"Oh, well," said Trinidad, offering an understanding smile.

Then Cornell asked, "So . . . do you two meet often?"

"A few other times," Porsche told him. "As needed."

Cornell was sitting on her right, and for the first time today, he held her hand. "As needed?"

"Didn't she mention it? I've followed my father into the business." Trinidad laughed quietly, earnestly.

"The business," said Cornell.

"Knowing odd facts, doing odd favors." He paused, watching an elderly woman shuffle past. Then, "I usually give my help across secure lines of communication. But sometimes it's nice to see my favorite cousin face-to-face."

"What kind of help?"

No one hurried to answer.

"Sorry," said Cornell. "Is that impolite?"

"Horribly, and I forgive you." Trinidad offered a gracious smile and wink, then said, *"Help* is a vague term, I know. What it means, in essence, is that if you're looking in the wrong places for information, perhaps I can suggest better places. But only occasionally, in special circumstances. Of course."

Cornell exhaled, then said, "You've got some enormous tools, I bet."

Again, silence.

"We were discussing those tools just yesterday, in fact. At least Timothy was." Cornell waited for a half-moment, then asked, "What makes a special circumstance?"

"Whatever happens," Trinidad replied, "no one should be able to point a finger at *us.*" He couldn't have sounded more patient. Offering a wise smile, he reminded everyone, "We have limits. Not strict limits. Not drawn in exact lines. But they're general guidelines that have been proven in countless situations."

"You want to remain hidden," Cornell mentioned. "I know. And you don't want to interfere in human affairs."

"Oh, we want to interfere. Just so long as we can avoid the perception of being busybodies."

"Either way," Cornell allowed, "you know your needs better than I do."

"I love Porsche." Trinidad leaned forward, his expression earnest. Determined. "You know, of course, that she was helping *us* when she met you. When she chose you. And she's chosen her current life. As long as her goals don't conflict with ours, and as long as *we* avoid everyone's ire, we can keep helping you."

"That sounds pretty vague," Cornell observed.

"We're exceptionally good with things vague," Trinidad countered.

Cornell was watching Trinidad's hands, watching the strong fingers tap the polished old wood. Then with a voice that Porsche could barely hear, he whispered, "I'm sorry. I think you're lying to me."

A light shone in Trinidad's eyes, but he said nothing.

"I think you're helping your cousin because you want her to succeed. You want the agency to be exposed. That's one of *your* goals, and it always has been."

Trinidad was wearing expensive cologne; Porsche suddenly noticed the odor.

"It's nothing that she's told me," Cornell allowed. "At least not directly. But I think that you people feel . . . how to put this . . . you feel *responsible* for certain things . . ."

That brought a broad smile and wink from Trinidad. Glancing at Porsche, he said, "You were right. He can cut straight through the bullshit, can't he?"

"He can," she sang out.

"That's what this is about, isn't it?" said Trinidad. "You came to ask permission to tell him the truth."

With her eyes, she said yes.

"Well," Trinidad allowed, "I guess you might as well."

It was a wondrous moment: Her two most devoted men sat flanking her, sharing the table that she intended to purchase for her newest family, and she couldn't remember ever feeling happy in quite this way.

"No wonder you love him," her cousin purred. "I guess I should try and love him, too. What do you think?"

While Porsche paid with cash, Trinidad slipped away unnoticed.

She and Cornell laid the antique table in the back of her truck, upside down, six chairs set among the upturned legs and every fragile surface protected with faded and stained old blankets brought for exactly that purpose.

Her cousin went unmentioned until they were on the road, Cornell at the wheel. With a careful voice, he asked, "When did you see him again? After Yellowstone, I mean."

She said nothing.

"What?" he asked, nonplussed. "Is that a secret, too?"

With an easy sharpness, she said, "I'm just counting, that's all."

Cornell dipped his head for a moment.

"Seventeen years," she reported, almost astonished by that number. "Nearly eighteen years."

"Half your life," he observed.

"Nearly."

After Father's bout with cancer, the families never found a suitable excuse to meet. As much as anything, it was the bad taste left by the brawl between father and son. Yet that brawl seemed to change the Vortunes. A couple of years later, Porsche learned that Uncle Jack and Trinidad had more than reconciled. The elder Vortune took an early retirement from Boeing, then left the earth on a routine security mission, taking his son with him. It was a healing adventure for them. Porsche both envied her cousin and missed him. But she and her family had their own little adventures, renting cabins in the Canadian wilderness, then walking through the nearby intrusions, visiting an assortment of relatives on a dozen different worlds.

When Trinidad came home, Porsche was attending college in Austin. He sent an encoded message, making a thin promise to pass through Texas soon and bump elbows with her. Then he congratulated her on her scholarship. "The jarrtees wouldn't believe it," he remarked with the usual sarcasm. "Because you can bounce a ball and throw it through a metal ring, people are willing to give you the secrets of the universe!"

At school she was the big star in a second-tier sport. Male athletes were more popular—or more notorious—yet Porsche managed to win her share of fans. The entire Neal clan would drive down from Dallas to cheer her on, and they'd frequently show at the road games. Her older brother, Leonard, Jr., brought his future wife to the spring tournament. Despite the losing effort and the endless distractions, Porsche realized immediately that the woman's blood ran thick with Few genes. It was that easy, she realized. That easy, and that sweet, too.

Porsche was an excellent student who leaped between majors, but after three years she left school without a degree. "Which is dangerous," her advisor warned. "Without qualifications, what can you possibly do in your future?"

She turned pro and was drafted early in the second round by the Cleveland Lakers. There was a women's team in Seattle, but by then Trinidad had left the earth on another extended trip. Aunt Kay and Uncle Jack would attend the occasional game, sitting close to the court, her aunt waving exactly as you'd expect a distant friend to wave, unsure if she was recognized. Uncle Jack, in contrast, preferred to play the grouch. After one game, the two of them met her, and Aunt Kay took it on herself to invite her secret niece out to a late dinner. But the team was flying to Honolulu in an hour, and gratefully, Porsche said that dinner would have to wait.

For the first time in her life, Porsche wasn't the best player on the court, or even on the team. Other women were closer to a human's limits than she was. Her fame-claim was her marketable name, in part, and because she played with speed and power. She had an official fan club; her presence meant ticket sales. Promotions and bonuses meant that she could tuck away enough money for the rest of her human life, and in a twist of irony, she was hired by a dying company to model with their sports cars, her image adorning a variety of men's magazines inside truck stops everywhere.

Porsche stuck with the sport until she stopped improving, her abilities polished by training and by experience until she could feel the first gnawings of age.

She retired without fanfare, in the off-season, at exactly the moment when it would garner the least attention.

Porsche went home to Dallas, briefly. Her baby brother, Donald, was marrying a talented, all-human woman named Linda— a perfect soul to usher into the Few. And of course she wanted to meet her older brother's twin sons, bouncing the chubby drool machines on her knees as she talked obliquely about her immediate future.

Bringing to bear an expertise polished on countless worlds, Porsche Neal soon vanished from public view.

The shrinking ranks of fans heard that she was traveling. An assortment of electronic footprints left the impression of a woman who was somewhere close but living in seclusion. Tax forms were signed and filed. E-mail was answered, but not quickly. There was even a face and voice that called old friends and teammates, looking and sounding exactly like Porsche yet never able to meet them in person, some excuse at the ready, and each excuse greased with a charm that left no lasting resentments.

By any measure, the genuine Porsche was far from the earth.

Long ago, she had promised herself that she would wander, and now she was keeping her word: She saw worlds famous to the Few, and uneverted wild worlds, and eventually she came to places that Trinidad had visited—with his father, or alone.

He was gone long before Porsche arrived, but people remembered her cousin, and they gave her the reheated compliments that he had enjoyed. She had a flexible soul, they said. She was durable and skeptical and as smart as smart helped a person, then she could stand on her courage. All good qualities, particularly for souls living on the brink of the Few.

"In other words," she admitted to Cornell, "they were patronizing me." She was riding beside him, her legs stretched out to keep the basketball knees happy. "The poor little pioneer girl from the wilderness . . . that's how they looked at me."

"The brink of the Few?" Cornell muttered.

He was driving slower than necessary, eyes focused straight ahead and both hands holding the steering wheel.

"The farthest I got was a minor administrative world." She paused, then added, "That's as far as Trinidad went, too."

"Okay."

"That's where I saw a map," she allowed. "It was a three-dimensional model of the many-dimensional universe. I couldn't comprehend most of what I was seeing, of course. But my host graciously tried to explain what he-she could understand at a glance—"

"He-she?"

"Some other time," she promised. Then she glanced back at her table and chairs, saying, "Trinidad had seen the same map. The same host had brought him there, which was a real privilege, and we were shown the same tiny feature. It was a whiff of colored smoke, at least to my eyes—just a tiny finger jutting out of a map that was bigger than most buildings—and he-she explained that the finger represented the earth and Jarrtee, plus almost every other world that I'd crossed on my very small travels."

"A damned big universe," Cornell ventured.

"Exactly."

She didn't mention that her host was also her lover, or that he-she had been Trinidad's lover, too. That second detail was a secret that she'd always kept from her cousin. Not out of guilt, she hoped. Certainly not out of remorse. But when it came to Trinidad, she felt an instinctive desire to keep a distance, to dilute down that relentless sense of familial intimacy.

"And you came back up the finger," Cornell prompted. Then laughing, he added, "To our little wilderness."

She'd returned to the earth at a prearranged time, using an intrusion in Kashmir. A passport and money had been hidden nearby, along with a small wardrobe and some Few-made tools.

After walking to the nearest village, she rode an ancient diesel-powered train to New Delhi, then took a scramjet to Dallas, skimming high enough above the atmosphere to tease the sky into uneverting, then everting again, most of the passengers too hardened to the miracle to even pretend interest.

Her older brother met her at DFW, and even though he acted pleasant, he seemed even more laconic than usual, saying maybe a dozen words before they reached their parents' house.

It was December; Christmas lights sparkled against the gray brick, and every house light was burning. Suddenly Porsche felt nervous, as if some animal sense told her that a trap was waiting. In a sense, there was. Leon couldn't stay. He and Donald and everyone else would come visit tomorrow, he promised. Then he promptly abandoned her at the curb, sealing his fate.

The great traveler—the durable strong soul that had embraced a hundred varied worlds—discovered that her legs were shaking from anticipation and nerves. It was a long walk, and exhausting, and while taking her last little step, the front door sprang open, a stranger standing behind the storm door, smiling and calling her name.

No, she realized, he wasn't a stranger. It had just been a lot of years, and who would have expected to see *him* here?

Mama-ma appeared, grayer but not gray. "You remember Mr. Vortune," she said brightly, her voice only a little forced. "We met him and his family up in Yellowstone . . . how long ago was that?"

No one answered the question.

"You know my wife, Kay," said Uncle Jack. "And Trinidad."

Aunt Kay was wearing an elegant dress, and the Vortune men were dressed in conservative business suits.

Everyone was trying hard to smile over cocktails.

Then almost as an afterthought, Mama-ma embraced her and squealed, "Oh, it's good to see you, darling. Home safe. We're all so glad!"

The Few had spent endless generations feigning calm in the vortex of surprise. But for an instant, for whatever reason, heredity and training failed Porsche. She said aloud, "Uncle." With the world watching, she said, "Cousin?" Then her uncle did exactly what he loved to do: He took charge. "The Asian air did you wonders, Miss Neal. Don't you think so, son?"

"I've seen her look better," was Trinidad's response.

Porsche stepped inside as Mama-ma tried to explain. The Vortunes were in town for a business convention, and wasn't it a wonderful coincidence? "Your father's in the kitchen," she reported. And as if to prove the assertion, Father stepped into the dining room, looking heavier than she remembered, wearing the same striped apron that he'd worn for nearly twenty years and waving a spatula as he shouted:

"Come give an old man a young hug!"

Aunt Kay waited nearby. She was still pretty, except she looked worn around her eyes, but the charm was unchanged. Taking Porsche's hand with her tiny hands, she squeezed hard and told her niece, "Dinner's still an hour away."

What did it matter?

"Maybe now?" she said. "What do you think, Jack?"

"Good time as any," her uncle allowed.

"What's happening?"

No one was watching them. Yet everyone felt obligated to read their lines, faithful to the very elaborate game.

"We've started a sporting goods store," her uncle confessed. "We're in town on business, and we thought this would be the perfect time to talk business with you. If you have a few minutes, that is."

She said nothing.

"If you're not too tired from traveling," Aunt Kay added.

Porsche guessed her lines. "I'm fine," she said. Then, "Where would be good?"

"The theater room," Mama-ma offered.

Uncle Jack ushered Porsche into the back of the house, Trinidad bringing up the rear. Once the door was closed, Uncle Jack instructed her to get comfortable. She sat at her own pace. The man who rightly blamed her for their family's hardships sat opposite her, and without warning, he conjured an unnatural smile, the eyes acquiring a cold, keen edge.

"We can talk," he promised.

The room was secure.

Trinidad sat on Uncle Jack's right, conspicuously saying nothing. The years had transformed him, creating the dutiful son.

"Let me just say it," her uncle began. "We're here to make a substantial and very important request."

"A request?"

"Humans," he said, with emphasis. He seemed to expect the word to explain everything. Then he took a breath, waiting a half-moment before saying, "They know about the intrusions."

"Since when?"

"Not long," he replied. "But the CEA has already managed to pry open several non-Few intrusions, and it's throwing resources and an insane amount of hope into the work—"

"How could they find even one?"

"Simple dumb luck." Her uncle's expression was grave, his voice holding no hope. "Officially, that's our position. In the past, on rare occasions, serendipity has given some amazingly primitive worlds the keys to the universe."

Porsche waited a half-moment, then said, "But you don't believe that—?"

Uncle Jack glanced at Trinidad, nodding.

His son leaned forward, with urgency. "There are some ominous coincidences at play here, Po-lee-een."

"Such as?"

"One of us may be involved."

"Involved?"

"One of us happened to vanish," Trinidad reported. "Just before the agency made its breakthrough."

"Who?"

"You don't know her," Uncle Jack assured her. Or warned her.

Trinidad showed a big grim smile, then explained, "A woman matching her description was killed in a hit-and-run accident. In California, not twenty miles from one of the agency's main labs.

The body was cremated before it could be claimed, but the physical evidence says the victim was one of ours."

Ours.

Porsche thought for a moment, then asked, "What else?"

"She was a run-of-the-mill courier," Trinidad reported. "When she vanished, she was transporting an assortment of machines, including a dozen basic keys."

Since the Few couldn't bring machinery across the intrusions, they had to build their keys and eavesdroppers and the rest of their paraphernalia on each of their worlds. The elaborate manufacturing centers—nano-factories usually no bigger than this room—were among their most important, deeply held secrets; Porsche had no idea where her own tools had been built, or by whom, or the technical specifics behind any of them.

A good courier would be just as ignorant, and precautions were always taken, insuring that precious ignorance.

"Is the agency using her keys?" she inquired.

Expecting that question, Trinidad said, "No," immediately. "From what we can tell, they're using their own big machines to pry open the intrusions."

"Wild intrusions," she repeated.

"Exactly," said Uncle Jack. "They've experimented with our glass disks, but of course basic keys don't help with them."

Sophisticated, encoded keys were required for them.

Trinidad said, "It is possible that there was a genuine accident, but the courier was injured. Not killed. A very specific head injury would have made her talkative, and if she'd had an alert audience—"

"It's happened before," Uncle Jack offered. "On a world or two."

"Or," Trinidad continued, "the answer is a lot simpler."

A stew of emotions welled up inside Porsche. Then a rational piece of her spoke. "If I wanted to abandon the Few, for whatever reasons, I'd probably stage my own death."

How many people actually betrayed the Few? She didn't know enough to make even a lousy guess.

For a long moment, no one spoke.

Then Uncle Jack said, "Whatever the reasons, the damage has been done. What matters now are the consequences."

Trinidad leaned even closer, telling her, "Human beings shouldn't be poking their sticks down strange holes."

"Exactly," said her uncle. "The social models are unanimous. If this technology comes too soon, human societies are in for chaotic disruptions. And if that technology is in the hands of just a few humans, then greed and desperation will make everything even worse."

"Every color of misery," Trinidad promised.

Porsche shook her head for a moment, then inquired, "So what's your request?"

"We need someone," said her cousin. "Someone to infiltrate the agency. Which isn't exactly a difficult trick, since the agency is carrying out a desperate search now for anyone with half an ounce of talent."

In an instant, she understood her Mama-ma's nervousness and Leon's chilly silence.

Softly, with a flat dry voice, she asked, "Why me?"

"Very few children immigrated to the earth," Uncle Jack reported. "You and your cousins are my two best candidates, as it happens. The right ages, and U.S. citizens, too. Though, frankly, you aren't my first choice, Porsche."

Trinidad winked at her, saying nothing.

"The problem with my son," her uncle continued, "is that the missing courier has had contact with me. On occasion."

"I wouldn't pass through the agency's security checks," Trinidad allowed.

Porsche had to laugh, for a moment.

"What's funny?" Uncle Jack asked.

"You," she said. "The situation. Everything."

Trinidad laughed quietly to himself.

"It's the irony," she explained. "We despise each other, yet here you are. Coming to me for help."

"Affection isn't a consideration," Uncle Jack warned her. "Trust matters, and I genuinely don't trust you."

"I suppose not."

"Except who else can I ask? Most of your cousins, like your two brothers, have homes and spouses, and children, too."

"The agency wants family-free recruits," said Trinidad.

Uncle Jack said, "You haven't been home . . . in how long?"

She glanced at her uncle, then her own hands.

"You owe your family a great debt," her uncle reminded her. "And, I think, you owe yourself just as great of a debt."

Porsche nodded, slowly, calmly.

"Join the agency, tell me what's happening on these wild worlds . . . and the debts will be paid. Eventually." He glanced at his son, then found Porsche's eyes again. "Afterwards, we won't have to like each other. But we can dislike one another as equals. Which, in my experience, is usually the best way to make peace."

Cornell and Porsche were nearly home.

The hills and windbreaks and occasional houses grew more familiar by the mile. Porsche found herself anticipating frozen ponds and the dilapidated bridges, and when she saw the old white farmhouse in the distance, she felt a palpable relief. The elderly structure had stood up to the wind for another day; shelter was in easy reach.

Since they had left the paved highway, neither had spoken.

Cornell adjusted his hands on the wheel, then asked, "Do you know? Was that courier responsible for you-know-what?"

"No one knows. Still."

He chewed on the words for a moment, then said, "Interesting."

"What is, darling?"

He smiled with a sideways glance. "If the agency had ever realized what you are, what would have happened to your folks and brothers?"

"They would have been protected. Before the agency could have acted, I hope."

"And you?"

"I was Trinidad's assignment. He was watching over me, just in case."

"On High Desert?"

"Just on the earth," she allowed.

"And what about now? He's still watching, isn't he?"

"Day and night."

Through the skeletal windbreak, they could see the metal outbuilding, and nearby, Nathan's old Chinese sedan and Timothy's bullet-shaped Brazilian sugar-burner.

"Has the debt been paid?"

"Mostly," Porsche admitted.

"But you didn't get your final answers, did you?" He removed his foot from the accelerator, allowing the rough road to slow their truck. "Is that what you're hoping for here? Timothy stumbles over a file that incriminates the courier, or clears her?"

"That would be nice, but it's very unlikely. Impossible, even."

"Because the Few have better tools than Timothy's." He turned the wheel with two fingers, creeping down the long dirt drive to the farmhouse. "And if the Few can't find the truth with their fancy tools . . . that implies . . . implies that they're up against someone who understands what you can do . . ."

Porsche said nothing.

With a confessional tone, Cornell admitted, "I've always wondered if it was something like this. Something bad."

She saw Nathan step out on the front porch, waving and smiling, shouting a string of incomprehensible words.

"Is that the secret you wanted to tell me?"

Her voice sounded distant and a little too stiff. "No," she said. "There's something else, too."

"Yeah?"

"After you and I got back from High Desert, I contacted my uncle. I explained what you wanted to do—investigating the agency, then expose them—and he thought it was a wonderful idea. But not for your reasons."

"What reasons, then?"

"If there is a traitor, and if the agency uses her, or him, to try to stop what we're doing—"

"She'll expose herself," Cornell muttered.

Porsche said, "That's the hope."

"In other words," he said, "we are bait."

Timothy emerged from the utility building, plainly relieved to have them home again.

"Worms on a hook," Cornell whispered with a bleak fascination.

Then Porsche turned to ask him, "What do you think? Should we tell the others?"

Cornell nearly spoke, coming close to giving a reflexive, "Of course we tell them." But then he paused, realizing that the circumstance had no easy answer. "Because of you," he remarked, "Timothy believes that he's perfectly safe. If he isn't, he might run off. Or at least, he'll pout like a seven-year-old."

"And Nathan?"

Cornell parked and waved at his father, then watched in the mirror as the gray-haired man walked around the back of the truck, lifting a blanket to see what they had purchased.

"For now," he said, "let's keep it our secret."

"Fine."

Over the thrumming of the engine, they heard Nathan shouting, "It's a beauty!"

Timothy stopped short of the truck, cold hands shoved into cold pockets. "Don't leave me alone with him again!" he screamed, with his suffering stance, his accusing eyes.

Cornell had another thought. "Is there anything else that you're keeping from me?" he asked.

Then almost as an afterthought, he said, "Porsche?"

She turned and kissed Cornell, kissed him with a tenderness that was unlike her, her mouth flush against his mouth for an age; then they pulled apart and found tears on their cheeks, damp and warm, fallen from anonymous ducts, and orphaned.

10

IN A MILITARY HOSPITAL AT AN UNDISCLOSED LOCATION, A MADMAN sat alone.

"A veteran of a different kind of war," declared the narrator.

Hawthorne's voice remained synthetic, but everything else about the segment couldn't have been more genuine. Without adequate staff on hand, the hospital had resorted to simple AI software running on heavily padded terminals—in effect, electronic psychiatrists. A few weeks ago, Timothy had opened a lightline to the patient and borrowed the security cameras to serve as eyes. Then Porsche had interviewed the patient, her voice translated into Hawthorne's deep rumblings. "Hello, sir," she had said to the patient. "I'd like to speak to you for a moment, sir. If I may."

A twisted, pitiful face gazed off in a random direction. Thinning red hair was cut short. He wore a simple hospital gown. Drugs and diet made his cheeks and neck puff out. The patient was perhaps twenty years old, or fifty, or anywhere in between. With a voice like shattering glass, he said, "Do you? Speak with me?"

She identified herself as a reporter, then confessed, "I'm eager to hear about your employer. We understand you once worked for Tangent, Incorporated."

The patient dipped his head, as if startled.

"Except I know there is no Tangent, Incorporated," she continued. "The company is a branch of the CEA. Isn't that right, sir?"

He took several deep, thorough breaths, then said, "I didn't tell you that."

"They hired you," she said, "and sent you far away."

"Maybe."

"To another world. Isn't that right?"

Again, he dipped his head. "High Desert, we called it."

"And something astonishing happened to you when you traveled to High Desert. Am I correct?"

Silence.

"You were changed. Physically changed. Am I right, sir?"

In a strong whisper, he said, "I was the same . . . inside . . . where you can't see; I was . . . I was me . . ."

"But I'm talking about what I can see."

Trembling hands covered his face, green eyes peering through white, sun-starved fingers. "Cross over," he allowed, "and your body changes. That's how you survive. You look alien, except you're always human. Even when you forget, you still are."

"What did you look like?"

"I had bodies. Six bodies. And I dragged my brain behind me."

"Is that how the aliens looked? That planet's natives?"

"I guess."

"What was your job on High Desert?"

"I hunted."

"For food. Is that what you mean?"

"Sometimes."

"What else did you hunt?"

"Them."

"Who?"

"Those aliens. The natives."

"The creatures shaped like you?"

"Yeah."

"And did you find them?"

Silence.

"Did you?"

The patient glanced at the camera fastened to the top of the terminal. Despite the puffy face, there was a wasted, raw-boned quality, particularly around the bright eyes.

"No," he finally admitted. "I never found them, no."

"How long were you stationed on High Desert?"

He considered the question, then admitted sadly, "I'm not sure."

"Where did you go?"

"I can't tell you."

"Did you visit the Breaks?"

He brightened suddenly. "You know about the Breaks?"

"And the Rumpled Mountains. Is that where you went? Into the Rumpleds?"

"Yes."

"Alone?"

He hesitated, then said, "No."

"What happened in the mountains?" A pause. "Something happened. I know it did, sir. I would very much appreciate it if you could tell me."

"We got lost."

"It's a strange, bleak landscape," was Porsche's assessment. "I find it easy to believe that someone would get lost."

"And hungry . . ."

"There's not much food on the Rumpleds, is there?"

"No."

"You found yourself in a famine." Her voice, and Hawthorne's, were more than sympathetic. There was a tangible appreciation for what the patient had endured. "You had to eat. You ate bravely . . . everything you could find, and that's the only reason you survived."

The eyes grew large, suffused with a hopefulness. "The others didn't. Eat. I told them to, but they couldn't make themselves!"

"Then you came back to this world," said Porsche. "Outside and inside, you were human again."

"Always, inside."

"I bet you looked like yourself, and sounded like yourself. Except sometimes, or maybe a lot of the time, you feel as if some part of you is still walking across that cold dead desert. Am I right about that?"

"Yes," he whispered.

"You went home," she continued. "Did you live alone?"

"Yes."

"And you were hungry, weren't you?"

Shame swirled with astonishment. "I ate something bad," he confessed.

"What did you eat?"

"Bugs."

"A lot of people eat insects," she offered.

"And a dog, too."

"Someone's pet dog?"

"I guess so."

"But those aren't bad things," she assured him. "What did you eat that was bad?"

Silence.

"On High Desert," said Porsche, "sometimes the hungriest people would consume one or two of their extra bodies. If they wanted to live, they had no choice."

"None," he whispered.

"Back home again, living in your own house again, and one day you woke up and discovered that you'd eaten every last scrap of food. Is that what happened?"

The patient nodded, gazing downward.

"Couldn't you go to the store?"

"No," he mouthed.

"Why couldn't you?"

"I couldn't remember . . . how to get to the store . . ."

"So what did you do next?"

Silence.

"Tell me," she said.

Nothing.

"I know what you did," she promised, her voice cracking. "But show it to me. I want to see it."

The patient lifted his pale white hand. Suddenly, the paleness of the fingers took a new significance, and when he rolled the fingers to the palm, making a fist, the hand creaked like tired furniture. Then his second hand grasped the first one's wrist, jerking once, then again, disarticulating the prosthetic hand from a bone gnawed clean of flesh.

In the distance, alarms sounded.

Disabling strobes began to fire.

Timothy killed the strobes and changed cameras. The patient was sobbing, fighting to cover his eyes with his partial forearm. For the first time, they could see him sitting in a sturdy wheelchair, his gown falling limply over the edge, no legs left to give it shape.

More than legs were missing.

According to a report uncovered by Timothy, the man's neighbors had heard his pitiful screams and called the police. Forcing his front door, the police found him wielding a steak knife in his surviving hand, fighting agony while attempting to saw off his testicles.

Another day of dedicated feasting, and he would have reached a vital organ.

A luscious last bite of liver, perhaps. Or the kidneys, maybe.

The man was someone who should never have passed through an intrusion, and as punishment, his soul had been left a mangled, mad ruin.

It was a madness unlike any other. A madness without cure.

"What that poor son of a bitch went through," said Cornell. "I know I'd go insane, if it happened to me."

"Would you?" Porsche replied.

"Wouldn't you?"

"No." She answered, then reconsidered. But she had to say it again, telling him, "No, I would survive it," because she couldn't envision any other answer.

Cornell lay beside her in the dark, conspicuously saying nothing.

Yet Porsche could imagine the madman lying in his invalid's bed, feeling the soft strong bindings around his good hand. She could practically hear him thinking of nothing but that glorious, inevitable moment when his nurses and orderlies forgot to secure him. Then with his own fingernails, he would tear at his chest, at the frail white flesh and living ribs and he would reach into the gore of his chest, and as he died, in that instant, he would take a cherished bite out of his own vivid red heart.

When they arrived at the farm and began to work, Porsche knew what they were fighting, and why, and everything that she had learned had simply reinforced what she knew about the enemy.

Whatever its shape, ruthless ambition was unacceptable.

Sentience without conscience didn't deserve the keys to the universe. What could be more self-evident?

Yet after the most wrenching days, Porsche would sit at the antique table, watching the others mix meals with idle conversation, and she would suddenly think of her birthworld—its relentless sense of clan and territory; its treasured paranoia and tradition-bound horrors—and what was wrong with her that she could actually miss such awful things?

One day, sitting at a very different table, she asked her companion, "Do you ever feel homesick?"

Trinidad was glancing over his shoulder, and perhaps he hadn't heard her. Or more likely, he thought the question was inappropriate, ignoring both it and her, waving at their waitress and half-shouting, "Miss? Cream? The real kind, if you please."

Another question came to mind.

"What is it with you and truck stops?" Porsche inquired.

Her cousin looked at her, revealing a broad smile. "It's obvious, isn't it?" Making a sweeping gesture, he said, "A pageant of the plain and potent, and all we have to do is sit and watch . . ."

"Is that so?"

"That, and I like the cuisine." He paused as the waitress appeared with his cream, throwing up a smile in thanks. The young woman—a nineteen-year-old child—seemed taken by her customer's face and manner. Did he need anything else? Trinidad said, "Eventually. But not now, thanks."

Porsche tried to look at the scene with her cousin's romanticism, but all she saw was a sloppy, virtually empty restaurant.

"Pretty."

She blinked, asking, "What's that?"

"The girl. Don't you think?" He laughed at his own lechery. "Different circumstances and I might try to build a friendship."

"No, you wouldn't."

"Why not? Spreading seed is basic to our nature."

"Human nature, or the Few's?"

"The seed's, actually." He rolled his eyes, then changed subjects. "I was hoping that you'd bring Cornell again."

"He's got a pressing assignment."

"Riding the agency's ass?"

"No," she confessed, "our toilet went critical last night. That takes precedence."

"I guess I can understand why." He started reaching for the floor, for his trim, nondescript briefcase. "Otherwise, how's the work going? Timothy and Nathan still at each other's throats?"

"That's blown over," she said hopefully.

"Well, good."

"Things are going well now. In another week or two, we'll be ready to wrap up."

"No shit." Trinidad wasn't particularly surprised, or interested. "Well," he began, "maybe you don't want this. Or need it. But here's my excuse for coming all this way. In the mood for a gift?"

She was handed a simple brown notebook made from flash paper and smart ignitors—the ignitors put to sleep, hopefully.

"I'd keep it closed till you're home," he advised.

"What's in it?"

"The official, unofficial policies of the CEA, including what's acceptable behavior for keeping the intrusions to themselves."

She laid her hand across the cover. "What behaviors?"

"Manipulation of the press. Intimidation of witnesses. And sweetest, how to maintain their independence from the government watchdogs."

She was astonished, and pleased. "This will delay things, I suppose—"

" 'Thank you, Trinidad,' " he coaxed.

"Thanks." She set the notebook on her lap, out of sight. "But isn't open charity against the rules?"

"Call my father, if you want." He showed his most charming smile. "Seriously, if anyone bothers to look, they'll find a perfectly legitimate path leading from the agency straight to you. The Few are not in the picture."

The youthful waitress was returning, balancing twin plates.

"Breakfast," Porsche warned.

"Perfect timing!"

Trinidad spent a moment flirting. Porsche looked out the window, watching the traffic pass on the highway below. A thin cold March rain was falling. She found herself wondering if it was raining at the farm, and was their roof leaking?

"No," said Trinidad suddenly. "I never feel homesick."

What was that?

The waitress had vanished. Leaning over an ostrich omelet, Trinidad's face looked buoyant and very boyish, save around the edges. "Homesick for Jarrtee? Never. On its worst day, the earth is a much better place."

"I know."

"Particularly now," he commented obliquely.

"What are you talking about?"

A look of mischievous joy ended with a wink. "Remember the Order of Fire? That bizarre faith that we belonged to for a day?"

"I remember."

Trinidad paused, sighed. "The Order's grown considerably since we left. In our City, and in the surrounding city-states, too."

"What of it?"

"The Order is fighting for political power. And I mean fighting. There's a genuine civil insurrection tearing through Jarrtee."

She shook her head. "I had no idea."

"And there's no reason you should even care," he assured her.

A mixture of vivid, conflicting feelings sprang on her. There was concern and grief, but mostly there was a secret glee. Yet she put on a proper face, saying, "I'm sorry to hear it."

Trinidad knew better. With a razored laugh, he told her, "Don't pretend. You're not that sorry."

She sighed, then asked, "How bad have things gotten?"

"It's bad enough that the Few have virtually abandoned the planet."

"Since when?"

"Over the last few years." He shrugged, saying, "I guess we were just a little ahead of our time, cousin."

The ironies rose up before her.

"My humble-free opinion?" he said. "I blame the jarrtees. They're a bunch of incestuous, doomed shits, if you want the truth."

He was insulting an entire species—the ultimate impropriety— yet Porsche couldn't help but nod and smile.

Trinidad snatched the bill. "My treat."

She stuffed the notebook into her bag, telling him, "I don't want us being forced off this world. Let's work to keep it stable. Agreed?"

"If this project of ours works out," he promised, "you'll be an old human woman playing basketball against your grandchildren. And probably beating them, too."

She didn't laugh as expected.

Instead, Porsche closed her eyes and took a deep, cleansing breath. "We leave a lot of worlds behind, don't we?"

"Of course." Her cousin laughed for both of them, stabbing at the egg and shaking his head in a dismissive fashion. "They're almost infinite, all in easy reach. If we're facing an insur-

mountable problem on one, plenty of others are ready for us."
It was the genetic mandate of the Few, and a cultural linchpin.

Porsche couldn't help but believe the logic in her blood,
even as a secret, traitorous voice whispered a very different
answer.

Hawthorne Klay appeared on the screen, conjured from the
blackness.

His professional reserve—the hallmark of his career—was
swamped by his obvious pain. After weeks of debate, including
several out-and-out arguments, they had decided to use the men-
tal patient at the end of the broadcast, delivering a final emotional blow before Hawthorne's concluding remarks.

Speaking to his audience of four, the apparition gave a quick
review. He repeated tales of corruption and cruelty, of fortunes
spent and goals unachieved—snatches of the more dramatic
video flanking him. Then in a very un-Hawthorne moment, his
voice broke, and he visibly gathered himself before saying:

"From this chair, I have reported the assassination of a president, the progress of many wars, and a litany of crimes of every
complexion, every scale. But what we have seen here tonight
staggers me. To think that a democracy like ours can knowingly
commit and condone these crimes . . . well, this is not my government, and this is not my nation.

"The people responsible should be tried in open court, then
punished in full.

"At the very least, the Cosmic Event Agency should be stripped
to the bone and reborn. And this wondrous technology—this ca-
pacity to move from world to world—should be given to all of
humankind.

"It should be given without charge, accompanied with our
heartfelt apologies and blessings.

"If human beings aren't mature enough to hold this power,
then we should fall together, as a species.

"I am Hawthorne Klay, wishing you . . .

". . . a good evening."

"And good evening to you," said Timothy, cutting the audio, a stream of fictional credits playing across the screen. Then, after a long pause, he asked the others, "Well . . . how do you like it?"

Except for the midmorning sun seeping through the occasional window, the utility building was unlit. People stretched in their chairs. No one seemed willing or able to give an opinion, which was remarkable. They were finished. Except for tweaks and polish, they were done working on the project, and the project was done working on them. Yet for the first time since last September, this strong-willed group could offer nothing but a relentless, introverted silence.

Finally, Nathan took the responsibility, telling everyone, "We should feel proud."

Pride was one of Porsche's emotions.

"Very proud," he trumpeted, rising to his feet and twisting his stiff back. "The truth is definitely going to win out."

Cornell rose, then stretched. In the partial light, he looked very much like his father, adjusting his spine as he steered them toward more pragmatic matters. "When can we broadcast? What's soonest, what's best?"

"We could go now, if we want." Timothy referred to the terminal in his lap. "But the ratings would be lousy. If we wait until eight o'clock tonight, we'd have the largest possible audience. Unless we hold off to Sunday night, then steal away *America Tonight*'s audience of fifty million. . . ."

"I vote for Sunday," said Cornell.

"That's what makes sense," Timothy replied.

"Or we go tonight, then repeat it in a few days," Nathan suggested, his voice almost giddy. "And keep repeating it until they yank us off the air—"

"As it is," Timothy interrupted, "we've got a running time of sixty-eight minutes. Ten minutes more than the original plan, thanks to Porsche's last-minute material." He paused, then told them, "I can show it once. I'm certain. And then they'll probably dynamite their emergency system, if that's what it takes to stop us."

"You're selling yourself short," Nathan warned.

Timothy gave a little laugh. "That's something I never hear."

Porsche stood, finally.

Eyes found her, then she said, "I think we should broadcast tonight." Then with a brisk smile, she added, "Like my coaches always told me, sometimes the easy two points are better than the spectacular three."

Cornell nodded thoughtfully, allowing, "Maybe it would be best."

"I'll hope for a reprise in a few days," Nathan said.

Suddenly, almost without warning, they realized that it had been decided.

"Tonight," four voices declared, in a chorus.

Then half-jokingly, half-seriously, Porsche injected a dose of pragmatism. "I guess we should think about packing now."

Timothy laughed hardest, then with an edgy voice asked, "Why bother?"

Everyone grew quiet.

He stepped close to Porsche, close enough that she could smell coffee on his breath. "Where you're going," he told her, "you can't exactly take your suitcase with you."

With her most reasonable voice, she said, "We're going to Nathan's house after the broadcast. That's the plan. And after a few days of hard sleep, we'll take a little drive down to Texas. Just as we've discussed for months, and of course you're welcome to join us. If that's what you want to do. . . ."

The man seemed puzzled, even surprised.

"I've always assumed that we'd just vanish. You know where."

No one spoke.

"You said you'd explain everything, too." He sounded like a little boy who feared being cheated. "Wouldn't this be a good time?"

"Tonight," she promised. "Right after the broadcast."

Then Nathan joined them, adding. "We'll show you something in the sky. Something I've had the pleasure of seeing for myself."

"No," Timothy replied. "I want more."

It was Cornell who responded, a bristling voice asking, "What do you mean?"

"I didn't come to this goddamn wasteland and work my ass off, risking everything, just for a 'thank you' and get sent home again." He spoke with a clear, practiced voice, never blinking, telling the others, "I want to step through. You know where. Just once, just so I can experience it."

"Are you sure?" asked Porsche.

"Remember the madman," Cornell cautioned. "There's that risk—"

"To my soul?" Then Timothy laughed, shaking his head as he said, "You don't realize it, do you? What people would give up just for one minute. . . .

"For a moment, just to be somewhere else!"

Porsche was stuffing socks into the last suitcase. Sunshine and a pleasant warm breeze poured through the bedroom window. Cornell was in his father's room, helping him sort and pack. Timothy was out in the utility building, adding final touches to the documentary. She was alone when she heard, "People are approaching." The voice was sudden and intimate, whispering deep in her right ear. "We don't recognize the vehicle, or the passengers."

Before Porsche spoke, she took a deep breath.

"How many onboard?"

"Three," the eavesdroppers reported. "Males. Two in the front seat. One behind."

"Armed?"

"They carry knives."

"What kind of knives?"

"Small. For filleting fish."

"They're fishermen?"

"Judging by their clothes and tackle, yes."

But Porsche wasn't reassured. She dropped the last ball of socks on the bedspread, then went next door. "Company coming, maybe."

Father and son looked at her with a sturdy indifference, as if trying to hold on to the domestic peace. Then Cornell gave a nod, turned, and said, "Why don't you keep packing, Dad? I'll be right back."

Nathan didn't say a word, his face turning to stone.

"The vehicle is slowing," said the eavesdroppers. "And now it is turning toward the house."

"Shit," she muttered, the stairs creaking underfoot.

"What is it?" asked Cornell.

"Nothing, maybe." It was unthinkable that the enemy would send three unarmed men. Besides, the Few-made defenses were awake, at the ready. Yet a nervous shiver passed beneath Porsche's skin as she stepped out onto the sloping porch. The vehicle was a big Ford, a sportsman's toy, its long and drab and very dusty body making a fishhook turn, then braking on the open ground just past her Humvee.

With a word, she could knock the passengers unconscious.

A few more words would bath them in a cleansing stream, making them forget the last ten minutes of their lives.

But she didn't use her weapons. Quietly, quietly, she said, "Walk with me," and stepped off the porch, Cornell hovering on her left.

The driver's window dropped.

A face emerged, a quick and too-friendly voice saying, "Hello, ma'am."

He was in his mid-twenties and called her *ma'am*. Reason enough to knock him senseless.

"I guess I'm lost," he continued, nothing about his face or his posture backing up those words. He seemed perfectly aware of his location, saying, "My friends and I are looking for a pond. Full of trophy bass, we've heard."

As promised, they were dressed like fishermen, their pocket-rich vests and north woods shirts looking too new, too bright, with three long fishing poles stuck in the back end, sure to be seen.

"The only ponds here are mud holes," said Cornell, his voice a little stiff, a little forced. "Bullhead and catfish, if that."

"Really," the driver replied, without interest.

The back window dropped, and another young man fired off his best smile. "Beautiful day," he offered.

"Too warm," the driver complained. "For May, that is."

Beside the driver sat someone older, his window already down, his body large and solid in appearance and unnaturally still. Porsche couldn't see his face. The back of his head was covered with a dark stubble. His neck was thicker than most thighs. With his right hand under his unseen chin, he was staring at the utility building, nothing subtle about his intentions. Obviously, the fishhook turn was for his benefit; he wanted a clear look at the target.

If they tried anything—if they brandished even one filleting knife—the defense systems would act in a microsecond, dropping electronic anvils on their heads.

For an instant, Porsche hoped the men would make that mistake.

But they were professionals. The driver just kept smiling, saying, "I guess we should do a better job reading our maps." But he didn't show her any map or ask for directions. "Sorry, ma'am. We'll get out of your way now."

The windows were rising, humming brightly.

Porsche moved, sprinting in front of the vehicle.

The older man had a square, simple face, as if he had decided at conception not to accept embellishments of any kind. He had the ruddy complexion of a European who had lived for years in the tropics. Tiny eyes were sunk into heavy bone. A calm and rugged and very wide mouth didn't bother to pretend any smile. He sneered at Porsche, and in the tiny eyes, for an instant, there was a glint of cold amusement.

She stared back at him, refusing to blink.

Then he was laughing, something suddenly funny, and he kept laughing until his window sank into its jamb.

She had recognized his face, easily.

It was the same face that Timothy had found near a murder scene, the same face that the farmer had known at a glance. These were brazen pricks, implying an ignorance. They didn't appreciate what they were up against. Again, she considered knocking them unconscious. But that would warn the agency, and there wouldn't be time to broadcast. Nothing mattered except making the broadcast, she was thinking. She was thinking clearly and quickly, only a sliver of herself watching the Ford accelerate, watching it move back toward the county road.

Cornell appeared beside her, or maybe he had always been there.

"Coincidence," he said, "or conspiracy?"

Either way, they had exactly one choice left to them.

11

A CLOUD OF SOFT CHOKING DUST SWALLOWED THE FISHERMEN.

Porsche never saw them vanish. She had already turned, sprinting for the utility building, grateful to see Timothy standing in the tiny east door. His long face wore a lost, almost baffled expression, eyes and the quizzical tilt of his head asking every imaginable question. Who were those men? What had happened? And of all people, why was Porsche scared?

"How soon?" she shouted.

"Soon?"

"To broadcast!" She slammed into the garage door, killing her momentum. "From right now, how soon?"

Timothy opened his mouth, then closed it. Then he glanced at Cornell, as if expecting some kind of translation.

Seconds mattered.

Porsche drove her flattened hand into his sternum, shoving him backward into the cool interior. "We're going now. Now!"

"Those men?" Timothy sputtered.

"One guess," she warned.

His eyes grew larger, but he couldn't quite comprehend. "On a weekday afternoon . . . we won't get the ratings . . ."

Cornell spoke, saying the man's name with a warning tone.

Timothy turned, blinked. "But we're safe here!" Then he

looked at Porsche with a wounded expression. "You can fend them off. You have your . . . your tricks . . ."

"What's your start-up time?" Cornell pressed. "From this second. Three minutes? Four?"

"Four, and forty seconds. About."

Porsche stepped away from both of them. "Status?" she asked the eavesdroppers.

"Our visitors," said the soft voice, "are continuing north at a responsible speed."

"What?" asked Cornell.

"We're all right," she reported. "For now, at least."

"Why wouldn't we be?" Timothy kept asking. He was moving toward the main terminal, almost strolling, doggedly determined not to worry. "They could launch scramjet missiles, and you'd just wish them away. You said it. You promised!"

Bullies with guns she could delay. A full-scale military assault was an entirely different monster.

Cornell joined Timothy. Glancing over her shoulder, Porsche saw him begin dissolving into the darkness. He said, "Would you get Dad?"

"Sure."

Nathan was standing on the front porch. "I was watching," he reported with a steady voice. "It was *them*, wasn't it?"

She said, "Absolutely."

The old man took the news with poise. A crisis was at the door, but a lifetime of paranoia left him able to accept the news.

"What should I do?" he inquired.

She hesitated, then decided. "The toolbox. Out by the basketball court—"

"I'll get it out," he promised.

"But keep the box closed. For now. Just wait for us."

"I'll be there," he promised, stepping down the sagging stairs.

Then she turned and jogged for a moment, pausing where the sun was brightest, where the newly leafed trees were farthest apart. A trio of lasers, each wearing a different kind of camouflage, came awake with a jarrtee word. Already focused on a specific part of the sky, they carried her next scrambled words on beams of coherent light.

"Trinidad," she whispered.

Then, "What's happening, cousin? What do you see?"

She waited for an instant, concentrating on the silence within her right ear. No response, no response . . . and finally, the expected voice arrived . . . probably no more than ten seconds after she said, "Trinidad."

"Cousin," she heard. "I'm looking, but nothing seems unusual."

"Nothing?"

"Not visually. Not on any government bands, agency-wise or otherwise." There was a pause, a distinct inhalation. Then he screamed, the single word—one of the few genuine universal words—twisted into a piercing, scalding roar:

"*SSSHHHHHEEEEEEEETTT!*"

Silence.

And once again, because it seemed like the absolute best thing to do at that instant, Porsche ran.

An industrial robot was on the television's main screen, standing waist-deep in fire and molten metal, a shiny can of deodorant clutched in one ceramic hand. "If it's strong enough for me," promised a harsh machine voice, "then it has all the power *you* will ever need."

"We're almost ready," said Cornell. A sideways glance, then, "Where's Dad?"

She told him.

The building had a back door. Cornell glanced at it, saying nothing.

Porsche asked her eavesdroppers for an update.

"No one is there," she heard. And she repeated it aloud.

"Ninety seconds till," Timothy announced. "Everything looks good. Perfect, even."

A slippery sensation passed through Porsche. Time seemed

too slow, and a focused, enraging impatience took hold of her. She noticed Cornell looking over Timothy's shoulder, rocking side to side. Timothy was hunkered over the terminal's keyboard, no buttons left to push, hands held lightly against his aching belly. Then something moved, something barely in her eye, and she half-turned, looking out the narrow east door, seeing nothing but the immobile brown tree trunks and the green branches nodding in the May breeze.

Again, Porsche asked if they had company.

"No," she heard. A whiff of irritation in the voice?

Impossible.

"Forty seconds," Timothy called out.

Three steps took her to the doorway, and she quietly asked herself, "What is it?"

Looking southeast, past the old windbreak, she watched the dirty brown field, and beyond, the perfectly empty, shockingly white graveled road.

"Thirty seconds!"

Within the range of her eavesdroppers, there was nothing. They were telling her exactly what she wanted to hear, and they were wrong. She felt it. It was exactly like having your lover claim his boundless devotion, but between the sweet words was that sense of doubt that he could never hear for himself.

"Fifteen seconds," two voices said, in ragged unison.

Porsche saw the odd motion again. Sudden, subtle. She found herself staring at the windbreak, at the dappled shadows. "Where are you?" More frustrated than fearful, she began to squint, urging the visitor to show itself. "Come on now . . . come on . . ."

"Five," said Timothy.

Cornell said, "Four."

Then both men said, "Three!"

And she heard a different voice. Quick and soft, and close, it felt as if a mouth was being pressed against her ear. "Porsche," it said with a delicate fondness.

Trinidad?

"Two!" the men were shouting, in the distance.

Milky white noise sputtered in her ear, then dissolved, the voice of her cousin shouting, "Trouble!"

"One!" Cornell cried out.

"Save yourself," Trinidad begged. Then she heard, "Porsche," again, something tacked on to the back of her name but some kind of brilliant shroud engulfing it, erasing it.

"Here we go," said Timothy, with excitement.

"Trinidad?" she called out. "What's happening?"

Cornell noticed Porsche standing in the open doorway, talking to herself, and he took a half-step, asking, "What is it?"

In a huge, tremulous voice, Timothy called out, "No!"

The others turned, looked.

"I don't understand!" he sputtered. "We're not . . ."

"What is it?" Cornell was repeating.

"This is . . . fuck . . .!"

Cornell's face was illuminated by the television screen. There was no sign of Hawthorne Klay; an ordinary afternoon news program was in midstride. Cornell was staring at the images, arms at his side, hands making fists, a baffled and very tired face framing a mouth that hung open, ready to speak as soon as words occurred to him.

Outside, wild birds were cackling. They had been cackling for several minutes, Porsche realized. Too late.

Again, she turned to look out into the bright day.

"This should work," said a furious voice. Timothy's voice. "I did everything right. Every fucking thing—!"

In the windbreak, in a synchronized motion, faceless men stepped from behind old walnut trees. Their features were hidden behind thick stockings that were green one moment, shadow-black the next. Gloved hands held stubby, big-barreled weapons. There were three faceless men, and following them were three more men. Armed. In motion. Making straight for the open door.

Porsche turned, screaming out, "Run!"

Then in her next breath, she used a single word, a human-ized jarrtee word, telling the Few-made defenses to drop the in-vaders, now.

Nothing changed.

The men continued to approach the metal building, showing not so much as a shred of urgency.

Again, she said the word.

Nothing.

She started to turn again, to look at Cornell and warn him again. But the television and every machine suddenly went dead, plunging the interior into darkness.

"What is it, what is it?" Timothy was chanting.

Then with a clear and determined voice, Cornell shouted, "We've got to go. Go!"

There was a soft thud followed by the shrill screech of metal being split open, and a fist-sized projectile burst through the garage door, dropping between Porsche and the others, a thick fountain of pink smoke dividing them.

"Get out the back!" she screamed.

There were more thuds, the blunt rounds driven into the steel. Ragged holes were punched into the long south wall, columns of smoky light pouring into the darkness. She glimpsed someone running. Maybe. Then she dropped to her knees, one hand grabbing the doorjamb, and peered outside in time to watch the faceless men firing another salvo, the jamb lurching as the entire building absorbed the blow.

If the enemy wanted her dead, she would be dead.

Porsche stood and stepped into plain view, hands raised up over her head.

The men lowered their guns, then with the casual scorn of school yard bullies, they began to trot toward her.

She waited for a half-moment, then ran.

Someone shouted: "Wasps! Use 'em!"

There was a *thud-ud-ud,* and a blunt blue-black machine streaked past her ear, slamming into the building, a paralyzing dose of amps pumped into the sheet metal, and lost.

She rounded the corner, sprinting beside the building's north side.

In the distance, over the warm, almost summery breeze, came the urgent *whump-whump* of helicopter rotors.

A point guard's instincts took hold.

A glance over her shoulder, and she saw a bulky figure bursting into view, aiming at her with a smooth professional calm.

Thud.

She responded, throwing her head down between her forearms and her weight pitching forward, the mechanical wasp passing close enough to leave the hair on her arms standing erect.

Wrestling gravity, she managed to straighten herself, then milked more speed out of her legs, looking out at the empty field as another man came around the corner, stepping directly into her path.

Porsche was close enough to make out a nose and long chin beneath the camouflage.

He was aiming his weapon. Slowly, then quickly.

Someone said, "Stop."

She sidestepped left, then right, and suddenly he was off balance, fighting his ample muscle and bone. Then she went left again and lifted her right elbow and made sure that she struck his chin, bone to bone, his head thrown back as she drove into his body, her right knee riding up between his legs, testicles absorbing the brunt of her momentum.

The man went limp.

Went down.

She rounded the corner and found the back door hanging open, a narcotic strawberry smoke pouring from inside. Barely breaking stride, she kept moving, crossing the yard and crashing into the windbreak, through junipers and bursting into the open again. Someone was running in her shadow. She heard him, felt him. Risking a half-glance, she saw a figure without any gun, arms pumping and his long legs closing the gap. She looked ahead, straight on. A fiery sprinter's pain blossomed in her lungs, spreading across her chest and pouring into her legs, congealing, making the legs heavy as stone, and as stiff, and hopelessly tired.

Against the sky, she saw the silhouette of the backboard and pole.

Someone was directly ahead of her. A male someone standing motionless on the stubble, and because she wanted it badly, she decided that it had to be Cornell.

Her pursuer grunted:

"Under . . . arrest . . . treason . . ."

Porsche couldn't outlast him. So she put on a surge, winning another step or two, then half-fell, half-squatted, trying to bounce off the lumpy earth.

Like in a thousand basketball drills, she reversed direction.

Charging the faceless man, she faked left before diving right.

But the man was too alert, or too tired to react. He bulled his way straight for her, dipping his head at the last instant, driving a bony broad shoulder into her body; suddenly Porsche was on her back with no memory of falling, lying on a bed of rotting stalks and fragrant dirt, the enemy straddling her, trying to grab her by the wrists.

An incandescent rage took her.

She pulled her right hand free and took a blind swipe, slicing off the mask, a familiar face framed by the hard blue sky.

The younger fisherman, the one who had sat in the back seat, wore a composed expression and a bloody cut above his eyes. The eyes were fastened to her eyes and a half-smile was building. Then his mouth opened, something exceedingly important to be said.

He never got the chance.

A metallic rectangle appeared in the sky. Porsche recognized its shape and the blue-gray color, though she couldn't remember from where. The rectangle came closer, grew larger. Then the man's head jerked sideways, taking the impact, and there was a hollow crash followed by tools banging, the old toolbox slipping off his skull, then dropping to the ground.

The fisherman shuddered, collapsed.

A voice came from a distant place, and Nathan's face appeared, grim and ashen.

"Where is he?"

Porsche tried to stand. Where was who?

The old man turned, staring back at the farmhouse and the utility building and the rising columns of strawberry smoke, and with trembling hands cupped around his mouth, he shouted, "Cornell? Cornell?"

A pair of exhausted wasps dove into the ground at his feet.

The fisherman was gripping the back of his head, his moans growing stronger.

Nathan stepped over the wasps, calling for his son again.

Porsche had mistaken him for Cornell. Cornell hadn't escaped, nor had Timothy, obviously, and she'd left them behind—

"Cornell?" the man cried out.

A black helicopter, seemingly carved from anthracite, rose up over the windbreak trees, then hovered.

Porsche grabbed Nathan by the arm. "We can't help him! Not now!"

He looked at her for an instant, his mouth working, no sound coming from it.

She let go and grabbed the toolbox, then she was running again, begging Nathan to follow her.

A hammer and screwdriver and a block of scrap pine were already set at the disk's center—a trick Nathan already knew, thank goodness. As they stepped onto the old glass, the sky filled with the starry glow of thousands of earth-rooted intrusions. Neither noticed. Armed men were racing across the open field. The helicopter revved its engine, dropped its nose, and came hard. Porsche didn't have any cushion. She opened the toolbox and grabbed the yellow handle of a second screwdriver, then sliced her finger on a bent nail. Then she shut the box and latched it, every motion precise and swift. Then she positioned it and the other five objects, building a ring around herself. When the ring was right, she felt it. There was an electric surge, and the six keys were suddenly locked in place. "Come here!" she shouted to Nathan, and she looked up once more, masked figures kneeling on the sunflower stubble, taking aim.

Without sound or genuine motion, the intrusion opened.

A squadron of wasps were launched, too late.

Porsche grabbed a thin hand, then pulled. Hard.

The disk around them vanished, engulfed by a rubbery black whirlpool that swirled beneath them.

She pushed Nathan, hard, forcing him downwards.

Then she returned, running carefully along the whirlpool's lip, grabbing each of the keys in turn and flinging them into that realm where nothing but sentience could endure.

Above her, with an explosive roar, the intrusion slammed shut.

And again, for a second time, Porsche had lost her home.

THE OLD WORLD

1

"... WORLD, WORLD ... A NEW WORLD ..."

The voice was soft and astonished; Nathan's new mouth struggling with a cackling language. He tried to say, "Porsche," and twisted it into gibberish. Then after a desperate deep breath, he exclaimed, "We need to climb! Climb!"

Climb was a weak translation.

Porsche was barely half the size of Nathan, her monkeyish body dressed in short golden fur, four long supple limbs ending in strong hands, and a prehensile tail that stood erect, displaying caution. She was standing on every hand, a phantom pain reminding her of her punctured human finger. Under her palms were the remnants of another disk, its glass shattered into shards and sand. The ground beyond was black as oil and littered with masses of rotting wood. In the distance, standing in a thin warm mist, were what passed here for trees.

"Climb," Nathan repeated, in despair.

They were surrounded by chocolate-colored tree trunks that rose high, erupting into a canopy of fat branches and overlapping leaves, nothing but a thin amber light falling on tiny them.

They lived in the canopy.

Porsche knew it, and felt it. Newly minted instincts screamed, telling both of them to climb. To ascend. Escape death's realm! Embrace the sky, and safety!

Again, Nathan attempted to say her name.

"Poo-chay."

His new face would have a passing resemblance to his human face—the intrusions did their best with each species—but whatever he was lay hidden under a male's hairy plume and the long white beard.

"Relax," Porsche advised. "We're safe here."

The coffee-colored eyes seemed to rattle around in their sockets. "Are you certain, Poo-chay?"

"What you're feeling is a reflex," she assured both of them.

Nathan gave a human nod, then whispered, "My son?"

"Alive," she promised. "They wanted to capture, not murder."

He picked up one of his front hands, holding it open before his face.

"We'll free him, and Timothy, too." She tried to sound utterly certain, adding, "and we'll make the agency pay . . ."

"Yes," he muttered. Curling his tail around his right leg and holding tight, he wondered aloud, "What could have gone so wrong?"

"I wish I knew, Nathan."

"We couldn't stop them, could we?"

She couldn't, no.

With his new old-man hands, he touched her face.

Porsche curled her tail around his tail, lending comfort. "If we're going to help anyone," she told him, "we need to find help here."

Nathan tugged on his beard, then his glorious plume, saying, "My first trip to another world, and I can't enjoy it." The hands dropped, and he added, "Anger. And fear. They feel the same here as there, don't they?"

The trees weren't trees, though they were alive.

Like coral reefs, they were built from smaller organisms knitted together into one magnificent community. Fungi reached

deep underground, monopolizing the flow of water and miner-
als to the world above. Long, long worms encased in polycar-
bonate shells formed the trunks. Only the canopy was vegetable,
feeding on brilliant sunshine and sending the excess calories
below as sugary syrups and proteins—a sophisticated, enduring
economy born from the soulless organisms.

They hurried to the nearest tree. Nathan grabbed the knobby
pseudobark, then hesitated, telling her sadly, "I'm not strong
enough to climb this."

But he intended to try, his tone implied.

"Human-old is different from being old here," Porsche assured. "Aboreal species anywhere are rugged. These bodies of
ours have redundancies. Extra muscle, heart, and bone."

He nodded, his tail trying for an optimistic tilt.

Then she was climbing, showing him several flavors of confidence. "When this mess is finished, we'll come again. For a real
visit."

"Yes?"

"This is a lovely world," she promised.

He said nothing.

Porsche's neck was long and limber. She easily looked down
the length of her golden back, showing Nathan her optimism.
"We'll take a vacation. With Cornell."

"Could we?"

"I can arrange it, yes."

"What about Timothy?" *Tee-moo-shay?*

"We'll bring him, too." She winked, human-style. "He's no natural, not like you Novak men. But he's got some talent, and this
isn't a strange world, either. Which is a big reason why it was
picked."

Nathan hesitated, then confessed, "I wasn't asking to include
Timothy."

She said nothing.

"Someone must have betrayed us." A pause. "Am I right?"

"Until I know Timothy did, he didn't. In my mind."

Nathan remained silent for a long while, concentrating on

the climb, working hard enough to pant. The air grew warmer and more humid, and they could hear the canopy—a chorus of buzzes and chirps punctuated with distant roars. A crust of lichen clung to the pseudobark. Epiphytes grew in the hollows, black-gold leaves straining out the last little meals of light. Then the trunk suddenly sprouted trees, some horizontal and most angling upwards, each tree adorned with its own bark and wood and ginger-colored leaves, an airborne jungle caressing their instincts, welcoming them, smelling like some long-forgotten home.

Porsche urged Nathan to rest.

Shivering despite the tropical heat, he was exhausted. But he ignored the offer, glancing down into the distance, then asking, "Which way?"

She hesitated, for an instant.

"Have you been here before? Are we lost, maybe?"

"No, and no." Nestled in the top of the trunk was a giant epiphyte, its bowl-like tissues filled to the brim with rainwater. Perched on the edge of the unexpected pond, she explained. "An associate came here for me. Months ago. Among other things, he left behind a little care package for us."

"Underwater?" Nathan inquired.

"Not anymore." A simple wooden ball broke the surface. Mechanisms inside it had watched them come through the intrusion, and when they were close enough, the ball had come out of hiding.

The ball had a threaded lid.

Inside were a map and various instructions, everything written in Trinidad's best script, in English. Plus there were four fabric pouches, each one filled with the local currency—ornately carved sticks of rare wood, their value determined by their feel and flavors.

The map aligned itself, pointing them in the best direction.

Porsche returned two of the pouches, resealed the ball, then forced it underwater, halfway burying it into pond's living floor.

They moved, crossing from limb to limb, and gradually, very

gradually, the canopy showed the symptoms of civilization. The overhead branches had been pruned, then reinforced with networks of fine cable. Elaborate nests were built in the high places, fashioned from gaudily-colored fabric. And with the nests came people—giant males, just a few of them, and multitudes of tiny females and their children, their bright chattering voices obscuring every other sound.

No one wore clothes, which was a blessing.

All seemed to accept the strangers moving among them, which was perfect.

Porsche spotted an open platform above, turned and told Nathan, "You're my father. We have come to visit distant relatives. Don't speak until someone talks to you, please. And try not to touch their tails with yours."

He nodded, then quietly, with a genuine fear, admitted, "I hope I don't do anything too wrong."

She looked at his dancing eyes, at the worried twisting of his tail, thinking that he was such a fine, sweet man.

"You'll do fine," she promised.

Then she laughed sadly, human-style. "I just pray that I'm a good enough daughter."

The public car was enormous and insubstantial, built of warm air and transparent foam laid over an aluminum skeleton, swinging on electrified cables strung above the canopy.

In shape and in motion, the car resembled an overgrown gibbon.

They paid with a stick, then entered the gibbon's chest. Nathan was quiet and compliant, nothing escaping his worried gaze. The floor was uneven, looking like so many branches laid side by side; the ceiling was adorned with hand- and tail-holds. With a beep and hiss, the doors closed themselves. Then the car was moving, leaping to an adjacent cable that rose even higher. The long swinging motions would have sickened humans, but Porsche, tucked inside her new physiology, found the sensation pleasant, even soothing. Long mechanical arms reached farther and farther, a blue bolt of lightning coming when a hooked hand found its grip. Gradually, the overhead canopy thinned, then vanished, and they could see the sky, a pure elemental blue to the east, and in the west a stack of fat white rain clouds, the small brilliant sun diving into a building storm.

"A brighter sun than ours," Porsche whispered, hoping to pull him out of his worries. "Isn't this place lovely, Nathan?"

The sun disappeared into the clouds; the world's everted face grew brighter. Turquoise seas balanced the golden lands. A tiny ice cap clung to the northern continent. Quietly, as if embarrassed, Nathan admitted, "The sky is special to me. Is that right?"

"These people worship their sky," she told him. "It means safety and comfort, and everything else good."

Nathan closed his eyes for a moment, then looked down. The jungle was every shade of yellow, nests linked into complexes and built along the sturdiest limbs. A human-born fear of heights suddenly latched hold, and he stiffened, asking with a secretive voice, "What do we call ourselves?"

She pulled her tail into a circle, smiling. "Maybe you already know, Nathan. Why don't you guess?"

With surprise and a genuine awe, he muttered, "Sky-lords."

"Very good, Father."

Nathan's hands played in his white beard, and with a cautious delight, he whispered, "What else do I know, daughter?"

"It depends on your talent."

"I have a little, I think." He spoke earnestly, like a man applying for a new job.

"I know you do," she said. "Concentrate."

With that encouragement, Nathan began to ignore their altitude, his eyes half-closing, his attentions focused momentarily on the strange, unexpected beauties of his mind.

Their destination was an elaborate nest set above a broad, strong river. They arrived with the afternoon rains, standing on the sheltered porch while Porsche, following Trinidad's elaborate instructions, struck chimes with a quartz hammer.

The curtainlike door was pulled aside.

Half a dozen young girls stood together, tails twisting into a Gordian knot, everyone gawking at the strangers.

"Is your great blessed father at home?" asked Porsche.

The girls were astonished that the old man hadn't spoken first. "Yes, he is home," one girl replied, no one making an effort to find him.

"I am one of your relatives," Porsche reported. "A very distant relative, and I'm very much in trouble."

The oldest girl mangled the name, "Trinidad." Then she asked hopefully, "Is he your blessed father's nephew?"

"He is."

The response was swift. With whoops and whistles, the mob left them, racing into the house, shouting, "They are here! They have come!"

Nathan peered inside. The floor lay at every pitch except horizontal, and there were doors in the ceiling leading to small rooms, little brown-eyed faces gazing down at them. Softly, very softly, he confessed, "I've always tried to imagine an alien's home."

"Have you?"

"This," he said, "I never pictured."

Suddenly an enormous male sky-lord appeared, stepping onto the porch and drawing the curtain closed behind him. His very long tail swished back and forth, betraying a worrisome giddiness. Powerful muscles rippled as he leaned close, sniffing the air, staring hard at Porsche, but never quite looking into her eyes. "I had given up on this girl," he said. "Her father's nephew promised that she would come before now."

"Events took longer than anticipated," she replied. Then she made curt introductions, their host touching Nathan's tail with his tail, the perfunctory gesture triggering another question.

"Was I told to expect two more visitors to come with the girl?"

Porsche admitted, "Events went sour."

The sky-lord's expression was curious, even suspicious. "This girl is a disappointment to me," he said over the drumming of the rain. "Her father's nephew promised that she was a confident girl. Afraid of nothing, he told me."

She didn't care what he saw in her now. "We came here for help," said Porsche, exasperation showing. "Did we make a wrong turn?"

"I intend to help," their host replied.

Then Nathan blurted out, "My son is in terrible danger." His face gave a human grimace, and his tail went limp, in desperation.

"Good sons are rare," said the sky-lord, apparently impressed.

Porsche remained silent, her thoughts private.

"On your world, is it the same?"

Nathan said, "Of course."

The sky-lord could look another male in the eye. "As I promised Trinidad, I have prepared a mock-bird. You should be home again before nightfall."

"Thank you," Nathan gushed. "Oh, thank you!"

"An honorable father," the sky-lord declared. "I will loan you one of my wives, and she will take you to the mock-bird. Will that suffice?"

"I think so," Nathan told him. "Will it, Porsche?"

"Yes. Thank you."

Then the big male addressed her once again, concluding with the words, "It's good to finally meet the girl. When she visits again, hopefully, she will have found her old confidence. Yes?"

The storm was pleasantly enormous, fat bolts of lightning coursing across the gray-black sky, bringing with it a kind of anonymity, the world narrowed to two or three arm-lengths in any direction, every sane person indoors and oblivious to the fools scurrying past, embroiled in some unimaginable errand.

Their guide—the borrowed wife—was tiny. Even Porsche dwarfed her. She wore an enormous rain hat that hid her face, and she barely spoke or looked at them. Racing along rope roads and rain-greased branches, she led them downward through the canopy, down to where Porsche could almost feel the ground underfoot.

Suddenly, the rain was passing.

Porsche saw ships moored on the river, engines sleeping, broad decks forested with masts that held the crews' nests high above the storm-tattered water. The riverbank was covered with great stone warehouses and floating docks, and as the last of the rain fell, there came sunshine, more liquid than any water and pouring over the three of them as they suddenly, unexpectedly turned between two warehouses.

The air in the alley was dripping and stale, almost suffocating.

The tiny woman paused, using coded words to speak with the hidden eavesdroppers. "Safe," she declared, then released half a dozen locks on a tall doorway.

Inside, hunkering in the darkness, was a large birdish shape, wings folded against its body, its nose dipped in apparent submission.

The mock-bird was large enough to carry three male sky-lords, plus an oversized female. Its fuel tanks were full, its systems waking in an instant. The autopilot was more sophisticated than the systems built locally, and it had been preprogrammed to take them to the wrong destination. Months ago, Trinidad gave Porsche the correct intrusion. And only when she had reset the pilot did their guide finally remove her rain hat, reaching inside and handing them the key.

The key was a child's puzzle, a swatch of colored fabric that could be folded into innumerable pictures—the most ordinary object imaginable.

Speaking to the ridged floor, their guide whispered, "My husband's wife wants to wish both of you well."

"And we wish you well," Porsche replied.

In the eyes and tail, for an instant, there was delight. Then with a breathless gravity, the tiny woman asked, "Is he well? Your father's nephew?"

"Very well, yes."

The woman's smile told everything.

Nathan coughed, then said, "Come visit us someday."

The woman's gaze lifted, her expression amused. Or offended. Or baffled, perhaps. "My husband's wife must leave first."

She turned, vanished.

Porsche and Nathan took their seats. With a word, the mock-bird ignited its jets and rose, hovering for a moment, then drifting through the doorway.

Only then, with a faint gray voice, did Nathan admit, "I really dislike flying."

There wasn't time for encouragement or a single platitude.

The jets roared, and the wings were dropped into position and locked. The mock-bird shot out from between the warehouses, and its nose tilted back eagerly, the last of the rain yielding to dry air and a brilliant, reborn sunshine.

Looking very tired, and amazed, Nathan stared down at the shrinking river, admitting to Porsche, and perhaps himself, "All of my interest in aliens and starships, and I've always been terrified of flying."

She took his hands, saying, "These people build wonderful planes."

The face behind the white fur tried to smile.

But it was a temporary comfort, and both knew it. Holding hands, they watched the golden land and the receding clouds as the machine climbed higher, its engines screaming, a genuine passion making it try to pierce the sacred sky.

The typical world possessed tens of billion of intrusions.

But it was a false abundance. Most intrusions led to dead moons and comets, or to living worlds too primitive to house sentient souls. Many of the rest were duplicates. Since the humans and sky-lords were neighbors, and since their worlds were large places equally twisted, they shared dozens of intrusions. But that was another false abundance: Most were difficult to use, located at sea or inside a glacier. The nearest suitable intrusion was to the west, in an isolated location, and even better, it had never been marked with a glass disk—the passageway easily opened with a single key.

A thinner, more ragged jungle rose beneath them, then dissolved into the raw bones of a mountain range. Tilting its wings, their mock-bird slowed and hovered, then settled with a cloud of rock dust, its jets cutting back, then dying.

Except for gray ruins on the nearby peak, the country was wilderness.

"What are those buildings?" Nathan inquired.

"Temples," Porsche recalled. "And observatories, too. Brave priests would come here to worship their sky, the moons, and stars. When they eventually learned to grind lenses, the priests built their telescopes inside their temples."

"Long ago," he guessed. "Judging by appearances."

"It was, yes."

They stepped outside as the sun began to set. The mountain air was thin and cold, their tropical bodies already suffering.

Intrigued, Nathan asked, "What happened when their sky changed?"

"I don't know the full history." She moved toward a pile of stones that looked much like every other pile of stones. Trinidad had stacked them, planning for today. "The simple history," she said, "is that the Change came too soon. The sky-lords had plenty of telescopes, but they lacked the mathematics to interpret what had happened. In the confusion, they blamed their own churches. There was a worldwide war. Twenty generations of fighting. And that was followed by an enormous Dark Age." Shivering, she picked up pieces of mudstone until she found Trinidad's mark—his name written in English. "According to my cousin, those temples have been empty for more than five thousand years."

"The follies of religion," was Nathan's verdict.

"Except the churches reformed and brought stability," she replied. "Today, they're the source of order and prosperity. And it was their priests who deciphered why the sky had changed.

And given time, the priests will learn about the intrusions, too."

Nathan gazed at the ruins for a long while.

Porsche moved away from the rock pile, counting her steps, then set the key into position and carefully stepped back again.

In the east, night was lapping against the mountain slopes. The dark countryside beyond was sprinkled with city lights, and above the jungle, the rich velvet black of empty water clung to the world's skin.

Porsche joined Nathan, wrapping her tail around his.

"What's on your mind?" she whispered.

"It has been quite a day," he began. A human astonishment made his eyes brighten, and he took a thin long breath, then said, "And do you know what really startles me?"

"What startles you?"

"Human beings, it seems, have done pretty well dealing with the Change. Better than these people, surely."

She waited a moment, then told the dear man, "Let's go."

Nathan nodded, turned, and took a last little walk on his newborn hands.

PORSCHE WAS STANDING IN A DAMP DARK BASEMENT, THE PERSISTENT flavor of concrete in her mouth and nostrils, her bare human feet recoiling when they touched the chill floor.

"Where are we?" asked Nathan.

Then he answered his own question.

"Earth, again," he muttered, gawking at his own furless, baby-soft body.

Weak fluorescent lights were buried in the ceiling. Four sets of clothes waited for them, each bearing a name tag, the PORSCHE tag flipping like a kite as a nearby vent began to blow.

Porsche pulled on panties, her remade finger aching where it had been pierced by the bent nail.

Nathan was watching. His eyes tracked down and up again, meeting her eyes, and he looked at the ceiling, squeaking quietly, "Sorry."

"No harm done." She half-smiled, pulling on heavy trousers, then a sports bra, two shirts, and heavy wool socks. Her footwear was top-of-the-line hiking boots. In her pockets were a Canadian passport, a wallet, and three flavors of dollars. She had a new, temporary identity. "Priscilla?" she called out. "Is this a joke?"

No answer; her voice rattled against the concrete, then vanished.

Nathan was dressing hastily, staring resolutely at the floor.

Again, Porsche reassured him that she had taken no offense.

He took a deep breath, gathering himself. "Perhaps my son mentioned," he began. "His mother was a very beautiful woman."

"Yes."

"Beautiful," he repeated, baffled by his good fortune. Then he risked eye contact, telling her, "You're almost as lovely, I think."

"Thank you, Nathan."

There were stairs at the far end of the basement, and a human shadow fell down them, followed by a familiar voice. Loud and insistent, and welcome, Trinidad said, "I'm glad you made it. We know what happened, and your friends are all right." Then, "Come on up. I'm afraid that we've got a lot to talk about."

The basement's cold gloom was replaced by overheated air and the relative brightness of a foggy day. Porsche found herself in a tall, expansive room, standing before a vast window, a wet green forest covering the land outside. "Strange trees," Nathan remarked. "Almost alien-looking." Then, as if to prove him right, a very peculiar animal strolled up to them, its doglike head attached to a long, partially striped body, dim dark eyes calmly examining them for treats.

"What is it?" Nathan sputtered.

"A Tasmanian wolf," Trinidad replied. He was sitting behind them, sitting in the middle of a long sofa, three steaming mugs on a tray set in front of him. "It's good to see you, cousin. Mr. Novak. How are you two?"

Porsche said, "Pissed, and worried."

"Everyone else is, too."

"Is that coffee?"

"Absolutely."

She took one of the warm mugs, then sat beside her cousin.

Nathan was exhausted. With his hands at his sides and his

shoulders slumping, he asked, "What kind of wolf?" Then, with a brittle tone, "And who are you?"

Trinidad introduced himself, using only his first name. "The creature is an extinct marsupial," he explained. "Human scientists managed to pull a viable cell from a museum hip bone, and they've cloned it several thousand times. Tweaking the offspring for genetic diversity, amiability, and gender. Some Australians like to keep them for pets."

"This is Australia," Nathan muttered.

"Tasmania. The home belongs to a friend. It was built just last year specifically to help us hide the intrusion."

"My son?"

"He's alive, and healthy. Try to keep that in mind, sir."

Nathan collapsed into a separate chair.

Finding nothing to eat, the marsupial strolled over to a drab blanket beside a wood-fueled stove, lying down near the heat.

"So where are they?" asked Porsche.

"California. They're being held at the agency's headquarters."

"And we've figured out what went wrong?"

"In part." With his voice slowing, Trinidad explained, "Some clever shit reprogrammed our machines, convincing them that we were the enemy."

Nathan stared at his own empty hands. "I don't understand. You have these amazing machines, yet the agency managed to disable them. How?"

"A perfectly valid question," growled a new voice.

Carrying a platter of sandwiches, Uncle Jack emerged from the adjacent kitchen.

"And who are you?" asked Nathan.

"I don't think you need to know," the man growled, neatly dispelling any illusions of generosity.

Still the prick. Yet Porsche was happy to see his plain face and his head of phony hair, his expertise and resources in easy reach.

Jack set the platter on the coffee table, then sat. "This was a lousy situation to put you in. But we assumed that we could defend the four of you. And not expose ourselves in the process."

"But if things went that wrong," said Nathan, "then the agency has to already know about the Few . . ." He paused, wrestling with the possibilities. "But even if they know about you . . . your existence . . . I don't understand how they can beat you . . ."

Together, father and son nodded.

"How could they fool your incredible machines?" Nathan continued. "Unless it wasn't *them* that did it! Oh, God! Is it . . . one of your own . . . ?"

No one spoke.

Nathan concentrated, shoving his way past clues and guesses and simple black fears. "A traitor. Among the Few." He pursed his lips, asking, "Do you have suspects?"

"Several," Uncle Jack conceded.

"A member of the Few . . . helping the agency." Nathan couldn't accept it. "I would think that would *never* happen."

Again, silence.

Then Trinidad leaned forward, meeting Nathan's eyes. "This is a private concern. I'm sure you appreciate why." Her cousin looked tired, age in his face and the barest trace of vulnerability in the compassionate voice. "You're part of a family, and one of your family members—one of your own—does something terrible. It's hard enough to admit it to yourself, much less to the outside world."

The Tasmanian wolf had returned, climbing onto the coffee table, nonchalantly eating the easy meats.

Nathan looked at his own hands again. "About my boy—"

"He's our first priority," said Uncle Jack. "I want you to know that, sir."

"And there's good coming out of this bullshit," Trinidad added. "We know a lot more about our enemies now. Thanks to the four of you, we're in a much stronger position."

Save for the gnashing of living knives, the room was silent.

The old man looked out the window for a long while.

"It's such a shame," he muttered.

"What's a shame?" asked Porsche.

"That we couldn't show our program." He was crying quietly,

with a certain haggard dignity. "The good we could have done, if we could have warned the world. . . ."

The wolf claimed the last sandwich, making its retreat to the blanket.

Nathan swallowed painfully. "How did they do that? Keep us from broadcasting, I mean."

"I don't know," Uncle Jack blurted.

"We're investigating," Trinidad purred.

Porsche said nothing. Nothing. She found herself watching the predator, studying the dull certainty of its eyes. Then she looked at her uncle, making him blink and stare off at the window for a moment. Then she glanced at Trinidad, something honest in his wide eyes, confirming what didn't need confirmation.

We weren't intended to make any broadcast.

She realized.

The Few themselves stopped us!

A private jet waited on a nearby landing strip. Three of them were climbing aboard; Uncle Jack would return home by other means.

"Believe me," he told Nathan. "We never anticipated this kind of disaster, but we will get your son back. That's a promise. If it takes subterfuge, fine. If there's a bargain to be struck, that's fine, too."

"Whatever works," said Trinidad.

"Threaten the bastards," was Nathan's advice.

"By diplomatic means, of course." Uncle Jack was working hard to sound optimistic. He ran a hand through his thick hair, then offered his other hand to Nathan. "Good-bye, sir. I wish I could tell you all the ways you've been helpful. And please, when you see him, tell Cornell thank you for me."

"I will," Nathan promised, shaking his hand vigorously.

Uncle Jack tried to take her hand, then thought better of it. "Have a safe flight, Miss Neal. I'll see you in a day or two."

Porsche didn't trust her mouth enough to speak. She climbed

into the plane, Nathan trailing after her. Father and son remained on the tarmac for a few moments, discussing everything, or nothing, hugging before they parted. Then Trinidad came up the folding stairs, one hand on the railing, his manner suddenly quiet, almost introverted.

The plane was larger than the mock-bird, less graceful and considerably faster.

Trinidad was their pilot until they were over the Pacific, streaking north at Mach 2. The automated galley prepared a small feast, and the three of them ate dinner in the luxurious cabin. Nathan picked at his food, then finally, with a great sigh, announced, "I'm very sorry. I really need to rest. For a minute, if I can."

Blankets and pillows were unpacked. After settling his guest, Trinidad invited Porsche into the cockpit.

"How's my family?" she asked immediately.

"Fine. All fine." He had expected the question, telling her, "The moment there was trouble, I alerted your parents and brothers. They're perfectly safe now."

"Where?"

"An appropriate location," he promised. "On that ranch in west Texas. Where you were acculturated."

Appropriate, and sad. They'd need new lives somewhere else on the earth, or they might even have to emigrate again. Porsche was at the heart of events—again—yet this time she didn't feel the same regrets. Everyone knew the risks. Everyone approved of her infiltrating the CEA, then applauded her work on the farm. She could recall moments when a brother or a sister-in-law took her aside to say, "You're doing good work," or from her parents, "It's wonderful that you and your uncle have finally declared a truce."

She bristled, for a moment.

Trinidad was watching her in the corner of his eye. Quietly, firmly, he said, "You know perfectly well. Sometimes, a lot of the time, it's best for us not to know too much."

"I realize that."

"You had an emotional stake in that digital fiction. I understand. You're feeling righteously pissed, aren't you?"

She was surprised by her anger, and worse, the acidic sense of betrayal.

"If it helps," he continued, "not everyone agreed with the decision. Some of us think that exposing the agency would be best. For everyone."

"What do you think?"

He smiled, wistfully. Then he began stroking the back of her head, much as a jarrtee would do to a dear friend.

Porsche felt a little sick, and suddenly very tired.

"Relax," was Trinidad's advice, moving his hand to her knee.

Hearing that word, she gratefully slouched back in her seat. A relentless weight was bearing down on her, trying to wring the last corporeal energies from her flesh.

"Sleep," said someone.

Trinidad?

Or herself?

"I'm too tired to sleep," she confessed, aching red eyes gazing out at the gray-blue Pacific. "I've been awake for weeks, it seems."

"Just like old times," Trinidad joked.

It took Porsche a moment to decipher the joke.

"What was that lullaby?" he inquired. "The one about the sun . . ."

She pursed her lips, waiting for the words to come.

Then Trinidad was singing for both of them, his voice smooth and soft, like a warm nest of freshly cut felt grass. 'Do not fear the sun,' he sang, in mangled jarrtee. 'Do not fear the sun, because it fears you, child. You, you, you. Do not fear the day, child, because it flees you when you awaken. And always, child, trust the night—'

" '—because it is yours, yours, yours,' " she managed, almost laughing. " 'Always trust the dark, because it is ours, ours, ours!' "

"You do remember!"

"Always," she whispered.

Night was sweeping across the world, reaching straight for Porsche. But before the sun could set behind their plane, her eyes had fallen shut, and her head dipped, and a pillow was Velcroed to her seat, supporting her head, its resident soul bathed in dreams.

She was still sound asleep when the wheels touched down, screaming against the hard white concrete.

Eyes fought gravity and the lingering, toxic fatigue.

It was day again. Early morning?

Trinidad glanced at her, not quite smiling. "We've arrived."

Nathan was awake and sitting behind Porsche, appearing rested but no less worried. Where were they? Squinting, she watched the flat land and the blurring shape of a metal outbuilding. It was a familiar building, and for a sleepy instant, in confusion, she thought they were back at the farm—an impossibility that kicked her into a useful panic. Then she was genuinely awake, realizing they were in Texas. This was the acculturation center. This is where she learned to be a good human, and it was the perfect place to assemble, then get on with the business of making things right.

The plane had slowed enough to turn, leaving the runway, several ranch buildings straight ahead of them, all in lousy repair.

People were standing in front of the old bunkhouse.

"Who are they?" Nathan inquired.

Mama-ma, and Father. And Leon, and Donald. Their spouses and children were flanking them. It was as if they were posing for a family portrait, everyone holding still until Porsche arrived. There were other faces, too. People who had come to help, no doubt. But instead of feeling thankful, Porsche suddenly pitched forward in her seat and began to tremble, only half-listening as Trinidad said, "It's good that you woke up," with a strange flat voice that seemed to persist long after his mouth had closed again.

Two more faces captured her gaze.

She had seen that nameless man just yesterday, although it

felt like months ago. She had seen him sitting in that sportsman's toy, wearing a ridiculous fishing vest and those deadly and very hard little eyes.

In contrast, the gray-haired woman standing off to one side had a name.

F. Smith.

Farrah to her friends, if she happened to have any.

What startled more than anything was how easily Porsche accepted this revelation, balancing it on top of other revelations. She barely made a sound, even when F. Smith made a gesture, giving a command, others being herded into view.

As the jets cut back and died, Trinidad turned, speaking to Nathan. "Remember the hope that we'd make some arrangement with our enemies? Well, that's what has happened. A good sturdy arrangement that benefits all parties. Assuming that everything goes well, of course."

Porsche watched her family part, allowing two more guests to walk slowly out into the sunshine.

Nathan cried out.

Cornell's face wore a vivid purple bruise, and he carried one arm gingerly against his side. Gazing up at the plane, he saw Porsche sitting in the cockpit, and she dropped her eyes immediately, staring at her own big hands and feet, taking a couple ragged breaths before saying:

"You're him, aren't you?"

"Him who?"

"The traitor."

Her cousin threw a gentle hand on her shoulder and squeezed, saying, "Do you remember? On Jarrtee, there's no such word as *traitor.*"

It was always plural.

Always *traitors.*

" 'One does wrong,' " he quoted with his very best jarrtee, " 'and surrounding the criminal are a thousand others, all busily looking the other way.' "

3

Three people were sitting at a long rectangular table, keeping as far apart as possible.

"It's good to be with you again, Miss Neal."

Silence.

"You look fit. As always."

Nothing.

"And mortified. But I guess under these circumstances, that's to be expected."

She kept her eyes down, giving nothing away.

"Your cousin tells me that you took a very roundabout route back to us. I'd love to hear about your adventures."

Porsche stared at the much shellacked, much abused tabletop. Years ago, she had sat at the same table, in the same cavernous, concrete-floored room, forced hypnosis feeding her a diet of cultural trivia. Television programs and famous personalities were staples; but if memory held true, this was where she had learned about communism. Particularly in Texas, that dying political faith was still loathed for its war on freedom. And now she was being held prisoner in the same room, by a supposedly democratic government. The irony, however feeble, made her break a little smile, and almost by accident, she looked up.

F. Smith was waiting.

"I know you have questions, Miss Neal. Feel free. That's what we're here for."

There were several minutes of unbroken silence, then Porsche turned, focusing squarely on Trinidad.

"Why?"

A broad, thoroughly unchastened grin blossomed on the handsome face, and he shrugged his shoulders. "Make a list of possible reasons," he offered. "Every one of them is a little bit true."

"You should know this," F. Smith interjected. "Your cousin has told us very little about your extended family, and almost nothing about your technologies. And to our credit, my people have respected those rules. We have a relationship of faith and genuine trust."

Porsche stared at her interrogator.

The woman was an imposing figure, even when she tried to reassure. Thick gray hair lay over linebacker eyes, and the deep voice matched her sturdy, don't-ever-cross-me face. "Faith," she repeated. "And trust. Two laudable qualities that your people have never shown us."

"What does that mean?"

"Said simply? It's disturbing to learn that strangers are living among us, in secret, acquiring wealth and power while pursuing their own obscure ends."

"Obscure?" Porsche snorted, then made herself laugh. "Ask my cousin. We don't harm anyone—"

"And I'm sure you're sincere." The bulldog face nodded, eyes unblinking. "I'm sure. Yet you can imagine a reasonable person's concerns. An advanced culture moves into this world, makes no attempt to contact us, and we learn about them only by chance. Which makes me wonder: Aren't we within our rights to take precautions?" She paused. "Assume, dear, that these roles were reversed. How would you react?"

"Would I take your family hostage? Never!"

F. Smith was the sturdiest piece of furniture in the room. After a long silence, she simply cleared her throat, then said, "I've always liked you. I mean that."

"We don't pose a threat to anyone."

"Comforting words, at first glance." She lifted her hands, flexed them, and laid them on the tabletop. "Okay, you're benign. But *benign* is a word applied to tumors. Benign tissue is never confused for a vital organ."

"A fair point," Trinidad said, amiably.

"For instance," the woman continued, "we know that you have a habit of sealing and locking the intrusions leading to friendly worlds. Worlds that offer intelligent life and new technologies. Why keep those things to yourself?"

"We've had hard experience," Porsche replied. "Species need to advance at their own perfect pace—"

"Cousin," Trinidad interrupted, "how about a moratorium on the platitudes?"

Porsche ignored him.

"How did you learn about us?" she asked F. Smith. "Was it *him*?"

"It's not my place to say," the woman replied. "But I'll tell you this: Several years ago, my people were contacted by someone offering to sell an impossible technology. That's how we learned to make a simple key that opens the easiest intrusions."

"It wasn't me," Trinidad promised, "and I don't know who it was."

Porsche refused to believe him. From here on, the simplest statement would always, always demand doubt and hard examination.

F. Smith continued, "Our benefactor never mentioned the Few. But once we opened our first intrusion, there were some obvious possibilities. If humans could dress like aliens and explore High Desert, why couldn't aliens stroll up and down our streets, too?"

"Humans can reason," said Trinidad, in mock warning.

"We could have used help in our explorations," the woman allowed, a grimness in her eyes and in the meaty lips. "Talent has always been our weakness. As you well know, Miss Neal. We tried to hire good people, yet hundreds died, many because they didn't have your kind of strength." She paused a moment. "You saw their suffering. You could have used your innate skills and helped us with our selection process. But instead, you remained mute, standing by while hundreds died needlessly—"

"Don't," Porsche snapped. "It was your project, your responsibility. And you knew that things were going wrong."

"A sensitive subject," F. Smith observed.

Porsche tried to remain silent, but a question leaked out, under pressure. "When did you learn about me?"

"When did we?" The woman enjoyed the moment, the suspense. "We used to play with the possibility. At meetings or lunch, someone would say, 'That Miss Neal is a little too good at this business.' You were excellent in the field. Independent. Mentally sound. Easily the best player on the team." She laughed, then added, "I protected you. Did you know that? There was talk about reexamining your life, putting your family under surveillance. But I told my superiors to leave you alone. An attitude that eventually brought me all sorts of embarrassment."

"Blame me for your embarrassment," Trinidad offered.

Carefully, in vivid detail, Porsche imagined flinging a basketball into her cousin's grinning face.

F. Smith asked, "Any more questions?"

"What do you want from me?"

"That's the important question, isn't it?" She pushed her chair away from the old table, wood screeching against concrete. Then she rose with a certain gravity, saying, "For now, I think we should take a little break. You'll want to see friends and family, I'm sure. Since the answer involves them, and we want to be fair."

"And I should leave, too." Trinidad jumped up, giving Porsche an obnoxious wink.

"Money, or revenge?" Porsche inquired.

"My motivation?" The traitor laughed, shaking his head and glancing up at the high ceiling. "It's the same as yours, cousin. All I've ever wanted, since before I was born, is to be the hero!"

Porsche sat alone for a few minutes, then Cornell appeared, wearing new jeans and a simple pullover shirt, and, feeling a kick of happiness, Porsche nearly made a joke.

"Did Aunt Farrah take you shopping?"

But she didn't say it, thankfully. Cornell turned, and she saw the deep purple-black bruises on his forehead and temple.

He took the chair on her right, sitting slowly and wincing.

"What's happening?" he whispered. Then in a louder voice, he asked, "Who in hell can I trust here?"

"Not me," she confided. "I've been wrong forever, it seems."

Her parents appeared, then her brothers. The four of them sat across from Porsche, gazing at her with a mixture of weary concern, puzzlement, and outrage.

"Are you two all right?" asked Father.

Porsche nodded, then glanced at Cornell. He was watching the ceiling, and she found herself following his eyes, spotting the tiny camera that had been bolted to one of the high beams. Everything seen and said was absorbed; why did she feel the slightest surprise?

Everyone looked up.

Mama-ma shouted, "Where's my nephew?"

Porsche told her what had happened, in brief.

"What do they want?" asked Leon. Her older brother looked exactly like a midlevel insurance executive, a little heavy and rather gray, as respectable as he was astonished. "Porsche? Do you have any idea what they're planning?"

Carefully, slowly, she took a cleansing breath. "In the short term," she said, "I think they want to see how we get along."

Donald pointed out, "Microcameras wouldn't be visible."

"That's the idea," Cornell offered. "They want us to know that they're watching. That they're in control."

People nodded, saying nothing.

Pulling his hand across his bare scalp, Father promised, "They won't learn much from us. Because we don't know much."

"We're ordinary citizens," Leon growled.

"I don't know how to build an automobile," Mama-ma boasted, "and I can't tell anyone how an intrusion key works."

"I don't even know where they're made," joked Father.

"Newark," Donald offered.

Quiet, forced laughter blossomed, then died.

Porsche kept thinking about her cousin. In his position, he had access to keys, including the six-sets that let them into friendly everted worlds. He could very well understand the theory behind them, at least well enough to sell the information to the agency . . . but F. Smith had gone to the trouble of claiming that Trinidad wasn't their original source—which might or might not be the truth.

Father caught her gaze.

He mouthed the word, "Jack?"

With a look, she said, "I don't know." If Uncle Jack had been captured—or worse, if he was an accomplice—this mess was even worse than it appeared. But if he was their ally and still at large, and he'd discovered the truth, he was probably already working on their release as well as his son's intricate punishment.

"We aren't worth much," Mama-ma declared, with a brittle pride. "Almost nothing, if they're thinking of ransoming us."

"Basic policy," Father echoed. "No ransoms."

A lie, Porsche knew. But really, how much could Uncle Jack offer in exchange for them?

"These people are short-term stupid," said Donald. "Push the Few too far, and we'll pick up and leave."

"And seal our intrusions behind us," his brother added.

"It's happened in the past," Mama-ma sang, happy to threaten. "And it will be humanity's loss."

Cornell sat motionless, withdrawn. But his eyes had a rattling, energized quality.

Porsche knew the look, touching him gingerly on a shoulder. "What is it?"

"Do you know what that camera sees?" he asked no one in particular. Half-smiling, half-grimacing, he warned, "It sees a room full of terrified people pretending not to be."

Father started to speak, eager to deny—

"No, sir," Cornell continued. Then he took Porsche's hand and kissed the back of it, and speaking into the bones, he said, "We should just shut up now. Shut up and bore them. And then maybe something will happen."

The bluster fell away to silence.

Twice they heard the distant rattle of helicopters arriving, then departing. Then after a long pause, the room's only door burst open, and Nathan stepped inside, followed by a pair of men dressed in black trousers and simple gray polo shirts, sidearms on their hips, and walking between them, a dazed and sorrowful Timothy Kleck.

Nathan saw no one but Cornell. Sitting next to him, he examined the bruises with a mixture of rage and vindication. "How are you?" he sputtered. Then before his son could answer, he added, "They're bastards, aren't they? Government bullies! I warned you, didn't I? A bunch of monsters!"

"I believe you, Dad."

Timothy took a seat at the far end of the table, alone. He wasn't injured, yet he seemed in worse shape than anyone. How could everything have gone so wrong? he was asking himself. Wide, haunted eyes examined his surroundings, then shot an accusing look at Porsche. Then, trying for hope, he fixed his attentions on the all-powerful guards, his mouth opening, fumbling for the magic words that would set him free.

But the words didn't exist, and the realization came slowly, painfully.

A few moments later, F. Smith reappeared, her face and manner like granite, pink and unreadable.

Trailing after her were two of the fishermen from the farm. Long scratches decorated one of their faces. He glanced at Porsche with a quick, utterly smug look, then held F. Smith's chair out for her, the picture of civility.

More guards entered, wearing the same black-and-gray garb, each man carrying several folding chairs that were arranged in neat rows. Middle-aged men and women filtered into view in the next few minutes, sitting in the new chairs. The atmosphere was more like a corporate meeting than an interrogation. There was coffee in cellulose mugs. Someone asked about the weather, and someone else mentioned the fire. What fire? Then Mama-ma spoke with a shrill voice, saying, "Where's my nephew? I want to see Trinidad!"

"I'm sorry," said a sudden voice. "He just departed."

The last fisherman made his entrance. Hard, tiny eyes burned above a cold smirk. He was wearing the same simple uniform but no sidearm, and he carried an electronic notebook in huge, bony hands.

No one spoke.

Even the bulldog woman regarded the man with a tangible respect.

"Finally, Miss Neal." The man approached, saying, "It's good to actually meet you. Officially, I mean."

She felt the hammering of her heart.

Walking behind her, the man said, "For those who don't know, my name is Latrobe. Benjamin Latrobe."

Father stiffened, growling, "What do you want?"

The question seemed to go unheard.

Latrobe continued walking to the far end of the table, then leaned over Timothy, speaking softly into an ear.

Timothy rose, and with a shredded dignity, moved his chair and himself out of the way.

Then Latrobe set his notebook on the table, staring at Porsche for a long moment, a serene disdain building.

Quietly, in a near-whisper, he said, "Before I explain what we want, Miss Neal, let me tell you why it is that you're going to do everything we ask."

A pause, then, "And why you will do it gladly."

No one spoke, or moved, or even breathed.

"Allegiance," said Latrobe. "Devotion." His eyes drifted over to Father as he asked, "What matters most to the Neals? A particular government? But that's preposterous. A particular planet? I don't believe so. As your wife said, you can leave the earth whenever you wish. And as for the human species . . . well, Mr. Neal, you haven't been one of us for even half your life. The universe is filled with viable species. A blessing for you, I'm sure. But the rest of us are a little more trapped in our circumstances, I think."

Everyone watched as Latrobe touched his notebook with a thick, delicate finger.

"The Few are what matters to you." He smiled at his hands. "I've had some long, fruitful discussions with Trinidad. On general matters, mostly. You're a vast and powerful family—despite that false-humble name—and despite the plethora of worlds and circumstances, you've managed to keep that sense of family. Which is noble, I think. I do." He paused, then asked, "Is my assessment fair, Mr. Neal?"

Father sighed. "It's a simple one."

"You're right. Everything has its complications." Latrobe read from his notebook's screen, then walked around the corner of the table, stopping behind Donald, taking his hand and lifting it with an easy, irresistible strength. Sunlight angling through one of the tiny windows danced on the golden wedding band. "A lovely wife, you have. Linda. But then again, Texas girls are natural beauties. Isn't that what people say?"

Silence.

"And you have sweet children, too. Your daughters Clare and Peggy. And Josh, too."

Her brother retrieved his hand, saying nothing.

"We won't tell you anything!" Father roared.

"I think you will," Latrobe countered. "You have alien souls, but you're saddled with human physiologies, human frailties. Give me the opportunity, and I'll wring every secret out of your synapses."

Porsche stared at the broad, amoral face.

"But you're mistaken. I don't care much about your technical wonders." He was amused, and serene. "Trinidad approached us with a very different offer. Very persuasive, and very specific. Your magic is impressive, but as he has pointed out to me—with a certain force—we really don't need your magic."

"What are you talking about?" Father asked.

"We want to make a leap of technology," Latrobe replied. "We're working for the chance to put this nation back at the helm of this little world." He shook his head, grinning as he said, "We'll leave the serious empire building to you, I think. For now."

Her parents winced, saying nothing.

"Now," said Latrobe, "I bet you know where this is going."

No one spoke.

"Really? No guesses, even?" He gave Father a solid, familiar pat on the shoulder, saying, "All I need is your daughter's help. Although everyone else will accompany us. If things go wrong, I want all of you in easy reach."

The voice was soft and filled with menace.

"Your sons and grandchildren, too." He gestured, saying, "Plus Mr. Kleck. And both of the Novaks, of course. Everyone is invited."

"To what?" Nathan growled.

Porsche knew.

Suddenly she was staring up at Latrobe, astonishment mixed with horror, plus a crystalline dose of tortured pride. Her cousin was an inventive monster—

Father noticed her expression. "What is it, Porsche?"

Because she could do nothing worse, she leaned over the table and stole away the surprise. "The CEA has been trying to find an advanced civilization. People with useful knowledge." She waited a half-moment, then said, "There's a perfect world. Exotic materials. Force fields and advanced engines. And powerful weapons, too."

Cornell saw it next. Or maybe first, and he had been holding his tongue.

"Jarrtee," he said. Badly, as always.

Latrobe nodded, adding, "Trinidad has shown us how to accomplish all of our goals, and in a matter of days."

The audience sitting on the folding chairs began to nod and smile, a feeling of self-congratulations washing over the table's bleak despair.

"Before this year is done," he continued, "the United States will have the means to achieve a one- or two-century jump on our competition. According to conservative predictions, by the end of the decade, we'll be spearheading the most incredible burst of technological change ever seen on this planet."

Porsche's first instinct was right: This *was* a corporate meeting.

"A few days," Latrobe repeated. "That's all I need from you people."

"And then?" Mama-ma squeaked.

"You'll go free, of course. With our thanks." If the man was lying, he did it easily.

"And if we won't help?" asked Porsche.

"You're the only person whose help we need," Latrobe reminded her. "If *you* refuse, I'll simply leave your family and the other conspirators behind. In the jarrtees' capable hands."

With a deep, cold voice, Nathan said, "Monster."

Latrobe shook his head. "No one here is a monster, Mr. Novak. But believe me, I know how to summon a monster when I need one.

"Which is true of everyone. If you think about it."

4

QUARTERS WERE ASSIGNED TO THE PRISONERS.

By chance or by plan, Porsche was given the same tiny room that she'd slept in years ago, and judging by appearances, the same very narrow bed. Cornell walked in after her and sat on the hard spring mattress, kicking up a sudden cloud of dust. Desiccated flakes of her skin drifted in that cloud. He remained motionless for a long moment, hands between his knees and his mouth more opened than closed; then he swallowed and looked up, asking, "Are you all right?"

A naked bulb made his bruises more vivid. She touched his face gingerly, then said, "No, I'm not."

"Neither am I." He almost laughed. "I'm being held against my will, and I hurt, and I'm very tired, and I'm pissed."

She sat down beside him, slowly, trying not to disturb the dust. "It was such a mess at the farm. I tried to find you—"

"I'm not blaming you, Porsche."

"I'm not apologizing."

"Besides," he said, "if I'd escaped, it would have just delayed the inevitable. Right?"

Sad, and true.

Cornell had a biting, cynical look when he wanted it. A dark laugh came welling up from deep inside.

"What's funny?" she asked.

"I am," he confessed. "All the things I worried about, and it never occurred to me, ever, that the trouble would come from inside such a perfect family."

The word *perfect* carried amusement and a whiff of bitterness.

Louder, without laughing, Cornell warned her, "They're probably listening to us now."

It was a certainty.

"I'm going to tell them exactly what I think," he vowed.

But she was honest first, tilting back her head, then shouting, "Trinidad! This isn't over yet!"

Late last summer, after returning from High Desert and resigning from the agency, Cornell and Porsche had paid a little visit to Texas.

The solitary child of a shattered family, Cornell found himself immersed in the Neal clan. They paraded around like some American ideal. A tenacious, very Texan form of cordiality held sway over every barbecue and basketball game. They adored her new boyfriend and tried to make him adore them, which was easy enough. And of course he couldn't help but worship Porsche—his alien-born lover, savior, and consummate mate.

"Consummate," he began to call her. From across the swimming pool or across the bed, he would say, "Come here, Miss Consummate," with a voice meant to sound teasing, but in truth was, in a sense, utterly honest.

It was the kind of relentless admiration that anyone would find intoxicating, and it was dangerous for both of them.

Porsche tried to warn him.

"First of all," she said, "I'm human. And there's no perfection in being human. Second of all, if you keep thinking this way, you're going to wake up some morning feeling cheated. My morning mouth hits you, and I'm not in a good mood, and you'll think to yourself, 'I'm in bed with a bitchy alien monster.'"

But warnings didn't change his mind.

Nor did anger or simply ignoring him.

What helped was Sunday service at the local Episcopal church. Cornell had been raised agnostic by a parent who distrusted any organized faith. Christmas was a secular holiday as contrived as Halloween. He hadn't seen more than a handful of Christian ceremonies. Yet he found himself suddenly thrown into the midst of hundreds of otherwise sane, top-drawer humans engaged in a shared delirium. It was sobering, and scary. Robes and candles and dusty hymns made for a fantastic show. But what astonished him most was how easily—indeed, how fervently—the Neal clan joined in with the general bullshit.

"Your father really belts out the Lord's Prayer," Cornell observed the next day, driving them out of Texas, heading north on I-35.

There was a delicate new bite to those words.

"What's wrong with the Lord's Prayer?" she asked.

"Nothing," he replied, but without heart. Then after a few more miles of red clay, he observed, "The priest, minister, whatever . . . he sure recognized your family."

Indeed, the moon-faced servant of God had singled out Porsche for a warm, "How have you been, darling?" followed by a cheery, "And I hope we see you again, soon."

"Of course Father Combs knows us," she replied. "We've been attending services since we moved to Lewisville."

"But do you believe?"

"In what?"

"In Christ as the Son of God!"

"Well," she began.

"And is he your personal Savior? And do you pray to Him while you're marching on another world?"

She said nothing, waiting.

"And how about the Trinity? Where do you stand on it? And Christian history? All that blood and guts . . . is it a good thing?"

Their eyes collided, something almost reproachful in his gaze. "Whenever you have answers, feel free."

"I should be agnostic. Is that what you're saying?"

"Maybe."

"You know our circumstances," she reminded him. "When we embrace a species, we embrace its society, too. In every way possible."

"Sure."

"Jewish. Muslim. Hindu. Each faith has its Few, and most of us try to be pious."

He fumed for another mile, then declared, "So it's just an elaborate game."

"So what's wrong with games?" she replied. "You don't know how we think, or how we choose to believe."

It was a pivotal moment.

At the time, Porsche thought it was the perfect moment. Cornell had found a flaw in the Neals' halo; suddenly they were hypocritical enough to be human. He never again called her Miss Consummate, which was all she wanted. And they continued north without further incidents, driving toward their shared and golden future.

But their conversation was never finished.

Months later, trapped in a room that she had never planned to see again, Porsche remembered how Cornell had repeated her words:

" 'You don't know how we think, or how we choose to believe.' "

"That's what I said," she admitted.

Then with a real prescience, Cornell asked, "But do you know what the others believe?"

"What others?"

"Your family," he said, laughing as if it were a joke. "Do you really, truly know what's happening inside their heads?"

Cornell lay on his side and coaxed Porsche onto hers, the two of them like nested spoons. His hands were firmly, even possessively cupped around her breasts. An ancient pillow, flat as a dish, had to be shared. When the overhead light was extinguished, the room seemed even smaller, and there came the sudden lucid memory of being twelve years old, lying in this exact flavor of darkness, feeling just a little homesick for a world that she had lost forever.

The irony was blatant: Her life was in retreat, moving back along its own curious past.

Tonight, the acculturation center.

And soon, Jarrtee.

In a whisper, Cornell asked, "How would they steal technology from the jarrtees?"

"It wouldn't be easy," she admitted. Imagining microphones in the walls, sewn into the mattress and crawling up their asses, she said, "In fact, I think it would be impossible."

Cornell waited for a moment, "They can't just steal machines and textbooks."

She told the listeners, "Only souls pass through the intrusions."

"Only souls," he echoed.

Then he said, "The bastards. They've got to kidnap people, don't they? The people with useful knowledge. . . ."

Trinidad had reported that Jarrtee was in turmoil, and that the Few had almost abandoned the world. Two key ingredients if you want to break into someone's house: Turmoil, and a lack of opponents.

"And somehow . . . somehow you're supposed to help them," Cornell muttered.

Somewhere else in the barracks, a child was throwing a fit. Its wailing was insistent and self-centered and ignorant; too many changes coming too fast, and nobody able to comfort it.

"They want to go there," said Cornell, "and abduct some poor old engineers and scientists . . . I bet . . ."

She shook her head.

"There's nothing gentle about the jarrtees," she warned. "Not their culture, not their species. And we're walking into their world wearing nothing. In every way, we are naked."

Let F. Smith chew on those words, she thought.

"It's a nightmare," her lover agreed. "Or a daymare, I suppose."

Porsche reached behind herself, offering a caress, a glancing hug.

"Whatever happens," he said, "I want to stay with you."

What was best, she decided, was to ignore those words.

He repeated them, then to the unseen, he said, "I'm a talent. Better than almost anyone else they'll find, except for the Neals. Isn't that right?"

Yes.

"Say yes, love."

She said, "You're a natural."

"I'm staying with you," he repeated, with force.

She was absolutely quiet, closing her eyes.

"They're holding my father, too," Cornell reminded her.

"I know."

"One thing these pricks understand," he muttered. "Most of us will do almost anything, if it means protecting our families."

THE PRISONERS WERE ROUSED BEFORE DAWN, APPLES AND WARM OAT-
meal laid out on the table where they had met yesterday, and
after the adults were laced with strong coffee, everyone was
loaded into a fleet of squat unmarked helicopters that roared off
into the half-lit sky, flying west one after another, too slow by a
long measure to outrace the sun.

Porsche sat with her back to the hull, between Cornell and a
muscular young soldier, perhaps Hispanic, dressed in the standard black and gray. Through a grimy armored window, she
could see the country beneath them, more flat than not, more
brown than green, and after years of drought, as empty as the
moon's far side.

"It looks a little like High Desert," she observed.

Cornell half-smiled, glancing at the soldier.

"I miss that world sometimes," she said.

"It was beautiful, in places," said Cornell, "and it never pretended to be kind."

The soldier squinted at a random crate, feigning indifference.

A dozen other soldiers faced one another over an assortment
of cellulose crates and overstuffed sacks. Nathan sat on the other
side of his son, buckled in, clinging to his ceiling strap. Captiv-
ity and the helicopter ride were doing their worst, yet if any-

thing, fear seemed to make Nathan younger. There was a gleam to his face. Without warning, he gave Porsche a surreptitious wink and smile, then stole Cornell's strap, too, bombarding the guards across from him with a lucid, accusing glare.

They reached the mountains gradually. There was a low blackness at first, too distant to seem rugged or even real. Then came a modest upheaval of stone and dark, drought-parched forest. Wanting a better view, Porsche asked permission to pee. The Hispanic soldier accompanied her up front. The toilet was set behind the cockpit, its tiny door sealed, the IN USE sign blinking red.

Porsche had to wait.

Through the tinted windows, she saw the true mountains and clouds of coarse black smoke suspended over them, riding on titanic columns of heat. Tangerine flames roared in the desiccated woods. The only sounds were the endless thrumming of the rotors and the winds that buffeted their machine, but Porsche had the impression that if their engines died, she would hear the gnawing roar of a wildfire, vast and selfish, growing even louder as they tumbled to earth.

The toilet door opened, a thickset man coming out sideways.

It was Latrobe. He stared at Porsche for a long moment, then conjured up a broad, complex smile.

"Pardon the smell," was all he said.

He claimed the seat behind the copilot, laughing, never giving her another look. Porsche stepped into the closet-sized toilet, shut the door, and did nothing. She stood before a sink too small to wash both hands at once, and she stared at her reflection in a plastic mirror. When she thought about everything, like now, she could almost feel that sense of being overwhelmed. But that was the trick. A person had to think in manageable bites. Gnaw at your problems like a fire gnaws. The world's forests couldn't vanish in one blaze, but given time, every splinter of wood is consumed by some kind of fire.

She flushed the chemical toilet, then stepped out again.

Latrobe was using his reader. With a sharp voice, she asked, "Doesn't it worry you? Going up against us, I mean."

The soldier took her by the shoulder, then an arm.

But Latrobe was amused, if anything. "You're saying what? That there might be some terrible retribution waiting for us?"

"Maybe."

"Well." He blanked the reader, saying, "Your cousin assures me that you won't. The Few aren't in the retribution business, first of all. And besides, we aren't going to harm any of you. Everyone comes home from this soon, and safe."

"And afterwards?"

"Everyone has what they want, more or less."

She made herself laugh, asking, "Do you actually believe Trinidad's promises?"

The face was inert, unreadable.

"I wouldn't believe him."

Latrobe narrowed his eyes. "I bet not."

"Wait," she warned. "Eventually, my cousin's going to disappoint you."

The face was utterly unconcerned, but something passed behind the eyes, making the meaty lips pull up grim for a moment. Then Latrobe gestured, telling the guard, "Miss Neal needs to be in her seat. Now."

She gave the burning mountains a quick last look, then let herself be pulled away.

When she saw Nathan again, she gave him a big, defiant wink.

They flew through smoke and into the brilliant scorched air beyond, the ground beneath them left black and simple. Miles had to be crossed before little islands of green emerged from the ash, growing larger and eventually knitting together, a sudden forest of ponderosa pine swaddling the slopes of an ancient mountain.

They rose with the long slope, then turned, half a dozen identical machines moving in a precise line.

Into her ear, Cornell asked, "Is this the place?"

Porsche watched the spinelike ridge, waiting for a flash of sunshine on black glass. But the pines hid the intrusion, and it didn't help being airborne, the perspective making the countryside unfamiliar.

A meadow appeared, and she imagined it with snow, and bonfires, and hot stew. Sadly, she admitted, "This is it."

The helicopters fishhooked and settled to earth. With a professional exuberance, the soldiers disembarked first. As she stepped onto the ladder, Porsche could smell smoke as well as dust and the cumulative stink of unwashed flesh. Tents had been erected near the forest, their mottled gray-brown fabric making them nearly invisible from above. In their gray crew shirts, in the sunshine, the soldiers looked like the hired help at someone's peculiar resort.

Cornell stayed with his father, one hand laid possessively on a shoulder.

Out of the mayhem of bodies and dust, a tall, dazed figure half-stumbled into view, his gray face turning aimlessly, outraged eyes trying to absorb enormous events.

Porsche shouted:

"Timothy!"

Hearing his name, Timothy paused, looking through her for a cold, hard moment. Then a soldier took him by the arm, and he seemed almost grateful, letting the man lead, glad for the guidance.

Nathan and Cornell were waiting for her. Nathan combed his shaggy white hair with one hand, then the other, accomplishing nothing. "I'm glad to be down," he announced. Then, "*They* set the fire, I bet."

"Let's go, Dad."

"To keep people away. I bet so." Nathan searched for an ally. "Do you agree with me, dear?"

More than privacy, a forest fire gave the operation a cover story. It explained the presence of a military-style camp in the New Mexican wilderness, and the persistent smoke would help hide what they were doing. She glanced up at the sky, wondering who might be watching.

A voice pushed its way through the fading roar of motors.

"Aunt Porsche! Did you see me?"

Nieces and nephews were escorting their mothers. Like youngsters on a field trip, the oldest were holding hands. One blond girl, spying her aunt, dropped her little brother's hand and came running, crying out, "I was in chopper machines, Aunt Porsche!"

"You were," she replied.

"Were you?"

"I was." Then, "Did you have fun, Clare?"

"Yeah," the five-year-old assured her. "I had a lot of fun."

"That's what matters," Porsche offered, feeling a pang in her belly now.

Clare's mother arrived, a winsome smile and shrug of the shoulders saying, in effect, "What a mess!"

Porsche asked about her husband.

"Donald's with your folks, and Leon." She took Clare by the hand, then wiped her daughter's face with a damp finger.

"How are you holding up, Linda?"

The question earned a moment's reflection.

The woman—a talent by birth; a Few by choice—showed the world her brave face, then with a quiet laugh, she said, "I'm not doing too badly," as if amused by her own durability.

Their destination was a large, heavily guarded tent surrounded by even larger tents. The interior had been warmed by trapped sunlight. A grayish light lay everywhere, staining people and objects with its color and identical waxy textures. Tables and cots had been set up according to someone's idea of utility. Perhaps the same person had thought of the children: Padded bats and soft balls were on the ground, still sealed in their plastic packages, begging to be opened.

"You've got to admire their energy," said Cornell, taking Porsche's hand.

"I admire nothing," Nathan grumbled. "Nothing."

Father and Mama-ma arrived, and the brothers, and Clare led the charge, every mobile child interrogating them about their flight and the huge fire, and the big men with the guns, too. Wasn't it amazing to be here? For the moment, it was a vacation. They were camping in the mountains. They couldn't think of it any other way.

Their grandfather seemed enormous and frail, his long face smiling one moment, then, without warning, verging on tears.

Mama-ma slapped her hands together, sweeping away their admirers with the promise of later fun. "Just now," she said, "the adults need to hold a meeting. Can you play with these toys now, please?"

Except the packages were tough to open. Penknives and keys had been taken from them, and the plastic was tougher than fingers and teeth.

Father called out, "Porsche!"

The children collected their aunt, Clare grabbing one arm and her twin boy cousins, Gregory and Mitchel, pushing Porsche toward the most remote corner of the tent.

Timothy sat nearby, glowering at a random point in space.

"Join us," Nathan called out, a plastic-wrapped turquoise-colored bat in one hand. "Mr. Kleck! We're holding a meeting over here."

The thin face flinched as if in pain, then looked in the opposite direction.

The Neals gave the Novaks surreptitious glances.

It was a slippery, subtle moment. Their faces weren't unfriendly, nor suspicious, yet the eyes appraised them with the frankness of bankers.

Exactly how far can we trust you? asked the eyes.

Porsche said nothing.

Cornell noticed everything, and he said nothing.

Nathan sat at the plastic table, announcing, "No Timothy, it seems."

There was a pause, then Father began. "Thoughts, anyone?"

No one spoke for a moment. Leon and Donald watched their children and harried wives. Their parents traded glances, forty years of marriage making words superfluous. Cornell took hold of two of Porsche's long fingers, clearing his throat, then gently asked, "Do you have any idea why he would do this?"

"He wants to be a hero," Porsche didn't say.

Nathan set the padded bat on the table, then asked point-blank, "How often does this happen to you people?"

The Neals bristled.

Then with stiff certainty, Mama-ma replied, "It never happens."

"Never," Leon added, for emphasis.

But how would we know? Porsche wondered. We barely know what the Few are doing on the earth!

"All right," Nathan persisted. "What is it that makes Trinidad so special?"

Special.

Once said, the word seemed to linger in the bright gray air.

Father glanced at Mama-ma, saying, "No, let me." Then with a mixture of authority and grim embarrassment, he said, "There have been incidents. Warnings. When he was a boy, and later."

Was he speaking to Nathan, or their captors?

"He's always been comfortable with lies," Father continued. "Grandiose notions. A certain self-possessed quality mixed with thrill-seeking." He sighed and looked at his daughter. "You were closest to him, once. How would you describe Trinidad?"

"Strong-willed," she admitted. "With a strong-willed father."

Embarrassment kept eating at her father. "He's my brother's boy, which is why I know what I do. Things not mentioned publically."

"Such as?" asked Donald.

Mama-ma touched Father on the forearm, lending encouragement.

"While we lived on Jarrtee," he continued, "the boy stole a full set of keys and tried to open an intrusion."

"When?" blurted Porsche, genuinely startled.

"It doesn't matter," Father claimed. "He didn't get the chance, and your uncle handled the incident privately."

The crime was worse than her disaster with Jey-im, but what bothered Porsche—what made her cold inside—was that she had never heard about it. Uncle Jack wouldn't tell her, naturally. But Trinidad hadn't hinted at it, much less boasted, and he was more her brother than were the two men sitting with her now.

"And it happened again here," Father admitted, squinting at a distant point. "After we saw their family in Yellowstone. . . ."

Even Mama-ma looked up, startled.

"The same stunt?" asked Leon.

"Except that time he succeeded." There was a slowly boiling rage that made it easy for Father to add, "That boy was a nightmare for my poor brother. He had to track him across worlds, then drag him home again. And afterwards, he had to embrace all the blame that he possibly could." His eyes returned, and he blinked again and again, grumbling, "I see now that Jack was too patient. Too kind."

"But Trinidad has been so much . . . better . . ." Mama-ma was trying to be gracious, or honest. "For years now, he's been a model son."

"Dear," Father purred, "I think the evidence says otherwise."

Silence.

"And my brother was so proud of him, too." He fidgeted, then said, "Obviously, he was too patient and much too forgiving—"

"Uncle Jack is neither of those things," Porsche snapped. "He can be a brutal fuck, frankly."

Wounded, Father claimed, "You've never understood him."

"And another thing," said Porsche. "How can we be sure that Trinidad's acting alone? That there isn't an accomplice?"

That brought an icy quiet, a deep introspection.

Porsche glanced at the children. The young Hispanic soldier was standing among them, calmly slicing open the plastic packages with a long military knife. In normal circumstances, he would look like any decent person. But she noticed his grim expression and how he never quite looked at the young faces, trying hard not to make them real.

Then Father summoned his usual hopefulness, telling everyone, "For the time being, I think we should cooperate with these people."

Everyone looked at him.

Then he pulled a hand across his mouth, saying, "And you're wrong about Jack, I think. I hope."

"When Jack finds Trinidad this time—" Mama-ma began.

There won't be any forgiveness, everyone thought to themselves, in a silent, prayful chorus.

6

SPARTAN MEALS WERE DELIVERED TO THE TENT, A COLD LUNCH FOL-
lowed by a bland dinner. The soldiers bringing the food were
bombarded with questions, and each left without betraying so
much as a meaningful look. Then night fell, and there was nothing to do but curl up on the hard cots. The midnight arrival of
another helicopter flotilla rattled nerves. By morning, they were
sharing the mountainside with at least three hundred soldiers.
Showers and toilets were available only by appointment. There
were no more clean clothes, and diapers were being rationed.
During breakfast, F. Smith and a pair of high-ranking souls paid
a visit, and the bulldog woman told the prisoners that everyone
would be embarking for Jarrtee as soon as the final arrangements could be made. Then she gave Porsche a little glance,
and without another word, she and her companions retreated.

The children's adventure in travel had already lost its lus-
ter. There were tantrums that morning, and in the afternoon, there was a bat-wielding fight between Clare—a fearless
little competitor—and her cousin Gregory.

The mood was little better among the adults.

Trinidad was the subject of endless discussions. Childhood
memories were resurrected, often more than once. Porsche of-

fered the occasional story or clarification, but most of the chatter came from her brothers. Finally, working together, their wives steered the conversation toward more immediate concerns. What was Jarrtee like, and how did its people live? Then they made the oldest children listen to the stories about the old home world. If everyone was going there, wasn't it reasonable to be forewarned?

Only Timothy didn't join in the general chatter. He sat alone in the loneliest corner of the tent, staring at the fabric walls or closing his eyes, feigning sleep.

Cornell tried to encourage him, but the man simply covered his face with both hands, ignoring the prattle.

In the late afternoon, Porsche approached. Timothy was lying on his back, on the desiccated earth, and she kneeled and said, "I know it's hard."

Nothing.

"And grossly unfair," she offered.

The man stirred, pulling his hands away from his face, blinking and looking past her, saying nothing.

"Blame me," she suggested. "I didn't keep my promises."

Timothy's face had the wasted quality of someone in the throes of a terminal illness. But the eyes became bright and strong, suddenly focusing squarely on her, and with a certain relish, he said, "Fuck you."

She took a turn at silence.

Then he groaned and covered his face with the crook of a long arm, telling her, "You couldn't make promises, and you fucking well can't take the blame, either. Bitch."

Porsche rose and turned.

Suddenly it was warm beneath the tent, and stale, and astonishingly bright; every person made to look small, drowning in the hot, brilliant air.

At dusk, the wind shifted, bringing the stink of a wildfire. Every breath tasted of black ash. Military rations had an unintended smoky flavor. Even in sleep, the fire laced its way into Porsche's dreams. Waking suddenly at two in the morning, she remembered seeing a smoldering ruin; she had been walking through the ashes, searching for something that she couldn't quite bring to mind.

"Po-lee-een," someone whispered.

She tried to sit up, discovering a hand on her arm.

"Po-lee-een," Trinidad repeated. He was squatting next to her cot, his breath without odor, his body freshly rebuilt after a transit through an intrusion. "Remember how we used to wander the City together?"

She nodded, smiling despite herself.

"Let's do it again. Like old times." The charming grin showed nothing malicious, nothing unkind. "How about now?"

She told him, "No."

Her cousin watched her in the filtered moonlight, measuring her.

"Give it up," was her advice.

"Do you think I can?"

"Easily." She waited for a moment, then added, "Just turn and walk away. I'm sure you can find someplace to hide."

"I probably could," he conceded.

A buoyant little hope was forming. She glanced at the motionless figure on the cot beside her, wishing that Cornell would stay asleep.

"Nobody would ever find me," Trinidad assured, something dreamy about his voice, his manner. Then he glanced over his shoulder, laughed, and shook his head. "Too bad I didn't think of that earlier."

A whistle sounded, piercing and close.

Soldiers carrying lanterns began to file inside, and the familiar voice of Farrah Smith called out, "It's time now. Everyone, please!"

"Too bad," her cousin repeated, mocking her.

And Cornell, apparently lying awake all this time, listening to everything, reached up and shoved Trinidad onto his butt. "Yeah," he concurred. "It's too bad."

Latrobe was waiting in the meadow, holding a mug to his face, steam rising as he sipped loudly, with exuberance, relishing the earthly treasure.

Porsche smelled coffee.

"Good morning to you, Miss Neal."

She said nothing.

"And Mr. Novak, too. Good idea. Keep close to your woman friend." Latrobe grinned. "We're glad for volunteers. Real talents like you are so rare."

Cornell looked tired, but composed. Wary, but unperturbed. With a quiet voice, he asked, "How much of a talent are you?"

"Fair," Latrobe answered.

A quiet, self-deprecating laugh took Porsche by surprise.

"He's being modest," was Trinidad's assessment. "He's not a pure talent, but he's got talent in his bones."

Latrobe finished his coffee, handing the mug to one of the nameless soldiers who seemed to be everywhere, eager for work. Then he whispered into the same man's ear, sparking him into a quick, determined trot.

The silhouettes of prisoners and guards swirled together inside the tent, in the lantern light. She didn't want to watch her family being herded along. "Are we going to stand here all morning?" she snapped. "Or are we getting to work?"

"Fine," said Latrobe. "Off to work then."

They walked uphill, armed men shadowing the foursome. Over the last few days, a roadlike trail had been pounded into the long ridge. Without snow, the landscape was unfamiliar. She had never been here before, she could tell herself. This was the wrong ridge, and probably the wrong mountain, and Trinidad was leading the agency into an elaborate, unimaginable trap.

For a few moments, she could almost believe that lie.

Then they arrived at the glass disk, black and slick and very familiar. Porsche recalled the nameless woman kneeling over the molten glass, warming her hands. She remembered her cousin throwing the snowball, striking her. It seemed like a pivotal moment, and if she could somehow change the play of those events . . . nothing would be any different today, she realized. Nothing would change.

Latrobe lifted his hand, saying, "We'll wait for a moment. I've asked someone else to join us."

With a quiet excitement, Cornell whispered, "Look."

To the east, crawling their way along the next line of mountains, were towering orange flames and a black wall of newborn smoke. The wind was in Porsche's face. She could smell the blaze, and even at this distance, she could see its relentless advance.

Anticipating a question, Latrobe promised, "This site is safe. No need to worry."

"It only looks like a wildfire," Trinidad added. "It's really about as tame as your backyard barbecue."

Nathan was right; the conflagration was planned.

The first murmur of people could be heard working its way up the ridge. "Who are we waiting for?" asked Cornell.

Latrobe strolled up to Cornell, and paused. He was shorter but more massive. Despite the chill mountain air, his shirt was opened down the front, dark matted hair covering his chest. "Frankly, I was thinking of using you. But you're a talent, and you have experience, and a good strong back—"

There was a sharp little moan from below.

Everyone turned, in one motion. Two men appeared, including the soldier who had taken Latrobe's coffee mug. With an exhausted voice, the second man asked, "How much farther?"

"You've arrived, Mr. Kleck."

Latrobe bounced forward, offering his hand.

Timothy stared at the hand, then at the glass disk. Then he took a long, clumsy step backward, in panic.

"Now, now," Latrobe clucked.

"What do you want with me?"

"Your scintillating company." The man had a bully's laugh.

"Well, whatever the reason, I asked you to join us. So why don't you join us? Please?"

Timothy glanced at Porsche, pleading with his eyes, his slope-shouldered stance.

Latrobe was behind him, one hand suddenly shoving him in the back. He relished his work. With a wrestler's instincts, he countered his victim's attempts to slip right or left. Dirt and rock slipped underfoot. Then Timothy's big feet were skating across glass, finding no purchase, slipping out ahead of him as his frantic keening voice began shouting, "No, no! Stop, please!"

In the center of the disk, six scrupulously ordinary objects— the keys—were set in a wide circle, held firmly in place by the invisible intrusion.

Timothy's feet slipped between two of the keys, suddenly vanishing.

His voice became louder, and senseless, finding a rhythm and holding it. He tried to strike Latrobe, long arms flailing, the fists glancing off the shoulders and a forearm and gallons of dark air. Then his body was inside the intrusion, and he looked downward, struck mute in an instant, gazing in terror at the image of twisting space.

With a flourish, Latrobe gave a final strong shove, and Timothy vanished.

He smiled, saying, "Your friend would appreciate some support from his friends. Since he's stuck now in a very strange place."

Then Latrobe stepped forward, vanishing.

And suddenly Porsche was running, charging past the guards and up onto the glass, leaping feet-first back into Jarrtee.

A FIERCE RAIN STRUCK PORSCHE'S FACE AND SLICK NEWBORN BODY, yet she barely noticed. Permeating the rain was a brutal wind, like a great hand shoving her sideways, and it was inconsequential. There was mud underfoot and a lush blue-black forest on all sides, but she saw none of it. Nothing existed but a searing white light that fell from everywhere, piercing the rain and trees, and the world. And Porsche looked at her own silver-white body, struck blind by the radiance, eyelids shutting in reflex, the full strong hands of a grown woman flung over the jarrtee face.

Lightning sliced overhead, seeping between the bones of her fingers.

A rolling thunder pressed down, forcing out breath and blood, and Porsche nearly stumbled, taking a half-step backward before she found her gait, prying her hands off her closed eyes, then reaching out, trying to see by touch.

Her right hand brushed against a jarrtee arm, then a jarrtee's robust neck.

Through her hand, she could feel the person screaming. Then the thunder dissolved, and she heard his scream, shrill and endless, and pitiful.

Porsche gave the neck a hard shake, and she shouted, "Quiet," again and again. Then she said, "Timothy," with her new mouth, the name mangled but recognizable. And pulling his ear hole to her mouth, she repeated, more softly, "Quiet."

He understood the word, the new language. The shock of that was enough to silence him.

"You are fine. Alive, and fine," Porsche assured him, opening her eyes enough to see his silhouette, thin for a jarrtee, utterly hairless, silhouetted against the rough, purple-black trunk of a twanya tree.

Her uncle had once stepped from behind that tree, startling her.

Someone else stepped from behind it now.

The jarrtee man was clothed in black pantaloons and a hooded gray-black shirt, his face covered with an impenetrable mask of night-colored glass. He was carrying two sets of clothes and twin masks, and without sound, he offered one of each to Porsche.

She dressed in a rush, fumbling with the jarrtee snaps before her fingers remembered the tricks. Then she held the mask against her face, and through tearing, sore eyes, saw maybe a dozen men emerging from the forest, a pair of them calmly and efficiently grabbing Timothy, each holding an arm and inexplicably dragging him toward the twanya tree.

Nothing about Timothy struggled, except for his face.

He fought to keep his eyes down, and closed, his newborn mouth managing to call out a single jarrtee word:

"Mercy!"

Nearby, a thickly built jarrtee man pulled on the second pair of pantaloons, then donned the day mask, fastening it to his face in an instant, every motion crisp and expert.

Latrobe.

He sounded like Latrobe, yet the voice was unmistakably jarrtee. As his shirt went over his head, he ordered Timothy secured. "But loosely. Nicely." His men pressed Timothy's back against the trunk, then stretched his arms out on either side, wrists and ankles lashed together with silken ropes. Adjusting the hood with one hand, he gestured with the other, saying, "Relax. It's almost over, relax!"

What was almost over?

He said, "Give him a drink. Now."

There was another searing bolt of lightning, but Porsche's mask absorbed and canceled the brutal glare.

Someone appeared on her right, eyes shut, walking out of the intrusion. She didn't need to hear a voice to know him. "Trinidad," she muttered, and for an instant, she was ready to fight. Fists and feet, if need be. Anything to hurt him. But a second figure emerged behind him, staggering with his first muddy step; in a louder voice, she cried out, "Cornell!"

Latrobe's men were prying open Timothy's mouth, forcing a spout down his throat and feeding him something liquid.

Suddenly she smelled a rich lard-and-blood stew.

More clothes and masks were brought for the newcomers. Porsche dressed Cornell, adjusting his mask and then readjusting her own mask. How did he feel? What could he see? He pointed, then said, "Timothy . . . what are they doing to him?"

She didn't know.

"Food will make him estivate faster," she offered. "But why they have to treat him that way . . . I wish I knew. . . ."

Timothy made a loud choking sound, a slice of clotted blood slipping from his lips and down his bare, unnippled chest.

"Enough!" was Latrobe's verdict. "Now, paint and puncture!"

Of all things, an umbrella was produced. One man held it over Timothy while two others cleaned and dried his chest. Then a template and ink gun appeared, and the gun screeched, air driving golden ink into the flesh with force enough that the man twisted in agony, his mouth gaping, lips rimmed with a vivid red goo.

Porsche advanced on Latrobe, shouting, "What are you doing?"

The other men closed ranks, and from beneath their shirts came blunt, deceptively simple looking weapons.

Jarrtee rip-guns, she realized.

Where was Trinidad? She scanned the gathering. He was dressing. No one kept her from him. Putting her mask flush against his mask, she shouted, "Did you get those weapons for them?"

"And more." She could hear the smile. "I can show you. Come see!"

The ink gun sputtered, died. The template was removed, exposing a complex and vaguely familiar insignia: The radiant reddish-gold blaze of the jarrtee sun. Then one man deftly forced the head forward and down, shoving a curled metal blade into the base of the neck, leaving a neat deep wound.

"Painted and punctured, sir!"

"Now wrap him," Latrobe called out.

The ropes were untied. The prisoner was smothered under a heavy anthracite-colored blanket. Then the blanket was cinched tight, and except for a lone sob, Timothy gave no sign of being awake, or even alive.

"Come see," Trinidad repeated, almost gleefully.

A muddy trail led downhill from the intrusion, boots and bare feet leaving overlapping tracks relentlessly filled with warm rainwater. The forest surrounding them couldn't be more lush, walls of foliage stacked against one another, fruits and flowers maturing in the afternoon light. Already, Porsche could feel her new body sensing the hour, the endless light, her flesh growing heavier with every step, reflexively descending into estivation.

Food and darkness would force Timothy there sooner. In a few minutes, perhaps. Which would be, in a sense, a blessing. The man wasn't any real talent. Unconscious, he would remain immune to the corrosive effects of being alien.

She glanced over her shoulder. Cornell and an armed man were following closely, and the rain kept pouring through the high, wind-tossed canopy, and for that moment, all she could think was that wearing the mask was another blessing.

Cornell couldn't see her face.

He had no idea how lost she felt just now.

Hidden in the forest was a tiny city.

Jarrtee military tents huddled beneath the largest trees, camouflaged with colors and chaotic patterns and electronic means that were purely jarrtee. "When the Few abandoned this world," Trinidad chimed, "we stockpiled a variety of equipment. For the night we returned, I suppose."

"And you borrowed from the stockpiles," she prompted.

"I took *everything*." He was nodding like a human, adding, "This entire area is swaddled in electronic camouflage. Unless a living patrol walks into camp, nobody can find us."

"Are there daytime patrols?"

"More than there used to be," he confessed. "But the City still keeps most of its forces on a normal nocturnal calendar."

Most of the tents were empty. But there was room for several hundred soldiers, perhaps more. Judging by the self-transporting crates and bulky sacks, there were enough arms to equip several companies of soldiers. She thought of people left behind in New Mexico. It wasn't an invasion force, but it was a force nonetheless. The only limits were the troops themselves. "If you bring them over," she asked, "how long before they lose their sanity?"

"The bulk of the troops? An earth day or two, maybe." Trinidad paused, then added, "If they are brought over, of course."

She tried to concentrate, to anticipate the plan.

Her cousin seemed to assume everything was transparently simple. "Of course they're just an emergency measure. A bit of firepower waiting in the wings."

She said nothing.

"Our operation centers on two dozen picked soldiers," he continued. "I helped Latrobe comb the military for the best available talents."

"The soldiers in the . . . in the rotor machines . . . ?" Cornell sputtered.

"Sturdy souls, all," Trinidad proclaimed.

Porsche felt less sturdy by the moment. She hesitated on the lee side of an enormous needle-nut tree, asking, "Am I suppose to estivate, too?"

"Not at all," her cousin replied, perplexed. "Why would we want that?"

A sturdy hospital lay half-buried in the mountainside, its roof built of green lumber and mud overlaid with ceramic armor. Inside, past a triple-sealed door, was a delicious volume of darkness. Porsche lifted her mask immediately. She could still feel the daylight, but it wasn't as insistent or intoxicating. Against the roof of her mouth, she smelled disinfectants and ozone and new odors that refused to trigger memories. A smooth-faced nurse or doctor welcomed Trinidad by name, a mixture of human and jarrtee smiles fading when she turned toward Porsche. "Remove your shirt," she commanded. "And turn your back to me."

Porsche looked at the trailing soldier, and obeyed.

"What about him?" asked the doctor, meaning Cornell.

"He gets the treatment, too," Trinidad replied, lifting his mask, his face exactly as Porsche had imagined it would be.

A chilling dose of electricity struck at the base of her neck, and she heard the distinct tearing sound as tight jarrtee skin was being cut open, just a little bit, giving the doctor a place to shove a cartridge no bigger than the final joint of a thumb.

"It's a hormone packet," Porsche guessed. "We wore them when we left Jarrtee."

"Yes," said Trinidad, "and no."

The doctor picked up an implement for suturing, then warned, "You'll probably earn a scar. I'm sorry."

Her voice was decidedly unsorry.

Porsche winced with the first suture, then asked Trinidad, "What do you mean, *no?*"

"When we were escaping, we used simple biorhythmic hormones," her cousin explained. "Crude, and short-term effective. But hormones fool the body only temporarily, with a great cost. In the years since, circadian studies have made enormous strides, and so have technical tricks like these masks." He paused, then added, "As it happens, the Order of Fire is responsible for most of these miracles."

The second suture brought more pain, but she sat motionless, showing nothing.

"What you're having implanted—what everyone in this camp

uses—is a package of hormones and stress peptides, plus the genetic machinations of a diurnal species. The Order employs a distant relative of ours." He paused, then asked, "Do you remember the terrors, Po-lee-een?"

"Jey-im and I used to study them," she replied.

"That's right. I had forgotten."

Trinidad was lying. She looked at him carefully, watching the eyes dance inside the big sockets, and she asked, "Am I diurnal now?"

"What you are," he replied, "is free. Your body is ready to be awake for a full forty cycles, day or night."

"This is what the Order does?"

"Routinely," he said. "Avidly. Religiously."

"The golden star. . . ." Cornell began. "You painted it on Timothy. . . ."

"It's the Order's symbol," Porsche offered. "We wore them, years ago. . . ."

"And to decent people across Jarrtee," said Trinidad, "it's the symbol of a terrible civil war."

The pressure against Porsche's neck lessened, vanished.

"Remember, cousin? How we grew up full of confidence in the jarrtee life? Generations came and went, but the City would always stand beside the Dawn Sea, and our blood would continue living happy, prescribed lives in the same homes, for unbroken millenia. . . ."

"Finished," the doctor announced.

"Cornell's next," Trinidad commanded, strolling in front of them.

The doctor held a laser scalpel in one hand, the nerve-deadener in the other. "Sit here, and tilt your head. Like that, yes."

Cornell sat beside Porsche, his profile tight and simple. With a matching voice, he asked, "What made everything change?"

"Jarrtee has always been just half a world," Trinidad replied. "People lived in the night, and that other realm, the mysterious day, was as inaccessible to us as the molten core under our feet."

"The day was an empty niche," Cornell offered.

"Essentially, yes."

"Hold still now," the doctor warned.

Porsche watched her make the quick incision.

"And secondly?" Cornell managed.

"The Order of Fire has been growing for a long time." Trinidad paused, looking speculatively at the shadowy ceiling. "It was always a borderline faith, but every city-state had some little chapter among its subclans. They were tolerated, in part, because the chapters served as conduits in times of disaster and war.

"The Order's evolution quickened when God-Stole-Our-Sky," he continued. "The stars had vanished, and suddenly it seemed very important to put aside territorial differences and start to share scientists and laboratories."

"When we emigrated," said Porsche, "the Order was still very small."

"Not as small as you'd think," Trinidad warned. "And it was widespread. And by jarrtee standards, it was remarkably united."

The doctor inserted a slick white cylinder into Cornell's neck, the motion deft, much-practiced. Then she collected the thick dribble of blood, filing it away. Why? And how many times had she performed the same operation?

"For the first time on this world," her cousin announced, "we have a community based on ideas, not genetics."

"But the Order still has to estivate," Porsche guessed.

"In shifts, yes. Like human sleep. Most estivate by night, but not all." Trinidad paused, sauntering over to Cornell and kneeling, making eye contact. "A new niche is being exploited. Can you guess the result?"

Porsche could feel the first rush of hormones. A morning hunger stirred in her stomach, and despite herself, she began to relax.

"Is it that simple?" she asked. "An implant in the neck?"

"The most devout believers undergo exotic surgeries," Trinidad allowed. "The eyes are modified. Pigments are added, and the body temperature is raised. Plus newborns are being genetically altered while they're inside their father's pouches."

"Normal people are scared," Cornell guessed.

"Like they've never been scared before. Yes."

"And who are we supposed to be?" asked Porsche.

Her cousin straightened, asking, "Where's that template, Doctor?"

"Beside the door." Her voice softening.

"Thanks."

Porsche watched the doctor as she watched Trinidad. It had been years since she had looked at a jarrtee face, but it was obvious, in a glance, that the woman and her cousin were lovers. Probably on two worlds and as two species.

"Each of us wears *this* on our chest."

The template showed a simple crown. Porsche instantly recognized the shape.

"Black ink," Trinidad added. "With coded markers to prove authenticity."

Boys wore crowns at the dawn feast; she mentioned it to Cornell, who growled, "I remember."

Trinidad pulled off his shirt, his platinum chest rippling with muscles and the overlapping jarrtee ribs. "The City uses special troops by day. Certain irregular units roam the mountains, helping to defend their people from the warriors of the sun."

"Using the enemy's own biochemical tricks," added the doctor, with delight.

"That's us," said Trinidad, squeaking out a little laugh. "We're great heroes to the City. We can move where we want by day, almost with impunity."

"Which is the idea, isn't it?" asked Porsche.

"Our employer wants knowledge," said Trinidad, sitting on Porsche's left. Then he bowed his head for the doctor, adding, "This world's finest minds are at the Master's School. They're estivating now. Estivating inside a new high-security facility deep beneath the City, as it happens."

No one spoke.

Then Trinidad confessed, "This has been a daunting project. It took months to collect the necessary equipment, Few-made and otherwise. It's taken months to recruit and train Latrobe's recruits and build this base camp, and of course we've made several dry runs into the City—"

"You should feel proud," said Porsche, lacing her voice with as much acid as she could manage. "I know I feel proud just knowing you."

In profile, Trinidad's face was calm, almost inert.

But his voice betrayed anger, breaking for an instant as he said, "What you don't know is so huge, Po-lee-een. Next to what you do!"

Their chests wore ink crowns, and their bodies were carried along by the sophisticated implants. Together, Cornell and Porsche put on their shirts and masks, then accompanied by the guard, stepped out into the temporary calm between storms.

Trinidad remained behind, speaking to the doctor for a moment.

Men were walking through camp, each of them towing a big jarrtee stretcher—silk and aerogel frames riding on float fields. On the first stretcher was a single passenger wrapped in a black blanket. *Timothy.* The other stretchers held two or three bodies, some long and some exceedingly short, and she looked at the strange parade for a very long moment before she could admit to herself, finally, who these people were.

"Please, miss," said one of the men. The soldier from the helicopter?

"Just order her to move," barked his companion, mangling a name afterwards. Alvarez? Was that what he called the soldier?

She looked at their masks, imagining the eyes behind them. Then she quietly and furiously asked, "Where are you taking these people?"

Someone gently grabbed her fist with his hand.

She expected Cornell, but found her cousin standing beside her instead. "All of them are doing fine, Po-lee-een. Fine."

She retrieved her fist.

"Would you rather have them awake and scared, or estivating in safe surroundings, unaware of everything?"

Cornell called out, "Which one's my father?"

No one responded.

"Don't worry about either family, Po-lee-een."

Timothy's stretcher was pulled past her, leaving the camp behind. "What about him?" she asked. "Where is he being taken?"

"That one I'm sorry about." Trinidad retreated a half-step, then admitted, "It was Latrobe's idea. I told him it's not necessary, but it could be worse. He originally wanted to use your boyfriend."

"Use him how?"

Cornell was moving from stretcher to stretcher, calling out, "Dad! Dad!"

"How?" she repeated.

"We need credibility once we reach the City." The voice hinted at complicated emotions. "We want to have a prisoner to offer to the security forces—"

"The insignia on his chest," she sputtered, "and the cutting of his neck—"

"Yes," her cousin replied. "That's what we like to do with our captives. The Defenders of the Dawn, I mean. They wrench out the implants, forcing them to estivate."

Porsche was ready to hit him.

It would do no good. But she was furious and tired of being tempted by helplessness, her arms almost shaking inside the wide sleeves, her endless nervous energies and the cumulative effects of hormones demanding action.

Then, another voice.

A strange voice, but familiar. Painfully familiar.

"Is that her?" said a jarrtee girl.

Porsche saw Latrobe strolling through the tent city, delicately holding a tiny hand that was connected to a walking stack of lumpy clothes. Staring out of the hood was an adult's long black mask.

"Aunt," she heard, in pure jarrtee. Then a mangled, half-human, "Porsche."

Clare.

Porsche sprinted toward her, and the girl tried to slip from Latrobe's grasp, shouting, "Let me go! Let me go!"

Latrobe lifted his free hand, in warning.

"Your niece demanded to see you," he explained. His voice was soft, almost purring. "And I thought you might appreciate the gesture."

Porsche made herself stop, made herself breathe.

"Hugs, hugs, Aunt Porsche. Please?"

Kneeling in the deep mud, she took the girl around her waist and pulled her hand free of Latrobe's hand, asking, "Do you know where you are, Clare?"

"Yes," she said, without hesitation. "This is one of those secret places."

"That's right."

"My mother said we were coming here," Clare reported, "but I'm not supposed to tell anyone about it afterwards."

"That's best," Porsche offered.

"I feel funny. Sleepy, and funny."

She said nothing, glancing up at Latrobe.

"Everyone will be here, waiting for us," he reported. "Waiting for you. Sleeping nice and sound, won't you, Clare?"

The girl said nothing.

"Fuck off," said Porsche, under her breath.

Cornell was nearby. He was unwrapping one of the blanketed figures. A pale old face suddenly lay exposed, the flesh permanently creased by hundreds of estivations that it had never experienced, the shape of the bones and something in the stance reminiscent of his father. Of poor Nathan.

"Everyone will be home again soon," Latrobe kept assuring Porsche.

Or himself.

"Know what, Aunt Porsche?"

She swallowed, then asked, "What, Clare?"

"I've got something pretty. This man gave it to me."

Porsche felt her heart ache and her blood clot, and she shuddered, asking, "What did he give you, Clare?"

"Look."

In a single motion, without a shred of embarrassment, Clare pulled her oversized shirt up to her face, exposing her chalky white chest and the brilliant ruddy-gold image of the sun, the fresh ink looking almost wet in the wet light.

"Pretty," said the shirt-muffled voice. "Isn't it pretty?"

Because nothing else would do any good, Porsche hugged her niece again, saying, "It's very pretty, dear. It's beautiful."

PORSCHE AND CORNELL WERE LED AWAY FROM THE TENTS, DOWN through the dripping woods.

The foliage was sun-fattened and sloppily exuberant, every long leaf polished to a black metallic sheen and every stem bowing under the cumulative weight. Masses of brilliant flowers promised the world gifts of cocktails and pollen. Cackling roars and musical wails filled the rain-saturated air. Sometimes there was a squawk or grunt underfoot, in warning, and sometimes there was nothing—no sound but the distinct impression of something behind the brush, calmly watching them pass.

Occasionally the lead soldier would pause, crouching as he lifted his free hand, waiting for an excuse to fire his rip-gun.

A trailing soldier caught Porsche's eye. His build and demeanor felt familiar, and there was something incriminating in the way he wouldn't look at her directly. Drifting back toward him, she asked, in a whisper, "Were you beside me in the helicopter?" Then, catching his scent against the roof of her mouth, "That other man called you . . . Alvarez, was it?"

He said nothing, and everything. Alvarez gripped the rip-gun until the handle creaked, and he tilted back his mask, as if expecting paratroopers to attack.

"Thank you," she offered. "For helping the children open their toys, I mean."

"Go on," he croaked. Then, "Ma'am."

They came upon a sudden mountain road. It was narrow, hacked from rock and titanic gray-green roots, and it was crowded with float-cars, armored and camouflaged, each one battered by collisions and cratered by rip-gun rounds. Porsche and Cornell were delivered to the smallest car, climbing up to the rear door, then down inside. A pair of masked figures sat in the front, on matching seats, singing a pop song popular on the earth ten years ago. When the door was sealed, sunlight dropping to an endurable glow, the driver lifted his mask and turned. "So how's the bass fishing here, Miss Neal?"

Beneath the jarrtee face were traces of his human appearance. "That ugly cut healed," she observed.

"Till I'm home again." He smiled only with his eyes, like a true jarrtee. "Isn't that how it works? Unless I'm gone for several weeks, in which case I'll have a sweet little scar."

There was a sudden *bang*.

The drivers dropped and sealed their masks, then struck the ceiling twice. The rear door opened with a little shriek, and a burly jarrtee climbed inside, shaking off the first drops of a fresh torrent. Filling a pivoting seat in the back end, Latrobe had barely settled when he barked, "Go!" And as they accelerated, following a tanklike vehicle, he lifted his mask and told the prisoners to do the same.

He was a simple-faced jarrtee, just as he had been a simple-faced human. But his eyes were no longer tiny, closing and opening again with a strange liquid satisfaction.

From beneath his robe, he produced an elegant piece of jarrtee engineering. A wrist cuff. "Precautions," he purred. "Show me your hands."

Porsche's left wrist was fastened to Cornell's right.

Latrobe sat back, totally at east. Gazing through a blackened side window, he said, "I forgot to ask. Have I mastered your old language?"

"You sound . . . reasonable . . ."

The man snorted, then said, "Better than reasonable, and you know it."

Cornell stared at Latrobe, then as if bored, closed his eyes.

The forest vanished abruptly. Below them, the entire rain-soaked slope had pulled free of the mountain, acres of mud and shattered tree trunks choking a narrow valley. The newest storm was already eroding the fresh slope. Sudden little streams carried silt, and gravity pulled at the streams, using the silt like the teeth on a power saw.

Then just as abruptly they were back under the canopy again, the storm blunted, no road beneath them, the way carpeted with felt grass and weedy flowers.

"Where's Trinidad?" asked Cornell.

Latrobe laughed. "Everywhere?"

The men up front laughed, too. It was an old joke.

"No, really. He's riding in that machine up ahead. We've laid down a line of eavesdroppers, from here to the City, and he's watching for trouble."

"I hope he's being helpful," she growled.

"Nothing but," said Latrobe, cheerfully.

Cornell's new hand felt slick and hot. Sometimes Porsche would glance at him, and sometimes she felt his eyes on her. But they avoided trading looks, and they never spoke to one another.

After a little while, Porsche looked back at Latrobe. "Can I ask something?"

"Maybe."

"Why bother with me?" She looked forward again, watching the colorless, endless rain turned to fog by the car's force field. "Trinidad has the Few-made tools, and he has the expertise. He knows this world as well as I do. Better, since he's obviously been here recently—"

"All true," said Latrobe.

"I'm weight. I'm a wild element. You're using more than a dozen hostages to keep me under control, and they must be a complication, too."

"You must be important," Latrobe assured.

"It's something that I offer, that Trinidad can't give you."

"Indeed," the singsong voice replied. "In fact, we went to considerable trouble to have your timetable and ours match up. Remember your cousin's extremely charitable gift? The agency's guidebook to acceptable mayhem?"

"It was a fake," Cornell groaned.

"Hardly, but that's not my point."

"You were delaying us," said Porsche. "You wanted us busy while you were getting everything set up here."

"It was your cousin's idea," Latrobe confessed.

"A good one," she grumbled.

A big hand casually patted her on the shoulder, as if trying to give comfort. "But what about your first question? What would make you so damned important for us to go to this incredible bother?"

"Tell me."

"Of course I'll tell," Latrobe responded. "Why else do you think you're here?"

The driver and his buddy were laughing again, almost cackling. Nothing in the world could be funnier, it seemed.

"There is a man," Latrobe began. "A jarrtee, naturally. He happens to live in your old City. The poor shit. He has a thankless job and a dull, dreary life. A marriage gone stale. Children who barely notice him. The kind of life that might drive someone to suicide, provided he had the courage.

"A few days ago—jarrtee days, I mean—the poor shit receives a very peculiar, utterly unexpected communication. A voice on an audio line refers to him by name, asking how he's been. 'Who are you?' he responds, although maybe he recognizes the voice. Just a little, maybe. 'Where are you?' he asks, trying to trace the call to its origin, and finding none.

"The voice won't identify itself, but it asks about the man. How is he? Is he happy? The voice hopes that he's happy, which is nice to hear. Then the voice apologizes. It apologizes for past sins, never exactly saying what those sins are, and it hopes that the man will find reason to forgive."

Porsche sat motionless, barely breathing.

"Jump ahead one jarrtee day," Latrobe continues. "Our poor fellow works an unpopular schedule because it means relative wealth for his ungrateful family, and on the positive note, he's learned that he prefers a measure of solitude. His job gives him that cherished solitude. And it's a rather important job, I should add."

He paused for an instant, then continued.

"Like I said, it's the next day. And again he receives another mysterious call. Again, audio only. But the voice talks to him for a long, long time, giving away its identity through what it knows. He might have suspected who it was, but now he knows. And the man finds himself thrilled to hear the woman."

No one spoke, or moved.

"Longing," said Latrobe.

He said, "The poor shit discovers a longing. A delicious romantic love. 'Are you nearby?' he asks her. She says, 'Yes.' 'Can I see you sometime?' But she's playing it coy, making no promises. 'It wouldn't be a good idea,' she warns. Then suddenly, as if frightened by her own romantic ideas, she says, 'I have to go now.'

" 'Will you call me again?' he asks.

" 'Maybe,' she concedes. But of course, she calls. That very next day, as it happens. At the usual time. Noon. The sun at its apex, and the world looking its most hellish."

"*She* is Trinidad," Porsche muttered.

"With his voice doctored, yes. But this time, the third time, there's a video image, too. Trinidad had his face doctored digitally—a trick that we backwoods humans could pull off—making him look like another. And he smiles at that poor lonely shit. 'I can't talk long,' Trinidad says. And the man asks, 'Where are you? Where have you been?' Then the poor shit calls her by the name that he hasn't used in years. 'Po-lee-een,' he calls out, 'I have missed you so much. So much!' "

More than anything, what chilled Porsche was the ease with which Latrobe mimicked the voices. In the voices, she could hear herself, and she could hear the deliberate and steady voice that she hadn't heard since she was a young girl.

"Jey-im," she whispered.

Cornell was staring at her, in astonishment.

Porsche settled deeper into her seat, numbed to the wobbling of their car and the relentless roar of the new storm. Then just as quickly, she collected herself, straightening her back to show resolve. With a glance over her shoulder, she asked, "How is Jey-im?"

"Eager," Latrobe offered. "Ecstatic, even."

The men in front were cackling like little children.

"Why not? His long-lost girlfriend is coming to see him." Latrobe smiled with the broad wet eyes. "It's all arranged. The time, the place. And what happens afterwards, too."

No one spoke.

Again, Latrobe patted her on the shoulder, lending strength. "You don't know this, but you made Jey-im a large promise. You told him that you can take him away from his bland circumstances. You're going to show him the way to an alien world. A beautiful, exciting wonderland—"

"But for a price," said Cornell.

"I forgot an important detail." Latrobe relished the moment. "Jey-im works the day shift as a high-ranking member of City security. It's his job to help defend certain estivating jarrtees in this time of civil unrest. Politicians are under his watch. And the wealthiest families. Not to mention the entire scientific establishment—"

"Shit," Cornell muttered.

"And Jey-im is willing to help us?" Porsche asked, halfway astonished.

"Without hesitation, it seems." Latrobe kept laughing, and his men with him. Eyes bounced in their big sockets as he joyfully asked, "Isn't it delicious? Two worlds, and such different worlds. Yet on both, men are willing to sell their souls for a piece of ass!"

LATROBE KEPT UP THE BRIEFING, PREPARING PORSCHE WITH THE smooth surety of an experienced coach. He quoted every word that Trinidad, wearing her face, had said to Jcy-im, and Jey-im's exact responses, and the tone of his voice, and the language of his body and adoring face. Then Latrobe paused, just for a half-instant, before asking, "Would you like to see that adoring face?" And from a blood-colored pouch, he pulled out the jarrtee equivalent of a snapshot, remarking, "I'm not the one to judge, but he strikes me as a respectable-looking man. Even handsome, almost."

Porsche stared at the holo image, seeing nothing. Then Cornell pulled the soft crystal sheet out of her hand, asking afterwards, "Can I?"

Latrobe began to laugh, and as an aside, he mentioned to Cornell, "As I understand it, that thing you're holding isn't just a photograph, it's some sort of camera, too. And it has a huge memory. And it's nearly indestructible. According to agency estimates, it will revolutionize photography on the earth—a twenty-billion-dollar business overnight, and every patent belonging to US industries."

No one spoke for a long while.

Then Latrobe resumed his work. With a narrowing focus, he

explained where they were going and what was expected of Porsche and of Jey-im, and sometimes he would interrupt himself, asking questions, testing her retention of important details, and inane ones, too.

Her answers were always crisp and correct. Yet Porsche felt detached, remote—as if someone else were borrowing her voice.

At one point, Porsche asked to see the photograph again.

Cornell handed it to her without comment.

As promised, Jey-im had an attractive, even appealing face. He was wearing nothing but his subclan markings, the colors washed out by the noon sunshine. His belly pouch had roughened lips—a telltale sign of having carried children. The wide black eyes showed a hopefulness suffused with an old despair. Porsche felt pity for the man, but at the same time, she was careful not to feel pity for herself. Or anger. Or anything else useless.

She handed back the photograph, then looked outside. Their little convoy had left the mountains behind, and in the open, the vehicles had moved apart from each other, as a tactical precaution. The roaring storm had fallen back to a gale-force calm, and she could see the long fields of day-ripened lappa nuts and oil grains, and once, the blockish, half-buried shapes of jarrtee homes. The homes were exactly as she remembered them, except for one sobering detail: Enormous automated rip-guns were set on the steep Tefloned roofs. In case the convoy belonged to the Order, the stubby barrels followed their progress, the house AIs ready to defend their estivating farmers.

When the convoy passed the houses, the wind suddenly strengthened, a high-pitched roar bringing a wall of steamy rain that crashed over them, erasing every trace of the outside world.

The men in the front weren't giggling anymore. Together, as a team, they were driving into the storm, using instruments to keep on course.

A palpable nervousness lay in the air. The briefing was finished, apparently. Latrobe began to contact the other vehicles in turn, speaking on scrambled channels, in a twisted English, asking questions and offering the same confident, comforting words. It wasn't just the weather that brought concern; a critical checkpoint lay ahead. If they wanted to enter the City uncontested, they had to pass through it. But if they missed the checkpoint, even by accident, they instantly became the enemy.

Cornell was looking straight ahead, staring into the maelstrom of furious air and water. Without looked at Porsche, he said, "The City is gone."

What?

"Washed to the sea," he announced. Then he half-laughed, glancing at her for an instant while admitting, "I can't believe anything could survive this weather."

She wanted the City destroyed, for an instant. She pictured them coming to a newborn shoreline, no one left to kidnap, and what choice would Latrobe have but to order them to turn and drive home?

But then she thought of the forty million dead and the fish gnawing on bloating bodies, and the daydream collapsed.

"Now you know why we're such great engineers," she mentioned, a whiff of pride in her voice.

The drivers were concentrating, hunkering over steering wheels with their shoulders tight and probably tired. Whenever the winds gusted, they would flinch, and the car would settle lower to the ground in response, sometimes slowing—and at least twice, when the howling reached its zenith, leaves and branches and muck and rock battered the force fields and armor, and the car just gave up, dropping to the ground and thrusting spikes into the pavement.

There was lightning, diluted by the protective windows but still relentlessly, piercingly bright.

Thunder followed, massive and sudden and rolling down to a sullen low roar that never quite died before the next bolt reenergized the air, shaking the car and its passengers with a god's malevolence.

Porsche found herself staring outside, nothing to say.

Sometimes she caught a glimpse of the armored truck ahead of them, tall and sturdy, and she imagined Trinidad sitting inside it, calmly orchestrating a multitude of Few-made eavesdroppers and weapons. No one else possessed such clear vision. Not in their convoy, or anywhere else in the City, most likely. And with that in mind, she placed her face against the window glass, mouthing words intended only for her cousin.

"You can't win," she warned him.

"If your father doesn't stop you," she assured, "someone else will. They won't let this go unpunished."

Then with her voice rising to a whisper, she said, "I don't understand you, Trinidad."

A sudden face appeared in the window.

Porsche flinched, for an instant. The black contours of the mask were bright with rain and a sudden flash of lightning. No emotion was betrayed, but one hand touched the glass curiously, silvery fingers outstretched, while the other hand lifted a rip-gun, tapping hard at the window with the stubby barrel, as if trying to break in.

"We've arrived," Latrobe announced.

The checkpoint.

Leaning forward, he placed his head between his prisoners, warning them, "Speak if they speak to you. But keep to the story. Understood?"

"What about the cuffs?" asked Cornell.

"What cuffs?"

Moments ago, on a signal, the bond around their wrists had dissolved, leaving nothing but the strong aroma of plastic and a ghostly pressure, Cornell and Porsche lifting their arms in the same motion, as if they were still lashed tightly together.

Everyone was ordered out into the rain, then told to stand in the open, masked faces pointed into the wind and their least favorite hands extended, palms up. Latrobe had positioned himself beside Porsche, and when the checkpoint's soldiers appeared, armed and swaggering, he placed his right hand firmly on the back of her head—a gesture of ownership, everyone warned that this big woman was his mistress.

She obeyed instructions, trying to act the part by tilting her head toward him; but beneath her mask, she allowed herself a tight, bitter grimace.

The ranking officer paused before them. Shouting over the rain, he asked, "How was the hunting?"

"Excellent," Latrobe replied.

A second officer held a needle-tipped probe, and with the crisp brutality of someone who did little else, she jabbed the needle into Porsche's upturned palm, drawing a million times more blood and tissue than required by the mandatory test.

In moments, Porsche's genetic material was examined, then matched against existing files.

Trinidad must have used Few techniques to build false identities. After that, it was a simple trick to alter the City's records, making files to match each member of the team. No one would doubt the sequencing of base pairs; certainly not the bored guards working in the midst of a terrific rainstorm.

"How many do you claim taken?" asked the first officer.

"Forty-three," Latrobe answered, with a tangible, well-practiced pride. He handed over a digital record of the fire-fights, adding, "We also have a prisoner for you."

That brought a surge of interest. The officer straightened, declaring, "It *was* a good hunt."

Porsche shook her sore hand.

"I see why you brought so many." Envy sharpened the officer's voice. His slick mask focused on Porsche for a moment. "A little vacation for the battle worn, is it?"

"With plenty of bounty money to spend," Latrobe replied.

"Show us what you have," the officer said, the demand wrapped in a false amiability. Then, "Come with us."

The officer was speaking to Porsche.

Glancing at a manifest displayed in a corner of his mask, he called her by her new name. "Po-lee-een," he said. "Keep me company, if you please."

Trinidad would have chosen the name.

He must have thought that Po-lee-een was too ordinary of a name to raise suspicions, if any suspicions remained. And the easy irony was too hard to resist.

Latrobe and the officer were walking together, Porsche remaining a half-step behind her supposed lover. She forced herself not to look back at Cornell. What mattered was playing this role to her best. Nothing was finished, nothing decided. Then she noticed Trinidad standing at attention like everyone else, his palm extended patiently, and she walked past him without looking toward his face, without even whispering the incandescent insults that kept swirling through her head.

The convoy's lead vehicle had its large doors propped open, seemingly for them. The trio climbed inside, into the room-sized cavity and out of the rain.

Porsche saw an armored box meant to hold munitions. Strapped to the top of the box—by his arms and legs—was a long and relatively frail jarrtee man, estivating on the brink of death.

She would recognize Timothy Kleck on any world.

The officer pulled off the blanket, examining the insignia that covered the narrow white chest, then fingered the gouged neck, and finally, he pried open both of the blind, old-fashioned eyes.

"A convert," was his verdict.

"But he has some rank," said Latrobe. "You'll see."

Stepping back, the officer quoted a modest sum, adding, "With more coming, if the judges' council upholds your claims."

Latrobe straightened his back. "That seems weak," he muttered. Then he added, "Sir," with a careful low voice.

The officer was accustomed to complaints. With a calm irritability, he said, "I see a hundred prisoners every day. Most haven't belonged to the Order for a single year. Maybe one prisoner, if that, reveals anything of substance under interrogation."

He was speaking to Latrobe but watching Porsche instead. "Either way, I can't authorize any larger payment. You know the policy. As soon as the City has measured this man's worth—"

"How soon?" Latrobe interrupted.

"Not very. I understand that they're backed up in security. Tomorrow morning is the soonest—"

"We never had this shit at the southern checkpoints," Latrobe spat. "Payment was quick and fair, always."

"I don't know how others work," the officer replied, immune to criticism.

"You're going to hold part of our bounty in your own tentacles, aren't you?"

The officer ignored him, approaching Porsche instead. "Do you think that I'm an unreasonable man?"

Was this a test?

"I am taking responsibility for this prisoner," he continued, "and that means that I accrue certain risks. What if he is innocent? I'm not claiming that's true. I don't know what's true. I've dealt with your group once or twice, and you play fair. But frankly, some of our irregulars have been known to kidnap good citizens, polish their skin clean, then decorate them to look like generals in the Order."

"I have soldiers to pay," Latrobe snarled. "For doing vital work under the sun, in the most miserable conditions imaginable."

The officer continued to ignore him.

Standing an arm's length from Porsche, he said, "You didn't answer me, Po-lee-een. Am I unreasonable?"

The man was testing her, but only for the most prosaic reasons. If she sided with him, then he would surely try to purchase her services from Latrobe. But why was Latrobe trying to piss him off? She thought for a moment, then understood. And to play along with the charade, she brought her mask close to the officer's mask, then said, "No, you aren't unreasonable. For being a cowardly pouch-fucked asshole."

The man's mask hid his features, but not his emotions.

He tried to stand taller, then gave a shrill command. "Take this prisoner!" he cried out.

Soldiers scrambled into the vehicle, moving fast.

Timothy was untied and carried carelessly by two soldiers. A third man held a computer in one hand, asking, "What is the prisoner's status, sir?"

The officer glanced at Latrobe, then Porsche.

"Suspected traitor," he replied. "Lowest priority."

In other words, Timothy would languish in a holding cell for a very long while, giving Latrobe and the others time to vanish.

"Weapons and munitions!" the officer shouted. "Surrender them, please! If you want your vacation now, I'd be advised that you hurry!"

They were disarmed, which had been expected: The City didn't relish the idea of armed irregulars roaming its streets, night or day. Timothy's stiff, immobile body was carried off into the rain, looking more like a sculpture than living tissue. Porsche found herself sitting in the car once again, cuffed to Cornell and moving into the City. Neither spoke, but with their masks removed, their black mood was obvious.

"Poor Mr. Kleck," Latrobe offered. "He awakens after dusk to find himself alone, trapped in a holding cell, inside an alien body, probably slated for a postmidnight interrogation."

Cornell was making fists, then squeezing, expending so much effort that his forearms trembled.

"It should be an interesting race," Latrobe continued. "Your friend isn't much of a talent, I would think. Insanity is guaranteed. But does he lose his sanity before the interrogators insert their electrodes and pump serums into his strange blood? Or is it the torture that pushes him off that cliff?"

Porsche didn't make fists or tremble with rage.

A strange calmness grew within her. Emotions were a currency, and she had none to spare.

In mutilated English, Cornell muttered, *"Cruel."* Then, *"You."* And finally, *"Fuck."*

Latrobe laughed amiably, patting him on the shoulder. "But I'm not the one who promised his safety. Am I?"

One driver giggled.

Otherwise, no one made a sound.

The spaceport passed on their right, the control tower surrounded by military vehicles, glistening ceramic runways stretching off into infinity, and one of the skeletal gantries calmly absorbing a titanic blue-white bolt of lightning.

Later, the convoy turned into an obscure alleyway, then pulled to a stop. Inside a long granite warehouse was a jumble of scrap machinery, and hidden inside a scrap tokamak were fresh weapons, rip-guns, and more powerful wonders wrapped tight inside electronic camouflage and simple oiled skins.

The weapons were handed out with a Christmas atmosphere.

A familiar figure appeared, rapping on the window glass with his knuckles, then climbing into the back with Latrobe.

Trinidad removed his mask, giving a half wink. "Good work at the checkpoint."

If anything, Porsche's calmness grew.

Latrobe asked, "Should you be here?"

"If things get complicated, I'll leave." Trinidad leaned back in the padded seat, saying, "No one suspects anything. Our route is clear. And our contact is already waiting. Eagerly waiting. And do you want to know how sweet our luck is? This is the last storm until dusk. Until we need it, the bad weather stays away."

The convoy was moving again, accelerating along a wide, otherwise empty avenue, the float mechanisms sending up geysers of gray rainwater.

Because he couldn't resist, Trinidad leaned forward, asking, "How does it feel to be back? Bittersweet?"

She said nothing.

"There aren't many changes that you can see. Even in the midst of civil war, jarrtees like to keep everything just so." Trinidad moved closer to Cornell, suspecting a better audience. "Look at that open field. Do you see it? That used to be a large, thriving neighborhood. But the Order sabotaged a shuttle, and that's where it impacted. Fully fueled, and the blast incinerated nearly nine thousand."

Porsche stared through the faltering rain, imagining the disaster.

Or maybe it had always been a field, and Trinidad was lying for no reason except that he could.

"I like the Order," he continued. "I know it's not the proper attitude for a member of the Few. All species are beautiful, but particularly those who are very kind and very dull."

In a tight, angry voice, Cornell asked, "Why are you talking to me?"

"Who says I am?" Trinidad leaned back again. "What I want to see is Jarrtee in another thousand years. I want to see who wins, and what's left. My vote goes toward the Order, though I don't think it'll be in charge. Something more placid, less daring, will grow out of it. But isn't that the way of rebellions? Like the United States. Conceived in a wave of idealism and latent power. Its pinnacle came in the last century, and since then . . . what? A long relentless decline, as inevitable as the need to piss three times in the night. Am I right?"

Latrobe responded. "When we bring out these scientists, everything changes."

"It will, it will," Trinidad sang.

The convoy was racing along the stone avenue, geysers flanking each vehicle.

Calmly, but with a whiff of bile at the edge of her voice, Porsche tried changing the topic.

"Just so I know," she said, "where is this meeting going to be held?"

Trinidad leaned forward again, close enough to taste her ear hole.

"You know where," he warned. "He's a romantic, and he needs privacy. A building left empty by day, and one with a strong sentimental hold—"

"The school," she muttered to herself.

"More precisely, the school's courtyard." Trinidad chuckled, saying, "You'll know exactly where to look for him, I think."

Porsche said nothing.

Her cousin leaned back and closed his eyes, laughing for a few moments. "Jey-im has been waiting in the rain for you. Where the terrors once built their nests. He looks so lovesick, Po-lee-een. So paranoid. So earnest."

"We should have dressed you up in drag," said Latrobe, his voice perfectly serious. "You could have fooled him, I bet. And we wouldn't have had to bother with *her.*"

"Except the poets on a million worlds are wrong," Trinidad countered. "Love is a lot of things, but it's never, ever blind."

$$\Large \epsilon\, 10 \,\epsilon$$

PORSCHE DIDN'T RECOGNIZE THE OLD FORTIFICATION AT A GLANCE. In memory, her former school was a place of darkness and simple pleasures wrapped within a child's perspective. But sitting inside the armored car, in daylight, the granite walls had an astonishing pinkness, the stainless-steel gates shone with a rapacious brilliance as the sun broke through the dying storm clouds, and there was something exceptionally bleak about the high smooth walls and the relentless lack of windows—not a jarrtee way of thinking, but it was hers.

"The west gate," said Trinidad, eyes closed in order to concentrate on a flood of data. "There's a small access door on the left. Unlocked. From there, I think you can find your way."

It was Latrobe who wished her "Good luck."

Porsche gave a little snort.

The cuffs dissolved again. Cornell lifted his freed arm, laid his hand across the back of her head, then turned her head, and with a forced calmness, he said, "Whatever happens . . ." and let his voice trail away, the last words left implied: "I love you."

A muddy rage was building. Porsche opened her mouth and said nothing, then took a deep breath and kissed him on the mouth—too lightly and too quickly—then removed his grasping hand and slowly, as if drugged, set the mask over her face once again.

The others donned their masks.

The overhead door opened with a screech, raw sunshine flowing into the cabin, buoying her up like water and depositing her on the flat wet paving stones outside; a mirror screech closed the door, and with a thin hiss, the car moved off to hide.

A firm shove opened the door, and it drifted shut once Porsche was inside.

She lifted her mask and quietly called out, "Hello."

The echo had a sharpness and an impatience, moving faster than any earthly echo, racing to the end of the ancient hallway and dashing back again, sounding like a stranger's voice, then taking a second lap, fading away in the end like a jarrtee question mark.

"Hello?" the building asked Porsche.

She walked on quiet feet, eyes adapting quickly to the gloom. Chill phosphorescent strips marked each classroom, and brighter strips illuminated doorways leading to the subbasements and the courtyard—escape routes for war and for earthquakes, respectively. Memories rose up from everywhere, yet nothing was where the mind expected it. She had always remembered how the floor was covered with tiny tiles—black-and-white; square and triangular—linked together to form seashells. But she had told Cornell that they looked like conch shells, which wasn't true. Pausing in front of the first familiar classroom, she stared at the floor, knowing that she had walked here barefoot hundreds and thousands of times. Yet instead of the expected ornate shell, she saw something relatively smooth, and simple, and worn. The remembered flourishes and much of its beauty had, it seemed, been conjured up by her homesick mind.

Above the room's locked door was a sloppy banner made of simple silk. Children had painted the big letters with the luminescent guts of nightflies. Their teacher must have given them specific instructions, but exuberance had won out. Each letter struggled to be larger and brighter than its neighbors. Dribbles and random flowers lent character. Porsche stared at the banner for an instant, struggling to read the City's dialect. And it didn't help that the flies' guts were tired of seeping light. Stepping closer, she consciously pulled her head to the right—to the beginning—and digested the words carefully, with the sturdy pace of a less-than-bright child.

"TO THE CITY, LOVE," she read. "TO THE ORDER OF FIRE, DEATH."

Porsche read the words a second time, just to be certain, then turned and began walking again, feeling someone or something urging her to hurry.

The building, perhaps.

Or more likely, Trinidad.

More banners dangled from the ceiling and above the doors, every class involved in the propaganda.

"THE ORDER WILL NOT STEAL OUR SOULS!" she read aloud, in a whisper.

Silently, she read, COOK THE INVADERS IN THEIR NESTS!

And over the door leading to the courtyard, she learned:

THE ORDER HIDES AMONG US: TRUST YOUR FRIENDS, BUT ONLY WITH YOUR SUSPICION!

Razored strips of sunlight slipped around the ancient aluminum door. Porsche secured her mask and shoved at the door, a staggering white-hot fire engulfing her. Squinting, she pushed against the light, navigating past the blurred outlines of twanya trees and leathery colo trees and a rank stand of black-black felt grass that roared at her with thousands of insect voices.

The jungle seemed shorter than before, and more impenetrable. She took one muddy path and found it blocked by a twisted mass of downed timber. The second path wandered off in the wrong direction entirely. Finally, she returned to the first path, obeying her instincts. Clever children had excavated a tunnel through the stack of rotting timber—a passage too small for adults. Porsche climbed instead, ignoring the masses of stinging vines and the nameless diurnal bloodsuckers, reaching the soft summit and finding a familiar face gazing up at her with a mixture of fury and surprise.

The terror was the size of a medium dog, and infinitely more menacing.

It wailed up at her with a piercing, chilling voice, its massive jaws opening like a rattlesnake's jaws, exposing the beautiful red flesh inside the long mouth, its long serrated canines shining like steel.

Porsche screamed back at it, lifting her arms high, trying to make herself look enormous, and fearless.

The terror didn't retreat, and it didn't have the chance to charge. It simply crumbled, knocked limp, a one-word command from Trinidad engaging a Few-made system, and suddenly the courtyard had fallen silent, not even the tiniest bug daring to squeak.

Porsche spoke first.

Not quite shouting, she said, "Jey-im," once, then again.

A muted voice came from somewhere below. "Po-lee-een? Is that you?"

She worked her way back to the ground, then followed the trail into a stand of young red trees.

"Is that you?" the quavering voice repeated.

Past the red trees was the familiar clearing, smaller and more constricted than she remembered. The jungle had crept closer in recent years. The sky was a window, brilliant but small. Porsche's very first thought was that the lovers who came here wouldn't be able to watch the sky as she had watched it. Then Jey-im appeared, standing in the brightness, and she realized that he had changed more than the clearing—in stature and weight, and showing the sculpting of time—yet strangely, she recognized him in an instant, and that despite the night-colored robe, despite the massive, doubly-thick mask.

"Po-lee-een," he muttered. "Is it?"

"Always," she replied.

But he acted skeptical, coming close but not quite touching

her, breathing hard for a few moments before asking, "Can we step into the shadows?" A security medallion hung around his neck, denoting his rank. "Can we show each other our faces?"

It was a painful ritual, thankfully brief.

Porsche clamped her eyes shut, then lifted her mask. In sympathy, Jey-im cupped his hands over her eyes, trying to protect them. Random colors swirled and faded away. She felt misery as well as a pair of thumbs wandering from her mouth to her cheeks and back again. Then a quiet, reverent voice gushed, "It *is* you," and he lowered her mask, admitting, "I had my doubts that you'd come."

"Of course I came," she countered. "Didn't I promise?"

He didn't answer, but instead said, "Now. Look at my face now."

She repeated the ritual, her hands flush against his rubbery eyes and her long, extremely strong thumbs playing over portions of his handsome face.

Blind now, wincing against the scorching light, Jey-im offered, "You're very beautiful still, I think."

Because it would help, she reflected his compliment. "And you're still very handsome, too."

Beneath her palms, the eyes began to smile, vibrating hard in their sockets. The man made a whistling sound, a kind of contented sigh, then clasped his white hands over hers, sucking air into his mouth once, then again. Much of jarrtee recognition was olfactory; it was one reason Trinidad couldn't keep pretending to be her. Then Jey-im suddenly pulled her hands to his chest, averting his face from the light, making her feel the feathery-quick beating of his hearts as he confessed, in agony, "I betrayed you . . . that one time . . . and for a long time I thought I did right . . ."

Once before, Jey-im had let her feel his honesty; she didn't intend to fall for that trick twice.

"Do you forgive me, Po-lee-een?"

"But I already have," she responded, avoiding the lie. Trinidad had accepted his apology for her, half a dozen times, at least.

"Please," he begged. "Forgive me now, please!"

Trapped, she whispered, "All right. I do."

"Yes?"

"Of course, yes!" She pulled her hands free, then slapped his mask into place. "But there's nothing to forgive. You were a child; I was an idiot. I'm the one who made the mistakes by telling you, and showing you—"

"Not mistakes!" he interrupted. "Now that I'm older and can understand . . . I mean, I'm thankful that you entrusted me with the truth."

Porsche took a short step backward, saying nothing.

"I've thought about you often. In the night, and by day, too. But always in secret, Po-lee-een." He seemed to come alive, talking about his devotion. "After I told my father what had happened, and all the security people, too . . . after that, I never again spoke about you or the sky that you showed me. Not to anyone. My wife knows nothing. My children, nothing. And I never even mentioned it again to my father."

Like an obedient dog, Jey-im had probably obeyed orders, but Porsche resisted the urge to cross-examine him.

Instead, she asked, "How is your father?"

There was a brief, telltale pause. Then he quietly admitted, "He died last year."

"I'm sorry," she offered, for no reason but politeness.

"There was an attack on the government," he explained. "The Order of Fire had set mines during the day—clever, undetectable mines—and several dozen administrators were killed the instant they sat at their stations."

The Order, it seemed, had a gift for surreal justice.

"It's just as I told you," he insisted, referring to past conversation. "This world has turned into a sad, wicked place. The fighting is endless. Not in the City, not yet. Here we just have incidents and bombings and mysterious disappearances. And we have carefully sanitized news. But at night, when the skies clear, people can see what's happening. Nuclear weapons and terrible energy beams are seen. Every night, another distant city-state burns itself into extinction. These creatures that we're fighting are everywhere, yet they aren't real enough to defeat. . . . which is their secret, I think. I think."

In different circumstances, Porsche could have told this timid man plenty.

But instead she simply conceded, "I see why you'd want to escape."

"I have nothing here anymore. Nothing worthwhile, surely."

"I know that," she reminded him.

Jey-im began to dance back and forth, years of pent-up emotion seeping out under pressure.

He asked, "Is it true? Can you take me to where you live?"

"Yes."

"Now?"

She shook her head, the human gesture baffling him. "Soon," she explained. "The intrusion is up in the mountains. When my work is finished, I can't see why you wouldn't be welcome."

The lie amazed Porsche.

She was stunned, simply stunned, to hear how easily she had told Jey-im what he was desperate to hear. Suddenly her words were hanging in the bright hot air, left to fend for themselves, and she could take a full step backward, waiting for her ex-lover to make the next move.

"This other world," he began uneasily. "Did you tell me about it?"

"No, I didn't."

"But what kind of place is it?" Liquid emotions passed across his face, and he confessed, "I wouldn't want anything too strange."

"It's not too different from Jarrtee," she told him. Then, fearing that might scare him, she added, "And in other ways, it is."

Jey-im acted disappointed, and afraid, and more than anything else, curious. He took a deep contemplative breath, then asked, "What is the world's name?"

"EE-arth," she managed, remembering when she had first heard that word. The moment; the speaker; the mood.

Jey-im didn't try repeating it. Instead, he took another careful breath, then asked, "What will I look like?"

There was bare ground beneath an old colo tree, and kneeling, she began to draw simple portraits in the mud—a woman first, then a taller man with his hand gripping the woman's head from behind. Neither figure wore clothes or hair. In crisp detail, she described humans, carefully mentioning everything that Jey-im would find comforting as well as everything comfortably strange.

There was a long pause.

Then, once again, Jey-im asked, "What was the world's name?"

She repeated the clumsy word, then added, "*Soil.* That's what the name means."

With two fingertips, he touched the male human's face, then the groin, smudging both features. "And if I don't like this soil-world?"

"Thousands more are in easy reach," she promised.

He rose. "And wherever I go . . . will you stay with me?"

With the smallest finger on her left hand, Porsche repaired the face, lending it a sorrowful grin.

"If you still love me, I mean. . . ."

Trinidad was watching. She could clearly feel the pressure of unseen eyes, the electric sense of anticipation.

"Please, Po-lee-een," he whispered, "tell me how you feel toward me."

Thankful for the mask, Porsche looked up and replied with a delicate firmness, "I have always loved you, Jey-im."

He sagged as if punched in the stomach.

"And I trust you," she assured. "Now that I can see you, and smell you."

"But something's wrong," he interjected. "Isn't it?"

"I came here with friends," she admitted.

"Yes?"

"We have a job to do. An important assignment."

Jey-im was silent.

"I told them about you. I've assured them that we can trust

you. But my companions . . . well, they know about the incident with us . . . how you betrayed me, and what happened as a
consequence—"

"Oh, shit," he muttered.

"They didn't even want me to meet with you. I had to fight
with them, and that was just to come here."

The man collapsed inside his robe.

"Trust," she repeated.

"I knew it—"

"What is that old expression? About trust and buildings?"

" 'What is beneath the ground, unseen, is what matters,' " he
quoted.

" 'And once the foundation is cracked,' " she continued, " 'the
building is forever in peril.' "

Jey-im stared at his empty hands, and after a long pause, he
asked, "Is there anything that I can do?"

"Prove yourself."

"Yes?"

"By helping us."

His masked face lifted. A dry, low voice asked, "How?"

"You have a remarkable job, as I understand it." A pause. "You
watch over how many Masters?"

"Three hundred and twenty-nine."

"The intellectual heart of the City," said Porsche.

Again, he looked at his hands.

"We don't need you," she threatened, "but if you did help us,
think how far that would go toward proving your worthiness."

The hands closed into frail, chalky fists.

"Without the others' approval, I can't take you with me."

"I suppose not," he whispered.

In the distance, over the prattle of insects and day birds, came
the warning scream of an angry terror.

Porsche placed her hand on one of the fists, saying, "I'm sure
you can guess what we need from you. So the question is: For me,
will you?"

The fists fell open, then dropped to his side.

With a mild, almost disinterested voice, Jey-im asked, "What will you do with them?"

"Great minds are precious," she promised. "Think what those scientists could accomplish, given adequate resources."

The head tilted, in surprise.

"That's all you want?" he said. "You just want to take them with you?"

"What else would we want?" Porsche countered, genuinely puzzled.

"I thought . . . I don't know," he sputtered. "Honestly, I don't know what you people need from us at all."

"But you will help us? You'll help me, won't you?"

Jey-im moved behind Porsche, then began to hug her, softly at first and then desperately. She could feel him shivering with emotion, and she felt the pointed pressure of his phallus, aroused and thrusting its way out of his body cavity, tapping against her strong jarrtee rump. Then she heard the shivering voice come across her shoulder, telling her, "What you want to do is to take people to a better world?"

She leaned backward, back onto his phallus, trusting him with her weight.

"Of course I'll help you," she heard, an incandescent joy building. "This is the kind of person I've become, Po-lee-een. Good, I hope I am. At least good enough."

The terrors were building their night nest.

Jey-im was leading her back into the school by a longer, easier route. A stand of mature trees had been uprooted in the last few years, probably beneath an irresistible gust of wind, and as they passed through the young clearing, Porsche saw a dozen terrors expertly weaving together thorny vines, then poisoning the barbed surfaces with toxic berries and their own infectious wastes.

Noticing her gaze, Jey-im slowed. "Remember how the terrors used to scare us?"

She said nothing.

"But we never actually saw them. Which was a big part of why we were scared." He laughed, carefree whistles sounding out of place. "Living in the day, like I do now . . . I get to see a lot of terrors. If you don't corner them, and if you don't posture, they're really nothing but noise and bluster."

She had caught him and passed him. There wasn't time to gawk at nature.

Jey-im's robe swished as he ran to pass her again.

The waiting door led into another portion of the school. In the sudden darkness, Jey-im pulled up his mask, and with a confessional tone, he told her, "People think our species is doomed. It's common knowledge. The Order is stronger every day. None of us will survive, most say, except the converted."

"Maybe not," she offered. "Apocalypse stories are nearly universal. What looks like the end rarely is."

Jey-im's head dipped, in shame.

"I'm sorry," he whined. "I'll try to be more original for you."

She didn't mean to insult.

But perhaps he wasn't insulted. Perhaps he was trying to rise to the challenge. After a long moment of contemplation, Jey-im asked, "What if the Order and the various city-states . . . what if we simply destroy each other?"

"Maybe so," she conceded.

They were in a portion of the school reserved for the oldest children. Porsche had rarely walked here, and she felt the instinctive sense of being the outsider. But Jey-im was comfortable, wading through dense clouds of nostalgia. Eyes smiling, he looked back at her, explaining, "I was just recalling one class. We had a master scientist come talk. In that room there, as if happens."

She was barely listening, concentrating on important problems.

"The scientist was very old, but still very brilliant," Jey-im continued. "He was a master in the Gargantuan—"

Cosmology, in essence.

"—but when he spoke to us, he spent most of his breath on the Minuscule."

Porsche said nothing.

"He talked about matter and its opposite. In the beginning, he told us, there was almost exactly as much of one as the other."

Silence. Then she prompted with a crisp, "And?"

"The particles annihilated each other perfectly. But there just happened to be a little more matter than antimatter. Which is the only reason there was anything left over to create us."

"I learned those same laws on the EE-arth," Porsche admitted, walking quickly over a floor decorated with tile fish. "In a place called TEEK-zas."

He continued, pressing toward some vital point. "That image has always troubled me, Po-lee-een. All that violence, and waste, and everything that is us is built out of the ash that happened to survive. We—the entire universe—were that close to nothingness."

Porsche was in the lead. The great steel gate and tiny access door were up ahead, and closing.

"I have a question," she heard.

Glancing over her shoulder, she felt a knifing pain that threatened to split her open.

"You'll be happier on the new world," she lied.

"I know I will be. But that's not my question."

"What is it?"

"If this war kills everyone—every city-state; every member of the Order—will I be able to return to Jarrtee?"

She slowed slightly. "Why do you ask?"

"Long ago, you told me how intrusions work . . . how they shape bodies to look like the local species. But if there aren't any more jarrtees, does the magic still work?"

Porsche stopped entirely.

Someone watching at a distance would assume that she was watching the access door, trying to guess if anyone was waiting on the other side. After a moment, and wearing a false disinterest, she told Jey-im, "The intrusions would eventually forget how to build jarrtees. But not right away. It takes a generation, usually."

"That's good," he replied, as if there could be any good in extinction. "And I suppose in the future, if something else intelligent were to evolve here . . . a new species of terror, maybe—"

Porsche turned abruptly, dropping Jey-im's mask for him, then she dropped and secured her own mask.

"We'll talk later," she promised.

"On EE-arth," he replied, full of hope.

"You said that very well," she lied. Then she opened the door, forever astonished by the brightness of the world, and after a quick string of breaths, she added, "I can't tell you how glad I am, being here with you again, Jey-im. After so long, I feel alive again!"

11

"I'VE SEEN YOU BEFORE," JEY-IM REMARKED.

Porsche assumed that he was referring to Trinidad, but after climbing into the car, and after removing the cumbersome mask, she realized that her cousin was sitting where Cornell had been sitting. Their new ally was staring back at Latrobe, of all people.

"We spoke once," said Jey-im.

"We did," Latrobe allowed.

"You asked if I knew the whereabouts of Master Ko-ee. And I said—"

" 'Her laboratory is in Yellow Compound, in the Fifth Section.' " The jarrtee eyes smiled, and the mouth attempted a human smile. "Did I thank you for your help?"

"Yes."

"Good."

Jey-im was puzzled, and wounded. "I thought it was strange," he told Porsche, in self-defense. "His medallion put him with a minor payroll bureau, but to me he looked like a soldier. Which is why I remember him, I suppose."

Trinidad reached across Porsche, shaking Jey-im and saying, "Don't be modest. We know you have a wonderful memory."

The compliment had its intended effect; Jey-im's eyes shook with joy.

Cornell was sitting in the back, next to Latrobe, his eyes conspicuously avoiding Porsche's.

Their car was already streaking down a flooded street. The other elements of their convoy were ahead and behind them, using parallel streets. Porsche couldn't guess how many Few-made eavesdroppers were positioned throughout the City, keeping tabs on everything, but it had to involve most of Trinidad's inventory.

"I suppose I should have sounded an alarm," Jey-im conceded, still bothered by his lack of vigilance.

Trinidad gave a whistling laugh, then supplied comfort. "If you'd tried to contact anyone, you would have reached me. That was one of our precautions."

"Oh." Jey-im considered those words. "I suppose you're right," he allowed.

Latrobe leaned forward, a thick hand patting Jey-im as he spoke to Porsche. "It happened during the last dusk. We were making a scouting trip, and I wanted to meet your good friend. If only for a moment."

"You're such clever people," Jey-im confessed, astonishment mixed with a knifing embarrassment.

"But you remember me, too," said Trinidad. "Think back to school, to Po-lee-een's family."

Jey-im stared at the face, then with feeling said, "I'm sorry."

"No? Are you certain?"

"Less and less. But I don't remember you."

Trinidad made a deep sound—an outraged sound—then said, "And I always thought that I was memorable. Can you believe it, cousin?"

Porsche said nothing.

Latrobe interrupted, saying, "Concentrate on what's waiting for us."

Cornell glanced at her, then just as quickly looked away, staring out at the blur of stone homes and high-pitched roofs.

Then Trinidad was speaking, using a torrent of technical terms and simple boasts to explain what he knew about the security measures waiting for them. He spoke of locks and alarms, and vast amounts of cold crust and diamond armor, plus the brigades of devoted guards, robotic and living. "You're clever and thorough and very paranoid people," was his verdict.

Jey-im seemed uncomfortable with the praise.

Then in the next breath, Trinidad promised, "I can get us past any guard, and I can punch holes in any mechanical failsafe. But I'd love your help dealing with that last trick of yours—"

Cornell spoke, finally.

"Explain the trick to me," he muttered.

Latrobe gave Cornell a warning glance. "No more questions," said the brilliant black eyes.

Trinidad was more amiable. Turning, he threw an arm over the back of his seat, saying, "It's very simple. Practically foolproof, even. When dawn approaches, the Masters are fed the best foods available. Then they're delivered to special showers and scrubbed clean. And I mean perfectly clean. No ink embellishments; no telltale odors. They're like newborns when they are led below, down and down into a subbasement that dwarfs every other facility like it on this world."

On Jarrtee, enlightenment arrives without illumination. Epiphanies are born out of a perfect darkness. And for the second time in the last little while, Porsche felt the darkness descend, an instant of clarity coming with her next breath.

"The Great Nest, they call it," said Trinidad, his voice almost booming. "Imagine the EE-arth's largest arena, then triple it and bury it. More than a kilometer deep, it's buried. It's resting on enormous shock absorbers, and it's clothed in the best armors, and the air is laced with enough EM noise to baffle the most determined eavesdropper. Then imagine half a million people filing into that facility, every last one of them similarly prepared for the event, the same perfect anonymity enforced for the best of reasons.

"No one knows where the Masters will estivate. The decisions are made at the last moment, by random means, no computer records kept. Half a million citizens lie down on a communal nest. Fattened Masters and fatter government officers, military leaders, and ordinary citizens—the winners of a lottery that has become popular in the last years—estivate as One, every face down, absolutely no easy way to decide who exactly is who."

There was a pause, then Cornell said, "But if there is an emergency—"

"If the unthinkable happens," Trinidad replied. "Exactly. The facility is threatened, and the day-shift jarrtees need to retrieve the most essential, unique souls from among all those inert bodies—"

"You know where to find the Masters," said Porsche, grasping Jey-im by his arm. "That's your importance."

With a thin pride, he replied, "For maps, I have always had a memory."

Silence.

Then Cornell challenged Trinidad, saying, "But you have to get us down there first. Right?"

"You think I can't?"

Jey-im glanced at one face, then the other. Why were these aliens at odds with each other? he was asking himself.

Trinidad showed everyone a human grin. Sharp teeth framed the thin milky lips, and the huge eyes drew closed.

Then, a soft whisper.

He gave a command, in mutilated English.

"After dinner," Trinidad told invisible machines, "I take out the trash."

There came a sudden peal of thunder, deep and relentless. By reflex, Porsche looked to the east; the next storm was rolling across the distant sea, black and malevolent, but not a trace of lightning squirting from it.

In the west, the sun was bleeding through the mountain-tattered clouds.

The thunder came again, louder and deep enough to be felt in the bones, and Cornell leaned forward, pointing straight ahead.

The Master's School was straight ahead.

A string of tall black-and-blood-colored pillars were jetting into the brilliant sunshine.

For a moment, Porsche simply watched the pillars, astonished by their sudden size and their unexpected, almost enchanting beauty. Then she reclaimed what remained of her calm, turning and looking at her cousin, carefully saying nothing.

"The Order," he said. "It must be attacking."

He didn't smirk or smile.

Finally, Trinidad had done something that left him feeling— for however brief the moment—small.

12

BENEATH THE SMOKE, THERE WAS A KIND OF NIGHT.

The float car slowed but never stopped. Porsche stared out into the swirling black clouds, emergency crews clad in refrigerated armor scurrying, battling wildfires inside the ancient laboratories. Quietly, pensively, Jey-im asked about the dead. How many were there? Trinidad responded with a laugh and a touch, and maybe a little too confidently, he promised, "The targets were empty. No one has even been bruised."

Latrobe handed out medallions. Identical to Jey-im's medallion, they worked inside the City proper, transmitting foolproof codes over short range, friendly souls able to glance at a mask and know a face, a name, and the vital rank.

"Just relax," was Latrobe's brisk advice. Then he returned to barking cryptic orders over his headset, positioning unseen vehicles and soldiers, orchestrating their assault.

Cornell glanced at Porsche.

How much worse can it get? asked the long dark eyes.

She shook her head, human-fashion. *I wish I knew.*

Trinidad had closed his eyes, leaning back as if napping. "On Saturday," he suddenly whispered, "I mowed the lawn."

Porsche braced for another blast, but nothing happened.

Yet Trinidad acted pleased. He blinked and smiled, then leaned close enough to kiss his cousin's ear hole, the softest imaginable voice suggesting, "Your friend wants to be happy. Help him, will you?"

Porsche sat motionless for a long moment, then forced herself to look at Jey-im.

Jey-im seemed tired and suddenly old. There was a whiteness to his flesh that no jarrtee would envy, and misery made him a little blind. Yet he sensed her gaze, and he spoke first. With a forced hopefulness, he asked, "Where is your home . . . on EE-arth?"

"I live on a farm," she answered.

"With your family?"

"No. I live alone." She said it once, then repeated herself.

He puzzled over the words, then asked, "Are there any city-states on the EE-arth?"

"Many," she assured him. "Small ones. Giant ones. Some are as large as the City."

"But you live alone?"

"It's a matter of choice." She glanced over her shoulder, watching the greasy smoke swirl in their wake. "Humans," she said, "are a flexible species."

"I would like to be that way. Flexible, to a degree."

Trinidad laughed without a sound, unnoticed by Jey-im.

"Do you have children, Po-lee-een?"

"None," she replied.

Jey-im found the news heartening, but he never said it. As he opened his mouth, the float car began to slow. Directly ahead was the shattered face of a newer building, and he muttered, "Oh," without emotion. Then he sighed, and with a genuine relief, he told everyone, "This is the place, my friends. The Great Nest."

A jarrtee kind of mayhem was in force.

People were sprinting back and forth; vivid curses hung in the scalding air; but there was an antlike tenacity to the scene, purpose and fate shared equally, and every mistake made together, as a team.

Latrobe gave his troops some final words. "Just like the drills," he said. "Keep it businesslike and crisp, then it's home again."

Their car had stopped. Once the masks were secured, every door lifted.

"Stay with us," the drivers advised Porsche, then Cornell, patting rip-guns carried on silk belts.

Jey-im was up ahead, walking between Latrobe and Trinidad, the first man holding him by the elbow while the other shouted instructions.

Porsche couldn't hear the words. The nearby fires roared like blast furnaces, and jarrtee alarms were sounding from everywhere—high-pitched whistles fluttering like heartbeats—and there was a sense that here, in this realm, words didn't have much worth anyway.

The Great Nest had at least one enormous entranceway, and titanic energies had melted stone and mortar, leaving it partway collapsed. But there was a plan to the destruction, like when one wooden block is carefully slipped from a child's house of blocks, distorting but not destroying.

A small lake of blackish magma lay cooling on their right.

Ahead of them, Latrobe and Jey-im were facing a dozen heavily armed guards.

Where was Trinidad?

"On the authority of the emergency office, section red," Jey-im was chanting, "I am taking charge. As of now!"

A guard asked Latrobe, "And who are you?"

Latrobe gave a name, a command code, then offered the guard his jeweled necklace, saying twice, "There isn't time for this shit!"

"We have to get the essential people out now!" Jey-im cried out. "Now!"

He sounded terrified.

It was a reasonable emotion, Porsche hoped.

Then came the electric crackle of the big float trucks that braked and stopped behind them. The rest of the convoy had arrived, driving out of the churning clouds with a massive, stark authority. Insignias had been added to the doors. Jeweled badges hung around every neck as the troops disembarked. Stretchers were unloaded, then activated. None of the troops were jarrtee, but their dry runs had taught them how to carry themselves. How to gesture; how to obey. Porsche didn't see one stumble. There was nothing in the entire show that was the least half-assed.

The jarrtee guards followed protocol, facing the invaders as they asked for confirmation from the City top offices.

Confirmation was swift and absolute.

Trinidad's cleverness had won again.

With a sudden surge, everyone moved downward into the enormous building, leaving behind the smoke and ceaseless alarms.

One of the guards—nearly a youngster, judging by the skittering voice behind the mask—walked beside Porsche, talking rapidly, fear wrapped tight in astonishment. "I heard we were hit by lasers. From somewhere across the world, I heard."

Throw an EM pulse at the sky, and most of its energy raced off into space, lost. But like the lights of a distant city, barely visible on the clearest, darkest nights, a thin portion of the pulse would arrive on target. Lasers would demand enormous energies, but otherwise, it was possible. Even probable, given the savageness of this war. And for people like the jarrtees, it had to be a terrifying prospect: The Order could deliver savage blows, and the attacks were launched from around the world—from places for which they had no names.

"Do you know what happened?" asked the guard.

Porsche said, "Maybe," with indifference.

No one else spoke.

Then the guard continued, pointing out, "This isn't my place. But aren't our people in greater danger, not less, if we bring them to the surface?"

Latrobe wheeled abruptly. "You're right. It isn't *your* place!"

"Yes, sir."

"If you're scared, run to the surface. Watch for the next barrage."

"Sir?"

"That's an order!"

On most worlds, bullies win the first fight. The guard stopped and sputtered apologies, perhaps hoping that the other guards would come to his defense. But no one would challenge a top-ranked security detail. Apologies made, the guard had no alternative but to make his retreat, dragging his shame with him.

A chastened silence took hold.

The sloping tunnel, deeper than any subbasement Porsche remembered, and dark enough for them to lift the masks, ended with an elevator larger than most houses. Its security had already been breached. Diamond doors had been pulled open, AI-triggered booby traps rendered insane, and at last, the remaining guards grew suspicious, lifting their weapons by reflex, too late.

Trinidad appeared behind them.

With the happy light voice that he used to tell jokes, he gave a one-word command, in twisted English.

"Sleep," he said.

Together, in a shared motion, the guards collapsed.

Jey-im gave a startled whistle. Otherwise, no one made the smallest sound, stepping deftly over the unconscious bodies and filing into the waiting elevator.

The doors remembered how to close. Then with a smooth, almost imperceptible hum, they began to drop, everyone lifting up on their toes, an earthly lightness coming to them as they plummeted into the depths.

Trinidad stepped casually up to Porsche and Cornell.

Latrobe was out of earshot, standing with Jey-im, feeding him praise and promises of the coming paradise.

Because there might never be another chance, Porsche stared

at her cousin's profile, willing him to look in her direction. Then, the question.

A single word, in mangled English.

"Why?"

Trinidad began to laugh. With a worn charm, he reminded Porsche, "I meant what I told you. Every answer you can imagine, you can apply to me."

She was standing between him and Cornell. It was Cornell who responded, reaching into his mind to find a scorching jarr-tee word. "Greed," he said. He accused. "The government is paying you—"

"Not a *dime,* frankly."

"No?"

"It's the truth." Trinidad pulled back his hood, then began to finger an ear hole. "I'm a patriot who's giving my time and expertise to help my adopted nation."

In a low, almost human voice, Cornell said, "Bullshit!"

"But I've asked for compensations," her cousin allowed. "A tiny percentage of the profits. A finder's fee, I consider it."

"How much?" asked Porsche.

"In the next twenty years, if the middle-of-the-road predictions hold, I should pocket somewhere around a hundred billion dollars."

She held herself motionless, then promised, "The Few won't let you."

"The Few won't care. Not enough to matter." He laughed abruptly, trying to prove his indifference. "I've protected the Few's technologies, and I've guarded most of our identities, too."

"And you've put your family at risk," she countered.

"*Your* family is barely at risk. In a couple of earth days, they'll be home again, and Clare will be talking about her fabulous little adventure."

She bristled when her niece was mentioned. "So you're not a traitor? Is that it?"

"In some eyes, I suppose I am. But you're assuming that I'm

unique, which I'm not. And you're pretending that the Few won't be satisfied until my ass is in some kind of prison, or dead."

"You're not unique," she echoed.

"Remember, Po-lee-een. Security is my field. My specialty. And with that comes knowledge. About past breeches, like mine, and the truly terrible offenses, too."

"Such as?"

"Let's just say that people like me, on the occasional world, have accomplished quite a lot."

There was a long, tense silence.

Then Trinidad gestured, remarking, "Your boyfriend needs reassurance. Give him a smile, will you?"

Jey-im was staring at her with passion and cold terror. Porsche obeyed, smiling but feeling so distant, so cold, that he surely wouldn't believe her smile.

Yet he seemed mollified, turning back to Latrobe again.

"What happens to Jey-im?" she asked.

"Maybe nothing. In all this chaos, the jarrtees will be hard-pressed to figure out who to blame."

"But people will be blamed," she reminded him. "You know how it'll be."

"I do. I certainly do." He smiled earnestly, saying, "The purge might take thousands before it's finished."

"Revenge against the jarrtees," she said. "That's another reason you're doing this, isn't it?"

"My favorite reason, at times." Trinidad stared at the nearest wall, laughing at his own simple dark reflection. "In the course of one afternoon, I'll steal the greatest minds in the City, leaving it weakened. Vulnerable. The City that decided I was a threat because I was an outsider . . . it's going to see that I was!"

The elevator was slowing, finally.

Quietly, almost delicately, Porsche pointed out, "You should blame me, if you're angry for the past."

"Oh, I forgave you long ago, cousin. Believe me."

But she didn't. Not one word.

Locking her legs against the deacceleration, she said, "You

and I both know what these scientists mean to the earth. What specialties they bring."

Amused silence.

"What?" Cornell asked. Then he answered his own question, saying in a too-loud voice, "Weapons."

"Rip-gun sales alone should earn me a small fortune," Trinidad conceded.

Then before she could say another word, the elevator had stopped, its inner doors parting, revealing a vaultlike door hanging open. In the distance was a vast chamber, lit by a single gray light and subdivided into thousands of compartments, each compartment armored and rigorously anonymous. And between the open door and the compartments were a company of elite troops, each soldier armed with enough weaponry to flatten a city block, and every last one of them lying on the scrupulously polished floor, on their backs, eyes half-opened in some shared daze.

Latrobe threw an arm around Jey-im, saying, "Now! Here's where you earn your key to a new world, sir."

The words sounded practiced, the voice deadly earnest.

"Po-lee-een?" Jey-im called out.

This wasn't the end, she told herself. And thinking of her family, she kept playing the game, abandoning Cornell and stepping up to Jey-im, managing a hopeful voice when she asked, "Where are these great minds, lover? You can show me."

The air was thick and old, felt grass and dust combining with the musty odor of thousands of inert bodies, and punctuated with the harsh stink of the dead.

Out of so many, Porsche realized, a few must have died while estivating.

Jey-im was steady, but slow. Walking at the lead, he would pause to examine a numbered post, and sometimes he would turn up one of the countless lancs running between the chambers. Porsche remained at his side. Latrobe shadowed them, impatience camouflaged with an officious attitude and a rigid posture. Porsche saw him glancing at his bare wrist, searching for a nonexistent watch. Then she looked at Jey-im, and for the first time, she asked, "How much farther?"

He stopped moments later, and pointed.

"Here."

Latrobe hesitated, glancing at Trinidad.

Her cousin squinted, his eavesdroppers able to pierce the EM noise and walls, but only well enough for him to say, "Maybe. Maybe."

Each chamber resembled a small bland jarrtee house, windowless and thickly built. Their chamber was utterly ordinary. Its doorway was decorated with old gods and the image of a famished sun, and it wore a simple mechanical lock meant to be opened from inside. Latrobe called up two men, then waved back the others. Shaped explosives were planted, then detonated, their energy and noise burrowing into the locking mechanism. Porsche barely heard the *pop,* and suddenly Latrobe was sprinting past her, trying to move like a human in the doubled gravity.

Porsche took smaller, cleaner strides.

Entering the chamber, she found Latrobe illuminated by a meek yellow lamp, standing over the naked motionless bodies, narrow and desiccated and always facedown. He had already rolled over two of the bodies, and with a breathless anger, he muttered, "Who the fuck are these people?"

The two bodies were tiny.

They were children.

Jey-im stepped into view. Suddenly he was the one who looked composed, in charge. With a quiet smooth voice, he said, "Wait."

Latrobe wheeled, grabbing him and lifting—

"Wait!" Porsche begged.

Then the man hesitated, perhaps realizing how far he was from home, and like it or not, how much he needed Jey-im's help.

"It's a standard precaution," Jey-im explained. "After I leave them, the Masters will exchange chambers with a neighbor. It's meant to slow down anyone who learns what I know."

"Which chamber!"

Then Trinidad appeared, saying, "It's straight across. I'm counting the right number of bodies. . . ."

Again, they punched out the lock; again, Latrobe did his mad dash into the dust-ladened chamber.

The greatest minds on the planet lay strewn about the floor, clothed in drab bodies that were more old than young—but never elderly—their skin left leathery and wrinkled by the long estivation. It was close enough to dusk that some of the bodies seemed to exhale as they were lifted onto the stretchers. One or two eyes danced behind their lids, navigating their way through dreams. But otherwise, the Masters were indistinguishable from corpses, and they were as manageable as cordwood.

The cordwood was piled five deep on the stretchers, heads and feet alternated, then everyone tied down with purple silk ropes.

Every facet of the operation had the crisp efficiency of a basketball drill.

In a convoy, the stretchers were taken back to the enormous elevator. Porsche and Cornell were given their own stretcher, their own precious cargo.

Latrobe and Trinidad kept close.

In the elevator, Latrobe said, "Just drop them on the floor. Do it."

And they went back again, everyone moving in a quick jarrtee jog with the stretchers floating between them.

They would make a single trip to the surface and the waiting trucks.

A dozen stretchers; sixty Masters at a time. Which meant half a dozen circuits before they could ascend to the surface again. Porsche made that simple calculation several times, trying to discern the perfect moment to escape. With Cornell. But when she managed to catch his eyes, he acted passive, resigned. In secret, she bristled, wishing she could say to him, "Listen. Trinidad can't look everywhere at once. If we can slip away, then lose ourselves in this maze, nobody will bother with us. And maybe we can find another way to the surface before the jarrtees regain control."

"What about Jey-im?" asked an imagined voice. It was Cornell's human voice; he called him *Jim*. "Are we planning to abandon Jim?"

She had no intention of abandoning anyone.

"You have no weapons," a new voice warned. "Not even one Few-made tool."

It was her father speaking, his tone reasoned and cautious, and insistent.

"What if the jarrtees find you?" he asked his bold daughter. "What good will you accomplish in prison?"

None.

"Help us," he beseeched. "Before you act, Po-lee-een . . . *think*."

Everything seemed to happen so smoothly, she kept thinking. But this was the easiest stretch. Trinidad's tools and the ally of surprise were giving them every advantage. But what about the return trip into the mountains? Dusk was approaching. Another set of storms were bearing down on them. When the City smelled what was happening, every available resource would be brought to bear on their tiny, body-ladened convoy.

With a chilling clarity, Porsche remembered how difficult it had been to move one family through those mountains, and that was in a time of peace.

And that was with the Few's cooperation, too.

Smiling in a grim human fashion, she wondered to herself: Do Latrobe and his team realize what kind of chance they're taking?

And if not, just imagine their surprise!

The final load of scientists was left tied to the stretchers.

The elevator began to rise, accelerating smoothly. Porsche was standing with Cornell, standing beside their stretcher, when Jey-im approached, trying to smile as he spoke with a perishable hope.

"Now we can be on our way."

She looked at the simple face for a long moment, wrestling for the perfect words.

There weren't any.

"On our way," he repeated, mostly to himself. Then he looked into her face and finally noticed something. He saw what he could have always seen, and in response, he straightened his back and glanced at Cornell, breathing audibly, swiftly and deeply, in mortal pain.

"No," he said, almost too softly to be heard. "No."

She hadn't touched Cornell, or spoken to him, or even exchanged the plainest of glances.

They had done nothing.

But Jey-im was surprised, and furious, and utterly at a loss about how to respond to this sudden epiphany. All of his strength was barely enough to turn him again, his eyes finding hers, and with a rising voice, he said, "You don't intend to take me. From the beginning . . . you have been manipulating me!"

"It wasn't me," she replied, by reflex.

"Oh, Po-lee-een!"

"That isn't my name anymore."

"What have I done?" Jey-im whispered. Then the voice lifted, turning hot and frightened. "What am I doing here? What was I thinking?"

Trinidad was approaching.

For an instant, Porsche was almost glad to see him.

"Your lady friend isn't entirely to blame," he told Jey-im, his voice nearly cheerful. "She's used you, yes. But be a little charitable . . . she had no choice."

The jarrtee groaned sharply, then with strong quick fists, he began to batter his own face.

A black astonishment held everyone motionless, mute.

Jey-im slumped to the floor, in agony. Scalding, iron-rich blood squirted from his battered flesh, and his screams were dressed in crimson bubbles, and he didn't stop until Porsche was on her knees, her hands grabbing his wrists as she clung to him, physically forcing him to stop.

She meant to speak, to offer the first helpful words that came to mind.

Nothing occurred to her.

It was Trinidad who spoke first.

"Jey-im," he said. Then he muttered the English word, "Sleep."

There was an electric sensation, sudden and delicate, and Jey-im pitched forward, limp and unconscious.

Porsche rolled him onto his back, then with the hem of his own robe, she began to mop up the darkening blood. From a distance, someone asked, "If we leave him here, what does it hurt?"

Latrobe was speaking.

"If the jarrtees find him, can they wake him?"

Trinidad shook his head. "It's a good Few stun. For several days, earth time, he'll be as useful as broken furniture."

Hands took hold of Porsche's hands. She found herself staring at four hands, recognizing none of them. Then she turned and realized that Cornell was pulling her to her feet again, saying in his quiet, cynical way, "At least it can't get any worse."

She said nothing, trying to obey her father's admonition to think.

Trinidad caught her gaze, something in his expression mesmerizing. His night-colored eyes were light-years deep, and they were utterly simple, suffused with a calm cold joy that made her angry, and determined, and focused.

"An important point lifts its gruesome head," her cousin sang. "Do you, Po-lee-een, know how fond I am of you?"

She gave a soft, astonished laugh.

"Well, I am. I adore you, and always have." He paused, then with a whisper of feeling added, "Which makes this especially hard."

"What's that?"

"I also know you," he warned. "I know how stubborn and self-righteous you can be. Which makes me wonder about the future."

She said nothing, waiting.

"I can defeat the jarrtees, easily, and I can make peace with the Few. But with you, my dear cousin . . . well, I have to wonder."

Porsche knew exactly where he was leading, and for an instant, she could almost hear his next words, and the grim, inevitable tone of his voice.

Why feel a powerful, almost crippling sense of shock?

"You won't let me rest," said Trinidad. "Will you?"

"Probably not," she admitted, in a whisper.

"Which leaves us where?"

Huddled together at the opposite end of the elevator, Latrobe and his soldiers were silent and nearly motionless. None seemed particularly surprised, which, if anything, infuriated Porsche even more.

"So you're going to kill me," she muttered.

Cornell edged closer, then hesitated.

Trinidad's eyes were turning milky, turning blind, some flavor of pain finally betraying itself.

"Po-lee-een," he muttered, "I really wish I had some choice here. But I don't, which means that all I can do is promise you . . . that I'll do everything in my power to see that the rest of your family returns home. Is that fair?"

She glared at him, saying nothing.

"Poor, poor Po-lee-een . . ." he sang.

She flung herself at him, and threw a fist—

And Trinidad retreated, too slowly, hands lifting and absorbing her first hard blow, then a muttered voice mangling the word, "Sleep," as he fell backward.

A mammoth surge of energy burrowed through her flesh, into her mind.

But what surprised Porsche was how much it was like a jarrtee's utter sleep, this sudden endless tumble into blackness!

13

PORSCHE AWOKE WITH A FAMILIAR SCENT IN HER MOUTH.

Her eyes opened gradually, first one and then the other, and she discovered that she could see by the soft glow of an infrared lamp. The lamp seemed to float, carried at a slow, stately pace. Straight above, shadows were cast by ornately decorated beams of olivine. She watched the shadows lengthen, then collapse in on themselves. She tried once to turn her head, hunting for the light's source, but her neck was fused, her body paralyzed for the moment. Or maybe, forever.

Obviously this wasn't the elevator, which implied that she was lying in her prison cell. And that left her frightened as well as strangely curious: Why would jailers bother to carve such an elegant ceiling?

Was it important to give the doomed a glimpse of beauty?

Again, Porsche inhaled, and again, there was that wonderfully familiar scent. Old stone and ageless humidity, the stink of perfumed fungi and the surviving aroma of a dawn feast combined to make an olfactory signature that meant *home*.

She blinked, then looked at the ceiling again.

Who would have guessed?

It was the oddest moment to be embarrassed, but Porsche was nothing else. This was the same feast room where she had once celebrated dusks and dawns. How many times had she regarded the ceiling from this odd vantage point? Then she managed to pry open her mouth, emitting a thin white keening sound that eventually, thankfully, got on someone's nerves.

"Quiet," she heard, the jarrtee voice furious and oversized, triggering more dusty memories.

Uncle Ka-ceen, she thought, in reflex.

"Relax," the man growled from somewhere nearby. "We're bringing you out of the stun now. Just relax."

Out of the stun; Trinidad could just as easily have killed her.

An unfamiliar voice—a woman's voice—said with a thinly veiled frustration, "And keep her from talking. Please."

Again, her uncle told her to relax and be quiet.

"Cornell," she muttered, the name distorted by her mouth and the effects of the stun. "Where is . . . Cornell?"

"Just this once," her uncle pleaded, "behave. Will you, please?"

Closing her mouth was as difficult as opening it.

Her uncle's face appeared, gazing down at her, smiling in a human fashion. He had the same intelligent and plain jarrtee face that Porsche remembered, but there were the inevitable traces of age, and behind the eyes, a palpable sense of crushing, now public burdens.

"Your friend is here," he said with a surprising warmth. "With us, and safe."

Again, Porsche opened her mouth.

"No," he warned preemptively.

"Cut her muscle activity," the unseen woman called out. "Make her relax, or let me—"

"Trinidad," Porsche muttered. Mangled. How could anyone understand her?

Yet her uncle nodded grimly, placing a warm hand over her mouth as he confessed, "I know. All about him."

Yes?

And to himself, with a nearly inaudible voice, "And probably always did."

* * *

The ceiling had belonged to them, but the feast table had always been another family's. Slowly sitting up on the slick marble, Porsche began to make out the holo portraits of strangers dangling in space, the chairs and mosaic rugs all wrong, and every other flourish conspiring to steal this space from its rightful if exceedingly absent owners.

Cornell lay at her feet, unconscious, whiskerlike probes piercing his smooth white scalp. Beyond him, unwired and tucked into a tight ball, was Jey-im. Sharing the table, the three of them resembled a cannibal's dusk feast.

"Who lives here now?" Porsche asked.

No one answered.

Instead, her uncle spoke with a grim pride, telling her, "You don't know how lucky you are. We just happened to find you and pull you out in time—"

"Thank you." On this world, and particularly in this house, she couldn't think of him as being anyone but Uncle Ka-ceen. "It was a good thing, Trinidad stunning us like he did. All things considered."

"He made a miscalculation," said the woman's voice. "Finally."

Porsche turned her head slowly, stiffly. A large jarrtee woman sat at one end of the table, her face illuminated by an infrared lamp and an autodoc. There was something odd about her, something decidedly familiar.

Porsche asked, "How much time has passed?"

"An eighth of a cycle," said her uncle.

"Where's Trinidad?"

He closed his eyes for a moment, blinked, and said, "We can't be sure. But he should be passing the spaceport now."

Cornell gave a lazy groan, and his right arm lifted, flexing once, then dropped slowly, as if exceedingly fragile.

"Does the City understand?" asked Porsche.

"People are beginning to comprehend, finally." With the thinnest trace of pleasure, he told her, "Your cousin has done a marvelous job, considering his resources. The jarrtees are reeling. Most of their day-troops are moving in the wrong directions.

And as far as we can tell, the high officials are blaming the Order. No one else."

The large woman touched the panel with an unnatural delicacy, gradually unscrambling Cornell's senses. By ignoring the conversation, she was making herself conspicuous.

"What's the Few planning?" asked Porsche. When no one answered, she reminded them, "My family is being held hostage."

Uncle Ka-ceen gave her a warning look, and with a gray worldliness, he said, "The issues are complicated."

The woman bent low, pretending to examine an obscure detail.

Then something very simple occurred to Porsche. "Wait. Trinidad told me that he had absconded *with everything* stockpiled by the Few!"

"Obviously not," was her uncle's reply.

"A second stockpile," Porsche answered, for herself. "As a precaution, I suppose. Is that it?"

"We live by our precautions," he purred.

Again, she looked at the feast room. "We're here for a reason."

"Obviously."

Cornell was waking, eyes forcing themselves open.

Gripping his closer hand with both of hers, Porsche made certain that he could see her face. "How do you feel, love?"

"You are . . . all right?" Cornell managed.

"I'm fine."

"You fell . . . unconscious . . . and we started to leave you!"

"Be quiet," the large woman rumbled.

"So I took a swing at the shit . . ."

A cloying stew of emotions struck Porsche. She was thrilled to have this romantic man defending her, and she was so very sorry for involving him, and there was a slippery anger, part of her wanting to ask, "What the hell good was that supposed to do? Both of us would have been in prison, and doomed!"

Instead, she shook her head, throwing the useless thoughts out of it.

"We kept our secret stockpile here," Porsche said, giving Uncle Ka-ceen a hard stare. "Before our family left?"

"No," he replied. "Others did it. After the City had searched this compound thoroughly."

The woman glanced up at him, for an instant.

"Once searched," he continued, "it was the perfect place to leave stores."

"A small stockpile," the woman informed her. "A fraction of what your cousin can wield, I'm afraid."

With a firm, reborn voice, Cornell asked, "Why can't I feel my legs?"

"Give me a moment," the woman snapped.

Porsche climbed off the table. Her own legs felt numb but strong enough. She walked stiffly to the doorway that led down to the subbasements. A security robot stood guard in the hallway. Larger and more heavily armed than the robots of her youth, it pivoted its head with a slick slow hum, buglike eyes regarding her for an instant before its mangled software decided that she did not exist, or that she was harmless.

The head turned forward again, watching for true enemies.

"Porsche?" she heard.

Cornell was trying to sit upright, finding himself staring at a pair of alien faces.

"This is Uncle Ka-ceen," she told him. Then gesturing at the woman, she said, "I don't think we've met."

"We have," the woman replied. "Once, years ago."

Suddenly and without doubts, Porsche recognized her.

Cornell spoke first. "I could hear you," he was telling her uncle. "You were talking about things being complicated."

"They are," he responded, with authority.

"What about the hostages?" Cornell asked. Then, "My father's in the mountains."

"We know that, yes."

"How are they?" Cornell snarled. "Do you know what's happening to them?"

The nameless woman spoke, looking only at Porsche. "We presume that they're safe. We know that they've been moved into the mountains west of the City, but unfortunately, our little stock of eavesdroppers is busy elsewhere."

"What about New Mexico?" Porsche asked. "Are we watching *there*?"

The older people traded glances, then Uncle Ka-ceen admitted, "We've focused quite a few resources on that intrusion, yes."

"But we have limits," the woman added.

"Are you going to help the hostages, or not?" Cornell demanded.

"When they come through the intrusion again," her uncle replied, "they'll be released immediately."

"You know that," Porsche said doubtfully.

"We've been in contact with the agency," the woman said, her voice carefully reassuring. "They've made certain promises, if their mission succeeds. . . ."

"Promises?" Cornell echoed.

"A diplomatic solution," the woman informed them.

Trinidad was right about one thing: Given proper motivation, the Few would gladly cut a deal.

Trading their own glances, Porsche and Cornell said nothing for a long moment. Then Cornell asked:

"What happens to us?"

"You'll be moved back along the route we took, eventually reaching the earth again." Uncle Ka-ceen wanted Porsche to see his smile, his earnest good intentions. "Your families will be waiting for you, hopefully."

Your families. The words cut into her guts. Weren't they his nephews, his own brother?

She shook her head, then gestured at the last unconscious figure. "What about Jey-im?"

"I'll wipe his memories as much as I can," the woman promised. "We'll leave him as he is, safe and near his family's compound."

And the security forces will question him, Porsche realized. And they'll eventually torture him, then execute him without a shred of dignity.

But the woman knew that already.

Porsche turned to her uncle, and with a quiet, rock-certain voice, she announced, "There's someone else that needs to be rescued. Timothy Kleck."

Both of them were taken by surprise. Uncle Ka-ceen almost shuddered, saying, "We assumed he was in the mountains."

Cornell explained what had happened.

Then Porsche exclaimed, "I won't leave him behind!"

There was a long, jagged silence.

"Uncle," she implored, "we have to rescue him."

Finally, the woman pushed back the strangers' chair and stood, stepping closer to Porsche as she asked, "Why would you assume that *he* is in charge of this operation?"

A sudden bright gloom grabbed hold of Porsche. She remembered when she met this woman in the New Mexican mountains, and how much she had disliked her, that childhood perception reborn in an instant.

With scorn, the nameless woman reminded everyone, "One of us has a son who has turned against us. Why should *he* hold command here?" She laughed loudly, the whistles rattling off the olivine ceiling. "Address me, Miss Neal. Mr. Novak. Every critical decision is mine."

Porsche was angry, and there was nowhere to let the anger escape. She held it deep inside, letting it burn, and with a careful and smooth and overly sweetened voice, she asked the nameless woman:

"Can we at least try to rescue our friend? Please?"

She appreciated the tone, but there was a wariness in the wide new eyes. "There is a responsibility here," she admitted. "We'll try to determine exactly what's happened to your friend, then *I* will decide. . . ."

Careful, Porsche warned herself. *Careful.*

"And if there is a way," the woman concluded, "I think we should make the effort."

With a flat, clean voice, Porsche said, "Thank you."

Cornell echoed her thanks.

"You're very welcome," the woman told them, smug with her power.

Uncle Ka-ceen said nothing, standing apart, motionless, staring at his own long, broad jarrtee feet as if nothing else in the universe mattered.

It was like being a child again, and it wasn't just the surroundings. Porsche found herself suddenly waiting while older souls did work with which she couldn't help, and like a fidgety youngster, she needed a distraction. That was her excuse, at least, asking permission to give Cornell a quick tour of her childhood home.

"Avoid the subbasements," was the woman's only restriction.

Porsche and Cornell strolled along the dimly lit hallways, drawing the occasional glance from a sentry, followed by determined indifference. She was an anomalous signal; she was a ghost. Taking her ghost lover's hand, she would point in a jarrtee fashion, using their shared hands to guide his eyes, and with whispers and emotion, she would tell little stories about the family that had once lived here.

The Neals' wing wasn't being used by the present owners.

Without furniture or mural rugs, the rooms resembled caves carved out of a granite mountain by some rigorous, exacting force of nature. Her own cubicle smelled musty and forlorned. Two adult bodies felt crowded. Twice, she reminded Cornell that she never lived here. Cubicles were intended to be private space and nothing more. The slitlike window was triple-sealed, but through the armor they could hear the muted roar of new rains and a well-rested wind. With a touch, Porsche opened the tiny closet where she had once lovingly stored her toys. The seams of its door were virtually invisible; a tattered piece of mirrored silk hung on its back side. The shelves within were exactly as she remembered; but someone had taken away her puzzles and hero dolls, and for a long moment, she was angry.

"You hid your toys," Cornell observed, his voice soft and airy, like a ghost's. "Was that normal?"

"For a jarrtee child," she replied. "Absolutely."

He kneeled and peered into the closet, then saw something in the mirror, and froze. A looming figure had appeared suddenly in the hallway. Without a sound, it stuck its head into the room, rip-guns in three hands and the fourth hand calmly grasping the cubicle's door, pulling it closed with a solid *click*.

Porsche heard the click twice—first in memory, then inside her expectant ears—and she remembered happy nights spent here, playing games with her favorite cousin, in the happy darkness.

Misunderstanding her silence, Cornell assured her, "It was just another sentry."

Then she was talking, without warning, and she listened to herself with a curious intensity. "I didn't tell you about this," she admitted. "Before. At the farm." She added, "I didn't think it was important, or necessary," and then she paused, her unconscious mind framing the next words.

"What is it?" whispered Cornell.

A bolt of lightning struck nearby, followed by an explosive crash. A thin stream of light seeped through a flaw in the window's armor, illuminating a narrow and very handsome jarrtee face. Porsche reached for the face as the darkness returned, finding the cheeks and eyes by memory.

"I shared a lover with Trinidad."

The face beneath her hand surprised her, barely flinching at the news.

"I mentioned the world to you. It's an administrative center for the Few. *Abyss*. That's a weak translation of its real name. But it's accurate enough. The world is an icebound ocean. Intelligence evolved without the help of free oxygen, and its sentient species has never been abundant. There are a few hundred true adults at the most, each huddled next to a different deep-ocean vent. Which is significant." She paused for a moment. "When the Few first arrived, it was impossible for us to hide among the teeming masses. There were no teeming masses. And better still, the Abyssians welcomed us. Within a short while, their entire population had converted. Within a few centuries, the Abyssian adults—vast and incomprehensibly intelligent organisms—were helping keep careful track of their intrusions and the multitude of local worlds, species, and customs.

"I was a subadult when I visited. Relatively small. Mobile. And compared to the adults, stupid. Which might be why I didn't understand what my lover told me."

Cornell waited for a half-moment, then took the bait. "What did he tell you?"

"Everything," she promised. Then with a whisper almost too soft to be heard over the muted sounds of rain, she told him, "We have only a few minutes. Listen . . . listen!"

Her lover was a full-grown Abyssian: A vast creature made of cold immobile flesh, intricate tentacles that fashioned machines of every sort, and through every part of his body, delicate networks of rigid, electrically conductive proteins. The proteins created a mind with more neural connections than a million human minds. "He," Porsche called the adult, but in reality, her lover contained both sexes, in abundance.

As a subadult, Porsche was simply female, and she was extremely small, too. "No bigger than a minke whale." When she came to Abyss, the adult called to her through the cold, acoustically transparent waters, asking for her name and origin. "For my records," he explained, sounding like every officious bureaucrat on every other world. But hearing that she was from the earth, he responded, "You possibly know a friend of mine . . . a certain young human male." Trinidad, of course. And learning the truth, he staged a quick, relentless courtship that was followed by a brief and staggeringly strange affair.

"I was Trinidad reborn," she admitted. "The adult kept assuring me that I looked and sounded like my departed cousin, and that I embodied some of his appealing personality. Though I lacked his charm, I was told. Then I was encouraged—ordered— to tell stories about my family, the worlds that I'd seen, and the people whom I'd met along the way.

"Adult Abyssians live through the experiences of others.

"They're rooted to one piece of ocean crust. They can't swim in their own seas, and none have ever tried crossing through an intrusion.

"Because there's no point in trying."

Porsche paused for a half-moment, then said, "Their souls are huge, and hugely complex. What are the chances that a neighboring world has evolved some sort of analogous mind?"

"Tiny," Cornell ventured.

"Tiny squared, and there's nowhere for them to go," she assured. "But on the other hand, they're ancient creatures with prodigious memories, plus a kind of godly wisdom, which means that eventually, sure as sure can be, they become boring as hell.

"I grew tired of being Trinidad's replacement, so I broke it off with the Abyssian." She shook her head in the darkness, remembering the darkness of that distant sea. "And to the creature's credit, he was gracious about it. He even said that he wasn't surprised, which may or may not have been the truth. You know how lovers can be, protecting their pride." She gave a half-laugh, then said, "He made a final request. 'Let me show you something wonderful,' he promised. 'Something that I'm not supposed to show just anyone.'

"That," Porsche announced, "is when I was shown the map of the Few's universe.

"The map was hidden inside the Abyssian, in a secret chamber surrounded by the mind itself. It was carved from light and odors and tactile sensations, and it was far too complicated for me to understand. Which my lover knew. He spoke to me as if I was an infant, telling me that I could, if I wanted, commit the map to memory under forced hypnosis, but I would never, ever comprehend its intricate geometry.

"The Few were spread across a vast area, he assured me.

"And himself too, I think.

" 'Nothing is larger,' he told me. 'Except the rest of the universe, of course.'

"There was a long silence, and I broke the spell. I asked, 'Did you show this map to Trinidad?'

" 'I very rarely show this to my lovers,' the Abyssian admitted. 'But he was very charming and very insistent . . . yes, I brought him here. Yes.'

"What was I to think?" Porsche asked.

Then she told Cornell how she was shown the complex twist of fuzz that contained the earth and Jarrtee and a few hundred thousand neighboring worlds, and beyond that fuzz was something that even a stupid soul could understand. Blackness. Emptiness. The Great Unknown.

"I think what happened," she told Cornell, and herself, "was that the Abyssian showed the precious map to Trinidad. My cousin used his charms, or maybe his lover's arrogance, which sounds exactly like Trinidad. Which is why I didn't think twice about it. He had seen the opportunity to go where he wasn't permitted, and he took it, and afterwards, he left his lover and Abyss, returning home again. Which was perfectly normal. And as ex-lovers will, the Abyssian must have thought of him. The sum total of their relationship was stored in that tremendous immobile mind, and he replayed each moment over and over again. . . ."

She paused for an instant, for a breath, then continued.

"I was being warned. Seeing the map was part of it. Words supplied the rest of my warning. But the Abyssian couldn't just say, 'This is what happened. This is what it means.' Because the Abyssian was embarrassed, undoubtedly. And angry in secret ways. And because he really couldn't claim, 'This is what it means.' My ex-lover was simply offering a possibility to me, not hard fact, and he/she dressed that possibility in camouflage that helped protect a colossal pride. . . .

"I glanced at the enormous map one last time, and the Abyssian touched the black unknown with one of his tentacles.

"And in passing—at least at the time I thought it was in passing—he asked a very strange—and when you think about it—a very obvious question.

" 'What if there is someone else?' he whispered. 'Someone exactly like the Few, but different?

" 'Expanding from world to world like us, but independent of us?

" 'And what if this is where the Few and the Others meet? At this little twist of worlds. Your earth. Jarrtee. Here. What would it mean, Porsche?' he asked me. Then with the most benign tone, the Abyssian suggested, 'Give it some thought. It might become important, someday. . . .' "

There was a pause.

It lasted for an instant, or an hour. Then the silence was broken when Cornell took the skeptic's pose, remarking, "You know, when people are shown random patterns of dots, their eyes and minds make up coherent pictures." He took a deep breath, then added, "Illusions. That's what they are."

Maybe the old Abyssian had been suffering from paranoid delusions.

Maybe.

Or more likely, Porsche herself was reading too much into a string of words and circumstances that weren't intended to mean anything at all.

Yet she was ready to counterattack, if only to convince herself that she wasn't imagining nonsense. If anyone in the Few could detect these mysterious Others, she would argue, why not an Abyssian who knows everything and has the quiet and the patience and the sheer time to contemplate what he knows? And if there were such things as the Others, then wouldn't they like to acquire an intricate, highly accurate map of the Few's empire? Forced hypnosis would be the avenue, and the agent would be . . . well, wouldn't it make perfect sense to employ a minor renegade like her cousin?

But Porsche didn't mention any of those fanciful logics.

Instead, she told Cornell, and herself, "I've never believed—never—that Trinidad is doing this for human money or simple revenge, or even both. I know him. At least I think I know him. And those answers just don't work."

"But if it's true," Cornell sputtered, "what does it mean?"

Many things. Some obvious, and others lying in wait like hungry tigers.

One obvious possibility reared up before Cornell, and he gasped, then managed to say, "Fuck," in jarrtee, then battered English.

Then, silence.

This time the silence was brief, and it was broken by the distinct sound of a door handle being turned, its titanium mechanism clicking gently as Porsche rose to her feet in a single smooth motion, and she glided over to the door, navigating in the darkness by memory, reaching toward the chill brass handle, grabbing it and feeling the little points of wear caused by a child's impatient hands. Years of being grabbed and yanked had left tiny marks, which was perhaps the only genuine trace of the little girl who had once treasured this delicious cave.

The handle and door were being pushed toward her, with force.

Porsche stepped back, bracing herself. The hallway lights seemed brilliant for an instant, causing her to squint, and a large jarrtee figure stepped toward her without warning, without sound.

She moved by instinct, kicking one of the solid ankles hard enough to make it fly, then letting gravity do the rest.

The man dropped on the floor with a pitiful grunt.

For the second time in his life, Uncle Ka-ceen was on his ass, knocked flat by his niece. But this time he wasn't angry, or embarrassed. He wore a pitiful expression built around milky blind eyes, and his voice matched his face, telling her, "I came to get you."

Softly and sloppily, he said, "We found your friend. And my superior thinks we can save him."

"Are you all right?" Porsche whispered.

"Not at all," he admitted, his breathing quick and useless. "I'm not seeing very much at the moment."

Misery brought the blindness.

With the frailest of whispers, Uncle Ka-ceen confessed, "I was listening to you . . . to everything. Everything."

He sat motionless for a long moment, probably wishing that he had beaten his son to death years ago, in Yellowstone.

Then with the trapped calm of a hero, he said:

"Take my hand. Take me where I have to go."

SALVATION

THE BUILDING HAD ONCE SERVED AS A SMALL NEIGHBORHOOD ZOO, its cages and sealed tanks designed to hold diurnal animals, deep-sea fish, and other creatures people never saw in the normal course of a night. Almost nothing had been changed to create a small prison. Suspected members of the Order were purged of biorhythmic hormones, tagged, and laid out, estivating in the dying light of the day. Every cage and drained aquarium was crowded with prisoners awaiting interrogation. The backlog looked enormous, but otherwise the building felt empty. Most of its guards had been sent off into the mountains, thrown into the desperate hunt for the kidnapped Masters. Only the interrogators were at full strength, but they weren't accomplishing anything; moments ago, Uncle Ka-ceen had stunned them, leaving their bodies lying limp on the floor of the main aquarium.

Bloodied prisoners sat along one glass wall, restrained by silk ropes and tangles of tubes and wires. None were Timothy. Porsche looked twice to make certain, and Cornell wiped clean a tall man's face, taking a hard look before he asked, "Where next?"

For every reason, time was short.

The four of them rushed from cell to cell, and Uncle Ka-ceen examined the coded tags, searching for a single prisoner brought through the proper checkpoint. It was frustrating work, and as the nameless woman liked to point out, "He might not be here. Records could be wrong, which means—"

"Nothing," Uncle Ka-ceen replied, glaring at the woman for a half-instant. "Mr. Kleck is here somewhere, and we'll find him."

"I certainly hope so," she offered, without hope.

No one had mentioned the Abyssian's speculation. Not in the woman's presence, they hadn't. And among themselves, they had said maybe twenty words, deciding only to keep secret what Porsche suspected.

For now.

The largest cage was packed, prisoners stacked three deep on the slick ceramic floor, and there was a thick, powerful stink in the close air. Bodies lying against the floor were ravaged by the jarrtee equivalent of bedsores—infected patches of blackened flesh, much of it rotting, fat green grubs enjoying the choicest portions. Hundreds of tags needed to be read. It would take too long. Porsche knew it, and standing back for a moment, she gazed at the motionless bodies, the scene possessing an inert and subdued dignity, utterly unexpected, and in a fashion, beautiful.

Life enduring every insult, every abuse.

"We can't leave him," Cornell whispered. "Not here. Not like this."

He could see the possibility looming, and he was hoping for Porsche's encouragement and conviction. But the best she could offer was silence and a purposeful nod.

"Low-grade prisoners," her uncle called out. "That's all that are here!"

If Timothy was here, he had been brought in recently. The guards would have carried him on a stretcher, and they were probably sloppy men, and hurried, and they despised their enemies.

She tried to read the bodies.

The angles of repose; the general mix of limbs and upturned faces.

She strode out to a stack of prisoners not far from a secondary door—a titanium door through which zookeepers might once have thrown meat and nuts to a band of terrors—and she grasped a spidery arm, yanking hard and finding the attached face, turning it up to the dim ceiling light as her uncle shouted out:

"I've already checked them over!"

It wasn't Timothy's face. She was wrong, and surprised. And an instant later, angry. Taking a step backward, her slippered foot clipped a sharp jarrtee chin, and she wheeled and glanced downward, staring at Timothy for several moments before the first sense of recognition struck.

"I have him. Here!"

Dubious, the woman asked Cornell, "Is it him?"

A nod. "Yes."

Timothy was buried beneath a layer of even newer prisoners, his tag tucked out of easy reach. With a laser knife, Uncle Ka-ceen cut the tag free. Then as an afterthought, he read the security code, shaking his head in a human fashion and laughing grimly.

"What's it say?" asked Cornell.

"It prescribes his interrogation," he explained. Then kneeling, he patted the long chalky face with a strange affection, adding, "You can't know it, son. But this is your lucky day."

Two figures lay unconscious in the back end of a little float car adorned with security emblems.

It was Jey-im who drew the nameless woman's attention. "What would be a likely place?" she asked Uncle Ka-ceen. "To leave him, I mean. Someplace where he will be found, but not too soon."

The last storm of the day was pummeling their car. Buildings were dark blotches against the gray of air and angry water. They could slow anywhere and dump Jey-im onto the pavement, and nobody would notice. They could stop and prop up his motionless body in the middle of a normally busy intersection, and the

poor man would stand alone for an eternity, the scant traffic seeing nothing in the mayhem.

But the woman seemed to need to act with some modicum of
decency. When Uncle Ka-ceen didn't reply immediately, she
turned on Porsche, trying for a reasonable voice that turned
shrill despite her best efforts.

"This gentleman made some unfortunate decisions," she reminded her. "And besides, the Few aren't responsible. The
agency holds the blame, and your cousin . . ."

"And so do I," Porsche added.

The woman discounted those words with a simple grunt.

"I could have warned him," Porsche explained, her own voice
crisp and certain. "A few words before we left the school, and his
life wouldn't be over now."

"And in the process," the woman countered, "you'd have
doomed your own family. Would that have been best?"

Porsche didn't say the obvious. How safe was her family as it
stood now, and what were their prospects?

Instead, she turned to her uncle, asking, "How's Trinidad?
What's the latest?"

He closed his eyes, listening to the prattle of eavesdroppers,
then after a little while, he announced, "The City still hasn't
found him. But it's doubling its search area, including sweeps of
the coastal mountains."

Their car was slowing.

The woman was pulling off into a building's rain shadow, and
with the calmest, coldest voice, she said, "This is where we'll leave
him. The jarrtee."

No one made a sound.

"Very well," she said. "I'll move the man myself."

Porsche said, "No."

Saying nothing, Cornell pulled a little closer to her.

Uncle Ka-ceen kept his mouth closed, feigning deafness.

Then the woman reached for Jey-im, and Porsche intercepted
her hand and held it tightly, staring hard at the cold black eyes,
saying, "No," with finality.

An electric moment passed.

Then the woman shrugged, human-style, and remarked, "I hope you have something reasonable in mind."

Porsche explained, in brief.

"I'm not going to be responsible for any of this," the woman growled. "It's your project, and all the blame is yours."

Porsche had to laugh.

"What have I been saying?" she asked, shaking her head in astonishment. "When have I said anything else?"

The last time Porsche was here, it was nearly dawn, the sky was clear, and she was accompanied by a young lover who would soon betray her.

This time, each of those geometries was neatly reversed.

She barely recognized the tiny courtyard. Lush weeds and an ankle-deep pond obscured the glass disk, and the surrounding compounds were shabby enough to look abandoned. Which they were, perhaps. Did security people still keep tabs on this intrusion? She asked, and her uncle, shouting over the drumming of rain, said, "Not for years, they haven't. The war demands all their attentions."

Uncle Ka-ceen and the woman were half-carrying, half-dragging Timothy Kleck.

Cornell and Porsche were following them, Jey-im strung between them, limp as mud and about as helpful.

"Hurry!" the woman implored everyone.

Porsche felt the glass beneath her, and as her foot skated forward, she kicked a day salamander. A fat golden tail flopped out of the water, vanishing with a sharp splash, and again she looked up, her own dose of paranoia making her scan the nearby windows, watching for masked faces.

The woman let Timothy fall into Uncle Ka-ceen's arms. From beneath her bulky shirt, she brought out six tiny statues molded from cultured diamonds.

Lightning crossed the sky, making the statues glitter and dance.

Then the woman was kneeling, trying to find the disk's center, and with a loud, happy voice, she told the world, "Another moment or two . . ."

Uncle Ka-ceen's face was hidden by his mask, but something about its angle and his posture told Porsche what he was doing. In another moment, he would lose the eavesdroppers. Which was why he was asking for a final update, his eyes closed beneath his impenetrable mask, his whispered commands obscured by the rain and tumbling white thunder.

"There!" the woman announced.

Then again, she told everyone, "Hurry!"

A gust of wind came barreling down the alley, thrashing the weeds and kicking up waves on the water. Porsche leaned into the wind. But Uncle Ka-ceen remained motionless, holding Timothy around the chest, the two of them immune to that elemental force.

Then the wind dropped to nothing.

"What?" Porsche asked, the sudden quiet making her voice seem loud. "What's wrong, Uncle?"

He didn't say anything.

He never moved so much as a finger.

Then the woman said, "Hurry," one last time. "We have people waiting for us on the other side." Then as if to sweeten the prospects, she added, "It's a dry world. Come with me, now!"

"Trinidad," Uncle Ka-ceen muttered.

"What about him?" asked Porsche.

There was a long pause that ended at no particular moment. Porsche heard nothing, then she heard her uncle's voice, and she realized that she had been hearing it for several moments, the words unclear, jarrtee mixed with ragged English and several other languages from worlds she couldn't identify.

Again, he whispered, "Trinidad."

The woman took hold of Cornell, tugging on his arm as she said, "Come with me. It will be all right."

"What's happening?" Porsche shouted.

"They just found him," her uncle reported, his voice suddenly strong. "The City found him. And the entire convoy."

Cornell took back his arm, asking, "What about their base camp?"

"They haven't found it," Uncle Ka-ceen reported. "Not yet, at least. But the City is screaming for reinforcements."

The woman decided on silence, for the moment.

Then Porsche said simply, "I'm staying here. I can't help anyone if I walk away from Jarrtee now."

"No," the woman replied. "You need to stay with us."

"I'm not going, either," Cornell promised.

The woman tried to touch his arm a second time, and he slapped her hand away, adding, "I'm tired of you."

"Take Timothy," said Porsche. "And Jey-im, too."

She was speaking to her uncle.

"Keep Jey-im stunned, I guess. Stunned, and innocent. I'll come get him as soon as possible."

"You two won't stand a chance," the woman warned them. "Minimal equipment. Just that little float car to drive . . . staying here is insanity!"

Uncle Ka-ceen turned to face her, and with a sudden composure, he asked, "Is the intrusion open?"

"Yes."

Then he said, "Good. Fine."

Without warning, he let Timothy slide down into the water and stepped over him, lifting both hands and giving the woman a single hard shove.

She stumbled, then seemed to fall into the pond's secret depths.

The water swirled, then grew still again. Then he calmly picked up Timothy and dropped him into the intrusion. He then lifted up Jey-im and half-flung him down again, making him vanish. And he finally kneeled and brought up each of the six intrusion keys, counting them twice, then handing them to Porsche while saying, "We might need these."

She nodded, speechless.

The tiny diamond statues portrayed heroes in the midst of their famous deeds. One of them was Po-lee-een, Porsche realized. Another was Ka-ceen, the great warrior who had personally slaughtered a thousand of the City's enemies with nothing but a steel blade. And the other four were named for her parents and her brothers.

"The witch let me camouflage these keys," Uncle Ka-ceen explained, a thin amusement breaking to the surface.

Then with a different voice, he said:

"Hurry."

As if they needed prompting.

PORSCHE DROVE, CORNELL SITTING TO HER RIGHT, NERVOUSLY PAS-
sive, and Uncle Ka-ceen behind them, his eyes more closed than
open, keeping careful watch over the world.

They would talk on occasion, but never for long.

Plans were discussed. Tactics were debated. Hypothetical problems were invented, then dissected and solved with a glossy ease
that left everyone feeling uncomfortable. The truth told, they
didn't know what would happen when they found Trinidad, or
even if they could reach the mountains. It became more and
more apparent that this was a pure gamble, an over-the back
full-court shot, and they wouldn't be able to even guess their
prospects for a long time to come.

Sometimes Porsche would talk about her cousin.

And the Abyssian's bizarre speculation.

Uncle Ka-ceen grew silent and cold in response, his face like
marble, very pale in the waning light.

Then Porsche took a deep breath and said, "Yellowstone."

She took a second breath, then aimed at a specific moment.
"After Trinidad and I talked about forbidden things. After the
two of you had your big fight. That next scene has always stuck
in my mind."

The man behind her didn't react. If anything, he grew even

more distant, one white hand stroking his bare head, the barest
tremor of the fingers betraying his true mood.

It was Cornell who asked:

"What scene stuck?"

Their fight was done, and Trinidad—bruised and still furious,
and thoroughly embarrassed—won comfort from his mother.
Aunt Kay had embraced him, pulling his head down against her
chest, and in plain view, she had whispered something into his
ear. Porsche didn't have any idea what she said. She considered
asking if her uncle had been eavesdropping, but he probably
hadn't been. And even if he had been, she doubted if anything
important was said.

"I guess what it was," she allowed, "was the way he leaned
against his mother." Porsche glanced at Cornell, but she was talking to her uncle. "I guess what bothered me—this is going to
sound awful—what bothered me was that sudden realization that
Trinidad had two parents. And the parent who mattered most
wasn't born into the Few, which was startling. And a little wrong,
I kept thinking."

There was a long silence broken by the distant rumble of
thunder.

"But that happened decades ago," said Cornell. "And the
Abyssian was years ago." He paused, then asked, "If you're right
about all of this, why figure it out now?"

Porsche glanced over her shoulder, her uncle evading her
eyes.

The truth told, she was proud of her cleverness, no matter
how belated it was.

No matter how gruesome the consequences.

"In part," she admitted, "it was coming back here and seeing
what the war was doing to Jarrtee. In part, it was Jey-im's apocalyptic mutterings. All at once it occurred to me that maybe, just
maybe, the Order isn't prospering because of its own bloody
merits." She hesitated, then said, "When we were in the school,
Jey-im mentioned the early beginnings of the universe. Matter
and antimatter collided, annihilating each other. Jey-im was

shaken by all that destruction. But I saw a different lesson. I kept thinking of traditional jarrtees fighting the Order, the two sides working hard for some type of mutual annihilation.

"What if there's something like the Few, but different?" she asked. "What if instead of slowly blending into a world's people, it takes a different attitude? It cultures disorder. Civil wars. Apocalyptic events that leave planets depopulated, at least temporarily.

"Intrusions are supposed to prevent invading armies. At least that's what the Few teach one another, isn't it? But what if there's only a hundred thousand jarrtees left alive in the near future, and they're scattered and weak, and disorganized? A few thousand naked soldiers are suddenly a force. And if the invaders can funnel a steady stream of souls into the empty world, they can quickly swamp the true natives."

She paused, taking a few quick breaths.

Then Cornell said, "What about the earth?"

"I've thought about it. A lot." She focused on the farthest point visible on the road, the rain slackening to where she could see nearly an earthly half-mile. "Maybe it means nothing. Pure coincidence, or whatever. But the twentieth century was so very bloody, so many nearly equal powers struggling for more power . . . right up until the Few arrived in an official basis, scouting out the species and societies . . . making ready to make a secret impact . . ."

"The world wars were manufactured?" Cornell replied, doubt mixed with a cold horror. "By this other group? Is that what you're saying?"

"I don't know what I believe," she confessed. "But the earth is at the very edge of the Few. And it is—if you think about it for about two seconds—pretty damned arrogant of us to believe that we're the only organized society of world-wandering souls."

Her uncle looked like a statue carved from pure opal.

She glanced at him, then admitted, "There was another clue. Trinidad gave it to me in Texas, after our capture. 'I want to be a hero,' he told me. And all of the sudden, walking with Jey-im in school, I saw the obvious glaring at me.

"A hero to whom?' I asked myself.

"That's when I saw Aunt Kay holding him on that mountain meadow, whispering encouragement to her son. I don't know what she told him, but I can guess. She said, 'Be patient. Be smart. And you'll be a hero eventually, I promise. . . .' "

She paused, then asked, "What is Trinidad doing here?"

Then she answered her own question. "In one operation, he's helping to weaken the strongest city-state on Jarrtee, and he's unbalancing decades of peace on the earth, too. Because if the agency can deliver those scientists, you know what kinds of technologies they'll win. Weapons. Wonderful, powerful new weapons. One world's horror contaminating its neighbor . . . and Trinidad . . . he's a great hero to those who matter most to him. . . . "

Uncle Ka-ceen leaned forward suddenly.

With a strong hand, he gripped her shoulder, and with a voice that couldn't be more frail, he said, "Enough, thank you. We've heard enough for now. Thank you."

There were two guard posts inside the City, unmanned save for robots unsuited for use on the front lines. A cursory examination of new medallions and identities was enough to have gates lifted and ritual words of encouragement offered for these trying times.

The third post was manned, and grumpy.

"You're lost," said the ranking guard, eyeing each of them in turn. "They want your unit up north."

Like Trinidad before him, Uncle Ka-ceen had dressed himself in the potent rank of a security official. He was exactly the kind of man who could whistle angrily, poke his head into the rain, then warn a lesser soul, "Our timetable isn't any of your fucking business, you dirty shit."

A jarrtee guard was the eternal master of his post.

Twenty-five years had changed nothing.

"Remain here," the man warned them. "We need a second look at you."

"Sleep," said Uncle Ka-ceen, in English. Then, "You shit."

The entire post was unconscious before he could complete his sentence, and before the last limp body struck the pavement, Porsche was accelerating, wringing everything out of their car's fierce little engine.

Dusk was settling over the world.

Pools of near-night gathered inside the deep valleys, and some of the night-blooming trees were already erupting into self-made light and perfume, begging a multitude of creatures to come admire them, feast on their abundance, then carry away their pollen even before the sun could set.

It was an ancient cheat.

And because it was ancient, it had a nobility.

Porsche felt energized by these little tastes of night. She drove fast along the narrow mountain roads, on the brink of recklessness, obeying her uncle's instructions and thinking about nothing but the driving, relishing that sense of focus.

"Slower," Uncle Ka-ceen warned.

She assumed a faltering courage. They had just crossed a forested ridge, rain and wind lashing at them, and the road plunged into the next valley. Porsche plunged with it, knowing that nothing counted now but covering as much distance as fast as possible—

"Stop!" her uncle called out. "Please!"

Reluctantly, Porsche applied the brakes. The float car twisted its force field, cutting into the steep slope and kicking up a fountain of mud and loose granite until their momentum belonged to the mountain. A momentary silence, as peaceful as it was misleading, caused her to turn and ask, "Why here?" But then she heard a wrong-sounding thunder, too close and too sharp, the explosive concussion hammering at them, then hesitating, then striking hard three more times, faster than beating hearts.

Somewhere below them, in that thick hot blue-black forest, people were eagerly and efficiently trying to kill one another.

Uncle Ka-ceen nearly closed his eyes, whispering commands, using their onboard eavesdroppers to measure what was happening.

Cornell sat erect, his face tired and his voice more tired.

"Are we in time?" he muttered.

The flat crack of a rip-gun came from nearby. Then, silence.

"What's happening?" he whispered.

"There's a standoff below us," Uncle Ka-ceen reported. "The convoy is surrounded by a few hundred of the City's troops. The humans are threatening to slaughter the Masters in their custody."

Porsche listened carefully, yet at the same time she felt very distant, very calm.

"How close are we to them?" asked Cornell.

"Less than a mile."

"Where's the intrusion?"

A hand appeared, gesturing at the next mountain to the west. "Another five miles, approximately."

Porsche felt as if she were standing on one of the remote mountaintops. "Do the jarrtees know about the base camp yet?" she inquired.

"I don't think so. But they have patrols everywhere."

She could guess Latrobe's thinking: Delay the enemy. Wait for reinforcements crossing over from the earth. Then fight their way to freedom. But naturally, the City was bringing up its own forces, too, preparing for a heavily choreographed assault— probably about two moments after the sun set.

She asked about the most important player. Trinidad.

"I don't know where he is," her uncle growled. "I can't find him through all the EM camouflage."

A tense silence descended.

Then she turned to stare at her uncle. His eyes were closed tight and moving fast beneath the chalky lids, as if dreaming. There was something sweet about his plain face, a quality that she'd never noticed before. The poor man was wrestling hard with what the eavesdroppers showed him—and worse, the horrible things that he could imagine, trying to find some escape from this bottomless, shame-riddled trap.

Porsche saw exactly one possibility, and it was only that.

A possibility.

"What kinds of tools do we have with us?" she asked. "Few-made, and otherwise."

Uncle Ka-ceen opened his eyes, recounting each item in turn.

Cornell made no motion, no sound.

She told them her plan, making little changes from what she had first imagined but the plan's bones left unaltered. Wasn't it obvious, this approach? Even inevitable?

Yet both of the men seemed surprised, then doubtful.

"You can't," said Cornell, by reflex.

"It won't work," Uncle Ka-ceen promised. "I can see twenty places where it could fall apart—"

"Fine," she interrupted. "Think of something better."

Silence.

Porsche fitted the mask over her face, then reached for the handle overhead, preparing to crack the door.

"Wait," she heard.

Uncle Ka-ceen handed her a piece of dried and sweetened twenty-five-year-old fat, telling her to swallow it.

She obeyed.

But it was Cornell who had said, "Wait."

And now he lifted her mask, saying, "For luck," as he bent close, managing a sloppy kiss before he told her, "See you in a little while."

He was working so very hard, trying to believe those final words.

THE SWEETENED FAT COVERED A PACKAGE OF FEW-MADE TOOLS, MOST of which did absolutely nothing. It was a package meant for security people, most of the com-ties leading to associates who had emigrated long ago. But she could speak to her uncle, if needed—a risky indulgence, since Trinidad might hear their prattle. And more important, Porsche could eavesdrop again. Not over large distances, and not where the EM camouflage was thickest. Yet she could see far enough to make out a jarrtee patrol working its way through the lush woods, and she could judge how far she could creep forward until there was the good chance of being spotted.

Settling into the undergrowth, into a rich bank of black mud, she heard a trillion furious insects screaming to the world: "Here, look here! Here she hides!"

The jarrtees noticed nothing, slipping off to the west.

Then Porsche rose again, and walked, and hesitated briefly, and walked again, trying hard to look as if she belonged there. Skirting the edge of a bomb crater, she could sense *something* nearby. It wore Few camouflage, but it wasn't invisible. Not to her. A sudden little voice told her to look to her right, and beware. She obeyed the voice. Then from her left, without warning, the oily black vegetation parted, a rip-gun leading the way, its grip attached to a masked figure whose shape and fluid mobility identified him in an instant.

It was the soldier who had sat stoically beside her in the helicopter and painstakingly opened the gifts intended for the children. *Alvarez.*

With the driest, smoothest voice she could manage, Porsche told the soldier, "I'm glad you're all right."

Those words took him by surprise, for an instant.

He paused in midstride.

"I want to see Latrobe," she announced. "I want to see him right now."

The young man scanned the forest behind Porsche, out of habit or fear, whispering quick questions through a secure channel.

"Tell him that time matters," she added.

The soldier whispered something about time.

Then, silence.

Instead of waiting for an answer, Porsche decided on impatience, walking past Alvarez while saying with a forced casualness, "Or shoot me, if you want. If I'm totally wrong about you."

The convoy looked like it had driven through a war.

Every armored vehicle sported fresh wounds and a crusted black frosting left from napalm. Porsche slowed her gait, brushing up against the soldier as she took a quick inventory. One of the small cars had vanished. With Trinidad on board? The possibility brought a stew of powerful emotions, then a blunt denial. Her cousin wouldn't let himself die that easily. Four wounded soldiers lay in an opened cargo hold, the platoon's medic laboring over the worst casualty, administering jarrtee medicines with a human's bedside manner. "You're doing fine," he said, without confidence. "Keep still. We'll be home soon."

Past the wounded, deep inside the hold, dozens of pure white bodies were stacked like firewood, faces and feet alternating to give the piles a semblance of balance.

The core of the City's genius looked utterly helpless, utterly pathetic.

As Porsche watched, one of the white arms twitched, brushing against another arm that jumped in turn, by reflex.

The Masters were beginning to rise out of their estivation.

"This way," Alvarez warned.

Porsche was escorted across an expanse of mud and rain-filled footprints. A battered little float car was tucked beneath an enormous twanya tree, and leaning against it was another wounded soldier. An exposed shoulder wore a jarrtee field dressing, and the iron-rich stink of blood lay against the roof of her mouth. Otherwise, Latrobe seemed remarkably healthy, his voice not loud but strong, his anger directed at people that no one could see. "I don't care how fucking tough it is. The bastards are bringing *everything.*" A pause, then, "No, I want relief in the hour. Leave a minimal crew in camp. Understand?"

"Having a bad day?" Porsche began to say.

Her lead foot kicked something firmer than mud, and drier. She looked down. A Master lay half-buried in the mud. A single round from a rip-gun—a fleck of metal shrouded in a force field—had torn through the man's head, the field's energies obliterating flesh and bone and probably making sand out of the rock far beneath them.

Lying next to the dead man were three more dead men, each executed with the same sick precision. It was their blood that Porsche could smell.

Four hostages, slaughtered in plain view, had earned the current truce.

"Come over here, Miss Neal." Latrobe beckoned with his good arm, his voice brushing charm before it found its true tone. "You were damned lucky to escape. Or did the City wake you up, and they're sending you to talk?"

It would be an interesting twist, but not interesting enough.

She told the truth instead. "No, the Few pulled us out in time. But you're right. I've been sent here to open a dialogue."

The face behind the mask was probably grimacing. An angry voice said, "A dialogue! Why in the fuck do you think we'd listen to you now?"

She didn't offer the obvious reasons.

Instead, Porsche asked her own question: "Where's Trinidad?"

Hearing his name, her cousin climbed from the car. "Hello, Po-lee-een!" He was uninjured, and unrepentant. His jaunty mood clashed with Latrobe's. "I'm making a guess," he began, each word framed with a whistled laugh. "My father managed to find you, didn't he? Which isn't really that enormous of a surprise, I guess."

She said nothing.

"What I'm asking myself," he said, "is why you've done something so stupid. What do you think you can accomplish here?"

She turned toward Latrobe, and said nothing.

"What?" Latrobe barked. "We're busy here . . . what?"

"A compromise. I came to offer you a deal." She waited for a half-moment, then gestured at Trinidad. "I don't want to talk to *him*. This is you and me. Assuming that you have the voice in decisions—"

"Fine," Trinidad offered. "Talk. I'll sit over here and pretend to be deaf."

A muted voice came from within Latrobe's mask. Someone was giving him an update, the voice soft and quick, and incomprehensible.

"All right," Latrobe told her. "I'm curious. I'll listen. What's this deal?"

"It's a lie!" her cousin cried out. "I guarantee it."

Latrobe's face was obscured by his mask, but when he glanced at Trinidad, for that instant, there was a palpable sense of frustration. The mission had become a nightmare. Promises of easy success were beginning to gnaw at him. It was the perfect moment, and Porsche mined it for all it was worth.

"I can give you worlds for almost nothing, and almost infinite resources, too."

She spoke, then waited for a moment.

Then anticipating his next question, Porsche added, "And best of all, it's a solution that the Few can tolerate. Maybe not embrace, but tolerate."

Latrobe hesitated, then said:

"What worlds are you giving us?"

"The earth's moon. And Mars. Every asteroid beyond. And in your lifetime, probably, the outer solar system, too."

Trinidad let out a scornful, high-pitched wail.

Latrobe's response was to look only at Porsche, waiting until the wail stopped, then telling her with a measured coolness, "Go on. Explain it to me."

"It's the nature of the intrusions," she began, "and it's the shape of the rebuilt universe, too. Every single body in space, no matter how insignificant, has at least one intrusion leading to somewhere else. A small asteroid, not more than a mile across, has hundreds and thousands of intrusions. Just like on the earth, most of those intrusions lead to dead places. But a few lead to living worlds. And if the asteroid is part of your solar system, there's a good chance—an almost one hundred percent chance—that at least one intrusion reaches directly to the earth itself."

There was a pause, then Latrobe said with a careful stiffness, "I know the general theory. Thank you."

"Then how about this? The earth and moon share tens of thousands of intrusions. The agency hasn't found any yet, but that's not surprising. The universe is a baffling maze. And why would you want to find such a thing? Because if you can identify just one intrusion that's in easy reach, and it reaches to an inhabited part of the moon, then a person doesn't need an expensive spaceship. Just step through the intrusion, neat and quick. Step through and your soul is transported, and a new body is built around it. But instead of being jarrtee or some other alien, you become human. Again. Because there is exactly one sentient organism living today on the moon, and it's human.

And since your human soul has very clear expectations, you actually become the same person that you are at home."

She paused, smiling beneath her mask.

"A neat little trick. Do you agree?"

Latrobe responded by glancing at Trinidad.

Before he could ask his question, her cousin said, "As far as it goes, she's telling the truth."

Latrobe turned back to Porsche, admitting, "I'm tired. I don't understand. Going from the earth to the moon might have uses. But how do we get the solar system out of this?"

"Send a team of humans and robots to Mars. A few humans and a lot of robots." She gestured, promising him, "Your country can easily manage that trick. Set down at a known intrusion that leads to the earth, then guide the robots as they build a city out of the native rock and ores. Teaching an intrusion about a local species is easy. I can tell you how to do it. When the Martian city is finished, your pioneers can step through and claim their apartments and houses. No long voyages in fancy ships required."

The audience wasn't an idiot. For a long while, Latrobe said nothing, obviously wrestling with the possibilities.

"The same trick works on asteroids," promised Porsche. "On the moons of Jupiter. Even with the gas giants themselves."

"Nonetheless," sang Trinidad, "it's difficult, difficult work."

Latrobe waved at both of them with his good arm, then demanded to know, "What happened to the Few's taboo about giving away technology?"

"This isn't new technology," she pointed out. "You know how to use the intrusions. And I guarantee you, the theory isn't going to surprise your scientists. Their problem has been that they don't have enough experience with intrusions. They don't know the geometry of things. But with help, we can revolutionize space travel in one little hour."

"The Few can," said Latrobe. "Or is it just you?"

"It's just me. For now, this is my offer, although I'm sure I'll get help."

"And the price?"

She was ready. "Release the jarrtees. Retreat off this world immediately. And give me my cousin as a token of gratitude."

Latrobe was staring at her, saying nothing.

She could guess the flow of his thoughts, then his next essential question.

Turning toward her cousin, he asked, "Is any of this bullshit? Is it?"

Trinidad shook his head, replying, "We've both seen solar systems that are tied together this way. It's not uncommon, no."

Which led Latrobe to the next obvious question:

"Why didn't you offer this before?"

In an instant, without hesitation, Trinidad assured him, "First of all, it's small slow potatoes that she's giving you. And secondly, I told Farrah about using local, short-distance intrusions, and the troubles involved, and we decided to wait until after this mission to discuss terms."

Was he lying? Porsche guessed that he was lying, and Latrobe was smart enough to see the possibilities.

"But you can give all of this to us, too?" asked Latrobe.

"Gladly. Easily."

"Because if you don't . . ." the man began.

"No," said Trinidad, one hand rising, and the index finger pointing skyward. "Threats don't impress me."

Latrobe took another half-moment to make his decision, then said, "All right. We continue as we planned it. Nothing changes."

To Alvarez, he said, "Take our guest back into custody, please."

With a rip-gun brushing against the back of her head, Porsche remained motionless, trying to keep a loose hold on her fear.

Trinidad seemed to float up to her, examining her insides with a Few-made sensor. The same tool signaled to her internal devices, deactivating each of them in turn; then a smiling, genuinely carefree voice said, "Nice try, Po-lee-een."

I know all about you, Porsche was thinking.

But she didn't say a word, except to whisper, "Your father

wanted me to deliver a message: He says that he's running out of patience with you."

Trinidad didn't react.

She could see him not reacting, holding himself motionless. Then the same smiling voice said, "Nice try. Again."

PORSCHE SAT IN THE BATTERED LITTLE CAR, ONE HAND CUFFED TO her seat, accompanied by a silent, pensive Alvarez, both watching helplessly as the enemy approached.

What began as pools of ink huddling beneath the burly leaves of a dusk-demon plant gradually grew into a linked body of seamless black. When the sun began to plunge behind the mountains, tendrils of blackness reached out, probing the wet gray light for weakness and a failure of will. When the storm clouds collided with the mountain ridge, the light fell to a thin late-dusk glow, and the enemy was emboldened, lifting itself off the ground, filling the drenched woods and lapping against the car itself. Porsche could almost feel it beneath the floor, a little cool and extraordinarily impatient, and with a voice that spoke to glands and hormones, she heard it say:

"Night. I am. Night. It is."

The jarrtees were sure to come now, and Latrobe's vaunted relief troops, coming all the way from New Mexico, were obviously late.

Corrosive worries ate at Porsche. She worried about her family. Were they still estivating safely at the base camp, innocent of the danger? And what about Cornell? She imagined him sitting beside her, and with a secret voice, she told him nothing of importance. Pure small talk; that's what she hungered for. Then she found herself thinking of Uncle Ka-ceen, and she felt something that wasn't exactly worry but was closer to pity, sickly sweet one moment, wrenchingly painful the next.

Where was Trinidad?

Looking out at the gathering night, she called his name.

Twice, she called for him. Her tone was angry and insistent; the soldier beside her pretended not to hear. Then as she opened her mouth again, there came a sudden clean roar that she didn't hear so much as she felt in her bones. A roar, then a *crack*. Then, a misleading silence. The silence lasted an instant, if that. A peacefulness held sway over the world. The night-girdled forest looked calm and confidently expectant, and then, with absolutely no warning, a piercing light came from every-where, slaughtering the blackness, chasing the last tattered relics of night into the crannies and the soil and into bodies of men.

Like an enormous hand, the explosion flowed down the mountainside, uprooting trees and consuming the leaves and branches left exposed.

The concussion drove the little car backward. Suddenly its windows were pitch-black, trying to choke off the light, and Porsche's mask did the same, leaving her blinded by too much brilliance, and then, by none.

A second blast was more distant, and if anything, louder.

She could barely hear the wrenching squeak of a door open-ing. A familiar voice said, "In," and a second voice said, "In." Two men had climbed into the front seats, and while they se-cured their door, the rear door opened wide, allowing two more voices to say, "In," and, "In." Then the last voice screamed, "Go! Punch it!"

Latrobe was laughing giddily as he said, "Go."

Blinking her wide eyes, Porsche fought to retrieve her vision. Blurred figures emerged from the fuzz, sitting beside her— Alvarez, still—and in front of her, and behind, and she turned just enough to see Trinidad, just enough to make certain that he would notice when she ignored him.

"Go!" Latrobe roared once more.

The drivers, in a chorus, screamed, "We're trying!"

The forest in front of them was burning, the soggy wood exploding into smoke and sloppy flames. For an instant, Porsche assumed that it was the City, that it had grown bored of waiting and had finally attacked. But Latrobe just kept laughing, the moment relentlessly funny, one of his big hands eventually patting her on the shoulder, something very fond and horrible about his touch.

"Our cavalry is here," he told her.

Then, speaking to everyone:

"We're almost home."

The blast had pushed over the timber in the same direction, mostly. The float car was leading the convoy, driving at an astonishing pace, using smoke for cover and the smoldering tree trunks as a kind of roadway. There was the steady angry sound of gunfire. Explosives detonated in the distance, then, nearby. Latrobe spoke to the heavy vehicles behind them, and after the close booms, he turned to Trinidad, snapping, "I thought they couldn't see us. You said!"

"Lucky shots," her cousin replied, his voice tight and a little slow. "Just a few lucky shots."

They reached the epicenter of the first blast, charred stumps sticking up out of the ashes, slowing their progress for a moment.

Using his eavesdroppers, Trinidad found the most perfect course, then shouted crisp instructions up at the drivers.

The drivers obeyed.

Watching the two men, Porsche saw none of the old jauntiness. Even with the help of the onboard AI, they were at the brink of their talent. The car was bouncing off burning logs, embers scattered by the force field, flaring up like bombs. The cabin temperature had passed scalding, stressing even a jarrtee's love of heat. The drivers were hunched forward. They were utterly silent. Every gram of their courage had been spent, nothing left now but a nervous, lizard-simple management of a thousand impossible jobs at once.

Porsche tested her cuffs.

Just for a moment, on the sly.

Then she almost looked at Alvarez, his attentions fused on the mayhem directly ahead of them.

The gunfire fell away to a distant, forgettable sound.

"See?" sang Trinidad. "Everything's fine."

They were climbing the long battered slope of a mountain, passing from one blast zone to the next. And the ground responded by growing steeper, the uprooted trees sometimes sliding loose in the muddy goo, one great old twanya tree falling past them, missing them by what seemed like, in that compression of time and emotion, the width of a hand.

"Reach the crest, and we're safe," Latrobe promised, his voice small. Almost vulnerable. "We've got several hundred friends waiting up there."

Porsche didn't allow herself to speak, or think.

Without warning, they emerged from the firestorm, the ground suddenly flat and the air brilliant. A ragged hole in the clouds exposed the sun. They seemed to be driving straight into the clean gold brilliance. Porsche squinted, stared. Two orblike shapes flanked the sun, mimicking its brilliance, and too late, she realized they were jarrtee airships waiting for this moment, half a dozen tiny missiles launched from each, each aimed at the minuscule command car.

Surgical doses of laser light evaporated the missiles.

A fusillade of light and explosives rose from the forest to the west, gutting the airships in the same instant, vacuum chambers imploding and the sparkling remnants of the aerogel armor falling, turning in the wind.

Latrobe shouted instructions, encouragements.

Trinidad was talking to eavesdroppers and other helpers, begging for every possible favor.

The forest was straight ahead, a wall of half-downed trees forcing them to turn and move parallel to the tangled mess, searching for any gap. Porsche glanced over her shoulder. The convoy stretched out behind them, each heavy truck making the same turn, following, gouts of earth and splintered wood proving that someone with a rip-gun was close enough to just miss.

A jarring turn, left.

Suddenly they were among trees, and an instant later, they were half-flying, the sinking sensation of a carnival ride lifting stomachs, hearts.

"Another two miles," Latrobe reported. To whom? "Go, go!" But their car didn't need urging. Skating on its force field, following the track of a recent mudflow, it was instantly moving too fast for jarrtee eyes to focus on anything. Darkness made them lift their masks. A blurring tunnel, black and oiled, sucked them down and down, and the pitch of the slope only grew steeper, the mudflow suddenly covered with a brown torrent of rainwater.

Finally, Latrobe said, "Slow."

But not too much. Porsche thought. Hoped.

The heavy trucks hurtled after them, braking in turn, geysers of filthy goo taking away their momentum.

Porsche turned to watch, feeling the pressure of the cuffs and mostly ignoring the armored truck that roared up to within inches of their ass.

She was watching her cousin, taking his measure.

Having no way of knowing if this was close to the right place— Trinidad had stolen her skills—she acted out of simple hope. This was a logical route, hope cried. And buoyed up by nothing more, she called to him. Twice. Loud, then louder. And when Trinidad didn't respond, she simply said it.

"I know all about you," she promised.

Nothing.

"What you are!" Porsche cried out. "I know."

The face turned toward her, the mouth opening, hesitating.

"There are the Few, and what?" she asked. Then again, she said, "Trinidad," before asking, "What exactly do you call yourselves?"

The eyes were incurious. Composed.

"The Others. That's what the old Abyssian called you," she was saying, excitement and fatigue making her mouth dry and clumsy.

Trinidad interrupted her, simply saying, "No."

What did *no* mean?

"We aren't the Others," he said with a soft gray tone. "You are."

Porsche felt herself falling emotionally, the magnitude of that single word—*we*—at once chilling and galvanizing her. I was right . . . it's real . . . I was right!

Latrobe spoke next, asking, "What are you chatting about?"

Granite statues were more animated than Trinidad. He was locked in place, incapable of uttering the simplest sound, his mind racing as he tried to deal with this crashing news.

Porsche aimed to cripple her opponent, with a single blow.

"Did you think we didn't know?" she cackled. "Is that what you thought?"

He didn't know what to believe, said his posture. His silence.

"You know what I've wanted to tell you?" she continued. "For so long . . . do you know what it is?"

A little voice managed to squeak, "What?"

"Cousin," she announced, "you are an arrogant, selfish shit!"

The arrogant shit suddenly sat forward, and after an instant of confusion, he screamed out, "Slow down! Now!"

In a single motion, the drivers looked back over their shoulders.

"Ahead," Trinidad warned. "Something's . . . ahead!"

Neither reacted.

It took Latrobe to say, "Do it," before they reluctantly braked.

A near-river was beneath the car, flattening where the mountainside became a sudden valley. They had passed into the next mountain's shadow, back in the embrace of night, and a familiar shape was standing in plain view, standing on their right, his body naked, his white flesh blackened by mud, hands filled with tools. But what Porsche saw was the thick stick that had been shoved into her uncle's birth-pouch, with obvious pain, the gesture carrying a powerful message recognized instantly by any jarrtee:

I regret the child whom I bore.

Beyond, drowned and uprooted timber created twin islands. There was exactly one way through, and the drivers steered for the gap, accelerating out of instinct, reasonably sensing an ambush waiting for them.

Again, Trinidad shouted for them to slow down.

Latrobe didn't echo the order. He was too busy or too uncertain about what was real, gazing at the strange apparition as they passed, the jarrtee face trying to twist itself into a human expression.

Only when they were between the islands, at the end, did the drivers realize that there was a trap here. Two men with a float car could have built it from the scattered debris. In minutes, with luck.

The trap itself lay beneath the water.

Uncle Ka-ceen had searched for the perfect intrusion, then with Cornell's help, he had anchored one of the diamond statues—a jarrtee hero—on top of it.

Six people were riding on a churning river, and the next moment, Jarrtee vanished, and they were screaming straight into the heart of a different maelstrom, black and vast, sucking them into its wild maw.

The habit of momentum continues inside intrusions.

There was no time to turn and retreat. In an instant, they reached that cleansing point where machinery evaporates, and weapons, and clothes as well as a set of jarrtee wristcuffs. Naked bodies spun wildly through the non-air. A twisting heat warned the flesh that it was dissolving. Porsche flailed with her arms, killing her spin, then reached out with the ghosts of her hands, trying to grapple with her defenseless cousin.

She meant to kick him, remorselessly kick him, until her feet turned to something else, and then she would make him suffer all the worse.

Nothing else mattered.

But Trinidad managed to grab hold of Alvarez, using him as a shield, then shoving the big man straight at her.

The collision was jarring, numbing.

An instant later, their limbs turned to tendrils, hundreds of them, and their bodies became masses of living, glowing goo, and the non-air thickened and cooled until it was water, a chill clean black ocean engulfing their newborn selves.

What they were was nothing like jarrtees, or humans.

Alvarez was unprepared, in total shock. With a language built of soft light, he made plaintive calls for strength, and please, god, for mercy.

Porsche ignored Trinidad. For the moment.

She embraced Alvarez, and in soothing colors, she told him to relax and trust her. Everything was fine, she promised. Then with eyes larger than windows, she studied their surroundings.

Meaning to distract him, she asked, "Have you ever seen the stars?"

In a thin dribble of light, Alvarez whispered, "Not really. . . . I was born . . . after the Change . . ."

"Well then," she told him, her voice emerald and gold, "you should look up . . . look up now . . . go on . . ."

FROM ACROSS THE WATER, A VOICE SHOUTED A WORD NEVER SEEN BEfore on that world.

It was the image of an extinct sports car, bright and sloppily rendered, and immediately recognizable. "Porsche," the voice cried out. Then in native words, "Are you there? Are you all right?"

"Here I am. I'm fine," she replied.

With white light, she simply spelled *Cornell.*

The intrusion was spitting out souls by the dozen. The quiet sea was cluttered suddenly with big gelatinous bodies, the Masters outnumbering everyone and most of them still unconscious, black and motionless, still mercifully estivating.

A hundred tendrils grasped Porsche, and she said, "Lover," with fond colors, accidentally stinging Cornell with the wrong type of tendrils.

He flinched, laughing.

Porsche apologized, then pulled away, spelling the word *Latrobe.*

Latrobe was nearby, watching in stunned amazement as his entire convoy crossed over to this nothing world. She approached the battered man, and again she offered to deal, adding the inarguable observation:

"You're beaten. Utterly."

"How did you . . . do it?" Latrobe asked. "How did you know where . . . where we would go?"

"We could guess," she admitted. "Plus my uncle was to contact the jarrtees, then coax their support in exchange for their Masters being released. Their troops left that route open, which helped—"

Latrobe exploded in colors, anguish mixed with rage.

Porsche began to scan the crowd for her cousin, and when the tantrum was ebbing, she repeated her terms. "The Masters will be returned to the City. You'll release my family and the other hostages. Plus I get Trinidad. Or else."

Brimming with anger, Latrobe asked, "And what do I get?"

"Your life, and freedom. And the solar system."

"Guaranteed?"

Cornell drifted closer, saying, "Ka-ceen struck a deal with the City. Just as Porsche had hoped he would."

"But if the jarrtees decide to throw all of us in prison?"

"Unthinkable," Porsche responded. "There's still several hundred heavily armed soldiers in the nearby mountains, and they're loyal to you."

"And how could I give them marching orders?" Latrobe asked.

"If he's given any reason, my uncle tells them to fight." She waited for a moment, hoping for the logic to sink home. "Besides, I think at this point, the City is unwilling to risk losing any more of its scientists. Which means that the only one that you have to trust is my uncle, and he wants nothing now but Trinidad."

Latrobe said nothing.

Cornell spoke. In calm colors, he warned, "Don't think about betraying us. Once we're back on the earth, we go free. Immediately. My father goes free. I do. Everyone."

Latrobe waited for a moment, then said, "Or what?"

"Our program about the agency is broadcast today, and not just on one network. It will be on every network worldwide."

It was a bluff, but a good one. For added punch, Porsche assured Latrobe, "The Few have it in their possession. If they don't get my family back again, the agency is going to be dragged out from under its rock."

Latrobe said nothing for a long moment.

A new voice reached across the water, tinged with the unfamiliar and delightful fear common to the doomed.

Trinidad said, "Latrobe," in trembling letters. "Are you going to let that woman push you around?"

In the end, it was Latrobe who had the sweet pleasure of beating Trinidad.

With stinging tendrils, he flooded her cousin's flesh with toxins, and with muscular tendrils, he tried to squeeze the life out of him.

Cornell, then Porsche, finally pulled Latrobe off his victim.

Gazing up at a thin dust of stars, the beaten man asked, "How soon can I be home? If I agree to your terms, that is."

"Right away," promised Porsche.

"All right," Latrobe replied, sounding as if he were impaled on a great hook. "Fuck you, and all right. . . ."

Little had changed on Jarrtee, and everything was different.

The first people emerged from the intrusion to find mud and drying timber. The jarrtees had diverted the temporary river with a bombardment. The forest was drenched in night, an innate excitement swirling with the fear. Uncle Ka-ceen appeared, and with a voice both calm and massive, he asked his niece for good news.

Porsche gave it to him, adding, "The Masters are just beginning to wake. I've told Latrobe and his men to bring them over."

"We'll leave them here. Safe. Then we'll walk up to our intrusion." In the darkness, the man was in his element. "I've convinced Latrobe's reinforcements that he's still in command and they should begin slowly withdrawing toward home. Which puts us back on the earth before them."

Good.

The man approached. His birth pouch was bleeding, but otherwise he seemed unharmed, inquiring with a chilling calm, "Where's my son?"

"Here."

Cornell was holding the criminal; walking out of the intrusion, they looked like dancing partners in desperate need of practice.

Ka-ceen approached, then hesitated.

He asked, "Why?"

The smirk came easily, the jarrtee face twisting itself into a human sneer. "Because," Trinidad replied, without shame. "Because I could."

Porsche expected her uncle to beat him, or worse.

But the older man simply nodded, a look of understanding washing away every other emotion, and with a gesture, he said to Porsche, "See to everything. Will you, please? I've got to confirm details with these various god-awful parties."

The base camp was nearly deserted. A handful of soldiers had been left behind, standing guard over Porsche's family and Nathan, and for a tense few moments, they seemed ready to injure their hostages. Latrobe's intervention kept Ka-ceen from stunning the lot of them, and it was Latrobe who gave final orders to his people, telling the guards to help move the hostages to the intrusion, and telling the distant soldiers to retreat to the intrusion as fast as possible. "The mission is over," he declared with a tight, small voice. "Things didn't work out, but I'm proud of every one of you. Now let's get out of here."

Porsche recognized the old twanya tree at a distance.

Walking beside her uncle and behind Trinidad, she apologized for a tiny crime from the past. "I'm sorry that I knocked you down like I did. When you stepped out from behind that tree trunk—"

"When was that?" asked Ka-ceen, honestly puzzled.

She explained, then thought to ask, "Don't you remember?"

"I do," Trinidad volunteered.

"Quiet," she warned.

Her uncle admitted, "I don't remember it, no."

Then as if it really mattered, he took his niece under his arm, assuring her, "It really wasn't that important, all things considered."

Just as they had years ago, they passed from Jarrtee into the middle of a New Mexican night.

The mountain camp was nearly deserted, and again, with a smoldering sure-handedness, Latrobe greased their journey through unfriendly country. Still naked, he confronted a sputtering, off-balanced Farrah Smith, laying out the terms of the agreement. At his insistence, the estivating hostages were carried back to their tent. Dressed in human physiologies, they woke while en route or shortly afterwards. Nathan demanded to know what had happened. He demanded to be given his clothes. He told everyone in earshot, "This is a travesty . . . a great injustice!" And when Cornell explained the truth, in brief, the old man took Porsche by the hand, shaking it as he said, "See? The truth perseveres!"

She considered arguing with him, then thought better of it.

Her uncle said something to Latrobe, and moments later, a phone was delivered to him. He called three nonexistent people in succession, then dialed a fourth number, telling the person at the other end, "It's done, and we've had a nominal resolution." He hesitated, listening to the voice on the other end. Then he lifted his free hand, adding, "I need you to do a favor for me. My wife. Find Kay, and keep her. Until I get there."

Porsche couldn't imagine a more terrible curse than foisting too much truth upon the world.

Again, her uncle made a request of Latrobe.

"Helicopters. Enough for my people, plus pilots. No one else."

Latrobe gave the appropriate orders, then, perhaps thinking he could salvage some good from a lousy situation, he mentioned, "It is possible, you know. That your people and mine have areas of common interest."

Her uncle didn't seem interested in responding.

It was Porsche who pointed out, "That's exactly what we've been telling you. Or didn't you hear us?"

Latrobe glowered at her.

But he had enough presence to shrug his shoulders, forcing himself to say, "I guess I didn't. Sorry."

Porsche was set to leave in the first helicopter.

Dressed in gray and black, she was walking through the tent, talking happily to her parents and the others, and a familiar voice said, "Aunt Porsche! Come here please!"

"You're awake," she told Clare. "How do you feel?"

"Tired," the little girl confessed. Then with a delicious joy, she added, "I just had a dream about you."

"Did you?"

"We were on another world. Everyone was. And it was very strange, but nice, too. You know? Fun."

"Other worlds usually are nice," Porsche promised.

The girl waved her closer, then with a conspirator's whisper, admitted, "It might have been a real place. I think."

"Maybe it was, Clare."

"But I won't tell anyone about it. All right?"

It was a golden moment, and chilling. Porsche could think of nothing to say but, "For now, it's a secret. It has to be."

Then she kissed her niece on her clean and damp, newly made forehead, and she rose again, her uncle and Cornell waiting for her, and her cousin standing between them, hands bound together, his stance and the unrepentant expression on his face making him look like a hero statue ready to be set at a public crossroads.

The forest fire had barely abated in their absence.

Porsche was riding inside a small attack helicopter, gazing down at the tangerine flames and thinking about everything. About nothing. Out of the blackness, over the thrumming of the rotors, her uncle screamed out the central question:

"What do you people want?"

Trinidad sat motionless beneath a weak yellow bulb, offering not so much as a glance in his father's direction.

But he kept smirking, knowing it drove the man crazy.

Porsche offered her interpretation, repeating the fable of matter and antimatter and their imperfect annihilation of each other. "The Others, or whatever they call themselves . . . they can conquer worlds by similar tricks," she said. "Where the Few work to coexist, the Others depopulate and destroy!"

She hoped for a reaction.

For anything.

What she got was a sturdy slow voice directed at the cabin's ceiling. "You think you understand," Trinidad growled. "You think you're clever, Po-lee-een. But you got lucky, that's all. You pieced together some clues and came up with a useful, wrong answer. That's it. That's all. So don't congratulate yourself too much, please."

She watched Trinidad, trying to decide if this was the truth.

Whatever that meant.

Her cousin seemed to be concentrating—an observation that would haunt her for a long, long time—and in those last moments, he barely seemed aware of what was happening around him. His father rose and walked toward him, a carefully cultured menace in his stance. He didn't have any Few-made tools; every device had been erased in his trip through the intrusion. But he had a military knife—another gift from Latrobe—and he acted as if he would use it, standing over his own son as he said something too soft for Porsche to make out.

Cornell was sitting closer to the father and son. He heard enough to glance at Porsche, and he was alarmed enough to start rising to his feet.

Porsche moved, but too late.

In a loud voice, Trinidad screamed, "Nothing's finished!"

His hands were bound before him. Knotted into one fist, he drove them into his father's belly. The knife fell, and Porsche moved. Too slowly. She thought that the knife was the target, and she dove and cut herself on the blade, retrieving it first. Then she looked up in time to see Trinidad opening an emergency hatch. Trinidad's father was doubled up on the floor. Cornell had chased her cousin, grappling with him as he fought to climb through the hatch. For a horrible endless moment, Cornell clinging to him, pulled out into the roaring smoky air with Trinidad . . . and she grabbed Cornell, not her cousin, pulling him back even as Cornell screamed:

"Get his hand . . . his hand!"

The hand, and everything else, had already vanished.

Porsche stuck her head out of the hatch, her long unkempt hair flying in the wind, and she looked below, at a great red wall of light and heat, a piece of her trying to see Trinidad's tiny impact, while the rest kept recalling the look on his face.

The Few weren't the only people to take precautions.

She told herself.

Against all odds, he had escaped.

SOMETIME BEFORE DAWN, ONE HUNDRED MILES DUE OF SEATTLE, KAY Vortune pulled into an all-night truck stop–chapel and filled her tank with high-test alcohol. Less than a day later, the clerk remembered her as a good-looking woman—for being grandmother-old, that is—and she was both pleasant and in no particular hurry. Surveillance cameras confirmed his assessment, at least about her mood. Lingering in front of the refrigerators, Kay seemed to wrack her brain before deciding on a protein-enriched sports drink. Standing in line at the counter, she added a piece of smoked salmon to her purchases, and she spoke to the clerk for ninety seconds, discussing the gentle rain and the un-gentle traffic, then giving him an extra two-dollar coin. "For your smile," she explained, offering her own smile with her tip. Then she returned to her car and pulled away without incident, no one seeing her again.

There was a man riding with Kay, the clerk claimed. He didn't actually see the rider, and perhaps it was a woman instead of a man. But he was certain that *someone* was in the passenger seat. Someone good-sized. Shown a photograph of Trinidad, the clerk said, "Not him," and then, "Maybe not him. I don't know."

The outdoor surveillance cameras had no record of Kay's visit. Each camera had failed five minutes before her arrival, then came back on line five minutes after she had departed—an easy enough trick, if there was indeed someone whose identity was to remain secret.

The state patrol found the Chinese-made sedan parked at a beach in Oregon, empty and locked. The Few stole the vehicle, and using forensic skills borrowed from a multitude of worlds, learned absolutely nothing of consequence.

Jack Vortune was present at every portion of the investigation, though he wasn't allowed any genuine powers.

Officially, he was enjoying what the Few euphemistically labeled *an opportunity for regeneration.*

Standing before the refrigerators, in exactly the spot where his wife of forty years had stood, he realized what she had been doing. Under the fluorescent lights, a person could see her face reflected in the glass doors and the polished aluminum frames, each face distorted but recognizable. Kay had been taking a last long look at herself. Her life as she knew it was over, and wherever she was going, she wouldn't likely see this face again.

The nature of the foe was hotly debated among the Few.

Kay and her oldest son could have been acting in tandem, without the help of any shadowy Others. What little evidence there was pointed to that comforting answer. Yet as a precaution, teams of security people were brought from neighboring worlds, given temporary identities, the best tools, and the authority necessary to chase every credible lead, and then, every slippery rumor.

Working unofficially, Jack Vortune handled his own investigation.

He searched the burnt forest in New Mexico, finding no trace of his son among the ashes. He interrogated his other children—*interrogate* was the only word for it—and after a lot of tearful nights and hard words, he learned that his wife had been a good if somewhat distant mother, and that her favorite child was her first-born. Finally, in despair, Jack borrowed a single intrusion key and searched the Oregon coast for his wife's escape route. But after visiting fifty wilderness worlds, he conceded that Kay was too smart to leave her car at a meaningful place. It even occurred to him that she might never have even left the earth, and today she was thoroughly human, hiding from him in plain view.

About the existence of the Others, Jack was of one mind. And in the company of his peers, he advocated a policy of relentless, aggressive vigilance.

Most found that attitude distasteful.

But he was tenacious, following his logic with the single-mindedness of a man who had lost hope and every shred of romantic love, and who could now look upon those qualities as being frailties. Nothing but the truth mattered, and the truth was—like it or not—going to win out in the end.

A PROMISE BROUGHT PORSCHE BACK TO JARRTEE.

The preliminary work was difficult, but the networks of Few-made tools left behind by her cousin and uncle were an immense help. There was a timetable that she barely met. Then at the appropriate time, she strolled down the familiar alleyway, entering the weedy and vacant courtyard as two men emerged from the intrusion. "So this is the famous Jarrtee night," said one of the men. Then he helped his companion walk to an overgrown stone bench, and he made him sit, asking, "Do you know who you are?"

"Jey-im," said the second man. Then, with a gasp, he said, "No, I'm not. My name is Loo-eek, and it always has been."

"Good," Cornell told him.

Porsche echoed that assessment, kneeling in front of the sitting man. "How do you feel, Loo-eek?"

Out of reflex, the eyes smiled.

A sad little voice said, "Sick. And tired."

"You've been stunned for too long," she allowed. "But it was for—"

"My own good," he said. "I know. Your friend says that I would have lost my sanity, if you hadn't done it."

And you would have remembered too much, she didn't say.

Too soon, Jey-im tried to stand.

Porsche helped hold him upright, whispering encouragements and crisp instructions. "There's an apartment not far from here," she said. "Its AI knows you. There's a subtle disguise that you should wear in public, and your new life story is waiting there. Learning it is your responsibility. I can't help you anymore."

"I know."

"But if you behave, and you're cautious enough, I don't think you'll have any trouble."

Loo-eek seemed to absorb the words, but he made no comment.

"This civil war helps us," Porsche admitted. "A lot of people have had to move and make new lives."

"I've lost my family," he said with a plaintive voice.

On Jarrtee, even adults could be orphaned.

"What about my world?" he asked with a cautious voice. "I know it's not big and important, but if things don't change, it may well die."

"We won't forget you," she said, knowing full well that she couldn't make promises. Yet if there was some group other than the Few, and if they were trying to willfully destroy the jarrtees . . . well, it only stood to reason that this place and these people would remain important. Perhaps even essential in whatever happened next.

She had no idea what would happen next.

Against the rules, the jarrtee man referred to her by name. "Po-lee-een," he whispered. "I wish I could walk these other worlds, Po-lee-een."

Cornell wisely stepped away, giving them a moment alone.

"With you, or not," he said. "It sounds like a wonderful adventure."

Porsche waited a moment, then responded.

"This is a huge and lovely world, and it's in terrible danger." She took a little breath, gesturing at the sky. "You are partly responsible for the terrible things happening now."

He squirmed, but he couldn't deny the words.

"When you contemplate adventure, think about what's happening here. A species is in the balance. An entire world. And what do you want to do? Take a walking tour of a universe that's much too big to embrace."

"That isn't fair, Po-lee-een!"

"You have a new life, a new vantage point," she told him. "Think. Work. And spend time with your neighbors." A sudden inspiration came thundering out of her mouth. "If there's any group that can help make peace, why not the orphans?"

The man responded with thoughtful silence.

And Porsche retreated, finally. She didn't look to see if her onetime lover was watching as she walked through the felt grass, heading for the intrusion. All she noticed was Cornell standing against a wall of thick foliage, stroking one blue-black blade with his platinum-white jarrtee hand, and suddenly, with the quietest of voices, she said, "We should leave."

"What?" Cornell replied. "You don't want to take a final look around?"

She shook her head, human-fashion.

"I did that already," she explained. "Years ago."

A WARM WIND GREETED THEM, STIRRING THE BASKETBALL NET INTO A quiet tune.

June had come to the farm. Glancing up at the sky, Cornell said, "A little after midnight, I think." In their absence, the farmer had plowed and planted his field, a tailored breed of soybean already thrusting its way out of the purified soil. The two of them set out for the farmhouse. They were comfortably naked, holding hands, whispering as they watched for anything threatening. For the time being, the Sky-lords would keep the intrusion open; should trouble come, an escape route would be waiting.

The kitchen light was burning, and as they approached the back door, they smelled the familiar stink of incinerated pizza.

Cornell knocked, entered.

"Dad?" he called out. "You here, Dad?"

Nothing.

Porsche followed him. They found their bedroom in perfect order, their clothing cleaned and folded, the old terminal wearing an antique dust cover, and every imaginable hiding place examined twenty times. As far as Porsche could see, the only thing missing was the pornography in the closet. And the steel box it came in, too.

As they dressed, a familiar voice came from outside. "Not there, old man! I want them *there*. Where I'm pointing!"

Nathan was out at the utility building, destroying Timothy's mood by helping load his equipment into a fat yellow truck.

It was impossible to decide which man was happier to see them.

Through a crushing fatigue, Timothy smiled, one long hand sweeping across his forehead. "How did your errand go?"

"Well enough," said Porsche.

"I was expecting you sooner," he confessed.

"We took a long way home," Cornell offered.

Timothy considered asking for details, then thought better of it. The last few weeks had left their mark. He didn't care about alien worlds or agencies running amuck, just so long as both left him alone.

In contrast, Nathan appeared rested. Rejuvenated.

Grasping Porsche's hand, he gave her arm a great tug. "I wish I could have gone with you."

"That makes both of us," Timothy whined.

Nathan ignored him. With a knowing nod, he said, *"They've* been watching us, but at a distance. And openly."

The agency, he meant.

"They'll park up on the county road. A couple men, usually. But they don't seem particularly interested in doing anything to us."

A truce had been declared between the agency and the Few. And in the meantime, each was trying mightily to decide what was in its best interests, and how each could achieve its ambitious goals.

Changing topics, Nathan asked, "So what's our plan now?"

Cornell told him the short-term plan. Porsche wanted time with her family; they were leaving for Texas in the morning, as soon as they could pack.

It was for Porsche to assure Timothy, "You're welcome to join us, of course."

A nervous laugh rattled down to a nervous shivering. "I don't think so," Timothy replied. "I'm retiring from this business. As soon as I can get my equipment loaded, I'm going back home again. To my home."

He didn't know about the Others.

Because it would be cruel to tell him everything, Porsche told him nothing. Extending her hand, she took his hand and shook it, wishing him well.

Timothy squeaked when he said, "About what you did . . . helping me . . . thank you . . ."

"You're welcome," she replied.

Timothy retrieved his hand, and as if treasuring her touch, he held it flush against his stomach, staring off into the distance, smiling at things only he could see.

Porsche made waffles in the early morning, using up the last eggs and milk in the refrigerator. The four of them ate at the dining room table, conversations brief and banal, then they cleaned the dishes and stored them neatly, in case the farmer happened to find another tenant for the house.

After a final round of good-byes, Timothy drove off in the rental truck, towing his Brazilian sugar-burner behind him.

Belongings were packed into suitcases, then loaded. Cornell drove the car they had come in, and Porsche drove her Humvee with Nathan beside her. The agency watchdogs were parked at the crest of the hill. Porsche decided on a neighborly wave, then eased the wheel to the left, her big tires missing the ugly sedan by nothing, nothing to see in the rearview camera but a cloud of swirling white dust.

They picked up the ancient interstate near Salinas. From there, it was a long straight drive south to Dallas.

Shrouded in electronic camouflage, Porsche told Nathan about her recent travels. "My people wanted to meet with me. To discuss possibilities. Plans." Then she told him about Trinidad and Aunt Kay and the possibilities of something like the Few, but different. After that bombshell was dealt with—in northern Oklahoma—she entrusted him with another secret.

"There's going to be a mission. An expedition, of sorts." She glanced over her shoulder, by reflex. "Past the areas mapped by the Few. Out as far as we can possibly go. Just to have a look around."

Calmly, soberly, Nathan said, "And you'll go, won't you?"

"Yes."

"And my son?"

"It's his decision. He has the talent and my blessing, too."

Silence.

Porsche looked out over the red clays and scrub timber, and after a few moments, she asked, "What are you thinking, Nathan?"

"I just realized something," he confessed. Then after a long pause, he told her, and himself, "I'm old. Too old to go with you, I'm afraid."

Porsche said nothing.

A warm hand took her closer hand, and she held it all the way to Oklahoma City.

Pulling up in front of her parents' house, just after the sun had set, Porsche sensed that something wasn't quite right. The front door had been left opened, but no one was waiting for them. With Cornell and Nathan in tow, she stuck her head inside the door and called out, "Mama-ma? Father?"

Nothing.

Then the answer came to her, and she relaxed. She even smiled. Creeping through the house, she spotted the familiar figure standing in the backyard. Her uncle wasn't doing much of a job of hiding, was he? She'd have to chide him for it, once everyone shouted:

"Surprise!"

Stepping through the back door, out onto the wood deck, she realized with an accelerating horror that this wasn't a homecoming party. A glance at the faces told her that much. Uncle Jack was staring at the swimming pool, his face red and glowering. Mama-ma was weeping quietly. Leon and Sally were embracing, their expressions simply desperate.

It was Father who approached, who took it on himself to tell her the news.

He looked ancient and worn-out, his plain face glistening with tears. With a cracking voice, he said, "Your uncle has been working . . . asking questions . . . which may or may not have anything to do with it . . ."

"With what?" Porsche asked.

Father swallowed, trying to find the words.

Her younger brother, Donald, was sitting off alone, calmly and steadily beating his head against the wooden privacy fence.

"Your sister-in-law has vanished," Father explained. "The same way Aunt Kay vanished, it seems."

Silently, Porsche reminded herself that she was a strong person.

"In fact," Father warned, "a lot of the Few's spouses, in a lot of places, have disappeared without any warning."

Cornell came close. "Oh, shit," he muttered. "Oh, shit . . ."

Then something else horrible occurred to Porsche, and watching Donald, watching him trying to beat himself unconscious, she forced herself to ask:

"What about the children?"

Father couldn't say it.

It was Uncle Jack who rose shakily to his feet, kicked aside spent beer cans, and looked into her eyes, saying, "Linda took Clare, and her other children, too."

Oh, god!

"All told," he reported with a slow dead voice, "almost a thousand children are missing. Taken. Lost."

Porsche looked down at the shimmering waters.

A woman's face was looking up at her, and for that moment, she didn't know the face. For a moment, she wanted to tell that woman not to worry, that everything would be all right. That she was strong enough to bear this thing.

Even if she wasn't, Porsche wanted to lie, telling that poor frail woman that she could endure this terrible day.

ABOUT THE AUTHOR

Gold Award winner of the first Writers of the Future contest, Robert Reed is the critically acclaimed author of seven previous novels: *The Remarkables, Down the Bright Way, Black Milk, The Hormone Jungle, The Leeshore, An Exaltation of Larks,* and *Beyond the Veil of Stars.* Reed is also a writer of short fiction, and two of his stories have been Hugo Award finalists: "Utility Man" in 1990 and "Decency" in 1997. He has had a number of short stories published in *Asimov's Science Fiction Magazine, The Magazine of Fantasy and Science Fiction,* and other major magazines. He has gained a reputation as a writer of hard SF with strong characters and intricate plots. His work has been compared to that of both Philip K. Dick and Ray Bradbury. He and his wife, Leslie, live in Lincoln, Nebraska.